THE FIRESTONE

. . . Is Mankind Ready?

Val Edward Simone

A Morningside Publishing Book

THE FIRESTONE ... Is Mankind Ready?
A Morningside Publishing, LLC Book

Text Copyright © 2014 by Val Edward Simone
All Rights Reserved.

Printed in the United States of America

Library of Congress Control Number: 2014956387

Printed Version
ISBN 978-1-936210-57-2

Cover Design: Val Edward Simone

For more books please visit:
www.morningsidepublishing.com
www.ekidslandpublishing.com

Dedication:
To the Sacred Naacal in all of us

With Special Thanks To:
Editor
Rita Samols

Musical Inspiration
Ernesto Cortazar II
Kevin Kern
Secret Garden
R. Carlos Nakai

THE
FIRESTONE

"When the Naacal civilization collapsed, humanity lost a race of special leaders. They were an inspiring nation of good people who chose to die with the secret of their wondrously terrible technology rather than share it and doom us all to live the horrors that brought about their own destruction. We owe them everything — our very existence."

~ Professor Hannibal Storm

CHAPTER 1

Jungle Village, Yucatan Peninsula, Mexico

"Never leave the sacred path."

Those five commanding words had been memorized by every Mayan child since the ancient days when the terrible gods lived in the surrounding jungle and the streaks of sacred fire crisscrossed the skies overhead.

"Disobey the commands of the gods and you will suffer the pain of their terrible wrath."

With these additional words of warning and his grandmother's trademark index finger wagging before his eyes, twelve-year-old Jesus Bolon began his every venture through the Yucatan jungle.

"The paths," she insisted, "were built by the gods to safely guide the Mayan people through the jungle. They are there also as a warning to those who might consider intruding onto their sanctified grounds."

Her words were ominous and serious.

"The gods," she continued, "are selfish and dreadful and they will not tolerate any intrusion whatsoever."

~ ~ ~ ~ ~

As she had done several times before, his grandmother had gotten him up at the crack of dawn and sent him immediately on the typical shopping trip.

She wanted the freshest fruits and vegetables from the carts of the vendors for a special meal for Jesus this day and it was always best to arrive very early, before the punishing sun had dried out the produce.

Today was special because it was Jesus' "compleaños," his birthday. He had forgotten about it.

Bending low, she brought her face close to his, and with a stern look she added, "Those foolish enough to ignore the commands of the gods and wander off the paths will be either consumed by the protective jungle around their sanctified land, or scorched to death by the consecrated flame."

Jesus nodded in full understanding.

"Good boy," his grandmother said, smiling. "Don't forget my words," she commanded.

Jesus again nodded in agreement and understanding.

"Now off you go," his grandmother said.

Jesus knew his grandmother spoke the truth, for he well understood that the lusciously thick, green foliage of the jungles of the Yucatan had existed unchanged for countless millennia. And that they stretched for several miles inland from the Gulf coastline, southward down hidden hillsides near Uxmal, the area known more commonly as the Puuc Hills region of Quintana Roo, and off into the heartland of other varied and mysterious landscapes. Protected by the green veil of a double canopy of vegetation, the lands of the gods had successfully remained hidden for millennia.

Even the evil men of ancient times who had invaded their land, speaking in their strange language, adorned in their metal headdresses and impenetrable body armor and wielding those frightful fire sticks, dared not penetrate the jungle after several of them entered and never returned.

Jesus knew very well that the jungle hid awful things.

As was typical for the Yucatan in mid-June, the beginning of the first rainy season of the year, a veil of mist wafted slowly over the valley. Formed as droplets in the rain-drenched air the night before, it had vaporized in the already blistering sun and was now slithering over the dense vegetation like a serpent seeking its prey.

The waking songs of the countless exotic birds with their contrasting harmonies echoed throughout the small, shallow valley. The ground foliage, thick and moist, was a special green color this time of day. These unique sights and sounds clearly spoke to both the mystery and the wonder of the jungle.

On this morning, the symphony of the birds was joined by the singing voice of Jesus, accompanied by the snap and crunch of breaking twigs and dry leaves under his zapatos as he made his way along the well-beaten path that had existed eons before his great-grandfather's great-great-great-grandfather.

~ ~ ~ ~ ~

After a time, growing a bit weary from his long hike, Jesus stopped next to a large rock that had worn over time to look like a little chair, perfect for the boy to sit upon and rest, as he had done so many times before.

He was running a bit behind. He'd attempted to pick up the pace, but the heat of this day was nearly stifling, not at all normal. He wondered if it was an omen

Being young, though, carried with it curiosities that demanded satisfaction despite any possible dreaded omens. He had dawdled along the path, stopping to study the ants at work, marching in a wandering line and carrying their heavy loads effortlessly back to their nest. Then there was the tiny Red Coffee snake crossing his path. For all its effort to look deadly by flattening its head and body, Jesus knew it was completely harmless, and being a boy and therefore a most naturally inquisitive creature, he just had to tease it a bit with a stick before allowing it to continue on.

Such officious distractions continually called out to him as he walked the long path to the market, slowing his progress.

Despite the white linen clothing that reflected the intense morning sun, Jesus was hot. He pulled his straw sombrero from his head and wiped a sleeve across his dusty forehead. Then he lifted the well-used white plastic water bottle emblazoned with the Nike swoosh from his shoulder bag, pulled open the plug, and squirted a stream of refreshing water into his throat.

Seconds later he heard a strange noise coming from somewhere behind the low hills to the southeast. He searched the sky for the source of the sound but could see nothing except the blazing sun rising up from the eastern horizon.

The noise grew louder. He could not readily identify it, and he, being a jungle boy, was unaccustomed to hearing anything that he could not immediately and easily identify. His father had taught him all the creature sounds of the jungle, especially those of the dangerous variety, and yet this was more of a scream, unlike anything he had ever heard before. His eyes strained against the morning sun to see this new beast. Louder and louder the screaming became, and then a new sound began, one that rose and fell. He became fearful, for it sounded as if the beast was in great agony.

He caught a glimpse of something dark and ominous rising from the top of a nearby hill and approaching directly out of the sun, a great flying beast descending straight toward him. His eyes opened wide in shock as the beast roared over his head, shouting in dreadful agony — screaming for its very life. The commercial airliner flashed over his head, all four of its engines fully engulfed in flames, its turbines churning and cutting out in their rhythmic death howls.

Jesus' eyes followed the airliner until it disappeared from view over the top of another hill just ahead of him, and a few seconds later a great explosion shattered the peace of the morning and a huge mushroom-shaped fireball rose up through the jungle canopy. The blast wave jetting across the ground nearly knocked him off his feet.

In his excitement he forgot the warnings of his grandmother. He stepped off the path.

Having now unwittingly ignored the commands of the gods, Jesus quickly dashed up the through the thick jungle until he crested the hilltop.

Emerging from the jungle onto the smoldering plateau, he found himself staring both frightfully and disbelievingly over the blast area of the crash. He stumbled through the last vestiges of virgin jungle and stepped gingerly onto the blackened and destroyed field, where small pieces of the jet lay scattered across the plateau. Even in his most horrific nightmares he had never dreamed of anything this terrible. But he had yet to see the most terrifying scene.

Hundreds of burning and shredded bodies were strewn everywhere he looked. He could clearly hear the hissing and sizzling of human flesh being seared by the flames.

Jesus wandered slowly out into the field, where he could view the complete destruction of the small plateau. Not one person was alive and the large jet was now reduced to small chunks of molten metal and smoldering fabric.

A moment later he caught a glimpse of something very large on the far side of the plateau. He couldn't make it out clearly through the billowing smoke, but his eyes became fixated on it.

He moved past the bodies and devastation without noticing anything more except what was being hidden in front of him. It was surely something he had never seen before.

Traveling the sacred path as he had done so many times in the past, he could practically do it blindfolded. All this time, however, he'd never had any idea that such a structure was present nearby. Through the columns of drifting smoke, he saw its immense size; he could not take it all in without turning his head.

Stepping through the final cloud of smoke, he stopped in front of the structure and stared up at it. The white marble walls and pillars, now glistening in the sun, still supported a domed marble roof which appeared undamaged despite the immensity of the explosion.

He, of course, had no concept of what this would mean to the archaeological world, nor could he understand the purpose of such an immense structure out here in the middle of the jungle. Nor could he imagine how long it had been here. But it looked ancient. And based upon the many stories recited by his grandmother, it was sure to be something terrible, created by the wrathful and unforgiving gods long, long ago.

He stared in utter amazement until, filled with a sudden terror, he recalled the stern warnings of his grandmother. Now, for his disobedience, he expected a wrath-filled suffering to visit down upon him, followed by a severe punishment for intruding on the hidden homeland of the furious and enraged gods — for stepping off the path.

CHAPTER 2

Los Angeles, California, U.S.A.

The underwater photographs were of ancient ruined structures planted firmly on the ocean floor, with smaller, broken pieces cluttering the surrounding area. Other photographs soon flashed on the screen as the voice of Professor Hannibal Storm, a mid-level staff archaeologist with UCLA's Cotsen Institute of Archaeology, blurted out a narration of the scenes. The loud, deliberate slap of the rubber-tipped pointer against the screen successfully aroused those boardroom executives who had drifted off. It was a technique he'd used many times in his classroom to regain the attention of drowsy students.

"... and moving around the projection of rock, we discovered these ruins," Hannibal announced. "After studying the markings here on the side, I'm sure it's the remnants of a man-made structure on a sunken land mass, but as the expedition is still photographing, it is impossible to say that these are, in fact, the ruins of some antediluvian civilization.

"However, the location of this site very accurately correlates with the coordinates given by Edgar Cayce, during one of his readings in December 1933, of the purported location of the expected ruins of Cayce's Atlantean island of Poseidia here, just off the coast of Bimini.

"Of course, even though it's common knowledge that this most definitely is *not* Atlantis, it *is* an ancient site that, to some, could have been, culturally speaking, an equal of Atlantis, and perhaps, as I suspect, even its predecessor.

"Upon my return to the site, I intend to prove it is a man-made structure and thus establish that this area was once above sea level, thereby giving full credence to my theories that ancient man had already constructed wonderful and technically complicated structures here in this part of the world thousands of years before the Egyptians learned to build mud huts."

Hannibal stood at the far end of the expansive black granite conference table in front of a display of photographs. His forty-three-year-old, well-built frame stood large in silhouette against the screen. But as the lights came up, his tired and tattered face, sporting a full day's growth of beard, failed to give anyone in the room much confidence in his report, let alone in him.

His messy brown collar-length hair flopping into his eyes and his haphazard, ill-fitting suit made him look more like a refugee from a homeless encampment who had wandered in off the street looking for a handout.

Despite his outward appearance, Hannibal Storm possessed one of the most intuitive minds in the world. And any considered description of him offered by someone in possession of more intimate knowledge of the man necessitated the words *genius* and *brilliant*.

Hannibal audibly exhaled and ran a hand through his hair while waiting patiently for a response from the man seated at the opposite end of the long conference table.

William Douglas Bernard, the self-indulging, arrogant, manipulative, and very powerful CEO of the company bearing his name, sat unmoved as Hannibal began nervously slapping his pointer into his palm.

Although many would aptly describe Bernard as an out-and-out tyrant, it was undeniable that he was a man who commanded respect. He was not to be toyed with and did not tolerate failure of any kind. Goal-oriented and success-driven, he offered little clemency to anyone who failed to meet his lofty expectations. Calling him a cruel taskmaster did not do the term sufficient justice.

It had been two months since Hannibal was given the money to begin his expedition. Now it was time for a status report and, hopefully, another check to continue the expedition.

Both male and female corporate minions — the court jesters of Bernard's empire — sat emotionless around the table, almost trance-like. God forbid they would ever verbally disagree with any decision made by Bernard on any issue, even if they mentally disagreed. There was no secret about their existence and duties. They were there only to stroke his ego and they knew it.

Despite Hannibal's friendly smile and most cordial behavior, not one set of sycophant eyes lifted to meet his. They sat like automatons, motionless, with blank expressions, staring straight ahead into space as they patiently awaited the faultless decision of their flawless leader.

Hannibal perspired profusely. He was a field guy, not an actor, not a showman. He was not given over to the necessities of polite and polished corporate behavior. Suits and ties were not his natural attire. In fact, he often came out of the field wearing torn and tattered jeans and safari shirts and smelling like the wilds he had just explored.

A few more silent seconds passed. Hannibal turned and stared at the photographs mounted on the display board behind him for a quick second, then turned back to Bernard. "Well, that's about it, Mister Bernard. What do ya think? Pretty exciting, huh?"

Without any further hesitation, Bernard dropped his pure gold ballpoint pen onto the stack of paperwork in front of him and stared directly into Hannibal's eyes. "What I think, Professor Storm, is that we wasted a million dollars on you. You promised me proof of Atlantis. I don't see proof. I see underwater structures that could be almost anything, but I don't see Atlantis."

"Well, it's not Atlantis. Atlantis isn't anywhere near the Caribbean. I made that very clear to you before taking on the expedition. What I said was that I believe this site to be a cousin nation of Atlantis, perhaps its predecessor. If I'm right, this will be bigger than Atlantis. Here is the proof. Look!"

"I am looking, Professor. I don't see anything that proves to me that it's Atlantis."

"Mister Bernard, it's *not* Atlantis. I wasn't *looking* for Atlantis. The photos! Look! Right here! The structure is man-made. Look at the lines, the architecture. Nature doesn't do this."

Hannibal picked up a stone sample, pulled a loupe from his pants pocket, and squinted through it at the stone.

"If you'll just take a moment, Mister Bernard, and look at this stone I pulled from near the structures, please. It's wonderful evidence of being formed above the ocean. That proves the ocean levels were much, much lower before the construction of the structures. Mister —"

The double doors to the conference room opened and Bernard's personal assistant entered. Walking up to Bernard, she bent close to him and whispered something in his ear.

Hannibal stopped talking and nervously waited.

The assistant finished speaking and walked out of the room, leaving the doors open behind her. Bernard thought for a few more seconds, then nodded and stood up. His underlings arose immediately, as protocol dictated whenever their "emperor" left or entered the room. He walked directly toward the open doors. "We're done, Professor."

"But sir —" Hannibal began, but Bernard was already going through the doors.

Immediately after His Magnificence had departed, his minion entourage followed him, still without looking at Hannibal, except for one young woman who stood glaring at him with contempt. "Time to get a real job, Professor," she said, and then she followed the others through the doors and was gone.

The meeting was obviously over and Hannibal was summarily abandoned in the conference room. He folded up his loupe with frustration and pushed it back into his pocket.

Today, it seemed, genius and brilliance were not enough to overcome the shortsightedness of a tyrannical benefactor.

A few hollow seconds passed and then a small, bespectacled, prissy man entered the room. He approached Hannibal directly, bearing a wicked grin, and pointed his thin index finger at him. "I told you," the Chihuahua of a man barked. "You have nothing, Professor. I'm calling Doctor Evans right now and canceling the rest of the expedition."

With that, the wee pretend man spun on his heels and sashayed out the door. A second later he stuck his head back into the room and snarled, "Now get out."

Hannibal quickly reached into his jacket pocket and withdrew a parking stub. "Can you validate?"

~ ~ ~ ~ ~

"Nice job, Hannibal!" he said to himself as he began to step out of the conference room, his arms filled with his presentation paraphernalia. "What a day! ... Dear God, what a year. ... Let's face it, what a *life*! It's just got to get better soon."

He gritted his teeth as he spied Dr. Richard Grendel, his longtime nemesis and funding competitor, standing near the reception desk. A young woman approached Grendel and handed him an envelope. "Here's your check, Doctor Grendel. I'm looking forward to your next video update. They just have me glued to my seat watching them. They're so exciting and informative. Good luck to you, sir," she said.

"Well, there goes getting better," Hannibal murmured, realizing now that there would be no way to avoid Grendel.

"Thank you, Tiffany," said Grendel. "That's so nice of you to acknowledge all our hard work thus far. I assure you, our forthcoming video will have you simply mesmerized. We're editing it now. It should be ready for release at the end of this week. I can't tell you all about it right now, but we've made some startling new discoveries. In fact, some of them are quite shocking."

At that moment he spotted Hannibal.

Grendel's smirk was practically audible as Hannibal exited awkwardly from the conference room.

"And speaking of shocking. Well, well, Hannibal Storm, as I live and breathe."

"Well, Richard Grendel, the fact that you're still breathing at all saddens me to no end."

Grendel chuckled. "Another failure, Hannibal? So sorry to hear that. Better luck next time, but I must admit you do look the part of a man beaten to a pulp. I don't blame you for not shaving. Being who and what you are, I'd be terrified of touching a razor too if I were you. As for me, well, I had to come in and pick up a check for the next phase of our exciting expedition. I'm very close to making an astounding discovery. Sorry I can't tell you more about it."

"So, you're finally mounting an expedition to search for your dick, huh, Dick?"

"That's so funny, Hannibal. I'll be laughing about it all the way to the bank to cash this check. No, seriously, I will." He pulled the check from its envelope and stared at it for a few seconds. "Wow! Will you look at all those zeroes. How about you, Hannibal? How many zeroes are you walking out of here with today? Oh, yeah — one. Your sorry-ass zero life."

"Bite me, Dick. If I were you, I wouldn't act so high and mighty. You haven't found anything of importance and you never will."

Grendel chuckled again. "I'm so sorry for you, Hannibal. I really am. By the way, I just heard a rumor about you possibly getting sacked from the institute. Not bringing in enough grant money, or something to that effect. Big institutions can be so cruel sometimes, don't ya think?"

"I'm sure you know all about that, Grendel. I'm more certain, though, that you're the one who started the rumor."

"Oh, Hannibal. That hurt to the core."

"If only it could kill."

"I'm serious, Hannibal. But then you already know that a professor without tenure is ... well, just fodder for the cannons, so to speak, the backs of which can only hope to support the real go-getters as we climb inexorably to the top. Gee, I hope it isn't true, though. You're needed around the institute — as a reminder of what not to do." Grendel chuckled once again.

"Go to hell, Dick. I've made more significant discoveries than all of you tenured assholes put together."

"Where are they, Hannibal? Where're your published papers? Oh, that's right. Nothing panned out. And now, once again, proved wrong, huh? It must really suck to be you, Hannibal."

"I'm not wrong. And institute brownnosers like you wouldn't know the truth if it sat on your faces. I'll be proven correct on everything. You'll see."

"Please, Hannibal. A global civilization that preceded all the other known civilizations by tens of thousands of years? Get real, ol' buddy. Nothing in any archaeological record supports your wild theory. It's just some fruitless imagined notion living an empty existence inside that Hannibal brain of yours. You know the place: where fantasy and fiction live hopelessly together in abundance, intertwined forever in utter irrelevancy.

"And that's only part of the problem, Hannibal. Your complete lack of discipline in the field got you what you deserved. You jump to wild conclusions based on incomplete evidence and flawed reasoning. You're a loose cannon out there, Hannibal, and it's all your own doing, or should I say your undoing, and it makes the rest of us look bad. Accept it, buddy. You're just not very good at this stuff. It's not your fault, but it's simply not in you to be successful. Sorry, old man. I'm just being bluntly honest with you. It's about time someone was."

"You're feeling pretty smug right now, Grendel. Enjoy it while you can, because you'll be regretting it all soon enough."

"You're a dreamer, Hannibal. You're a wannabe archaeologist and it's time for you to wake up. You'll never make any kind of meaningful discovery and you'll never get tenure anywhere. Hey, here's an idea, though. Maybe you should become a fiction writer. They can propose something outrageous and there's no demand that they prove any of it. Besides, you're good at fantasy thinking, right?"

"As opposed to you, Grendel the realist, eh? Yeah, well, you might be real good at finding your own ass, but that's about it. You haven't discovered anything but tidbits. Nothing of real consequence."

"Maybe so, Hannibal. But I look *good* finding those tidbits. That's your other problem, buddy, you know that? You lack showmanship."

"There's a lot more to archaeology than putting on a pretty show, Grendel."

"There it is. You just don't get it, do you? *The show is everything*, Hannibal. That's really all there is to it. Our benefactors want to watch an intriguing performance, an exciting show that will startle, amaze, and wow the viewers, bring in the numbers and the big bucks. You lack that necessary understanding, Hannibal. You think it's all about the discovery. Well, ol' buddy, it isn't. But you don't get it, and that's why you'll ultimately fail.

"Look at me, though, Hannibal. I've got the face, the talent, the brains, and the presentation. I've got the whole package and I've got it in spades. More importantly, I understand that it's all a show. You, on the other hand ... well, look in the mirror, buddy. All your sad truths are right there staring woefully back at you."

Grendel glanced at his watch.

"Oops! Gotta get to the bank. So sorry, Hannibal, but I just don't have any more time for you, buddy." Grendel put the check into the inside breast pocket of his sports jacket and patted it lightly. "Have a shitty day, Hannibal." He turned and departed the room, chuckling smugly.

"It's just got to get better now," Hannibal said.

CHAPTER 3

Hannibal's beat-up car was smoking as he pulled into the parking stall of his apartment building and stopped. He turned the key off, but the motor continued coughing, sputtering, and choking for several more moments. Finally, with one final clunk — a death knell — it ground to a halt.

Gathering up what he could hold of his presentation paraphernalia, including his well-worn briefcase, tripod, and photograph albums, he kicked the creaking rear car door closed and sauntered across the parking lot toward the building.

It was then that he noticed the sheriff's car and civilian workers stacking familiar-looking furniture onto the lawn next to the curb.

Kindly Mrs. Morrison, the building manager, greeted him with her usual gentle smile, her meticulously coifed gray hair neatly stacked on her small head. At least fifty pounds overweight, she still presented a pleasant and friendly vision in her mid-calf-length skirt and flower-printed blouse.

"Good evening, Professor," she said warmly.

"Good evening, Mrs. Morrison. What's going on?"

"You're being evicted, dear. Sheriff's Deputy Thompson has the notice for you."

Deputy Thompson stepped up to Hannibal and handed him a folded piece of paper. Arms full, Hannibal had a difficult time grasping the paper, so the deputy stuffed it between the pages of a photo album, saying, "Hannibal Storm, this is an eviction notice signed by the court. You, sir, shall cease and desist occupying your apartment immediately."

Hannibal turned to Mrs. Morrison, who still wore a sweet, loving smile. "But Mrs. Morrison, why?

"Because, dear, you haven't paid your rent for five months and you're a worthless bum."

"But —"

She waddled away, glancing over her shoulder. "Find someone else to mooch off of, Professor. Have a nice day, dear."

Hannibal stepped up to where his belongings were being stacked and opened his arms, dropping his presentation materials on top of the rest.

He walked into the building and up the two flights of stairs, passing workmen carrying his possessions down, and into his apartment.

He was shocked to see all his belongings being removed, boxed, and carried out by strangers.

He glanced at the ceiling. "It's gonna get better now, right?"

His head dropped in dejection just as a voice from behind startled him.

"Hi there, Hannibal. How's it hanging?"

"Shit on a stick!" he bellowed. He turned his eyes skyward once again. "Haven't you got anything better to do than dump on me?"

He forced himself to turn around and stared at the two government men wearing identical mirrored Foster Grant sunglasses, standing in the center of the hallway, their hands folded neatly and comfortably in front of them.

"Dumping on you is what I do, Hannibal. It's my job," one of the men replied with a wide grin.

"I wasn't talking to you, Jackson."

"Oh. My bad," replied Agent Jackson, stepping into the apartment.

"When I said 'shit on a stick,' *that's* when I was talking to you."

"Ever the same Hannibal, I see. The only real constant in the universe."

"Oh, Christ!" Hannibal grumbled. "This is all I need right now. I thought I told you bastards to stay outa my life. Now go to hell!"

"Hey, I love your décor, Hannibal. What is it? Early Atlantis?"

Every available wall space and floor space of the apartment was covered with photographs, sketches, artifacts, stone carvings, and other paraphernalia looking Atlantean, although it was all now systematically being taken down and placed into large boxes.

"At least my walls aren't covered by playmates of the month like yours are, Jackson."

"To each his own, Professor."

Hannibal went to his refrigerator and pulled out a beer. He cracked the top and took a long swallow. "I'd offer a beer to you guys, but you're leaving. So please, respectfully and politely: *Get the hell out!*"

Jackson chuckled lightly. "We'd like you to accompany us, Hannibal," he said, calmly and deliberately.

"And I told you both to go to hell, remember, Jackson? When I first saw you, I looked at you and said, *'Go to hell'!'*

"It's good to see I can still count on you, Hannibal," replied Jackson with another smirk.

"I quit working with you assholes a long time ago, Jackson. Do you recall that? You think you can just show up anytime you get into your wee little minds to do so?"

"Come on, Hannibal. You know better than that. Once in, you're *never* out."

"I was never 'in,' Jackson, you idiot. The CIA used me a couple times to confirm some findings. That's it. You know that. That doesn't make me 'in.' Jesus Christ, get real. I was young and stupid when I let Kirby talk me into doing those favors for him. I didn't know what I was doing."

"Well, Hannibal, look at it this way. Now you're *old* and stupid and you apparently still don't know what you're doing." Jackson chuckled smugly, casting a spiteful eye around Hannibal's dismantled apartment.

Hannibal finished his beer and tossed the empty can to the floor, not even trying to aim for the trash can. "I've had a very bad day, Jackson, and it doesn't seem to be getting any better at the moment. I'm not in the mood to spar with you right now."

"I know all about it, Hannibal. Bernard's a tough ol' bastard. Now look at this, getting yourself evicted. It certainly hasn't been a good day. I can see that. So, let's go. We don't have a lot of time."

"I've got my life being dumped out on the street, Jackson. I don't think I'll be going anywhere with you tonight."

"Well, technically speaking, ol' buddy, it's being dumped on the lawn, but I can take care of that."

"Here we go," muttered Hannibal. "Thanks, but no thanks. I don't want to owe you or the agency anything. I'm done. I got out for a reason and I have no desire to get back in. Not that I was ever 'in' in the first place."

"I can stop all of this, Hannibal. All you have to do is come with us. That's it."

"It's never 'it' with you guys. Do you think I'm an idiot?"

Jackson cut Hannibal a patronizing look. His right eyebrow arched upwards.

"Eat shit, Jackson."

"Just come with us and I'll put an end to all of this."

Hannibal considered Jackson's words as he watched the movers continue taking his home and world apart. Finally he looked at Jackson.

"What do I have to do?"

"Simply take a short drive with us. That's it. If I can't convince you, I'll drop you off anywhere you want and you can come back here to your little Atlantean paradise, courtesy of your ol' loving and generous Uncle Sam."

"Don't do this, Jackson. I'm in no mood for your bullshit."

"That's all you have to do, Hannibal. A quick ride. What do you say?"

Hannibal thought about the offer as another mover came into the room and picked up yet another morsel of his life.

"Doesn't look like I have a choice, does it?"

"Not from where I'm standing."

"Fine, Jackson. I'll do it. You're a real bastard, you know that?"

"Whatever, Hannibal. I'll just have a word with the sheriff and the manager and be right back."

Jackson departed, leaving his colleague standing still and staring at Hannibal.

Hannibal reached into the refrigerator again and pulled out another beer.

"Want a beer, Edwards?"

"No, thanks, Hannibal. I'm on duty."

"Good, because this is the last one."

Edwards grinned.

~ ~ ~ ~ ~

Several minutes later, men began bringing in the furniture they had just taken out. Mrs. Morrison toddled past his door with a large handful of cash in her hand, stopping to stick her head in and smile that special smile towards Hannibal

"Glad you're staying, Professor."

"Are we square, Mrs. Morrison?"

"Oh yes, dear. That nice young man just paid your back rent in full, another year in advance, plus a very nice bonus. You can go now. I'll see to it that everything is put back into your apartment and it's locked up."

"Thanks, Mrs. Morrison."

"Think nothing of it, dear. You *do* have special friends, I'll say that for you."

"Low friends in even lower places, it seems."

"Ta ta," said Mrs. Morrison. She turned and walked away, thumbing through the bills in her hand, just as Jackson walked into the apartment.

"We gotta go, Hannibal. Now."

"Where we 'gotta go' to, Jackson?"

"I'm not at liberty to say at the moment. Let me just say this. Poseidon Deliberate Jupiter."

Hannibal's expression became serious. "What did you say?"

"I said 'Poseidon Deliberate Jupiter.'"

Hannibal immediately tossed his half-full can of beer back over his head and into the sink and wiped his coat sleeve across his mouth. "Well, come on, let's go, Jackson. What the hell you waiting for?"

~ ~ ~ ~ ~

The black government-issued Chevrolet Tahoe sped down the open California highway. Inside the SUV, Hannibal rubbed his hands nervously as he attempted to interrogate Agent Jackson.

"When? When did you find it? No! Where? *Where* did you find it? Was it where I said it would be?"

"Hannibal, you'll have all your questions answered in a few hours."

"Come on, Jackson. Answer me, damnit. Where was it?"

"Hannibal, you know the drill."

"Ah, don't be a chickenshit, Jackson. This could be the biggest discovery ever. Do you know what this means? If it's there and it's intact. My god, Jackson! Was it intact? Oh, did you arrange —"

"Yes, she'll meet you at Edwards."

"Edwards Air Force Base? Oh, great! Wow! What if it's intact, Jackson? Can you imagine the possibilities?"

"Hannibal, I'm sure you'll find all your answers when you get there. Now shut up. You're driving me crazy!"

Hannibal reached out and grabbed Jackson by his shoulders and shook him excitedly. "Thanks, buddy. You just made my day."

Jackson let Hannibal shake him. He said nothing, just shook his head. Hannibal sat back in the seat and laughed. "It's getting better. Yeah, so how you doin' now, Hannibal?" He asked himself.

Jackson stared at him and shook his head. "You're very weird, Hannibal."

~ ~ ~ ~ ~

The Tahoe stopped alongside the Gulfstream G-5. Hannibal thrust open the door and climbed out. He looked at his watch anxiously and then yelled, "Where is she, Jackson? It's just like a woman, you know."

Traci Jefferson stepped through the Gulfstream hatch. "What's just like a woman, Hannibal?" she asked.

Hannibal cringed and then walked toward the aircraft. Climbing the short stairs, he smiled sheepishly. "Women are always on time, Traci. That's what I meant."

"Yeah, right, Hannibal. Well, at least there's one dependable constant in the universe."

"That's what Jackson said." Hannibal squeezed past Traci and entered the plane.

"It's been a while, honey. Marry anybody lately?"

"Ah, geez. It's gonna be a long flight."

CHAPTER 4

The jet, airborne for the past three hours, was at 32,500 feet on a southeasterly heading, with Traci and Hannibal its only passengers.

Sitting across from one another in the tan, plush leather seats of the sleek corporate jet, Traci eyed Hannibal intently as he dabbed at a large wet stain on the crotch of his pants. "I knew you were still angry."

"Oh, don't be silly, Hannibal. I told you, it just slipped from my hand."

Hannibal finished dabbing himself and tossed the napkin onto the table next to him.

He sat silently, studying Traci's exquisite form — her thin, shapely legs, her petite frame, perfectly constructed face, and blonde hair, beautifully coifed. Something fondly remembered crossed his face in the form of a slight smile.

"You're staring again, Hannibal."

"I always stare at you, honey."

"It's not going to work this time, Hannibal. You're avoiding the real issue. It's killing you, I know it. I'm impressed, though. I didn't think you could hold out this long."

"I don't know what you're talking about. I'm staring because you're still a knockout."

"I'm pretty, am I?"

"You know you are, Traci."

"Pretty enough to leave standing at the altar?"

"I knew you were still pissed."

"It hurt, Hannibal. You left me standing there in front of everyone. Remember?"

"It was an emergency! I explained that to you. Several times already, I might add. It was located right where I thought it should be. Imagine how I felt, to find an intact Mayan seal complete with inscription, two hundred feet below sea level right off the coast, right where I said it should be."

"It wasn't a Mayan seal, Hannibal. It was an engraved piece of tin dropped overboard from a cruise ship."

"But it *could* have been an ancient artifact of great importance. I'm sorry. For the millionth time, I'm sorry. Okay?"

"Oh, Hannibal, if I didn't still care for you, I'd ... I'd ... well, I'd punch you in the nose."

"If it'll stop you from tossing drinks at me, go ahead."

"Stop mocking me!"

"I'm not."

"It wouldn't do any good anyway. I learned a long time ago that if I ever got between Hannibal Storm and an archaeological find, I'd lose every time."

"Then why are you still so angry? You know the position I'm in with the institute."

"I know all about it, Hannibal."

"I'm sure you do. Well, it doesn't really matter anymore. I think I'm going to be sacked pretty soon."

"I know all about that too, Hannibal. I know everything about you, you loveable goof."

"I'm not a goof."

"You are to me."

"Fine. Whatever."

"You have grown some, though, over the past year. I'll have to give you some credit for that, I guess. The old Hannibal would have been badgering me about what brought him here from the moment he set eyes on me. Maybe there's some hope for you after all."

"I'm the same guy. You just never took the time to try and understand me."

"Don't go there, Hannibal. Don't you even start down that highway, buster."

"I'm sorry, Traci. You're right."

"How dare you say that to me. To me, of all people."

"Here we go again. I said I was sorry. Do you need to toss another drink in my lap to feel better?"

"I really hate you right now, Hannibal."

"You love me. You know it."

"And that's what really makes me hate you. It's a disease."

"And there's no cure for it, right?"

"Shut the hell up! Just shut up, Hannibal."

"Fine. I'll just sit here, then."

Traci studied him for a good long while. Finally, she smiled slyly. "It's killing you, isn't it? Not to know why I've brought you here. You're dying to know."

"I'm curious, that's all."

"Yeah, right."

"I'm serious. I'm wondering what we're doing on a corporate jet. I didn't know the CIA flew corporate jets these days."

"Come on, Hannibal. You know I left the agency last year after you dumped me."

"I know you've developed a new cover. And I didn't dump you. You dumped me. Get your facts straight."

"I really hate you, and no, I left the agency."

"Bullshit."

"Well, I left active duty. I'm still working with the agency, but in a different capacity now."

"That's more like it. So what's your new 'capacity'?"

"I work for Grindstone Energy Technologies now."

"Tell me something I don't already know, like what you do for them."

"Hannibal, I'm the CEO. We're on a Grindstone jet."

"Whoa! Moving up in the world, huh?"

"Sort of had to. *We* weren't going anywhere."

"Ah, geez."

"Sorry. That was unnecessary."

"Well, congratulations. On the CEO thing. I didn't know that."

"Thanks."

"Tell me, Traci, what does the CEO of an alternative energy company have to do with the CIA? Better yet, what are we doing heading south?"

"I was right, wasn't I? It's killing you not to know. Well, sorry. I can't say right now."

"Oh, really hush-hush, huh? Obviously, I was right. Grindstone is a cover. So what's up?"

"Let's chat more about it after we land."

"Well, what is our cover story? Are we using our real names today, or are we into disguises and secret code names?"

"I think we can dispense with all that for now."

"You know what I mean. What the hell is going on?"

"Sorry, dear. I just can't take any chances on this one."

"You've never taken any real chances in your life."

"I took one with you and look what happened."

"You're just not going to give up on it, are you? You're gonna keep banging on me about that forever. That was a year ago, for crying out loud."

"You're right. It was a long time ago. I should get over it. You obviously aren't troubled by it."

"Here we go again."

"Okay. You're right. Sorry. Let's leave it alone. Let's talk about something else."

"Fine. So what does Grindstone have to do with the CIA?"

"Okay, Hannibal, you win. Grindstone has a contract with the government to find alternative energy sources."

"Yeah, right."

"I'm serious."

"Fine. So why are we heading deep into Mexico?"

"Let's just say for now that Grindstone has a unique contract with the government and leave it at that. Okay?"

"Okay. For now. So why did you use our code words?"

"Because I knew it would get you here." Traci smirked as she pulled her briefcase up and set it on her lap.

"Then you *did* find it?"

"No, dear. Your precious Cave of Golden Seals has not been located."

"The cave isn't in Mexico anyway. So why are we heading into Mexico? Why this hugger-mugger routine?"

"Look at this and tell me it's not just as important as the Cave of Golden Seals."

She opened her briefcase and pulled out a file. Opening it, she said, "Yesterday morning a large commercial airliner went down in the Yucatan. It was fully fueled when it went down, having just taken off from Cancun minutes before. The resulting fireball burned away a large portion of very thick jungle growth and exposed this."

She pulled out an 8 x 10 color photograph and handed it to Hannibal.

"It looks like some kind of ancient ruin," Hannibal said, studying the photo closely. "A temple, maybe."

"Well, look at this." Traci handed him another photo, a relative close-up of the structure, a small portion of it scorched and blackened from the fire. She pointed to a particular spot on the photograph and added, "Right here. What do you think?"

Hannibal reached into his pocket and withdrew the loupe. Holding both close to his eye, he studied the photograph closely.

"I see you still carry that loupe with you."

"Yes."

"That's been the problem, Hannibal. You and that loupe."

"Don't go there, Traci. You know it was a gift from Andy Anderson. It's a loupe. That's all it is and ever has been."

"You care more about that loupe than you ever cared about me."

"Do we really have to do this right now?" replied Hannibal, still studying the photograph.

The expression of surprise on his face nearly said it all. "My god!"

"What, Hannibal? You recognize something?"

"It appears to be a temple of ancient origin ... but I don't understand. What does this have to do with energy sources? Why is Grindstone interested in ancient temples?"

"Hannibal, please. What is this?" said Traci, pointing to a specific spot on the photo. It was a unique symbol engraved above the entrance to the structure. "What is this right here?"

Hannibal moved the loupe over it and studied it carefully. "You don't know?"

"That's why you're here. We don't know. It's a symbol, obviously, but no one has any idea what it might represent. The head Mexican archaeologist said he's never seen it before." Traci reached into her briefcase and pulled out a third photograph. "Here. Here's a blowup. Do you know what it is?"

Clearly now, Hannibal could see the symbol — a double triangle holding a set of three hexagons descending toward a circle composed of red, orange, green, yellow, and blue interlocking crescents. Each shape was an inlay of semi-precious stones. Hannibal brought the photo close to his face and stared at it.

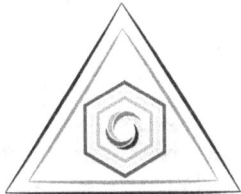

He moved the loupe over it and stared at it for some time in silence.

The extended silence was too long for Traci. "Do you recognize it, Hannibal? Is it a temple of Atlantis? ... Hannibal? ... Hannibal?" Hannibal continued his mesmerized stare and did not respond. "HANNIBAL — do you recognize it?"

Hannibal continued his inspection a few more seconds and finally looked up. The distant look in his eye intrigued Traci.

"It's NOT Atlantis," he scoffed. "How many times do I need to say it? Atlantis is not in this part of the world, not in the New World. But ... Lemurian or Lemurian-like remnants should be located somewhere around here."

"Lemuria? Okay. ... Well, is it Lemurian?"

Hannibal leaned back against the seat and thoughtfully scratched at his chin with his little finger. "Maybe."

"Maybe?"

"Have you ever heard of the 1893 Herzog Expedition?" he asked as he folded his loupe and returned it to his pocket.

Traci shook her head.

"In July 1893, based on a secret report discovered by an unacknowledged fellow researcher, a team of archaeologists and anthropologists, headed by Dr. Harold Herzog from the University of Washington's Anthropology Department, set out on a huge expedition to the Yucatan. After two years of searching, they discovered what Herzog reportedly believed to be genuine proof of what he called an 'Atlantean' ruin.

"The Mexican government at the time was very much opposed to the removal of any of the artifacts, but it has been rumored that Herzog managed to smuggle several of the articles out of the country anyway. At least that's the story.

"These articles were said to have been engraved with special markings. I've seen sketches of some of them, but they were at best only second- or third-generation copies.

"Some of them, as I recall, were almost identical to this one. The original sketches were reportedly lost in a fire decades ago. As for the articles themselves, no one can say for sure what they were. Some people swear they were some kind of stone. Some say they were special tablets. We'll probably never know for sure. They reportedly disappeared about the same time the sketches burned."

"What about Herzog?"

"Dead. The entire expedition team, with one exception, died when their boat sank somewhere off the Yucatan coast while returning from the dig to Corpus Christi. Some say the boat sank under mysterious circumstances. Who knows anymore? It was a long time ago."

"How did the articles survive the sinking?"

"They were supposedly smuggled out long before the team was scheduled to return."

"You think it's this structure Herzog found?"

"Impossible to say. All the records, maps, charts ... everything, apparently, was destroyed in the fire. Besides, it doesn't really matter anymore. All the new data indicates that Atlantis, or what passed for Atlantis, is not located in this part of the world. Some believe it may have been located on what we now know as the Greek island of Santorini and was destroyed during the eruption of the Santorini volcano, then known as Thera, about three thousand years ago. I've also heard it said that Atlantis was actually the island of Crete and was destroyed by a tsunami created by the Thera eruption. No one of worth today really believes that Atlantis is anywhere near the New World, although some still insist that it was located in the Atlantic Ocean and that the southwestern shores and mountaintops of the continent make up parts of the Bahamas, Bimini, Cuba, places like that.

"I think that's all hogwash, but the underwater land masses near Bimini *are* quite old. The structures I've seen and photographed near there show *every* indication of being man-made, although some would argue that they're just natural formations."

"Are you talking about the Bimini Road structure? The one that looks like a roadway under the water?"

"No. I'm talking about other structures. You probably wouldn't have heard of them. They've not been publicized. Something about them has most governments scared or worried. Which is why I think Bernard pulled the plug on me. He's such a horse's ass," he added heatedly.

Traci dropped her hand onto Hannibal's knee. "Hannibal, dear, focus, please. Focus."

Hannibal calmed himself. "Well, he *is* a horse's ass."

"What about the structures?"

"The structures indicate at the very least that part of the island was above water some time ago. When exactly, I haven't yet made a determination, but I'll tell you this: *If that blind, stupid bastard hadn't cut off my financing —*"

"Hannibal, please, dear. I *really* need you to concentrate here. This is really important."

Hannibal sat back in his seat and took a few deep breaths. After several smaller breaths, he said, "Fine. I'm calm. I'm calm. Look, Trace, I believe the structures are only part of some larger network of structures that may have been connected, in some lesser way, perhaps, to the Lemurian civilization."

"What part is that? Isn't Lemuria supposed to have existed somewhere in the Pacific Ocean?"

"Lemuria. Land of Mu. That never existed. At least it didn't exist in the way that Churchward described it. No, that theory lost acceptance when tectonic plate shifting became the accepted theory for the cause of land shifts. Besides, all the evidence for a sunken continent in the Pacific Ocean doesn't exist ... and really, it never existed."

"Wait! Who is Churchward?"

"Colonel James Churchward. He was a British-born occult writer. In 1926, at the age of 75, he published *The Lost Continent of Mu: Motherland of Man*. In that book he claimed to have proved the existence of a lost continent called Mu, or Lemuria, in the Pacific Ocean. According to Churchward, Mu extended from a little north of Hawaii southward to somewhere around Fiji. Now we know it isn't possible that a continent like that ever existed because of the model of plate tectonics. The model itself builds on the concept of continental drift, which was developed during the first few decades of the twentieth century. *BUT!*" Hannibal slid excitedly to the edge of the seat as he continued. "Churchward insisted that he had identified a race of people who lived there. He called them the Naacal."

"Not the Lemurians?"

"No. The Naacal. Well, they're the same race, but Lemuria ... oh, it doesn't matter right now. Listen to me. He said he'd discovered information indicating that this civilization was fully flourishing some fifty thousand years ago, and that they were technologically more advanced than we are today, and here's the punch line. He believed he had evidence that the ancient civilizations of India, Babylon, Persia, Egypt, and, listen carefully, the *Mayans* were all remnants of the Mu civilization — the descendants of the Naacal."

"Wait a minute! Now you're saying that Churchward was right?"

"Partially, correct. I'm saying he figured out a part of it, but never quite put it all together. We know now that, geologically speaking, no continent of Mu ever existed, but the technology of the ancients *had* to have come from somewhere and no one has ever fully explained the sudden advance in similar building technology and other technologies that were used to create and sustain entire ancient civilizations right after the end of the Ice Age. Both Egyptians and Mayans built pyramids, and there are other pyramids all over the world, from China to Bosnia —"

"But the Egyptian and Mayan pyramids look totally different!"

"Do they really? If you consider the lack of building materials and the fact that the Mayans faced sheer cliffs and had heavy jungle to contend with, might that not explain the slight differences in building techniques, materials used, and the overall scale differential?

"The Egyptians built bigger because they had better resources and easier terrain to contend with. But both civilizations looked to pyramids. In fact, most of the world looked to pyramids. Think about it. Why? Why would civilizations all over the world, with no apparent knowledge of each other, build the same structure — unless they all had the same foundational knowledge from the same original source?"

"I don't know, Hannibal. I think you're stretching a bit."

"Maybe. Maybe not. Look, Churchward claimed to have gained his knowledge of the Naacal from a priest in India. He claimed that the priest taught him a language that had been dead for centuries. The priest was said to have shown him several ancient tablets written by the Naacal, but they weren't complete. In fact, they were only pieces of a larger lost tablet, but he claimed, after studying the records of other ancient civilizations including the Mayans, that the basis for the story was substantially supported. He also claimed that the Egyptian sun god, Ra, R-a, was just a different spelling of the Naacal word for the sun, R-a-h. So there's a connection. It's there somewhere."

Traci leaned back in her chair and scratched at her chin. "Hmm. Is that so?"

"You still don't believe it, do you?"

"It's not that. I just think it might be a simple coincidence."

"Try this, then. What if there was a global civilization that once existed? Wouldn't that end all the archaeological speculation?"

"I guess so, but I just don't see it, Hannibal."

"Are you serious? Let's take a look at some very interesting points of comparison between, let's say, the Americas and Egypt, for example: Both societies built pyramids of stone aligned with the cardinal points on a compass. Both cultures built temples using megalithic stones weighing tens of tons and joined them with absolute precision. Both used royal headdresses that are very similar. Both used construction techniques that incorporated L-shaped corners and utilized similar metal clamps that held the stones together even during vicious earthquakes. And finally, both cultures used mummification to preserve their dead. Does this seem to you to be simple coincidence?"

"When you put it like that, no."

"Of course not. The only explanation is that there was once a global civilization that existed and maintained very close contact all over the globe."

"And you think it could be the Naacal?"

"Does it sound so crazy?"

"Okay, Hannibal. You make a good argument, but what does that have to do with this symbol here?" Traci pointed to the symbol in the photograph.

"Honestly, at this moment I just don't know exactly. I'm more taken with the architecture of the structure. I mean it has no apparent relationship with anything Mayan or Aztec. It's unique and completely unexpected." Hannibal picked up the enlarged photo of the symbol again and studied it for several minutes in silence. Finally he looked up at Traci and smiled a Cheshire cat smile.

"What?" asked Traci.

Hannibal rolled his eyes and looked up at the ceiling of the aircraft.

"What, Hannibal? Give it up."

Hannibal returned his gaze to the photograph. "Well, I'm not saying I know what it is, but getting back to Herzog, I heard a rumor, just a rumor, mind you, but I heard that what Herzog was actually looking for was the *tuaoi*."

"Tua what?"

"Try this. Two'-uh-oy."

"Okay. What's a tuaoi, Hannibal?"

"The Great Crystal. A large crystal. Immense, really. It was the catalyst device for producing wireless power. Apparently both the Naacal and, supposedly, the Atlanteans — who were actually Lemurians, or more specifically, one of the Naacal nations — perfected this form of energy."

"Are you talking about a firestone? An actual firestone?"

"Yes. Nice to see that Grindstone keeps up on this stuff. A firestone, yes. But that's a misnomer. There was no fire, per se. It produced power, or rather it channeled power based on the zero-point energy theory. It was like a power station, the generating crystal which gathered together the power created by the electromagnetic forces of the earth and focused it into useable, wireless energy. It was, in action, a wireless power station. It produced the energy necessary to power their homes, their ground transportation systems, their commerce and industrial manufacturing, and, of course, their spacecraft and watercraft."

Traci reacted with startled amazement. "Spacecraft, Hannibal? Now you're jerking my chain."

"No! Not at all. It's said that while the Naacal were more practiced at it, both civilizations, the Naacal and the Atlanteans, had access to space travel. And that would make sense, since they were one and the same people. Both had spaceports, where the spacecraft ascended from and returned to."

Traci laughed. "Okay, Hannibal. That was a good one. You almost had me on that one."

"I'm serious, Traci. Supposedly, the firestone had tremendous power. It could cause objects to defy gravity, or it powered separate anti-gravity devices. I think that's what Herzog found and, ultimately, what caused his death. His murder."

"Let me see if I get this — wait! You're saying Herzog was murdered?"

"The details of the sinking have been a source of speculation within certain circles for decades. The weather was reportedly clear. The seas were known to be calm on that particular day and yet the ship sank. You can imagine what was being speculated."

"But there's no proof that the sinking was intentional, right?"

"Nothing that would make it into court. But the lone survivor, someone named Billings, I think, gave a pretty clear account of something gone awry aboard the ship just before it sank. Of course, all those records have disappeared as well. So there's no way to verify any of what I'm saying."

"What happened to the survivor?"

"He died back in early 1950s, I believe. At least that's what I remember hearing."

"So, maybe Herzog found the firestone and was murdered for it? Why?"

"Let me put it this way," Hannibal said. "The best minds in the world today are stumped as to how the firestone could be used, let alone believing that it *was* used, if it existed at all. It's thought that the Naacal very effectively used the energy produced by the firestone to power their airplanes, boats, submarines, and even their spacecraft miles from the original source. Perhaps thousands of miles away. Is that significant enough?"

"I don't understand exactly."

"Okay. Imagine possessing the knowledge of *unlimited, free, wireless power*, capable of powering homes, businesses, cars, factories. Free, limitless, and renewable power. It would be worth hundreds of billions."

"Tens of trillions, you mean."

"No doubt an inconceivable amount of money. Imagine the power held by the nation that controlled this technology. It certainly would be worth killing for. I believe nations would even risk a horrible war to possess the knowledge and power of the firestone. If that's what this symbol even means. Of course, this symbol could have nothing at all to do with the Herzog expedition or the firestone. Hell, it could be a sign for a bakery, for all I know."

The pilot's voice on the intercom interrupted them. "Folks, please fasten your seat belts. We are beginning our descent into Cancun. Ms. Jefferson, we're told that your helicopter is standing by."

CHAPTER 5

The helicopter completed a perfect landing. The door popped open and Traci and Hannibal exited. Bending at the waist to avoid the whirling blades, they made their way toward a structure hidden by an enormous tent and surrounded by several uniformed soldiers of the Mexican army packing suitable defensive firepower.

The area still looked like a war zone, minus the bodies, of course, with parts of the destroyed airliner left exactly as they had fallen.

Hannibal immediately spotted young Jesus Bolon standing alone near some crates. He walked over and smiled down at him.

"Hey, kid. How are you doing? You know, maybe this isn't the place for you."

Jesus just stared back at Hannibal with dark, sullen eyes.

Hannibal repeated his words in Mayan. Jesus nodded, but remained where he was.

Traci walked up behind Hannibal.

"Should he be here, Trace?"

"His name is Jesus Bolon, Hannibal. He witnessed the crash. He's the one who first saw the structure over there, and he's been here ever since we arrived. I don't think he's gonna leave anytime soon either."

"Damn! He saw the bodies too?"

"He was first on the scene, Hannibal."

"Christ! Nothing will ever be normal for him again."

"Look around, Hannibal. It's pretty much the same for everyone here, I think."

~ ~ ~ ~ ~

The surrounding area, with several individual tents lined up in neat rows, bustled with the activity of every scientific and investigative variety. Teams of white-coated people scurried about, some with notepads, some with shovels, some with other tools and brushes. From Hannibal's cynical perspective it seemed like barely controlled chaos.

As they neared the guarded entrance, CIA Agent Kirby Hansen exited the tented structure. He saw them and waved. Trotting toward them and past the guards, he stopped short and grinned. "Well, well, as I live and breathe. The Storm blows in. It's about time. What do you think, Hannibal?"

Hannibal stepped up to Kirby and punched him squarely in the jaw, sending him sprawling backwards into the dirt. The guards immediately reacted, but Kirby held up his hand in a halting motion. He rubbed his chin, shook the cobwebs from his brain, and wiggled his jaw as he sat up.

"I still think you're an asshole, Kirby."

Kirby looked up, smiling at Hannibal. "Are you still sore about that little incident?"

"'Little' incident?!"

Kirby chuckled. "Damn, Hannibal. That was five years ago. Can't you get over it?"

"He seems to have gotten over *our* little incident."

"Don't you start in on me, too."

Traci just grinned.

"Well, I see you can still take care of yourself, partner. Good right cross. It's a beauty, huh? The structure, I mean."

Kirby jumped to his feet and turned to stare at it.

"Yeah, Kirby. It's something, all right. When can I see it?"

"How about now? Get the clean suit on and have a look."

Kirby looked at Traci. "Hi, Trace."

"Hi, Kirby."

Kirby just grinned and bumped up his eyebrows.

~ ~ ~ ~ ~

The clean suits were fancy versions of bulky hazmat suits, designed to prevent any further contamination of the structure, and Hannibal adapted to his quickly.

"Hey, Hannibal. Traci fill you in?" asked Kirby as he walked into the clean room.

"I'm sure she didn't tell me everything. What's the CIA doing here in Mexico?"

"Need to know, partner. Only what you need to know."

"Well, then, what do I need to know about this?"

"Hell. Nothing ... everything. I don't really know anything about what's goin' on myself, partner."

Hannibal stopped Kirby by grabbing his arm. "You know everything about this operation. You always know exactly what's 'goin' on,' and I'm not your *partner* anymore."

"I'm serious, Hannibal. I'm in the dark on this one."

Hannibal scoffed. "Okay, fine. I don't need your help. I'll figure it out on my own."

"That's why you're here, Hannibal."

"Bullshit!"

"I'm tellin' you, partner. This one has got the high-muckety-mucks in an uproar. I only got here late yesterday afternoon myself. As soon as I arrived, I was told to get your ass here ASAP. That's all I know. Oh, except that a Doctor Hector Gonzalez will be flying in this afternoon to head the investigation. You know him?"

"I know him. Good man. Well respected. So what do the spooks want with me, then? It looks like you got everyone you need here already."

Kirby looked around to see if anyone might be listening. There was no one. He pulled Hannibal close to him. "The emblem, Hannibal. The emblem above the door. They want you to decipher it before the Mexicans do."

"Why?"

"Don't know, partner. They just want it done."

"Bullshit. I know you, Kirby. You're in deep on this one."

"Hey, partner. I mean it. This one's a blur. I gotta go. Have a look around. You're cleared everywhere. Keep me posted. Good luck. Thanks, Traci. Good job." Kirby disappeared from the clean room.

Traci looked at Hannibal. "You ready?"

"As I can be, I guess." Then he shouted toward the door, "And we're not *partners!*"

Hannibal grabbed Traci's hand and followed Kirby's path out of the clean room and to the entrance of the main tent.

He took a deep breath and walked through the entrance. They turned a corner, went through an airlock, and found themselves at the main entrance to the structure. Hannibal froze on the spot and stared up at the emblem over the door.

"It looks as if it were installed an hour ago. It's in pristine condition. How's that possible?" He stared at the symbol.

Traci nudged him. "What are you thinking?"

"I'm thinking we ought to go inside and have a look around."

From the open ten-foot-square marble door, which could be moved easily back and forth with only one finger, Hannibal could see that the interior was made almost completely of precision-fitted white marble and stone with colorful stone-chip mosaics decorating every wall. The area was brilliantly lit by klieg lights powered by large generators outside the structure.

Hannibal estimated the exterior of the structure to be approximately forty feet by forty feet, with a roof that towered at least twenty feet above them and finished in a dome.

As they entered the structure they saw that its inside was a hexagon, with every detail of the ornate and colorful interior clearly and brightly exposed by the powerful lights. The immaculate condition of the building's interior stunned Hannibal.

In the center of the room sat what appeared to be an altar made of the purest white marble, also in a hexagonal shape, each of the six sides proportionate and parallel to the interior walls of the structure.

The flooring was also of intricate design using, again, the finest white and black marble. A large yellow-tile sunburst was centered in the floor of the room, encircling the altar-like structure, with six grand radials that exploded outward to the walls, while lesser radials spanned the spaces between the larger ones, their lengths equal to the radius of the sun's body. On the ceiling directly over the alter was an inlay of gold depicting a blazing sun, half the size of the dome, shining benevolently over the mosaics of a beautiful and graceful people and a rich and prosperous landscape, its rays proportional to the rays on the floor.

The mosaics were made of different-colored chips of highly polished limestone, granite, and marble, and were still extremely vibrant. Every wall had two different scenes presumably depicting the lifestyle of the time. Some pictures showed flying craft descending to the earth. Some were of water activities and various types of watercraft, both surface and subsurface forms. Others illustrated a more common life, such as a farmer attending his abundantly producing field and a factory worker constructing something of use. Each scene was tied to the adjacent ones by a yellow line which tied directly to the sunbursts on both the floor and the ceiling. One section of the wall portrayed two groups of people apparently in battle with each other. These people were touched by both sets of rays, one emanating from the golden sun above and the other from the sunburst set into the floor. One group of people was apparently of a red race while the other was black.

Hannibal wandered around looking up at the dome and then down at the yellow-tile sun. "Two suns?" The question was meant for him alone.

Traci tugged on his arm. "Hannibal. Is this real?"

Hannibal only nodded as he continued his walk slowly around the structure, his eyes glued in amazement to every detail. Finally he turned back toward the altar-like structure. "Look at this, Traci."

They approached the structure in the center of the room and peered down into the hexagonal hole, about five feet deep and five feet across and empty.

"What is it?"

"Well, Trace, I'm not certain, but I do believe it's a hole."

"Be serious, please."

"How can you expect me to know what it is? I'm looking at it for the first time, just like you."

"I'm sorry, but you're supposed to be the expert."

"I *am* an expert in the things I know, but this is something I've never seen before. I don't think anyone has seen this in millennia, if my guess is correct."

"What guess? You know what this is, don't you?"

"I'm not sure."

"Fine. Just tell me what you *think* it might be. Please, Hannibal. This could be very important."

"I think it's where a crystal was seated. Note the hexagonal shape. That's the shape of a perfect crystal. But wow! It would have to be a giant crystal to fit in there. It would explain the two suns, though."

"Two suns?"

"That's what I asked myself. But I think I understand now."

Hannibal pointed up to the gold disk on the ceiling and then back down, to the yellow sun surrounding the altar. "I think that's the physical sun above and this one down here represents the crystal's radiation pattern of energy. But I'm only guessing."

"The firestone?"

"No, it's too small for the firestone."

"How do you know that?"

"I don't, but legend says the firestone was immense. This is big, but I wouldn't call it immense."

"Then what?"

"I can't say right now. Give me some time to think."

Hannibal walked around the room and took note of the section of the wall representing the warring factions. He studied the area for several seconds. "If this is Lemurian, then these two groups of people might represent the Children of the Law of One and the Sons of Belial."

"Who?"

Hannibal continued his slow walk around the room, stopping to study each of the mosaics before responding. "They were the two basic groups widely regarded as being responsible for beginning the aggression that eventually destroyed the Lemurian civilization."

"Lemurian, not Naacal?"

"They're the same, Lemurian and Naacal. They're the same race of people."

"But one group of people is red and the other is black."

"The Naacal would have been Indian. The other group shown was actually the same. The black color, according to the legends, represents their dark spirit. The Sons of Belial are always depicted as black or dark. It represents the blackness of their hearts, the darkness of their minds, the emptiness of their souls."

"I see. That makes sense. But how did they destroy their civilization? They weren't destroyed by earthquakes and volcanoes, like Atlantis?"

"Sort of, but it was the aggression of these two factions that was at the heart of their destruction."

"You mean the destruction was man-made?"

"Yes, that's what the legends say."

"Just to be clear, Hannibal, we're talking legend, not fact, correct?"

"Legend, yes."

"Okay. Please continue."

"The Children of the Law of One were purportedly the pure souls of thought which remained true to the creative spirit as they projected themselves into material form. They never forgot their source, if you will. The Sons of Belial, on the other hand — Belial means the personification of evil and devout wickedness — were the souls that projected themselves into earthly form seeking only that which would gratify their own fleshly desires and lusts. Eventually, the Sons of Belial became completely encased in their earthly form and lost the ability to move from the spirit world into the flesh and vice versa. As they became permanently separated from the creative spirit, they became despondent."

"So they started a war?"

"Not right away, or at least that's how the story goes."

"Tell me, Hannibal. I'm fascinated. Please tell me the whole story, from the beginning. I don't understand."

"It's a long story."

"We have the time. I need to understand this."

"It's not a happy story, Traci. In fact, it's a story of true shame. It's a story of a very painful moment in the history of mankind."

"The *legend* of mankind, right?"

"Yeah, the legend."

"Okay, tell me, Hannibal. From the beginning, please."

"Here goes. It's very simple. Let us begin with the word 'all.' Everything here is all there is. All is everything. We are all that ever was or ever will be. Before the universe, there was nothing but us and we were one. There was, in essence, then, only I. But it was our desire that we should be more, so that we could converse together, but it was not possible to speak separately, for we were but only one — a singular consciousness, if you will.

"And so we divided ourselves into many and we created, in this division, the physical plane. Still, we were so well connected, one to the other, on the other levels that every individual thought was still our own, collectively speaking. We could not escape the whole and think anything that was separate from the One. And so, some parts of us, wishing to put some separation between us for the sole purpose of discovering new and independent thoughts, projected ourselves into the physical plane. But in separating ourselves from the One, the Singular Consciousness, we found ourselves instantly separated from the One and lacking the knowledge of how to get back to the One. We had now become *they* and *us*: separate beings. This is what has been called the First Falling."

"Is this the story of the Devil, the heavenly war, and one-third of the angels being cast down to earth by God?"

"It may have been the basis for the story, Traci. If not this exact story, it may have come from a story like this, but you must understand, they were not cast down by God. They separated from the One only to expand the One into many so as to enjoy each new individual created from out of the One differently."

"This is pretty deep for me, Hannibal."

"I'm explaining it as simply as I can."

"Okay. Go on."

"They had no desire to permanently separate themselves from the Singular Consciousness and they cried mournfully that they had separated and could not find their way back.

"There was no war in heaven, as you might call it. The separation occurred as an act of love, done in love. But no matter how it was done, or for what reason, they could not find their way back home, so to speak. And so the rest of us, wishing to rescue ourselves, our kin as it were, from the separation, mounted a rescue. This resulted in what has become known as the Second Falling.

"In the midst of the rescue, the rescuers became partially encased in the matter of the physical plane. Thus they *fell* also; hence, the Second Falling. So once again, in love's quest, we lost more of ourselves to the entrapments of the physical plane, but not before we sufficiently instilled in our Second Fallers the know-how to find their way back into the Singular Consciousness. How this was accomplished is still debated, but it also may explain why all the fallen didn't just become evil right away. The *Seconds*, as some call the Second Fallers, still possessed the spark of the Singular Consciousness."

"So that's the story of the creation of man?"

"One of them ... at least a part of it."

"How does it relate to this structure?"

"I have no idea, Traci. I'm just suggesting that it might be related."

"Well, what about the firestone? How does that relate to the story?"

"Like this. After the Second Falling, the rescuers, who were part of the Children of the Law of One, or the Sons of Light, as they are sometimes called, coexisted on the earth with the *others* for a very long time."

"Wait, Hannibal. Who were the *others?* Weren't they the same people?"

"Yes, but the *others* consisted of those who, although originally being part of both the First and Second Fallers, had, after a time, given in fully to the temptation of the physical plane, had become fully encased in the physical form. They, who would eventually become known as the Sons of Belial, having come from the stars, so to speak, and now found themselves trapped, became an angry people."

"Hannibal! You mean they were extraterrestrials?"

"Look, Trace, this is going to take some time. It'll take a lot longer than it has to if you keep interrupting me."

"Sorry, Hannibal, but if you're suggesting that this planet was seeded by a group of ill-mannered extraterrestrials —"

"I'm not suggesting anything. I'm trying to tell you the legend as I understand it. May I continue?"

"Fine. Sorry."

"Anyway. The beings on the earth at that time can best be described as two souls born of the same great Loving Source, God, as this source is often called today.

"However, over time, the Sons of Belial, having given themselves further to the physical plane, began thinking very differently than their counterparts from the Law of One, the Sons of Light.

"The Sons of Light maintained their devotion and allegiance to the Source. Thus they retained their ability to move back and forth between spirit and flesh, although, because of the falling, they were not able to stay in the spirit for very long. This caused more strife between them and the Sons of Belial, for those beings had lost even that temporary ability.

"In the great many years that followed while living upon the earth together, the two factions grew further apart until one faction moved away to live in the land to the west."

"Where is this land?"

"For Christ's sake, Traci!"

"I'm sorry, but I'm just not following you."

"It was an island nation, Traci. One group lived on the eastern portion and the other moved to the western side, okay?"

"Okay. Please continue. I'm sorry. This is very deep stuff."

"I know, but this is the only way I can explain it. Anyway, these people became horribly segregated over time and soon factional border skirmishes became more frequent. But for the most part, each party stayed on its own side and they existed mostly in harmony.

"Meanwhile, over the centuries both managed to build large civilizations. During this building time, it has been suggested by certain scholars, both factions, working together in some limited fashion, discovered wireless power through the use of large crystals."

"Finally, we're getting to the crystals."

"Hey, you said you wanted to hear the whole story."

"I know. Now I'm beginning to understand. Continue, please."

"The harmony didn't last. The Sons of Belial grew more and more jealous of the Sons of Light and their ability to communicate with the Source, God, at will.

"Finally, the Sons of Belial sent a message that they wanted the Sons of Light to leave the island or face a great war. The end of peace was now inevitable. It was only a matter of precious time before a confrontation would take place.

"The Sons of Light, however, ignored the warning and refused either to leave or to fight."

"How was that possible? How could they escape the inevitability of a fight yet continue to live on the island? It makes no sense."

"Here's where things get fuzzy for any scholar, including me. The Sons of Belial gave a specific time and date when the Sons of Light were to either leave the island or fight the war. The High Priest of the Sons of Light was supposedly very wise and powerful, and extremely adept in the ways of firestone technology.

"It is said that he suggested an ingenious way to remain on the island and yet avoid the war. The king, eager to save his people and retain their home, quickly agreed.

"It's not certain what that plan was, but it was said to involve the firestone, something never before tried and something that the firestone was never meant to do.

"At the appointed hour on the appointed day, both factions gathered on the field of battle. No one knows what happened after that."

"What the *hell*, Hannibal!"

"That's it. That's all that's known."

"What the hell kind of ending is that?!"

"No one knows what happened, Trace, except that the firestone was used and it went tragically wrong. The misuse of the power destroyed the island."

"You need to work on your storytelling skills, dude. That ending sucks."

"Sucks or not, that's all I know."

"Fine. But it's the last time I ask you to tell me a story. So, what about this building? What do you think it is? Someplace where the firestone was kept?"

"I've been leading up to this."

"You lead for shit, Hannibal. Get on with it. What the hell is this building?"

"Calm down, Traci."

"Calm down, nothing. What a crappy ending to an intriguing story."

"I'm sorry. Look, I think this building is a part of the story. And if I'm not mistaken, an intrinsic part."

"I should know better by now, but I'll bite. How is it intrinsic to the story?"

"I think these mosaics are telling us what actually happened to the Naacal, or at least explaining what *could* have happened to them. If they represent the Naacal at all. For all I know, they could represent anyone."

"How so?"

"How so what?"

"You said the mosaics are telling us something. How so? How do you know?"

"Look at these battle scenes."

"So now you're saying these drawings are depicting a war?"

"I'm not saying anything, but see the differences between these people here in this scene and in this scene. Do you see it?"

Traci's eyes scanned the different scenes and noted the differences Hannibal had pointed out. The people depicted in one scene varied slightly in both manner and physical form, but only slightly; it was difficult to see that the changes were significant. "Yes, I see the differences. But could this scene not have been created by a different artist than this one? Could it be that simple?"

"It could, I suppose, but look at the other scenes around the room; they're virtually identical."

"Perhaps the one artist died and left the work unfinished. The next artist's technique was slightly different."

"You may be right, Trace, but I don't think so. The people are changed. They're larger relative to the other scenes."

"I see that, but so what?"

"I think their size depicts their growth."

"They grew bigger?"

"Not physically, but in wisdom. See how they almost *look* smarter. See how their eyes are wider open, their skin almost looks softer, the lines in their faces are fainter."

"Yes. I see that."

"I think the incident caused them to grow in wisdom. I think that's what is depicted here."

"Wow, Hannibal. When you reach, you really reach. How can you come to such a conclusion? It just looks to me like a different artist finished the work."

"You might be right, but from what I understand, their conflict became the foundation of good versus evil, one of the very first references to man's invention of God and Satan and the basis for all religions as we know them today."

"Man created God? I think you have it backwards, dear."

"Man created the concept of a singular God, Traci. The further back in history you go, the more references you find to the "gods," not a singular entity, but many. And let me also point out that the main gods were attributed to the female side of nature, the Sacred Feminine. In fact, the ancients held the Creator to be female — again, the Sacred Feminine — because creation has always been tied to the female nature. There's a whole other story about that, but let's not get into that for the moment."

"Yeah, let's not go there, please. I'm confused enough. And besides that, I don't want to listen to another disappointing story from you."

"You're a hard woman, Traci Jefferson."

"You helped make me that way. But I don't want to go *there* right now. Tell me this instead. Why doesn't the world know about the Naacal's existence?"

"It does. There are references to them all throughout the ancient texts."

"But a civilization that old and that technologically advanced, you'd think they'd have left more behind than just references in old texts and pictures on some ancient temple walls."

Hannibal pointed to the structure. "Maybe they did."

"But if they were as great as you say, I would expect more to be known about them. Much more."

"Maybe what's left is all there is. Maybe they weren't as great as we think they were. Maybe all they left is a stark reminder of just what corruption and misuse of power can lead to. Maybe they left enough behind to give us a lesson of how not to live."

"How could an entire civilization, its people and its land, just disappear? Wouldn't there be more signs?"

"Maybe the lack of signs is what's most important."

"Wouldn't destruction on that scale require enormous power?"

"Power on a scale unknown today. The technologies we possess only scratch the surface of the power that was commonly in use by the Naacal — if the stories about them are to be believed. If the stories are in fact true, then this structure might be the only thing that survived."

"How could an island sink into the ocean and not leave a trace?"

"Honey, we've explored more of the universe than we have our own ocean floors. For all I know, a whole darn intact city could be sitting on the bottom of the ocean under a few feet of mud, just waiting for discovery."

"Where do you think the island was?"

"I have no idea. I've been searching for years for that answer."

Traci leaned forward and stared down into the hole.

"Do you believe the stories, Hannibal? Do you think this is where a crystal rested?"

"I'm pretty sure something of the sort was in there. As I said, it's hexagonal and that is the form of a perfect crystal, so it *is* possible."

"Isn't it kind of strange to have a power crystal in an altar? It's like the crystal was venerated as a god."

"I don't think it's an altar, Traci. At least that's what I'm coming to believe."

"It's not?"

"No. Look at these mosaics again. What do you see?"

"Beautiful pictures of a beautiful race of people."

"Look deeper. See the depictions? What do you see now?"

"Oh, Hannibal, I'm not good at this. I give up. What am I supposed to be seeing?"

"The illustrations on these walls do not relate to anything religious. There's no deity here. No sign of a godlike figure or anything which could be construed as a supreme being. I may be wrong, but I believe we're standing in a power station."

"A power station!"

"Look at these walls. What do you see?

"Come on, Hannibal. My brain's about to explode."

"Describe what you see."

"Well, let's see. I see a farmer. I see a boat, an airplane. I can't believe I'm saying that I see an airplane, but there it is. I see a —"

"You're missing the larger point, Traci. Concentrate on the bigger picture. What you see are depictions of their commerce, their industry, their agriculture, and military applications of wirelessly transmitted power. Power transmitted through this and other power stations to receiving crystals."

Traci's expression brightened. "You're right! My god, you're right, Hannibal! I see it now."

Hannibal walked around the perimeter of the room and pointed out each scene as he moved. "Look. The rays of the power source up there on the ceiling touch every scene in this room. Just as the power produced by the firestone touched everyone's life in the land. See how everyone is joined by the power of the firestone? Even in battle. See here, these warring factions are joined together; regardless of their conflict, they are eternally joined. In death or life, these people were forever connected by the undeniable power of the firestone."

"You're incredible, Hannibal."

"Or it could be something else entirely, but right now I have no other ideas about what that could be."

"No, Hannibal. You're onto it. But how could one station reach out to so many?"

A new thought struck Hannibal. "Follow me!"

Hannibal and Traci dashed out of the room and stripped the clean suits from their bodies. As they exited the large tent, Hannibal's eyes searched the immediate compound for Kirby. He finally spotted him standing in a group at the far side of the area. He trotted over. "*Kirby!* I need a map. Do you have a topographical map of this area?"

"Yeah. We've got one in that tent over there." Kirby pointed to a distant tent. "Why?"

Hannibal ignored the question and made a dash to the tent, disappearing into it. By the time Kirby and Traci caught up to him, Hannibal was tracing the map with his finger.

"What, Hannibal? What have you got?" asked Traci.

Hannibal eyes opened wide with excitement. "We need a chopper!"

CHAPTER 6

The helicopter flew low over the jungle canopy. Hannibal sat in the seat next to the pilot. With the map folded neatly on his lap, he searched the jungle below for something, although he did not know exactly what it was.

He glanced down at the map and then out toward the jungle again. He smiled, slapped the map, and said to the pilot, pointing toward a spot in the jungle, "Head over there to that hill, please."

The pilot nodded and turned the helicopter.

As they came close to where Hannibal had pointed, his eyes searched the jungle below for something as yet unseen. The pilot drifted the helicopter slowly over the hilltop as Hannibal's eyes continued their search. A small, flat clearing, many yards below the summit, finally came into view.

"Put us down there, please."

The pilot nodded. A minute or two later the chopper sat on the ground with its spinning blades winding down to a stop. Kirby, Traci, and Hannibal exited the aircraft and moved toward the summit of the hill approximately four hundred feet away through thick jungle undergrowth.

When they reached the crest of the hill, Hannibal laid the map on the ground and placed a compass on the map. He turned the compass slowly until he saw what he needed to see. He looked up and stared straight ahead and then grinned.

"Would you mind telling me what the hell is going on?"

"Need to know, Kirby. Only what you need to know."

"Come on, Hannibal. What is it?"

Hannibal pointed to the map. "What do you see here?"

"I don't get it."

Hannibal carefully corrected the compass to an exact setting. "Kirby, concentrate. What do you see?"

Kirby's eyes lit up. "I see a reciprocal vector directly back toward the structure."

"Damn right, and at this altitude, if the jungle was clearer, you'd have a line of sight directly back to it."

"I get it," Traci interjected. "You think there are other power stations and they're set up on line of sight?"

"Yes. Exactly. Although I'm not a physicist, I know a little something about it. The beam would go straight out from the source. Factoring in the curvature of the earth, the Coriolis effect, and the way gravity bends light at this altitude, I figure this spot is about as far as the beam of energy could go without flying straight out into space."

"So you think there might be another station in the area? Is that what you're saying?"

"You got it, Kirby. If I'm right, somewhere around here we should find another structure similar to or exactly like the other one. Traci, you look over that way. Kirby, you take that direction. I'll look over there."

The three split up and disappeared into the jungle.

~ ~ ~ ~ ~

After several minutes Kirby encountered an unusual formation of rocks, seemingly stacked on top of each other. He pulled a machete from its sheath on his belt and began to cut away the thick vines. After a few chops he realized that the formation was just a natural clump of rocks, uniquely eroded over time by the area's typically heavy rainfall.

~ ~ ~ ~ ~

Traci carefully stepped through the foliage, maneuvering through and around large vines and fallen logs. Her eyes nervously searched the jungle around her with each step. Nearing a log, she placed her hand against a tree and raised her left leg to step over the obstruction. Sensing a nearby presence, she turned her head.

~ ~ ~ ~ ~

Hannibal was kicking around at some undergrowth when he heard Traci's scream. It was so loud it could have easily awakened a dead Mayan had there been one in the area.

Hannibal snickered, then hollered, "Snake or monkey?"

"Snake! Damn python!"

"Yeah, that'll do it."

~ ~ ~ ~ ~

Traci gingerly backed away from the python and had just taken a step over the log when she heard Hannibal scream even louder and then curse.

"Snake?" she shouted.

"Yep. Damn big one, too!"

Traci chuckled and swung her other leg over the log. "Must be this one's mate."

"Must be."

"See anything yet?"

"Yeah. A damn big snake."

"Hannibal." Traci chuckled.

"No, I don't see — *hello!*"

~ ~ ~ ~ ~

Hannibal had noticed the large piece of marble from a small glint of sunlight reflecting off its polished surface. He bent low and lifted several heavy vines up off it.

"Kirby?" he shouted.

"Yeah?"

"Can we get some men over here to clear some of this jungle away? I think I found something."

Kirby and Traci rushed to where Hannibal was scratching the ground with his foot.

"What did you find, partner?"

"We're not partners, Kirby."

"Yeah, whatever. What did you find?"

"Duh, I don't know, Kirby. That's why I want some workers to clear this crap away. Okay?"

"You're sure getting crabby in your old age," Traci said.

"Isn't he, though?" Kirby chortled.

"Don't you think this is a pretty small area for another power station?"

"I agree with Traci, Hannibal. It doesn't look anything like the other one."

"If we clear the area, we'll know. Why are you both resisting so much? This is my job. Let me do my job, for Christ's sake. Neither of you have the experience I have when it comes to things like this. When something is found, digging uncovers it. And then everyone can see if it's important or not."

Traci winced. "It will cost a lot of money to get this area cleared, Hannibal. I'm just asking you if you really think it's necessary. That's all."

"I can't answer that, Traci, but here's a piece of white marble. Do you see any other white marble around here? I don't. Don't you think we should check it out?"

"But where's the structure, partner? I don't see any structure."

"Maybe it collapsed."

"Where's the rubble, then?"

"Maybe it was removed to build something else."

"But wouldn't the foundation footprint still be here?"

"If we have the area cleared, Kirby, maybe I could answer that question with a bit more certainty. How can I tell without clearing it?"

"Look, partner, I'm not trying to be disagreeable, but I don't see anything accept the one piece of white marble under your foot. That could have been dropped here by anyone."

"I have to agree with Kirby, Hannibal. It's just a flat piece of ground. There's nothing to indicate that anything was ever built here."

Hannibal kicked at the dirt in disgust. In doing so, the expanse of the marble grew larger. "Look at this! I'm telling you guys, something is here."

He dropped to his knees and began wiping the dirt off the marble. "Look."

"I'll be damned!" said Kirby. He dropped to his knees and began helping Hannibal scrape away the soil covering the flat marble.

Within ten minutes, they had cleared away enough dirt to see that the marble was the foundation of a large structure. When they reached a miter joint they stopped.

"Okay," admitted Kirby, standing up and rubbing dirt from his hands. "Okay, Hannibal. I'm convinced." He opened his satellite phone and dialed. "This is Kirby. Bring men with shovels and machetes. ... How many? ... *All* of them! NOW!"

~ ~ ~ ~ ~

It took ten men a little over three hours to clear the marble hexagon, which had a diameter of exactly fifty-five feet. The five-foot-wide white stones glistened brightly in the afternoon sun. The stones appeared to be a portion of the foundation of a much larger structure.

Hannibal stared at the foundation and then asked Kirby, "Do you have your digital measuring laser?"

Kirby pulled the instrument from his back pocket and handed it to Hannibal.

Hannibal walked around until he found a flat stone. Handing it to Kirby, he said, "Hold this stone right here, perpendicular against the edge of the foundation, just like that." Kirby did as he was bid.

Hannibal walked to the other side of the exposed marble foundation and set the laser down, turned it on, lined up the laser dot on the stone surface held by Kirby, and pushed the button. He brought the screen up in front of him and read it aloud. "Fifteen point one eight one five meters. That's incredible!"

"Why?" asked Traci.

Hannibal finished calculating in his head. "It's exactly twenty-nine cubits. That means these people measured distances the same way Egyptians measured them. We archaeologists know that the Egyptians used the cubit as the standard unit of measure, but there has never been found a measuring device with which to establish the standard length of a cubit. It has been reported that a cubit is between eighteen and twenty-one inches, and from the measuring rods discovered in some Egyptian tombs, it would appear to be between twenty point six and twenty point eight inches.

"Understanding the great precision with which they built the pyramids, mathematicians backed into the length of the cubit by using the measurement of the great pyramid itself — the relationship of the base to its height. From their work they deduced an Egyptian cubit to be point five two three five meters, or twenty point six one zero two inches. We just measured the marble foundation here from side to side and found it to be fifteen point one eight one five meters. That means it's exactly twenty-nine cubits. Now, there remains some controversy over the cubit's true length, but it's clear to me that the mathematicians got it right. And it's also clear that the Naacal were using the cubit long before the Egyptians. So when we refer to an Egyptian cubit, we're actually talking about the original cubit — the Naacal cubit, I believe."

"If these structures are Naacal."

"Yeah, Trace. If they're Naacal."

"You did that calculation in your head?"

"Yeah, Kirby. But what's important is that whoever built this, they were clearly using the cubit long before the Egyptians. That's for sure."

"Not to be quarrelsome, Hannibal," said Traci, "but you're assuming these structures to be older than the Egyptian civilization. What if these were built after the Egyptians?"

"Not likely, dear. There's no mention of these types of structures anywhere in recorded history that has been discovered so far. It is therefore more likely to assume that this energy system preceded recorded history and was subsequently lost before history was written down and saved for public consumption."

"Makes sense to me," said Kirby.

"Well done, Hannibal. You continue to surprise me," said Traci.

"Don't get too excited. We need to clear more of this structure before we know what it is that we've found."

"I've just sent the text. They'll be here within a few hours. I'm having generators and klieg lights lifted in by chopper. By tomorrow morning they should have this place pretty well uncovered, but I think you've found another power station. Just like you thought."

"Let's not get ahead of ourselves, Kirby. It looks nothing like the footprint of the station. This is only about a quarter the size of the other structure."

"Okay. So what is it?"

"Gee, buddy. I don't know. Let me look it up here in my Official Ancient Ruins and Artifacts Handbook. I'm sure it's in here somewhere ... oops, guess not. *How the hell do I know what it is, Kirby?* I'm looking at it for the first time. Just like you. Look, you guys, I'm betting no one's seen this in thousands of years. I don't know what it is. You'll have to be patient until we uncover this completely. Usually digs like this take a whole year to uncover. It's normally very slow work. We're tearing into this like crazy. This is not the way to do this."

"Partner, we don't have a year to uncover this. I got management crawling up my ass."

"I understand, Kirby, but you'll have to give me a bit more time to identify what this is with any degree of certainty. Until then, I'm just guessing off the top of my head."

Kirby fell quiet and stared at the ground.

Hannibal noticed. "What, Kirby? You got something?"

Kirby looked up and grimaced. "You did that calculation in your *head?*"

CHAPTER 7

Dr. Andy Anderson, the highly respected senior geologist for the Geological Society of Australia, sat quietly at his desk in the city of Cairns, dutifully studying the charts and readings of the quake that had occurred two days earlier. Its epicenter was in the MacDonnell Range, located in the Northern Territory of Central Australia nearly thirty miles west of the town of Alice Springs.

He well understood that most earthquakes in Australia occurred along or very near the continent's edge, but on rare occasions throughout Australia's history, quakes had been recorded deep inland.

Two such quakes in recent times, occurring near Alice Springs, came immediately to mind. The Marryat Creek quake of 1986, measuring 5.9 on the Richter scale, shook the ground some 186 miles south of Alice Springs. The quake of 1988, located primarily near Tennant Creek, almost 295 miles north of Alice Springs, measured about 6.5 in strength.

Remarkably, both quakes left little evidence of their occurrence except very minor damage to some nearby buildings. And that had already been fully repaired.

This latest quake, however, a record-setting 8.2, was extraordinarily large for this area and it commanded Andy's deepest concentration. The reports and seismic data were crystal clear on the matter. The ground shook violently for 59 seconds and was keenly felt as far away as Uluru, a small town some 145 miles southeast of Alice Springs, but other than that, it remained fairly localized. The quake happened at 0528 hours. It must have been a pretty rude awakening for the townspeople of "the Alice." Because of its great depth, this quake also produced very little surface damage in the town's vicinity.

Nevertheless, the MacDonnell mountain range had reportedly suffered catastrophic change. A previously unknown fault line suddenly and ferociously shifted, leaving a 103-foot-high rift along the south side of the range, extending almost ten miles in an east-west direction from the epicenter.

From the data which lay before him, it was clear that the land on the south side had subsided. A five-mile-wide patch of apparently weakly supported crust simply sank away under the abrupt harmonic vibrations produced by the quake. Anderson immediately suspected the phenomenon of liquefaction as one of the main factors in the subsidence scenario. But liquefaction, he understood, required saturated and unconsolidated sediments transforming into a substance akin to a liquid when vibrated by a large quake. To his knowledge the water table in that region was much too deep to cause saturation. The area consisted more of an arid desert-like sedimentary material, very dry and compact. The data thus contradicted itself and made no sense to him.

It would have made much more sense if the data revealed an upward shifting of the strata resulting from the range being uplifted from the pressure created by two plates colliding. But a singular downward shift was contrary to anything he had ever seen in that area before. Landscapes typically change slowly, a few inches at a time over many years, not hundreds of feet in a single instant. And for the MacDonnell Range, not downward.

During his methodical study of the available data, he had grown suspicious toward all the typical causes, and now he was convinced that beneath the surface of all the data lay another reason for such a dramatic downward shift. The catalyst for such a subsidence in the shallow crust had yet to reveal itself, and he passionately wanted to understand it.

When all was said and done, he was certain of one immutable fact. He wasn't going to discover the true cause sitting on his bum in that office. He was an outdoorsy kind of guy anyway, had been so since he was a child running up mountains and along sharp ridges, picking up interesting rocks. Being assigned to the regional office and confined to reviewing data sent in from his field geologists was unsatisfactory to him.

Andy's boss, Jake O'Connell, had brought Andy in from the field because of his age. It was a question of safety and liability for the society. The rugged mountains and jagged ridges, the ruthless heat of the summers and the bitter, freezing cold of the winters was no place for a man of seventy-nine. Out in the field, an old man was vulnerable to stumbling and falling down in desolate areas many miles from any medical facility.

In O'Connell's words, "One would have to seriously question the wisdom and sanity of any man who would still want to do field work at that age."

To Andy, no man sitting behind a desk could call himself a true geologist. The proper study of geology was done in the field, with hands soiled and roughened by pick and shovel and rock hammer, by walking the ground and climbing the escarpments and studying the granules of broken rock with a loupe while sweating under the blazing sun or shivering from the cold. In fact, Andy was noted to have replied to a young geologist candidate's question of what lies in the outdoors for a geologist in this way: "A real geologist, young man, sweats it out in the hot sun, crawling over rocks and crashing down slippery slopes in pursuit of his truth. He gets his hands dirty, his muscles exhausted, and enjoys it no other way."

To most, it was a hands-on type of job. To Andy, it was much more than that; it was a love affair. The feel of hard, weathered rock beneath his boots, the windswept sand in his mouth, the sweat dripping from his forehead were like a tender kiss and embrace from a beautiful, loving woman. His love was the dirt, the rocks, the land.

His phone rang.

He growled, wishing that he was in the field miles away from any telephone. He picked up the receiver. "Anderson here," he said.

As he listened, his demeanor softened. "Hello, Hannibal," he said. "It's so good to hear your voice again, my boy. Yes, I have been following your latest quest. The formations in Bimini certainly do look interesting, but the findings in the west Cuban waters look the most promising. How goes your progress, mate? ... In Mexico! What are you doing there? ... White marble? In Mexico? In the Yucatan? Impossible, mate. White onyx is widely scattered throughout Mexico, but not white marble. And you should know the difference, mate. Are you sure it's marble and not quartzite? There's a distinct difference between the two, as you should know too. You were one of my best students at the Udub [an affectionate local term for the University of Washington]. You would have made a fine geologist if your calling wasn't archaeology. ... So you're certain it's white marble, then? ... Well, if it is, it must have been brought in from some other area. White stalagmitic onyx is found in Tecali, of course, but that's about thirty-five miles from Mexico City. I've never heard of white onyx up in the Yucatan, let alone white marble. There's mostly limestone up there. ... No, Hannibal, it's not native to that area. I'm certain. It must have been imported. What are you studying? ... You can't say? Why? ... Ah, you're back with them government types again, huh? ... Well, all I can say is what I've said. White marble could not be native to that area, so it must have been imported. ... Okay, my friend. Hey, keep searching that western area of the Caribbean and don't be surprised if you find something extraordinary there. I'm certain you're onto something in those waters. ... Okay, Hannibal. ... Yes. You're welcome. G'day, my boy."

Andy hung up the phone, thought a few seconds, and then shook his head. "Blimey, that's where the action is. Out in the field. Not behind this bloody desk."

He picked up the phone and dialed.

"Grace. Get me a ticket to the Alice. ... I don't care what the old man wants. Book the flight. I want to leave today."

~ ~ ~ ~ ~

Hannibal walked the cleared hexagon of white marble slowly. His study of it seemed methodical, but he had been 'methodically' studying it for over two hours, ignoring every question put to him by the others. They had stopped asking questions forty-five minutes before. He kicked at the dirt-filled center and nodded occasionally, as if considering a thought he had been hiding from the others.

The hexagon had been cleared and excavated very carefully. The ground had been dug two feet down around the marble blockwork and it appeared to Hannibal that the marble continued even deeper.

At Hannibal's insistence, every shovelful of excavated dirt lifted from the site had been vigilantly sifted for any other clues. Just because time was an issue didn't mean that Hannibal was going to abandon proper excavation etiquette. The sift box had failed to yield anything of importance thus far. And so the receipt of any retrieved answers fell either to Hannibal's keen power of reason and observation or to a plain and simple scholarly guess. Even Dr. Hector Gonzalez just walked the marble hexagon scratching at his chin in confused amazement.

Finally, Hannibal stopped in his tracks. He looked up at Kirby and then back down at his feet. He then moved to the center of the hexagon.

"Have the men dig here," he said. "Dig out the hexagon center ... carefully, though."

"Why? What are you thinking?"

"I'm thinking we should dig out the hexagon, Kirby."

"Fine. Fine." In fluent Spanish Kirby ordered two field workers to dig where Hannibal had indicated.

Dutifully, the men began shoveling as Hannibal walked over to Traci.

"Okay, darling. What's going through that Hannibal brain of yours? Why dig it out?"

"Well, my darling, I have a feeling we'll have the answer to that question just as soon they dig out the area. But I'm betting we'll find a hexagonal hole in the center of the larger one."

"A hole for another crystal?"

"Yes. If I'm correct, we have just located a distribution station."

"I'm not following you."

"We found what I initially believed to be a power station, but I'm guessing now that it might be merely an in-line boosting station instead, with a crystal that boosted the beam along a path. This site, then, is simply a distribution hub, a broader directional distribution point. And I'm also betting that if we follow the radials indicated in the boosting station, we'll find others along the same radial patterns."

"Oh, my, darling! I'm following you now. Wouldn't that be something."

One of the worker's shovels hit an obstruction. He called out excitedly and Dr. Gonzalez rushed to investigate while Hannibal stood quiet.

Twenty minutes more and all were standing around a hexagonal hole in the white marble extending down nearly three full cubits, or nearly five feet.

"You're good, Hannibal, ol' buddy. How did you know?"

"I'm damned brilliant, Kirby. That's how I knew."

Kirby smirked. "You really have a hard time accepting a compliment, don't you?"

"Depends."

"Well, like it or not, partner, you have one coming. And yeah, I know, we're not partners. I got it."

Hannibal grinned. "There seems to be some hope for you after all, partner."

"Partners, huh?"

"Just kidding."

~ ~ ~ ~ ~

An hour later, after more work around the outside base, a second outer ring of marble blocks was uncovered, this one a full cubit in width. Now with the entire hexagon cleaned out, they could see how the nearly three-foot-high pedestal was surrounded by more inlaid patterns of colored stone pressed into a flat surface a full cubit below the new outer ring depicting other radial patterns.

"A distribution station," said Traci, "I would never have guessed. Okay, Hannibal, you officially get the gold star. Now do you have any idea where we might find the other stations in the network?"

"I think I do."

"Great! I'm all ears."

"If I'm correct, and I usually am about these things." He paused and grinned.

"Please, Hannibal."

Hannibal continued. "I'm guessing the patterns are already given to us. I think the radials are exactly as they're depicted on the outer ring. Follow them and I'm guessing you'll find the rest in due course."

~ ~ ~ ~ ~

Hannibal dropped the phone into its cradle and stared at the blank wall of his seedy Mexican hotel room. Traci walked into the room through the open door.

"Hannibal? Any luck?"

"Yeah."

"Well?"

"He confirmed it."

"Who confirmed what?"

"Doctor Honeycutt."

"Who's Doctor Honeycutt and what are you talking about? ... Hannibal? Where are you?"

Hannibal looked up at Traci with a strange expression. "I'm here."

"No, you're not."

"He confirmed it."

"Talk to me, Hannibal. Who's Doctor Honeycutt?"

Hannibal turned his eyes to the floor and stared at the chipped terra-cotta. He poked at it with the tip of his boot and remained silent, in deep thought.

"Hannibal! Don't do this to me. Talk to me."

Hannibal glanced up into her eyes. "Sorry, hon. Doctor Honeycutt is a friend of mine up in Seattle. He's the foremost authority on the geology of the southwest U.S. and Mexico. He confirmed what Andy told me. There's no white marble in Mexico. If it's here, he says, then it had to be imported."

"Well, now. All we have to do is find out from where. How do we do that?"

"We have it ... uh ... tested." His eyes drifted back to the floor.

"Are you okay?"

He shifted his eyes back to Traci. "Yeah. Sorry. My mind is just reeling from all this. Do you realize that we've already rewritten history? Everything everyone ever knew or thought was true about how long man has been in the western hemisphere has just been trashed."

"Do you have any idea of how long ago those structures were built?"

"No. But we can perform radiometric dating and determine that. For sedimentary rocks younger than, say, fifty thousand years, we use the carbon fourteen method. In this case we'll need to find something organic, something containing carbon, from under the structures. We can test that. That'll give us an idea of the age of the structures — how long ago they were built."

"How can we do that?"

"We dig under them, Traci."

"I'll get someone on that."

"Kirby's already got some men digging under the boosting station."

"Great. Now what do we do about the marble?"

"We send off pieces of it to the lab for testing."

"Which lab?"

"The Colorado School of Mines in Golden, Colorado. They have an excellent geochemistry lab. I think they would be able to test the crystalline structure and tell us where it most likely came from."

"Isn't marble just marble?"

"No. Each type of marble is unique. The structure of the marble is like a fingerprint. This is some of the purest, whitest marble I've ever seen. Have you ever seen the Jefferson Monument or the Tomb of the Unknown Soldier in D.C.?"

"Sure, several times. Why?"

"Those structures are made from Yule marble, named after George Yule, the mining engineer who discovered it — or, should I say, rediscovered it — in the 1870s. It's a uniquely white marble from Marble, Colorado. One of the purest, whitest marbles in the world."

"Are you saying the marble from the boosting and distribution stations is from Colorado?"

"I've been researching sources of white marble throughout this hemisphere. The closest source of this quality of marble is Marble, Colorado."

"You think this marble was quarried in Colorado? Do you know how far away that is from here?"

"As a matter of fact, I do. It's approximately one thousand six hundred fifty miles away, as the crow flies."

"Do you hear yourself? That's a *long* way to transport marble. And from the size of some of those blocks, my god, Hannibal. Some of those blocks must weigh tens of tons. How would that be possible thousands of years ago?"

"I would imagine it would be pretty simple if the builders had the ability to fly or defy gravity. More importantly, though, if the blocks did come from Colorado, there should be traces of an ancient quarrying operation somewhere in the town's surrounding hills."

"Do you know anyone in Marble who could check it out?"

"No, but I do know Raymond Potestio, a professor at the School of Mines. He's their leading professor of geochemistry. He might be able to put us in touch with someone down at Marble. Hell, he might be able to identify the stone himself. Let's have Kirby get a piece of marble ready to ship to the school. I'll call Professor Potestio and prepare him to receive it."

Traci smiled. "I like you like this, Hannibal. So serious, so dedicated, so ... professorial. I've never really seen this side of you before."

"So you don't think I'm a dunce like every other archaeologist in the world?"

Traci chuckled lightly and hugged him. "Darling, I think you're smarter than all the others put together."

"Thanks."

Then she became serious. She thought for a while before speaking. "Hannibal, do you think about me once in a while?"

"No. Not really."

There was noticeable hurt in her voice and expression as she asked, "You don't?"

"No, Traci, not just once in a while. I think about you every minute of every day," Hannibal said with a wry smile.

Through her own cynical smile she replied, "You're a real jerk, Hannibal. You know that?"

"I hear that a lot. I think that's why you're still in love with me."

"Maybe, but you're still a jerk."

"That only makes me more loveable."

CHAPTER 8

Dr. Andy Anderson walked along the new rift very near the epicenter of the mighty quake, shaking his head. "My god," he said aloud. "The incredible power it took to do this."

He stopped and stared upward at the sheer cliff that now towered over a hundred feet above him. He had strolled along this path many times before and had even taken some chips of rock with his rock hammer from a particular outcropping that now loomed well above him.

Something caught his eye. A bright glimmer several yards away down in the bottom of a small chasm. He strained his eyes to see it clearly and then almost fainted when he realized what he was looking at.

The white marble was surely out of place against the red quartzite of the MacDonnell Range.

From his many years in the field, he knew that these mountains were made up of several rock types. Predominantly they consisted of red quartzite, giving the range its bright red color, but there existed also granite, sandstone, and siltstone. Several fossils he had found embedded in the rock gave proof that a great inland sea once covered central Australia, hence he knew also of the large deposits of limestone, but nowhere in this region was there any sign of the existence of white marble. And this marble was so purely white that he was certain it had to have been imported over a vast distance and placed here.

The quality of the marble reminded him instantly of Makrana marble, typically found and quarried in the Neharkhan region of India. Makrana marble had been chosen to build the great Taj Mahal in Agra.

The Neharkhan quarries, to his knowledge, were the closest quarries that could have produced this exquisitely white marble. He would, of course, perform extensive testing on this magnificent calcite rock to confirm what he already suspected. Still, the sheer feat of transporting this tremendous block of marble over such an immense distance must have been an unimaginable undertaking. The thought of such a feat dazzled him.

Upon closer examination, he decided that it might be some kind of support column. But a support column for what? While pondering that question, he spied another buried block of marble some fifty feet away from the first. It was barely visible under all the rubble and he considered that it might even be a part of the first block.

Seeing this marble generated another question. Why use marble from an immense distance away when you've got a mountain of granite on the site?

Then the real questions began bombarding his brain. *Who* brought this marble to this region? *How* was the marble transported here to central Australia, an area some 580 miles at a minimum from the ocean, over land extremely difficult to traverse even today with modern transportation equipment, not to mention the sea and land journey from the Neharkhan region, if in fact that is where it came from?

For *what purpose* did someone find it necessary to bring such blocks here? Two more important questions then stirred within his head. *Who buried such great blocks and why were they buried in the first place?*

Just when he thought he had asked all the important questions, two more intriguing ones filled his mind. Why had Hannibal Storm asked him about white marble in Mexico? And was there any correlation between what he had just found here and what Hannibal had obviously discovered in Mexico?

~ ~ ~ ~ ~

Dr. Anderson, always prepared for most contingencies when he made it out to the field, finished tying the nylon climbing rope to a large stake that he had pounded into the ground near the edge of the chasm. He slipped his backpack on, tightened his rappelling harness, and tossed the other end of the rope into the hole. Gripping the rope, he dropped off the edge of the thirty-foot cliff.

He descended effortlessly to the bottom, unhooked himself from the D ring, and slowly made his way toward the first marble block. Reaching out and touching it, he found that it was perfectly honed. He found a small chip of it on the ground and peered at it through his loupe.

"Yep," he said to himself. "Pure calcite."

Working his way over toward the second anomaly, crawling at times on his hands and knees across the craggy, razor-sharp chips and broken blocks of quartzite, he was able to get to the other block and remove just enough debris to confirm it as white marble. It appeared to be an equally large block independent of the first.

He ran his hand over its surface and felt the faint polishing marks, which confirmed that these blocks had been quarried and honed by ancient stonemasons and transported to this spot. But who were these masons and when were these blocks of marble quarried and honed?

Working his way around the block, he pushed some dirt away with his hand. Since it was somewhat soft, he dropped his backpack and removed a small military shovel, screwed down the handle, and began removing dirt from the top of the block.

Within an hour he had cleared away a good portion of the dirt and moved to where he thought the end of the block was. At that precise moment the ground gave way and he found himself on his back, desperately clinging to a nearby protrusion of red granite. The ground had fallen away into blackness.

Gathering all his strength, he pulled himself back up to the edge of the collapse and peered down into a deep hole. It was too dark to see anything, but it did appear to be a gentle slope. To his amazement, the landslide had exposed the white marble blocks as support columns for a large cavern.

"What in bloody hell do we have here?" he asked aloud.

He pulled a small flashlight from his front pocket, flicked it on, and aimed it into the hole. It was, as he'd suspected, a very gentle slope downward into the darkness.

Being a most curious and bold fellow, he descended into the darkness. His flashlight exposed no immediate danger, but he cautiously continued a few feet at a time, moving only as far as he could clearly see ahead of him, sliding on his rump down the slope. It took him the better part of ten minutes to reach the bottom, where he was able to stand up.

He calculated his vertical descent to be almost two hundred feet. At the edge of what his flashlight could illuminate, he noticed that the terrain ahead appeared to be sandy, flat, and stable. The ceiling of the limestone cave was well above him. He guessed it to be over fifty feet above his head. In some places it looked to be even higher.

He did not notice any of the usual formations common in limestone caves, no stalagmites or stalactites. He also saw no water dripping from the ceiling, another common trait for such caves, but he heard the sound of water in the distance, beyond the illumination range of the small flashlight.

He reached into his backpack and withdrew his helmet, put it on his head, and turned on the lamp. The more powerful helmet lamp now lit up the cave well enough to see several yards ahead. He walked toward what he thought might be a larger cavern.

After about fifty yards, he discovered the source of the water sound. It was a small river with a lazy current, about fifteen to twenty feet across and at most a couple of feet deep. He waded across it with no difficulty.

Once on the other side, what he saw next literally brought him to his knees in wonder and amazement. He saw footprints, some shod and others bare, with toe prints clearly visible. Some were large, while others were very small. He reached out and gently touched one of the prints. The sand was soft. He guessed that the footprint had either remained unchanged over a very long time or had been made only minutes before his arrival.

He aimed his helmet lamp in the opposite direction of the footprints, but he saw no one. He reached into his shirt pocket and withdrew a small camera, shot several pictures of the footprints, and then returned it to his shirt pocket. He stood up and walked around the footprints, remaining off to the side as he followed them toward the cavern opening.

After almost a hundred yards, he reached the opening. His lamp followed the footprints until he saw many more prints, as fresh-looking as the first, heading in different directions.

He raised his head. In doing so, the light of the helmet lamp clearly illuminated what lay ahead of him. It was then that the full revelation of his discovery jolted him. "Oh, bloody hell!" he exclaimed.

~ ~ ~ ~ ~

"The results are in," said Hannibal to Traci and Kirby, both of whom had just walked into his hotel room.

"It's about time. It only took them two weeks," said Kirby. "So what's the verdict?"

"He confirmed that it's nearly pure calcite. Ninety-nine point five percent calcite. Further tests confirmed that it's Yule marble from Colorado. So it seems a fitting choice for the Naacal to choose this marble to build their power stations."

"That's really amazing," replied Kirby.

"That's astonishing," added Traci.

"There's more. Professor Potestio located the ancient quarry. He said he had never thought to check out that portion of the mountain before and everyone had just assumed that segment of the mountain had simply fractured and broken away eons ago. After checking, though, the professor found definite tool marks, providing strong confirmation that someone quarried the marble. Based on his tests, he's determined that the marble cliff was last quarried a little over twenty-five thousand years ago. The archaeological timeline for human habitation of the western hemisphere has just been shattered by more than thirteen thousand years. More importantly, it's my belief that if we bother to go looking for them, we'll find other boosting-station foundations somewhere in the U.S."

"I'm afraid to ask now, but do you have any idea of where to look for them?" asked Kirby.

"I'm guessing along the radials, like all the others. If we keep finding others and follow their radials, I believe we'll eventually get up into the U.S. From there, who knows what we'll find."

"Well, then, I guess I'd better go check in with my boss and let him know what you think."

"Say hello to Jack for me."

"Who?" asked Kirby with a distant expression.

"Jack. Your boss. Remember him?"

"Oh, yeah, Jack. Sure, Hannibal. I will." Kirby turned and left the room.

"Something's not right with him," said Hannibal.

"Why do you say that?"

"I don't know. It's just a feeling."

"A feeling like what, Hannibal?"

"I can't say for sure. He just seems strange to me."

Traci chuckled. "You both seem strange to me. I can see why he was your partner. Birds of a feather and all."

"That's what I really miss about you, Traci. Your keen sense of wit and humor."

"Ah, come on, dear. I'm just messing with you. You know I've always been attracted to your little oddities."

"I'm not odd."

"If you say so ..."

The phone rang again. Hannibal answered.

"Hannibal Storm here. Hello, Professor. What? ... Why is that? ... I understand. ... I don't know. That's a long way to go without more information, Andy. Can you give me a little more? ... I see. Well, right now I'm sort of on an important find. I don't know if I can get away at the moment. Let me call you back later today. ... You have? Are you sure? When? ... Okay, Andy. I'll be there, I promise. I'll call you this afternoon. Goodbye."

"Well. Now I'm as curious as can be. What was that all about? Was that your professor friend from Australia? The one who gave you the loupe?"

"Yeah. Do you think Kirby can get me back to Los Angeles quickly?

"I'm sure he can, but what's up?"

"Andy wants me to come to Australia. He purchased a ticket for Friday from LAX."

"That's tomorrow. Whatever for?"

"He wouldn't say on the phone. He just said it was a most urgent matter and I needed to be on that flight."

"But you can't go. You know that, right?"

"What are you talking about? Of course I can go. I'm going."

"Fine. I'll have to get packed, then."

"No, Traci. He was adamant about me coming alone."

"Well, you can forget about that, Hannibal. I'm coming with you."

"He said alone and I'm going alone."

"You can't. You're too important to our work here. I can't let you do that."

"Then you've got my resignation."

"Nice try, Hannibal. You know it doesn't work that way."

"I don't care how it's supposed to work. Andy said he needed me and I'm going to Australia ... and I'm going alone."

"Listen to me, Hannibal. I know Andy is important to you, but I can't allow it. Your work here is more important."

"You can't *allow* it? I'm not working for you."

"Be logical, Hannibal. Please."

"No! You're not going to drag me into another one of your arguments."

Traci bit her lip and kept silent.

Hannibal stood up and began stuffing clothes into a suitcase.

"While I'm gone, I want you and Kirby to go back to the boosting station and map the radials. See if some of the radials are directed toward the U.S. I suspect you'll find several that are. I would concentrate my search on the highest peaks along those radials. I'm betting that you'll either find a boosting station or one of the distribution hubs like we just found. ... Are you listening?"

Traci remained still and silent.

"Good. You're listening. It's very important that you do as I say. The answer is in the small distribution stations, I think. Find their trail and it should lead you back to the Firestone or at least in its direction. You got that?"

Traci stared without emotion.

"Good girl."

"Hannibal!" Traci said in a low, controlled, calm but firm voice. "Listen very carefully to *me* now and try to get this through that Hannibal skull of yours. You're *not* going anywhere. Understand?"

CHAPTER 9

Having crossed the International Date Line, Hannibal found himself in front of Charlie's Inn on the main street of Alice Springs at midday on Saturday. It was already a scorcher. The 24-hour commercial flight and additional three-hour ride in the small private plane that got him to the local airport had left him with aches and pains. He tugged his suitcase from the backseat of the taxi and shut the door.

The funny thing still bouncing around in Hannibal's mind was how Traci thought she had him under her control. It took only one phone call to Kirby, threatening to resign and walk away, for her to understand that she actually had no power over him. And after Kirby finished a private chat with Traci, she even calmly offered her satellite phone to him. She did, however, plead with him to stay in contact. Hannibal agreed, and Kirby made arrangements for him to get back to Los Angeles that afternoon without any more argument.

Hannibal hadn't expected her to react so calmly about the whole matter. It was a curious close to what he thought might end up being a real deal breaker. But here he was in Australia, with not only her satellite phone but also her blessing and a goodbye kiss on his cheek.

"Thanks for the ride," said Hannibal, reaching into the passenger window and handing the driver some bills.

A moment later he stood on the sidewalk and wiped a shirt sleeve across his sweat-beaded brow.

Located at the southern end of the Northern Territory, in an area often referred to as Central Australia and straddling the usually dry Todd River on the northern side of the MacDonnell Range, Alice Springs boasted of being the largest town, with the best water supply, for hundreds of miles around in that arid, scrubby grassland.

Charlie's Inn was a favorite hotel for most tourists, but Hannibal wasn't interested in sightseeing.

Walking up to the desk, he introduced himself to the striking blonde on-duty manager.

"Oh, yes, Mr. Storm. We've been expecting you. I have a package for you as well. Could you please sign here for it." She handed him a tablet.

"Sure." He signed the paper, picked up the box, and shook it. "Have you seen Professor Anderson?"

"Not in the last few days, sir."

"Not in the last few days? Doesn't that seem odd?"

"When he checked in a couple of weeks ago, he told us he might be away for days at a time."

"I see. Okay. Thank you."

"You're welcome, sir. Enjoy your stay. Do you need any help with your bags?"

"No, thanks. I'm good."

Hannibal made his way to his room, balancing the box on his shoulder and dragging his suitcase behind. After opening the door, he moved over to the bed and set the box down.

"What have you left for me, Andy?" he whispered.

Breaking the seal and opening the flaps, he peered into the box. There he found a map with a hand-drawn red ink trail marked on it, a compass, a very large survival knife in a hard plastic sheath, two large candles, an extra-large box of "strike anywhere" matches, a caving helmet equipped with a high-powered LED lamp, a climbing harness, and a very large flashlight, with several extra D-size batteries, all stacked on top of a brand new vinyl backpack.

Under the backpack were explicit handwritten driving directions along with a map and instructions not to tell another living soul where he was going — those last words underlined for emphasis.

"Now *this* is going to be interesting," Hannibal said.

~ ~ ~ ~ ~

Forty minutes later, he pulled the rented SUV over to the side of the road and behind a large boulder, as the directions instructed. As he did, he noticed another SUV already parked there. He stopped just behind it, got out, and looked around. Not seeing another living thing, he put on his caving helmet and tossed his backpack across his shoulder. He oriented the map to the proper direction and confidently set out westward, as the map indicated.

Within minutes he found the rift and the rope, one end tied to a stake pounded securely into the ground and the other end disappearing over the edge of a small cliff. He tugged on the rope several times, testing its strength, and then slipped into the climbing harness, affixed the rope through the D ring, and dropped over the edge.

Thirty feet down, he settled gently onto the solid ground and unbuckled himself from the harness, allowing it to drop to the ground at his feet. He immediately noticed the footprints leading to an opening in the cliff face and then spied the odd block of white marble. His mind flashed back to the Yucatan and the marble he had seen there.

"What do we have here?" he muttered.

The tracks were easy to follow, for there were plenty of them. They all looked to be made by the same type of boot. Studying them carefully, he noticed that in one set, what looked like the latest set, a foot dragged. Not well versed in the techniques of tracking, he was not sure which foot was dragging, but if he were forced to make a guess, it would be the left.

Arriving at the sloped area, he squatted and peered down into the darkness. The slope seemed gentle enough. Skid marks into the blackness seemed to indicate that the good doctor had indeed gone this way.

Hannibal realized that he held only questions in his head. To discover the answers, he needed to gather his courage and make the descent into the eerie blackness.

Flicking on the flashlight, he sat firmly on the slope and inched his way down into the hole.

His careful descent took him a good long while, but upon reaching the bottom without incident, he stood up. Only a faint glow from the opening above penetrated the dark; the blackness that lay ahead of him was almost blinding in its intensity. He reached up and clicked on his helmet light. That was better. He had no trouble finding the drag marks in the soft sand and so he followed them deeper into the cavern.

About three hundred feet in, he clearly heard the sound of running water. A minute later, he found the end of the tracks at the river's edge, but the drag trail continued directly into the water.

"Andy, my friend, just what the hell were you doing?"

He forded the shallow river slowly, confirming that the depth was passable, and then picked up the drag trail once again for another seventy-five feet or so. It was then that he found its source.

Sitting on the sand, leaned up against a boulder, was the body of his good friend, its vacant eyes open and staring into the emptiness of death's void.

A pen was still in Anderson's right hand and a note lay on his lap. Hannibal picked it up and read it.

> *"Stroke. Lucky right handed. Footprints 25,000+/- years. Certain. Take camera follow footprints. You were right. I want remain here. You'll know where. Be great. I know you will. Tell no one. Reseal. World not ready to know truth."*

Hannibal noted that Anderson's backpack was filled with several bricks of C-4 and remote detonators. He guessed it would be well more than enough to reseal the cavern. He also noted several packets of meals-ready-to-eat and several canteens of fresh water, as well as assorted cooking supplies. It looked as if Anderson had planned an extended stay in the cavern, never counting on his age doing him in.

He noticed Anderson's satellite phone hanging off his belt. He unhooked it and looked at the face of it. Four missed calls and he recognized the incoming phone numbers. Three were from Andy's office, but one was from Kirby Hansen's satellite phone. *Why would Kirby be calling Andy Anderson?* he thought.

He purposely hadn't told Kirby who he was meeting here in Australia, just that it was urgent he come. He hadn't even told Traci everything Andy had said to him on the phone. Then he thought more about it. Perhaps there was no mystery at all. Traci had obviously told Kirby who he was meeting with. Well, no matter, he reasoned. There was nothing he could do about it now. He stuffed the phone into Andy's backpack and slung it over his shoulder.

Hannibal patted Anderson's head and closed his staring eyes.

"Sleep well, old friend. Your task is done. I'll take it from here."

He moved next to the ancient footprints and squatted down. He laid his right hand onto one of the tracks.

"Wow! Could have been made today."

He stood up and followed the ancient tracks in the sand back toward the larger opening deeper into the cavern, stepping to the side so as not to step on them, preserving them as any archaeologist would.

As he reached the cavern's larger opening, he stopped abruptly and stared blankly at what he could not believe existed.

"Oh my!" he exclaimed.

Even the strong beam from his helmet's LED lamp was not enough to penetrate the full depth of the cavern, but it was enough to expose a sight he could only have imagined before today.

"Andy, my friend, what did you find?"

In the white light, a large hand-carved limestone building stood directly in front of him, stretching upward toward the ceiling of the cavern.

His mouth agape in awe, he started toward the building. In only a few steps he realized that there were many other structures in line with the first, stretching back into the darkness. He clearly saw that it was larger than anything ever discovered on earth before from that time period, but the helmet light was not bright enough to see just how large the city truly was.

When he reached the doorway to the first building and peered inside, he got the impression that it was someone's home. Stepping inside the first room, he felt as if he was stepping into a living room. As he looked about the room, his light caught several wooden chairs, benches, and stone protrusions built along the limestone walls in different sizes and widths and placed at different levels; his mind pictured them as some kind of shelving. The walls were absent any decorations except for the distinctly painted stripes and floral and geometric patterns near the ceiling.

"Andy, this is going to change the world!"

Moving methodically around the lodging, he discovered that the building contained many rooms. He concluded that it must have been the home of a large family, and suspected that it might even have been several generations of the family living together.

He knew that in olden times the elderly were revered, not pushed aside when they had become less able or infirm. The old were nearly deified. They held great power and wonderful wisdom, and provided welcomed guidance to the young. They were treated with the utmost respect in all things. It would, therefore, have been quite normal for families to take care of several generations of family members in one home.

Hannibal easily pictured such a family living here under this roof, with both sides of the family living as a unit. Having been brought together through marriage, their expanded family was as one. Hannibal believed that these must have been beautiful times for humanity.

In several of the rooms he found disintegrated matting he believed was once bedding. In one particular room, he noticed a large stone shelf that he believed was a bed shelf, a place of respect, probably originally softened by plant material or cloth and used as someone's off-the-floor bed — perhaps where the patriarchal and matriarchal heads of the family slept.

An idea came to him. He smiled and went back to Anderson's body, scooped it up and placed it over his shoulder, then carried it to the stone shelf. He laid Anderson down gently on the shelf and folded his hands reverently across his body at his waist.

He put his hand on a now clammy and cold forehead and looked into the expired face.

"Here you are, my friend. I think these people would have felt honored that you chose to spend your eternal rest here in their home."

He then ran back and retrieved Anderson's helmet and jacket and placed them on top of his friend's body. "The Egyptian pharaohs had their belongings placed with them for their journey into the afterlife. You should have nothing less, my friend."

Returning to the open area outside the home, he opened his own pack and pulled out a large flashlight. He knew now why Anderson had put it in the box. He flicked it on and the powerful light shot out into the cavern.

What he saw startled him.

"Oh my god, you have *got* to be joking."

The cavern was at least forty to fifty feet high in most places. But that wasn't what shocked him. It was the sheer expanse of the city.

The light from this flashlight, although extremely powerful, was still not adequate enough to expose it all. Hannibal squared his back to the near building and stepped off the depth of the city. After nearly a thousand yards he came to the end wall, coming to stand in front of another limestone-hewn building.

"My god. How did you build such a city? And why build it underground? Who were you?" Of course, he didn't expect anyone to answer him, but he wished they were still alive to have the discussion.

Starting at one side of the city, he repeated his method, to find out how wide the city was. A little over four hundred yards later, he was standing at the far side of the cavern and in front of another building.

"This is incredible!"

From his quick study of the design, he concluded that it was the presumed intent of the builders that everyone should have a view of the city center. It seemed logical. Perhaps it was how they conducted town meetings, as it were — an efficient gathering of all people for the necessary purposes of managing the city or to communicate important notices.

As he strolled around the great city, he found no merchant areas. From that he concluded that the city center was also where the people gathered each day to prepare food and create cloth and other items needed by the community.

From what he had seen and understood about other ancient cultures, the center was where the city gathered, not necessarily to sell anything, but to come together, period. It was the center of their lives, their people, their ways. It was the center of all things, and everyone had a view of it. Everyone, through this view, was a part of the greater society.

He couldn't be certain, of course, but it appeared that everyone contributed to the welfare of the community without compensation, or that compensation was made by having enough to eat, clothing to wear, and other essentials that were created here, each person assigned a given task to perform for the welfare of everyone else. Each had a job to perform. Each could depend on the efforts of another for the things not produced or provided by themselves.

He envisioned, based upon his experience, that each person contributed in the way that they were best suited. All had what they needed and they in turn created what others needed.

He found further proof of his theory when he located great fire pits and food preparation benches in the heart of the center. He figured that the entire city prepared their food together, cooked it together, and ate their meals together. They were truly one people, living as one.

The more he saw how the buildings were built, with rooms but absent any individualized cooking facilities, the more he came to believe his theory. These people lived together in true bliss and harmony. There may have been some individualism, but it was minimal. They were a united people in almost every phase of their lives. They must have been a very strong and close people, Hannibal concluded.

"Whoever you were," he said aloud, partly hoping they would hear him, "you were lovely people. And wherever you are now, I hope it's worthy of who you were."

CHAPTER 10

Two hours passed quickly for Hannibal as he searched the city, concluding, or at least guessing, that this was a city that could have comfortably held at least five thousand people.

Then he stumbled upon a great white marble foundation. And in the center of the foundation was another hexagonal hole. From the similar design he had unearthed in the Yucatan jungle, he surmised that it once held a distribution crystal. It must have been a massive crystal, at least fifteen to twenty feet high, for the hole was massive as well, and almost six feet deep.

It all was coming together for Hannibal now. His theory of an extremely ancient global civilization had to be correct.

~ ~ ~ ~ ~

Walking the perimeter of this once great city, he came upon a structure that looked like none of the others. It was a perfect square made completely out of blocks of the red granite common to the region. It was not carved out of the surrounding limestone like all the other structures; it was built here, one block at a time.

Hannibal walked off the size and estimated each side to be approximately fifty feet long and at least twenty feet high. A granite door was placed in the center of one side — the side facing the city center.

The door was sealed with some sort of natural sealant. He pulled on the handle, but it would not budge. Whatever the sealant was made of, it had held the door tightly shut for some 25,000 years, if Anderson's estimate was correct.

He pulled out Anderson's camera and snapped several pictures, then pulled out the survival knife, the one he had found in the box prepared by Anderson, from his pocket. Withdrawing it from its scabbard, he began digging at the seal. He was amazed at how pliable the material was. As he began pulling pieces of it out of the crack around the door, he found that it rolled easily in his hand, as if it had been put there only days before.

It took him nearly an hour to remove enough of the sealant to allow him to budge the door. And when he did, to his complete amazement, the heavy granite door, which he guessed measured ten feet square, opened so smoothly that it took virtually no effort to open. He was stunned to see that the door was fully four feet thick, the same thickness as the walls of the structure. It must have weighed several tons, but he could literally use one finger to open it. How that could be confounded him. But it was what he found inside that stunned him even more.

Aided by his helmet lamp and his huge flashlight, he saw stone shelving lining every wall from floor to ceiling. The shelving was about two feet wide and about one foot thick and spaced two feet apart. Each shelf was filled to capacity with a combination of both papyrus scrolls, stored horizontally within stone boxes with dividing pieces every two feet, and engraved stone tablets measuring about two feet by four feet.

"Papyrus. So you had some contact with Egypt, huh? How much more of the world did you know about?"

He was convinced that Anderson had not seen this but still knew that the city housed something of extraordinary importance.

He delicately picked up one of the scrolls and started to unroll it, and was shocked to learn that it unrolled as if it had been rolled that morning. The material was completely without damage and was still moist and supple.

If Anderson was correct about the age of this place and these scrolls were placed in this vault all those years ago, the sealant had flawlessly kept all air out. This vault was a treasure trove of human knowledge left by a people now dead for hundreds of centuries and yet it was as if they had written their words on those scrolls that morning.

Unrolling the scroll, he began to look at the writing and was surprised that he could understand much of the language. He then realized it contained elements of Mayan, ancient Sumerian, and Navajo. "Navajo?" he said aloud. "How can this be Navajo? The Navajo language was only a spoken language until just a few decades ago." Still, those few words, sounded out, were most definitely Navajo.

There were other symbols he did not understand at all. It was then that he realized what he had discovered. He was reading the original language of these people — the language of the Naacal.

He surmised that when they, for some reason or another, left this underground city and ventured out into other lands, their language evolved into dialects departing from their original source. Thus, over time the Mayans developed their own language, the Sumerians developed theirs, and, of course, the Navajo established their own language as well. But each was born out of the original root language — the language written here, the long-silent text staring back at him now desiring to shout its story to the world.

In the center of the room he noticed wooden and stone benches and stone tables, upon which he imagined the scholars of those days had most likely sat reading and penning these works of knowledge and wisdom.

Hannibal sat down on one of the stone benches and unrolled the scroll completely, revealing the marvel of the text — the words which had flowed from the mind of an ancient author.

Although he could not read it all, of course, he understood enough that he knew this particular scroll concerned a story of how an individual or a group of people traveled across vast open waters and found another land. From its tone, he guessed it might have been a travelogue of some kind.

He rolled it up and returned it to the exact spot where he had found it and then strolled around the library until he noticed something extremely interesting. From symbols engraved on a particular set of stone boxes he recognized the words he could best translate as *critical, urgent,* or perhaps *very,* or *highly necessary.*

He fished around the scrolls, unrolling one and then another, scanning the symbols and reading briefly what he could of them.

He repeated this several times until he found one scroll which nearly floored him.

He could not decipher all of the symbols, but those he could seemed to provide information regarding the tuaoi — the Great Firestone.

Sitting down at the stone table again, he studied the scroll in great depth. Soon he grew frustrated with his inability to comprehend the full text of the Naacal language that spread out before him across the table.

Three specific sketches caught his eye, however, and they staggered him. Although he had difficulty understanding their relationship to the rest of the text, there was no doubt as to what they symbolized. The first was clearly the Flower of the Wholeness of Life — a 64-sided tetrahedron crystal. The second one, another familiar symbol, could only be that for zero-point radiant energy — the torus, the blueprint by which nature forms energy into matter. The third drawing was, no doubt, the Vector Equilibrium, the underlying structure of the torus itself.

Just how these symbols fit into the Naacal story, whether there was a simple physical or a more metaphysical connection, he couldn't tell, but he decided that he needed to record this scroll. He laid it out and photographed it as completely as he could before rolling it up and continuing his search through the box.

Quickly discovering other scrolls with critical information regarding the Naacal people and their history, he noted that they were filled with a wealth of knowledge concerning their way of life, the workings of their society, and their religion. In all, he found twenty scrolls of particular importance.

Then he scoured the many stone tablets in a section of the library he realized could literally change the history of mankind for better or worse, depending on how the information would be received and implemented by the mainstream archaeological society.

Looking through another bin, he discovered what he thought looked like music scrolls containing a complete symphony, if he could call it that. In the same bin, he also discovered incredible still-life paintings using wonderfully vibrant colors of all sorts. He photographed every scroll in the bin.

He then noted an odd little stone tablet sitting alone on a shelf, about twelve inches square, looking more like a piece to a giant jigsaw puzzle. None of the other stone tablets looked anything like it. He stuffed it into his backpack, thinking that it merited further study and it was small enough to carry with him.

The familiar warble of a satellite phone momentarily distracted him, but it was some distance away, buried in one of the backpacks he had left outside near the main entrance to the city. He initially ignored it, but then realized that it might be Anderson's satellite phone, for he rarely went anywhere without it.

Out here in the depth of Central Australia, regular cell phone service was nearly impossible, except in and near "the Alice." Then he wondered how a sat phone could work at all in a cave, not having a line of sight with the satellite above.

"Ah, damn!" he muttered, realizing that the phone was one of the newest models, a hybrid with two operating systems in it so that it could act as both a cell phone and a full satellite phone, a new system for governments. But then, what was Andy doing with such a sophisticated phone?

He dashed out to where he had dropped Andy's backpack and grabbed the phone, still ringing. Looking at the display, he saw that it was Anderson's office calling. Suddenly he realized that the returning signal could be used as a GPS signal locator, one of the primary benefits of being both a cellphone and a satellite phone. He flicked it off.

Just then his own hybrid phone started ringing, echoing throughout the cavern in such a way that it sounded as if it was right next to him. He had forgotten about it.

He sprinted back to the vault and turned off his phone after discovering, by the caller id that it was Traci calling. "Not now, honey. Not now. I'm sorry."

Hannibal thought a moment and then realized that if someone had been tracing either of the signals, it was too late. They would have a fix on his location. But if he was lucky, they had not yet thought of that procedure.

By his watch, he determined that it was near sundown. He had been there all day and hadn't even thought about the time.

He gathered up his belongings and shut the vault door, worried about the contents now exposed to the air and how long they would remain undamaged by the elements. In the short time he had studied the scrolls and tablets, he clearly understood the importance of what the vault contained. He had to preserve it. But how?

He then thought of a solution. He had to reseal the vault as best he could. That meant he needed to get back to town and purchase some silicone caulking and backer rod to permanently reseal the door. He had plenty of photographs of the scrolls and tablets, but he knew that the vault must contain other wisdom and knowledge far beyond anything he had already found. But was Andy right? Was mankind not ready to know the rest of the secrets contained in the vault?

From his time as a CIA support operative, he understood and was trained well enough to use the C-4 Anderson's backpack provided. After resealing the vault door, he would then seal the entire cavern.

A frightening thought came to him. Was it possible that someone would find the cavern before he could seal it? Yes, all things were possible, but was it likely? He could not answer that, but he then thought of something he could do before it got dark to even further minimize such a possibility.

He jogged out of the cave, reconfigured the climbing harness, and climbed out of the chasm. He walked along the rift's edge until he spotted what he had hoped he would find: an extra-deep section of it. He returned to the SUVs and looked around for any signs of human presence. Not a soul anywhere. He pulled the keys to Anderson's SUV from his pocket, having retrieved them from Anderson's body, and started the engine. He drove near the edge of that extra-deep section, put the SUV in park, and took his time wiping down any areas he thought he and Andy might have touched. It took him the better part of ten minutes to wipe the SUV down, then using a rag, he put the truck in gear and let it go over the cliff.

After it went over, he suddenly realized his mistake.

"Oh shit! Hannibal, you're a dumb ass. Don't explode, you son of a bitch! Don't you dare explode!"

He hit the ground in anticipation of an explosion that did not occur.

"It always explodes in the movies," he muttered. "Don't explode. Don't you dare," he commanded.

He heard the engine cough and then die.

"Okay. Yes! That's what I'm talking about! Thank you. Thank you, you son of a bitch."

Just then he spotted a dust cloud approaching from the direction of Alice Springs. It was a car moving along the road toward him. His SUV was hidden behind the large boulder, so he wasn't concerned that it would be seen if the car kept moving. He was more worried that it might be a ranger or the police. If it was either, then he was screwed.

Perhaps they had received a call from Anderson's office and they were out looking for him. It would be necessary for them to check out anything that looked strange or out of place.

Now panic set in. He leapt to his feet and raced back toward his SUV. He might have to hightail it out of there in the hopes of leading them away from the rift. Perhaps they would ask him about Anderson once they knew who he was. He could explain that Anderson had never showed.

The thought of the SUV exploding returned. "No," he said, trying to reassure himself. "The motor died. There's no heat being generated. Come on, Hannibal, get control of yourself." He relaxed as he watched the cloud of dust growing closer. "But the engine still could be hot enough to ignite gasoline if it was leaking — stop it, Hannibal. Stop it!"

As he reached the boulder he saw the cloud of dust growing larger. Within minutes, he saw the car. It was not the police or the ranger patrol. It was an ordinary vehicle, probably tourists driving along the road, out to see the effects of the latest earthquake. He looked back toward the vehicle. No smoke. No fire.

"It's good, Hannibal. Everything is cool. Nothing to worry about."

Seconds later he heard the engine of the approaching vehicle. It didn't change pitch. It was cruising along. Then the car zipped past him at high speed and disappeared around a bend in the road and was gone.

"Jesus, Hannibal. You're one lucky son of a bitch."

CHAPTER 11

The explosion was loud, the column of smoke enormous and black as hell, especially against the cloudless sky. It startled him. He turned back to see the huge column of smoke rising from the rift.

"Hannibal, you're an *idiot!*"

The smoke would be a dead giveaway if anyone spotted it. The sun was dropping quickly. In only a few minutes it would be gone and the black smoke would blend into the night sky — he would be saved.

His eyes searched the sky and the landscape. He saw no other vehicles or aircraft in the area.

"You got lucky, Hannibal. Don't do something that stupid again, you jerk."

Minutes later, the sun was gone and the twilight rendered the smoke a non-factor. He certainly had acted foolishly, but he had escaped a bullet. Or had he? He finally reasoned that only time would answer that question.

For now, he thought, he would head back to the hotel and act as if nothing unusual had happened this day. He'd get cleaned up and eat some dinner as if all was normal. He would then retire to his room to study the photographs on his laptop. First, though, he had to tidy things up in the cavern.

~ ~ ~ ~ ~

He pulled up in front of a hardware store on Main Street and parked.

A little while later he exited the store carrying fifty tubes of silicone sealant and a fifty-foot roll of quarter-inch polyethylene backer rod. He tossed them into the backseat of the SUV and slammed the door closed.

Minutes later he pulled into the Charlie's Inn parking lot and stopped. He shoved his gear as well as Anderson's down onto the floor and put extra clothing over the top of them.

Walking into the lobby, he was immediately greeted by the same cute manager.

"Did you have a nice day, sir?"

"A very nice day. Thank you."

"Did you take in the sights and explore our beautiful area?"

"I did. I hiked all over the place. Tomorrow I'm going to get an earlier start and make an even nicer day of it."

"Were you able to contact Professor Anderson?"

"No. I was not able to. Has he shown up yet?"

"No, sir. I'm afraid not. The police stopped by to look at his room earlier. They asked me to have you call them when you returned, seeing that you know him and all."

"Of course. Where is the police station?"

"Just go out the door and turn left. The station is about three blocks down on the same side of the street."

"Great. I'll just clean up a bit and then take a walk down there to speak with them in person."

"I'm sure they'd appreciate it."

"Not a problem. Thank you for letting me know."

"Of course, sir. Have a nice evening."

"You too."

When Hannibal got to his room, he immediately removed the memory chip from the camera and taped it to the back of a dresser drawer. He then took a shower, dressed, and walked down the street to the police station.

Walking up to the desk, he introduced himself to the duty sergeant. He was immediately escorted to a private office and asked to take a seat and wait.

A burly detective walked in the door several minutes later and introduced himself. "Hi. I'm Detective Arnie Callson. Thank you so much for coming down personally."

Hannibal couldn't help but notice the drab, rough appearance of the man before him. His khaki shirt and shorts looked as if they had never seen an iron. His hair must have been frightened of a comb, and his face hadn't seen a razor in at least two or three days.

"You're quite welcome. I hope I can help."

"Doctor Hannibal Storm. Is that correct?"

"It is."

"Yeah, you're a doctor of archaeology, I understand. Is that correct?"

"That's correct. Have you any idea what's happened to Andy?"

"Andy?"

"Professor Andrew Anderson. I call him Andy."

"Oh, yeah. Right. No, we haven't located him yet. Can you tell me anything?"

"Not really. I got a call from him the other day while I was on a dig in Mexico. He sounded very worried about something. Well, maybe 'worried' is inaccurate. He sounded very excited."

"Excited, not worried?"

"Excited, yes."

"Not worried?"

"I'm an archaeologist, Detective, not an English professor. He was excited."

"But there is a difference, wouldn't you agree?"

"Yes. And I would characterize our conversation best by saying that he sounded excited about something. Knowing him as I do, I would say that he'd discovered something interesting and was excited for me to see it."

"Okay, that makes sense. He was excited. Can you tell me anything else?"

"I don't know what to tell you, Detective."

"Why do you think he would call an archaeologist from America down to the Alice, Doctor? I mean, why wouldn't he contact an Australian archaeologist?"

"I can't say for sure, but Andy and I go back a long time. Almost twenty years. We used to do a lot of exploring together. Maybe he just felt more comfortable calling me."

"I see. But you spoke with him before coming down, yeah?"

"As I said, he called me. He told me he had a ticket for me to come to Alice Springs and he'd catch up with me down here.

When I showed up at the inn, I found out he'd left a box full of spelunking equipment for me."

"Spelunking equipment?"

"Yes. He and I used to do a lot of cave exploring together in the old days, when he was teaching up at the University of Washington in Seattle. When I saw the equipment, I thought he had found another interesting cave he wanted to explore with me."

"Sounds pretty trivial to have you rush all the way to the Alice to explore caves, doesn't it?"

"Exactly. So it had to be pretty important. I suspect it was very important. He must have seen something incredible in a cave. That would be my guess, at least."

"I see. I suppose he could have discovered something like that. Makes sense with what he boxed up for you."

"It does. I just hope he shows up soon. He tends to get lost in his discoveries, so maybe he just got carried away and forgot to meet me."

"Yeah. Perhaps that's it. Have you known him to stay out of contact with his office for several days at a time?"

"He's a geologist, Detective. He's done it many times in the past. Weeks at a time. You know, most of those guys lose track of themselves when they get around rocks. When I was training with him, we'd be gone for days sometimes, in the remotest parts of the state, just looking at rocks and formations. So no, it's not unusual at all, but he is an old man and that bothers me."

"I see."

"I just hope he's okay. He's nearly eighty."

"Right," said the detective. "He's an old sort to be running around in the mountains, ain't he?"

"Yep."

"So you never met him at Charlie's, you said?"

"No. He left a message at the desk asking me to meet him out west of town at that old bend in the road."

"You still have that message?"

"I'm sorry, I don't. Didn't think I needed to hang on to it."

"Yeah, right. That's too bad."

"You know where the road makes a V, just before it heads south into the mountains?"

"Yeah, I know the place. Is that where you were supposed to meet?"

"Yes."

"But he never arrived?"

"No. I waited for over two hours before I gave up and spent the next several hours walking around searching for him."

"And?"

"Nothing. Not a hint of him. After it got dark, I gave up and came back. Of course, I didn't want to alarm anyone unnecessarily, so I told the manager at Charlie's that I was out just hiking around."

"You did?"

"Yes. I don't think we should panic anyone just yet, do you? I mean, did I do the right thing? I'm not too good at this secret squirrel stuff."

"Secret squirrel, did you say?"

"Yeah. Ah, it's an American thing. An old cartoon show for kids."

"Ahh."

"So. Did I do the right thing?"

"How's that?"

"Telling the manager —"

"Yes. Sorry. Yeah. There's no use starting a panic at this point."

"Have you contacted his office, Detective? Maybe he was called back on an emergency."

"Wouldn't he have contacted you if he was?"

"Yeah. Come to think of it, I guess he would have, huh?"

"Well, according to the manager of the hotel, he's been missing for a couple days at least. I guess we'd probably better organize a search party. Do you have a cell phone, Doctor Storm?"

"Yes, I certainly do. Would you like my number?"

"Yes. Absolutely." Hannibal recited the number to the detective and he scribbled it down.

"Have you received any calls since you've been here, Doctor?"

"You know, to tell you the truth, I forgot to turn on my sat phone today. Let me check."

Hannibal pulled out his satellite phone and turned it on. Seconds later he got a missed-call signal.

"A missed call."

"Pretty nice phone, that. A bit pricey for us down here, though. You must have quite a budget at the university."

"For some things, I guess."

Hannibal pushed some buttons and Traci's phone number came up. He showed it to the detective. "My girlfriend. Well, actually, my fiancée. Well, ex-fiancée, I should say."

"You're no longer getting married?"

"No. She's a little pissed at the moment. You know how women are."

"Yeah, I'm afraid I do. My wife's a little pissed at me right now also."

"Too many nights out with the boys?"

"Too many nights working late, mate."

"Ahh. That'll do it also."

"Well, thanks for stopping in, Doctor Storm. If you hear from Professor Anderson, please call me immediately. Here's my card with my number."

"I'll certainly do that, Detective."

"What are you going to do tomorrow, Doctor?"

"Well, if I don't hear from Andy tonight, I thought I'd take advantage of what time I have and really do some exploring around the area. My flight doesn't leave for three more days. I heard you had quite a shaker recently. I saw some evidence of it today. I thought I'd check it out a little closer. That would be all right, wouldn't it?"

"Certainly, Doctor. It was a hell of a shake, mate. Scared the bejesus out of me, it did."

"I live in Los Angles, Detective Callson. We're used to them."

"You can have 'em. They're pretty scary to us down here. On the coast they get 'em frequently, but here in the Alice we don't experience 'em too much. I wouldn't care to experience another one like that, I'll tell ya."

"I bet. Well, thanks, Detective. Let's hope we all hear from Andy real soon."

"I'll let you know if we do. You do the same."

Hannibal and the detective shook hands and Hannibal walked out of the office, down the street to a little restaurant, and had dinner. He acted as normal as he could. All the while, the photographs of the scrolls and tablets were beckoning him — haunting him.

CHAPTER 12

The computer screen resolution was clear and crisp. It wasn't the same as having the scrolls and tablets sitting in front of him, but it was plenty good enough for what Hannibal Storm needed. To be safe, he first saved the photographs onto a flash drive. He then connected with his private and secure computer at UCLA through his client file transfer protocol program — FTP, as it was called in the industry — and uploaded them all to that system. Including the camera's chip, he had saved the photographs on three different storage devices. He felt protected.

Sitting in his room in Charlie's Inn very late into the evening, he translated as many of the symbols as he could from the scroll which appeared to contain the information about the tuaoi. He couldn't translate it all, but he was shocked to learn that the deciphered major coordinates on the tablet appeared to provide a rudimentary location of the Great Firestone somewhere in the southwestern United States.

He thought it best to keep the information to himself for the time being. No telling what more those scrolls and tablets might have to say.

His eyes began to droop; it was too late to continue. If he wanted to get out to the cavern early in the morning and seal it all back up, he'd better get some badly needed sleep. So the computer went off, the lights went out, and Hannibal drifted quickly into a well-earned sleep.

~ ~ ~ ~ ~

Before the sun peeked above the eastern horizon, Hannibal was in his SUV heading for the cavern. He left early for two reasons. He didn't want anyone to see him leave the hotel. Like the police, for instance. Secondly, if someone were to follow him, like the police for instance, it would be very difficult not to use headlights, considering the dangerous curves in the road leading out to the cavern. If someone were to follow using headlights, he would be certain to see them and would adjust his route accordingly.

No one saw him leave the hotel; the late-night manager was sound asleep and Hannibal tiptoed past without disturbing him. He saw no one waiting near the parking lot, and no one followed him. His shrewd thinking now allowed him the opportunity to take care of what he needed to do.

Once inside the vault again, he photographed every tablet that looked even remotely important, every scroll in which he could find anything remotely interesting regarding the Naacal and their history, their language, their philosophy, and the location of any other cities, camps, or villages. After several hours, he felt he could do no more. It was time to make sure the vault was as hermetically sealed as he could make it.

With fresh batteries in his helmet lamp, he completely resealed the door to the vault by first pressing the polyethylene backer rod into the crack around the door and filling in the rest of the joint with generous squeezings of silicone. Then he ran a rag wetted with mineral spirits to finish the sealing by smoothing out the joint. It took him only twenty minutes to finish, but the seal was solid and complete. It might not last 25,000 years, but it was the best he could do.

He laid the rest of his supplies next to the door and walked away, knowing there was nothing more he could do to protect the room.

Then a terrible thought occurred to him. What if the clerk at the hardware store reported the odd American purchasing fifty tubes of caulking? How was he going to explain that away? What would an American archaeologist be doing with fifty tubes of clear silicone caulking?

Hannibal understood that Alice Springs was an isolated town and that any outsider would garner special attention whether he wanted it or not. Did the clerk notice Hannibal's purchase? Or, as he suddenly hoped, did the recent earthquake spur sales of caulking to seal up cracks caused by the shaker? Was it so unusual after a strong quake to purchase that type of product?

The only thing Hannibal could do right now was proceed with his plan. If he was confronted by Detective Callson about his purchase, then he might have to either confess or do something more drastic. He wondered how long it might take for the people of Alice Springs to miss one of their more prominent and senior detectives. He hated to think about having to do anything to the man, but this secret was more critical to the world than the life of one police detective, or even one geologist. If confronted, Hannibal Storm might have to become a murderer in order to save the world.

So far, Hannibal had been very fortunate. He just hoped his luck would hold out a while longer — at least until he got back to the States.

He pulled Andy's sat phone from his backpack and thought about turning it on to see if Kirby had called again but decided against it. If the professor's phone signal was being monitored, he would be caught in his planned deception. He decided to leave it turned off. He opened the back of the phone and removed the battery. He then tossed the parts into Andy's backpack and laid it on top of Andy's body, reasoning that it was better lost forever than found. He knew Andy would have approved of his actions.

His heart suddenly sank. He grabbed his own satellite phone and noticed he had forgotten to turn it off that morning before leaving.

If someone was monitoring his phone, his destination was already compromised. He clicked it off quickly.

"Damn!" he hissed.

~ ~ ~ ~ ~

A sound caught his attention. He couldn't be certain, but it sounded like rocks clicking together. It was faint, but Hannibal heard it quite clearly. Someone was in the cavern with him. He clicked off his helmet light immediately.

He stiffened. Perhaps it was the detective. Perhaps he had followed Hannibal out here after all. He began to panic. Had Detective Callson, by chance, bugged his car? Was he clever enough to do that? Was he deceitful enough to even think about it?

The next question his mind raised sent shivers down his spine. What would happen to him if he was found with Andy's body? No doubt about it, he reasoned, his goose would be cooked.

Sure, it could be proven that Andy had died of natural causes, but Hannibal would be guilty of covering up his death. Well, maybe not, he thought. He could always tell the detective that he had found the body only this morning. But still, by then, the cavern would have given up its secrets forever.

Of course, trying to keep it hidden was down the drain anyway if someone was in the cavern with him.

He kept low and behind the stone entrance to the home, his eyes searching for any movement. It was so black he couldn't even see his hand in front of his face.

He heard more sounds, like shuffling footsteps in the heavy sand of the cavern floor.

He was certain of it now. Someone else was in the cavern and they were coming closer. The more he listened, the more he was certain that there was more than one person. The detective and his partner, he instantly reasoned.

He thought about it and wondered if he was capable of killing them. Then he considered that he might have to do just that to keep the world safe. The thought crossed his mind that this day might be his last. Perhaps they would overcome him. They carried guns. He didn't.

He considered coming clean with the officers, but something in his mind told him to remain hidden and silent.

He was glad he did.

The beams from two powerful flashlights crisscrossed the darkness. They were still a ways away from where Hannibal hid. Then he heard the splashing of water. They were fording the stream and coming toward him, most likely following the footprints just as he had.

What a shame, he thought. Those footprints had remained untouched for tens of thousands of years. Archaeologically speaking, they were invaluable and should have been isolated and preserved. And here some dolt of a detective and his partner were stomping all over them, forever destroying any historical value they might have had to future archaeologists. What asses. Boorish, idiotic asses.

The flashlight beams crisscrossed the cavern again as the intruders continued directly toward the city. Hannibal remained as still as he could, but he knew that eventually whoever it was would discover him by following his tracks.

A new thought struck him. What if these intruders weren't the detective and his partner but rather some people willing to kill him to keep the secret of this city for themselves? If it was someone like that approaching and not the police, he was a dead man for sure.

He tried to recall what the professor had left him in the box. He remembered. The survival knife! The huge survival knife. But wait a second. He'd left that with the caulking supplies outside the vault. *Damn!* his mind screamed at him.

The intruders were still a good distance away, though, and he thought that it might just be possible to get to the vault before they came close enough to spot him. If he was quiet, it should work out, he reasoned. After fetching the knife, there were other buildings very near the vault that he could scurry into and hide.

He made his move and, as silently as possible, scurried toward the vault. His boots shifted the sandy floor no matter how softly he tried to walk, and the acoustics in the cavern would have been most appreciated by any orchestra conductor. He was making too much noise, but he had to get to that knife. It might be his only chance to protect himself. The old adage about bringing a knife to a gunfight entered his mind.

He shook his head, trying to rid it of all negative thoughts. If he hid well enough, he might surprise whoever came to harm him. A good plunge of the knife in under the ribs would certainly stop a fight before it could ever begin. Of course, he would need a bit of luck to then put down the second person, but he'd worry about that when he had to.

Skulking along toward the vault in the absolute blackness was nearly impossible, but moving along the stone building faces made it doable. He tried recalling just how far away the vault was from the professor's body.

Damn! he thought. The vault was about halfway toward the rear of the cavern — at least five hundred yards away. This was not going to be easy, but he recalled nothing that would trip him up along the way. The ground was smooth and flat.

It was just damned dark, darkness unlike any he had ever encountered before. Then he remembered what Andy had told him about precautions to take when spelunking. Always carry far more batteries and flashlights than you think you would ever need because the darkness underground was unlike anything normal people could ever imagine. Andy had said that after some time in this kind of darkness, months actually, the light- and color-reception rods and cones in the cells of the eye could eventually die, causing permanent blindness.

It was not going to be months, he hoped, but with the intruders moving up on him, he didn't dare flick on his own flashlight. Instead, he felt along the buildings, slowly working his way toward the vault. Good thing for him, every now and then the glare of their flashlights flickered, exposing their position. He was still well ahead of them, but the truth of it began to frighten him — they were drawing closer quickly. They could move faster than he could because they weren't trying to hide. It was now a race to see who would get to the vault first.

He managed to stay just ahead of the intruders' beams of light and then, finally, he felt the now familiar granite walls of the vault. He was very close and so he got down on his hands and knees and crawled until his hand touched the vinyl of the backpack. The beams were now bouncing all around him. He fought against the strap that kept the pack closed until he found the right clasp and flicked it open.

His right hand dove into the pack and quickly found the plastic scabbard. A second later he clasped the knife's handle. He withdrew it from the pack and pulled it from the scabbard.

It was all good, but it was too late. The flashlight beams were directly on his back.

"Stop!" barked one of the intruders.

He dropped the knife and turned his head. He saw nothing but the bright beam of the flashlight. He moved his hand to block the light. That also was too late.

He felt the blow against the side of his head, and then the lights went out completely, along with any thoughts he might have had floating around his brain.

~ ~ ~ ~ ~

He stirred. He heard voices. Faint at first, almost distant, as if in a dream. They became louder. He couldn't understand them at first, but then recognized the singsong of Chinese. He heard other noises as well, scraping noises.

He tried to sit up, and almost made it until a foot to his chest sent him back to the sandy cavern floor.

"You stop! You do not move!" It was a Chinese male voice.

Hannibal tried to focus his eyes, but couldn't. "Who are you?" he asked.

"You not worry about us. You be quiet, okay? You sit still and you do not die, okay?""

After a minute or two more, his eyes finally focused and he saw two Chinese men trying to pull the caulking from the vault door.

"Stop that!" Hannibal shouted. "Don't do that! You'll destroy everything."

One of the men stopped his work, pulled a handgun from his belt, and pointed it directly at Hannibal. His face a fierce stare, he pulled back the hammer and aimed carefully.

"You asses!" said Hannibal.

The two shots weren't very loud, he thought. Not as loud as he'd expected, at least. And there was no burst of fire from the muzzle before him, but there were two flashes from his left. Another two blasts of light and sound, and both Chinese men dropped to the ground, their fallen flashlights illuminating the rhythmic streams of blood pumping out into the sand from chest and head wounds.

Traci's face was the next thing he saw.

"What are you doing here, Trace?" he said, still groggy.

"Saving your ass as usual, honey."

"You followed me all the way out here?"

"My private jet can go just about anywhere, honey."

"Private ... Geez. The life."

"Lucky for you I did follow you."

She began untying the bindings of his hands.

"Who are those guys?"

"Chinese agents, Hannibal."

"What are they doing here?"

"I think they were going to kidnap you."

"But why? How did they find me?"

"Hannibal, please don't be naïve. The word, I'm sure, is out about you and what's happening in the Yucatan. Whether you like it or not, lover, you're a hot commodity."

She finished untying his hands and helped him to his feet.

"And the thing about satellite phones, sweetie," she coyly added, "they can easily be traced. Especially ones with a tracker chip inside them, like yours. Unfortunately, they can be traced by just about anyone who has the technology to do so."

"I don't understand. You bugged your sat phone?"

"Of course. How do you think I found you? More to the point, how do you think *they* found you?"

"But it was *your* sat phone."

"I know. Sorry, honey. It was Kirby's idea. I borrowed Kirby's sat phone."

"Well, that explains it. And it explains the call to Andy's phone, too."

"I didn't call Andy, Hannibal, but you left me little choice but to track you."

"You didn't call Andy?"

"No. I was tracking you just fine until you turned off your phone. Glad the Chinese found you first. It was easy to track them."

"Wait a minute! I was the bait? You were using me as *bait?*"

"Sorry again, Hannibal. But as I said, you gave me no choice."

"You set me up!"

"It turned out okay, didn't it?"

"Tell that to my head, after I find it. It's around here somewhere. In pieces, I think."

"Gee, Hannibal. You should have told me what you were gonna do here. It's really not my fault, you know?"

"I didn't know I was going to end up here. I followed a map from Andy."

"Well, honey, that's how shit happens. What happened to Andy, Hannibal?"

"He's dead. Died of a stroke down here. I put him inside one of the houses. This is where he wanted to be buried."

"I see. Do the police know about it?"

"No, and I wasn't planning on telling them either."

"That's good. I don't need to be involved in this. What is this, anyway?"

"Do you see what's all around you?"

"Yes, I do, and I must say it's truly breathtaking. But what is it?"

"We don't need to have anyone else down here mucking it up."

"I understand, but what is it?"

"Just as soon as I find what's left of my brains, I'll tell ya."

"Really sorry, Hannibal, but I had to watch what they were doing before I showed myself."

"As it worked out, Trace, I'm glad you followed me."

"Me, too. So tell me. What is this all about?"

CHAPTER 13

Over the next thirty minutes, Hannibal told Traci the complete story.

"Can I see the inside of the vault?"

"No. It needs to remain sealed. The scrolls are too important to risk any damage to them."

"Okay, I understand. Besides, you've got plenty of photos, right? I guess that will have to do."

~ ~ ~ ~ ~

After repairing the seal on the door where the Chinese agents had scraped it off, Hannibal and Traci went to the room where the body of Professor Anderson lay.

"I'm sorry about your friend, Hannibal," said Traci, staring down at Andy's body.

"Yeah, me too, but what are we going to do about this? I suppose we could take the body back with us, but I really hate to do that."

"Let's not. Leave him here in peace. Leave him as a mystery. Nobody needs to know. He has no wife, right?"

"No, she died years ago. He never had any kids either. His brother died a decade ago. His parents are long dead. He really had no one." Hannibal thought for a moment. "Geez, that's really sad. I never thought about it. He really was all alone. He just had his work."

"Yeah, it's sad, but it solves our problem. Unless someone else finds this cavern."

"That won't happen. I know where lots of C-4 is."

"Oh!"

~ ~ ~ ~ ~

With the charges in position, he and Traci bade goodbye to the underground city and to his dear friend. He pushed the button.

The explosion was huge and the result was sure. The collapse of the surrounding wall completely sealed the cavern as if it had never been there at all. Someone looking at it, as geologists very well could in the near future, would see just collapsed rock, as if the earthquake had caused it all. He had even taken great care to effectively cover the protruding end of the white marble entrance columns.

Hannibal then suggested that they bury the intruders' vehicle the same way he had taken care of Anderson's.

It went much smoother this time. No hot engine. No explosion.

They carefully erased the tire marks with branches off nearby bushes. Peering down into the crevice, they could barely see the tail ends of the vehicles. With any luck at all they would not be found for years. But even if they were discovered, there was nothing to tie them to the sealed cavern.

"When can I see the photos you took?"

"Just as soon as we get back to the inn, hon. Where are you staying?"

"Same place as you."

"Clever."

~ ~ ~ ~ ~

Once back at the inn's parking lot, they immediately started for Hannibal's room. They didn't get far.

"Doctor! Doctor Storm!"

Hannibal turned and saw Detective Callson approaching.

"I've been looking for you, Doctor. Can we speak?"

"Sure. Have you found Andy yet, Detective Callson?"

"Who, may I ask, is this?"

"Sorry, Detective. This is Traci Jefferson. I told you about her yesterday."

"Ah, the ex-girlfriend. I thought you said she was pissed at you."

"I am pissed at him. And you are Detective Callson?"

"I am, ma'am. I'm surprised to see you here."

"I'm pissed, Detective. But I still love him."

"Sounds like me and the missus."

"Have you found him, Detective?"

"'Fraid not, Doctor. Not a trace of him. May I ask where you've been this morning?"

"Doing like I said. Wandering about, looking at the earthquake damage to the hills."

"Somethin', ain't it?"

"Sure is. Didn't affect much here in the Alice, though, I see."

"Right. We got lucky, we did. When did you get into town, Miss Jefferson?"

"Late last night. I wasn't going to come, but I always seem to miss him when he's gone. So here I am."

"That's right nice you have the time to drop what you're doing and rush out here with your guy."

"Yes. I am fortunate."

"May I ask what you do for a living?"

"Am I being interrogated, Detective?"

"I'm sorry, miss. No. Not at all. I'm just the curious type. I guess it comes with the job. You don't need to answer if you don't want to."

"I was kidding, Detective. I'm CEO of a corporation that searches for alternative energy sources."

"I see. Sounds interesting."

"It's very interesting, and it gives me time to rush away, as you say, with my guy when I want to."

"If you'll excuse us, Detective, we're a bit hungry. Going to get a bite. Would you care to join us?"

"No, thank you, Doctor. I gotta get back to the office. Lots of work to do. We're finally organizing a search party to look for your friend."

"Can we help?"

"No, thanks. We've got our ways of doing things down here. I'll let you know if we find him."

"Okay, thanks. When you do find him, give 'im hell for me."

"I'll do that. G'day, Miss Jefferson."

"Good day, Detective."

Detective Callson turned and walked away.

"Well, that went well, I think. Of course, if they do locate Andy, the whole gig is over." said Hannibal.

"I don't think they will. I *am* a bit hungry, though."

~ ~ ~ ~ ~

At lunch, Hannibal fell silent as thoughts raced around his head.

He felt good about covering their tracks from the cavern. He was certain they had left nothing behind to incriminate themselves. Traci knew her business as well. Now they only needed to get on Traci's corporate jet and head back to L.A.

Then something else slid through his mind.

"Hey, Traci. I've been having some strange thoughts lately. I know this is going to sound odd, but have you noticed anything different about Kirby lately?"

"You mentioned that before. Why?"

"I don't really know. I'm getting bad feelings about him."

"Are you still hanging onto the grudge about him leaving you behind in Iraq?"

"No. Well, yes. I'll probably always hold a grudge about that. I damned near died. But it's not about that."

"Well, what then?"

"It's like he has some hidden agenda. I don't think I trust him right now."

"He's a Company man, Hannibal. You don't trust anyone at the Company. Not even me, I think, sometimes."

"I trust you, Traci. Why would you say something like that?"

"Never mind. As for Kirby, you haven't gotten along with him for quite a while, Hannibal."

"He's an ass sometimes, but we're friends, I guess, in our own way, and I've never thought I couldn't trust him."

"Not even after he ran out on you? Are you serious?"

"I know. It pissed me off, but he really did the right thing. Getting that critical data back to the CIA when he did was the right thing to do."

"Wow! Listen to you."

"I'll deny it if you ever tell him what I just said."

"Your secret's safe with me, dear. So what do you think has changed?"

"I can't quite put my finger on it."

"Well, then, just keep quiet about it until you do."

"It's a trust thing. A gut feeling."

"You mean like you and me?"

"You're just not going to drop it, are you?"

"You made your choice, Hannibal. The Mayans over me. I get it."

"No, you don't get it. I don't think you ever will understand me."

"At least I tried."

"And I tried, too. Damnit, Trace. I'm an archaeologist, I'm sorry. You knew that coming into the relationship. So why were you so surprised?"

"I thought I mattered more."

"You do. You did, at least."

"That's not enough, Hannibal. You hurt me badly."

"Once again, I'm sorry, but I'm sorrier that you won't let me be me."

"I don't want to argue, Hannibal."

"Then don't start arguing about something that happened over a year ago."

"You make it hard to love you, Hannibal."

"Anything new on the power station?"

"That's it? That's all you have to say?"

"I give up."

"I know. You give up so easily when it comes to talking about us."

"I was just curious about the power station."

"Let's not talk about that right now. I don't know who might be listening."

"Okay. Have it your way."

Traci fell silent. Hannibal sat fiddling with his hair.

"Women," he finally blurted out. "Can't live with 'em, can't get caught disposing of their bodies." A wry smile crossed his face.

"That goes two ways, buster."

"Yes, it does."

"And right now, dear, you owe me."

"Yes, I do. Thanks for saving my bacon, by the way."

Hannibal chuckled. Traci joined in.

"Anytime, Storm."

"What do you say I chase you around the room for a bit?"

"I'm too tired to run. How about we just screw our brains out and then get some sleep."

"I can do that."

~ ~ ~ ~ ~

The phone rang.

It was the inn's manager informing Hannibal that Traci's pilot was waiting at the Alice Springs airport for the return flight to Los Angeles.

Hannibal immediately notified Detective Callson that they would be leaving for home and left his home and office phone numbers should Andy show up. Of course if he did, Hannibal thought, Detective Callson would have the fright of his life.

CHAPTER 14

A day and a half later, Hannibal and Traci arrived at his apartment in Los Angeles, dead tired but with no one the wiser about their harrowing ordeal. Apparently even the hardware clerk had taken no special notice of the American buying fifty tubes of silicone.

For all his worry, the incident passed into memory without fanfare or untimely announcement.

~ ~ ~ ~ ~

He dropped his armload of mail, including a large box, onto the kitchen table. Mrs. Morrison had been keeping his mail for him while he was gone, and the kitchen table was the only available space amid the hodgepodge of cluttered confusion that was his home.

Traci dragged in and looked around.

"Fire the maid, did ya?"

She shrugged her shoulders and plopped down on the sofa after sliding aside some displaced artifacts.

"Private jet or no private jet, that's a long way to travel within three days. Even for the man I love."

"You can say that again."

Hannibal looked around.

"I gotta get this place straightened up. But not today."

His sat phone rang.

He glanced at the face of the phone. He recognized the number. "It's Kirby calling."

"So answer it."

"It's your phone, remember."

"Hannibal, please."

He answered. "What do you want, Kirby? I just walked through the door and I'm beat. ... Yeah. She's sitting on the sofa all wiped out, too. What the hell do you want? ... I don't care what they found right now. Call me tomorrow. ... I know it's Traci's phone. ... Well, then, call *her* tomorrow. Just make it tomorrow, no matter what. ... What? ... No! I don't want you here tonight. ... Hello? Hello?!"

Hannibal hung up the phone. "Sure, Kirby. Come right on over. No problem," he said sarcastically.

"What did he want?"

"He found something, or somebody found something. I don't know and I don't care. Oh, and he's coming over."

"Wonderful."

Hannibal lay back in his chair and closed his eyes. He was in need of sleep and lots of it. Instead, he was about to have company.

Opening his weary eyes, he glanced around again at the chaos that was his apartment. In complete disarray, his valued possessions were scattered about the room haphazardly, without structure, without purpose or direction. Completely out of control. Tossed there by the police-hired movers without any care at all — a seeming junk pile of useless artifacts important only to him, lying about without objective or function.

Then he saw it all instantly, clearly, for the first time — his apartment was a physical representation of his life, a microcosm of what his horrid, dysfunctional existence was like at that very moment.

He understood himself in the midst of it, a valuable researcher and thinker, possessing a brilliant mind full of knowledge and potential, but now only a cluttered lump of disorganized chaos and uncertainty.

The artifacts, the sum total of the experiences and beliefs that made up his life, were important only to him. Only *he* saw the real value in them. His life lacked any true structure or purpose. There was no order to anything, either around him or within him. Maybe what everyone had said about him was right. He was a wild man living in an open wilderness without any borders or guiding structure, a feral mustang, racing madly to nowhere.

Or maybe all of this thinking was just the haunted ramblings of a sleep-deprived mind. He glanced over at Traci, who had fallen asleep. He couldn't figure her out either. What the hell did she see in him? She could have any guy she wanted. She apparently still wanted him. Nothing made any sense, and that seemed par for the course he was on.

It was his last memory before tumbling into the rabbit hole of a deep sleep.

~ ~ ~ ~ ~

The doorbell rang.

He woke up with a start and began to get up to open the door, but Kirby pushed the door open, rushed in, and then slammed the door shut.

"Sure. Come on in. Make yourself comfortable," he said, still seated.

"I don't have time to play right now, Hannibal. I don't have time for anything humorous at all."

Hannibal saw that Kirby was extremely serious as he paced around the room, tripping over everything, completely ignoring the mess.

Traci woke up and stared dumbly at Kirby.

"What happened in Australia, Hannibal?"

"Nothing much."

"Did you say anything to Anderson about the Yucatan before you left?"

"Of course not. Why?"

"Come on, Hannibal," Kirby said, rubbing his hands together nervously. "Tell me the truth."

"No. I said nothing. Well, I just asked him if white marble was a stone native to Mexico. But you know that already."

"Is that the truth? Is that all you said?"

"Yes. Why? What's got you so worked up? You're like a pacing tiger."

"Bad stuff, Hannibal. Bad stuff happened while you were both away."

"What's going on?"

"They found Doctor Gonzalez's body yesterday. They believe he was murdered."

"Hector? Someone killed Hector?"

"Yes."

"Why the hell would anyone kill Hector? He was just a gentle, simple, honest, hardworking archaeologist."

"Doesn't matter now. He's dead."

"Where did they find him?"

"Does it really matter, Hannibal?"

"Yeah, Kirby. It matters."

"Somewhere near where you found the distribution station. The smaller one. The one out in the jungle."

"They're both out in the jungle, Kirby, but yeah, I understand. It figures." He rose exhaustedly out of his chair and began to pace.

"What figures? What the hell are you talking about? You expected this? Is that what you're saying?"

"Let's just say, Kirby, that I'm not surprised."

"Why? Come on, Hannibal. Tell me."

"There's only one reason I can think of. He found something special."

"How do you know that?"

"What other reason would there be for killing one of Mexico's most prominent archaeologists, one of the most visible men in the field and also one of the gentlest men I've ever known?"

"Yeah, he was a nice guy. So what? Lots of nice guys die every day. What did he find?

"I got him killed. *We* got him killed," Hannibal said.

"What are you talking about?" asked Traci.

"What we found out there in the jungle. It got him killed."

"It's not our fault, partner."

"Kirby, you just don't get it, do you?"

"Get what?"

"When good people are allowed to die without justification, we are all guilty of murder."

"I don't have time for all the high-and-mighty sentiment, Hannibal."

"Then make time, Kirby, because you're just as guilty as I am. And now I know we could all be guilty of destroying the world if we find the firestone."

"I can't worry about those implications until we locate the firestone and secure it. That's my job now, Hannibal — securing the firestone. I'm sorry about Doctor Gonzalez, I really am, but I've got to find out what he knew — what got him killed. And I've got to know if you said anything to Anderson."

"I said nothing to Andy about what we're doing in the Yucatan."

"You didn't speak to Doctor Gonzalez?"

"No! Of course not. How could I? I was sitting in the middle of Australia."

Kirby ran both hands nervously through his hair. "I got a message on my phone from him yesterday morning — early."

Startled by Kirby's words, Hannibal shot a glance at the CIA man. "Who? Who did you get a message from? Andy?"

"No, of course not. I meant Doctor Gonzalez. Why? Do you know something you're not telling me?"

"I know lots of things you don't know, Kirby. I'm smarter than you."

"I don't have time for this sparring shit, Hannibal. What aren't you telling me?"

"That you're a really nice guy, Kirby, but I was holding that one close to my chest."

"Hannibal! Knock it off. Do you know something about Doctor Gonzalez's murder? Yes or no?"

"No. I don't know anything, but he must have found something extraordinary and whoever killed him must have been trying to get their hands on it. So you got a message from Hector on the day he died?"

"Yes."

"And you weren't going to tell me this?"

"I'm telling you now, Hannibal."

"You talked to him?"

"No. He only left a message. He sounded very excited. He said he wanted to call you but didn't have your number. He asked me for it, but I obviously didn't get the chance to chat with him about it. He said that only you would understand. That he had information extremely critical to your theory."

"Critical to my theory?"

"Yes."

"What theory? I mean, which one?"

"He didn't say."

"Did you call him back?"

"No."

"Why?"

"I just told you, I didn't get the chance. But there was something strange about the message. It was like he got cut off in the middle of his call."

"Do you still have the message on your phone?"

"No. I deleted it by mistake."

"Damn. Well, do your CIA thing. Call the phone company and have them retrieve it. Or hell, call the NSA. Aren't they keeping everything nowadays?"

"I suppose I could, but I don't really need it. Hannibal, I think I heard him being killed."

"How's that, Kirby?"

"He was talking and then I heard a whoosh sound. Then silence for a moment. Then there were some indistinguishable background voices. I couldn't understand what was being said. Then the line went dead, like someone crushed his satellite phone. I tried to replay it, but deleted it by mistake. I got a bit nervous, I guess. Anyway, I called it in immediately. The Mexican authorities found Hector's body several hours later. I got a call from their offices telling me that there were no signs of a struggle."

"And you believed them?"

"No, Trace. I most certainly didn't."

"A cover-up?"

"It's sure looking that way. I got a call from one of my assets down there who saw the body. He said Doctor Gonzalez had a tiny puncture wound on the right side of his neck, like a syringe had been used on him. But it wasn't a needle. I mean it wasn't a syringe. Just the puncture mark, you know, with a reddening welt around the wound."

"It wasn't a syringe, Kirby," said Hannibal. "It was a dart. Probably poisoned. I'm betting curare or something like it."

"What makes you think that?" asked Traci.

"The whoosh sound. I bet it was a dart from a blowgun or a powered dart gun."

"Ah. Right. Of course. Why didn't I think of that?"

Kirby looked odd.

"What, Kirby? You know something else, don't you?"

"It *was* a dart, Hannibal. My asset told me. A dart dipped in curare. How did you know?"

"Blowguns were in common use throughout the region for centuries. At least they were a long time ago. They were introduced through migration up out of the Amazon."

"How do you know that, Hannibal?"

"Oh, let me see, Kirby. Maybe because ... I'm an *archaeologist*?"

"Hannibal, please," said Traci. "Try to be civil. It was a fair question."

"Okay, Hannibal. I'm sure you're right," said Kirby. "But you said '*were* common.'"

"Yeah. They're not too common anymore. They discovered better ways to kill people, I guess. Were there any tracks?" Hannibal asked.

"Duh, Hannibal. It was dig site. Of course there were tracks."

"Don't *you* start now, Kirby," said Traci. "My god, I wish you two would just grow up."

"Sorry, Trace," said Kirby. "He brings it out in me."

"Tell me about it."

"Glad I'm having some effect on you two. I should have asked, Were there any *unusual* tracks, Kirby?"

"I don't know. Hundreds of photos have been taken by the Mexican forensic team."

"Can we get our hands on them?"

"Probably not. If there's a cover-up going on, they'll most likely seal everything or deny such photos were ever taken. You know how it works. Would they help?"

"I don't know, Kirby. It might be better to have the photos than not to have them, though, right?"

"I guess so. But it's clear he was murdered. There's no question about it."

Hannibal thumbed at his nose. "Did they search his office yet?"

"I had my own team head there immediately after hearing about his death. That was yesterday."

"Can you call and ask if they found anything?" asked Traci.

"Don't have to. My lead guy called me while I was on my way over here. His office was ransacked. His laptop was missing as well."

"Someone ransacked a field office? And got away with it? That means professionals. Anything else missing?"

"Yeah, all the handwritten notes he made out in the field."

"Do you know what Hector was doing just before he died? I mean, do you know what he was working on besides the distribution station?"

"No clue, Hannibal. He'd been keeping a really low profile since you left. He wasn't sharing much with me. But I do know that he was very excited about something. Excited enough to want to call you. His phone message confirmed that. What are we going to do now?"

"Nothing we can do, as I see it. It's up to the Mexican government, isn't it?"

"Not really. We're funding it. We can call the shots to a large degree, now that their guy's gone."

"What about the cover-up, then?"

"I'm guessing someone way above my pay grade is calling the shots on that."

"Can we get access to the site?"

"I don't know. I can check. If they balk, I'll dial up the pressure."

"Come to think of it, I'm not sure heading down there right away would do us any good," said Hannibal. "We wouldn't know where to start looking for anything. Hell, we wouldn't know *what* to look for. If only I knew what got him excited."

"Well, that's about it. I just wanted to bring you up to speed. When you're ready to go back down there, let me know and I'll arrange it. It's getting ugly down there, though. I know that much, partner."

"We're still not partners, Kirby."

"Stop it, Hannibal!" said Traci. "Geez! You're like a spoiled child."

"That's okay, Traci," said Kirby. "I know he's joking."

"No, Kirby. I'm not."

Kirby smirked.

"He's stubborn about it, Trace, but I know him too well to take offense."

"That's too bad. Because I'm doing my best to offend you."

Kirby chuckled.

"Promise you'll never change, Hannibal. Anyway, welcome back. I'm calmer now, knowing you didn't tell him anything. Anderson, that is. Get some rest, you two. I'll let you know if anything changes."

He left and Hannibal collapsed back into his chair.

"Something's going on, Traci. And it's not good. I think he's got a hidden agenda."

"Like I said before, he's a Company man. There's always a hidden agenda with the Company. But you know that already. Hell, I had many hidden agendas when I worked for them."

"You still do."

"I meant when I worked directly for them."

"Yeah. Like I said, you still do."

"Hannibal, I don't want to spar with you right now. I'm really exhausted. I can't think anymore. ... By the way, I'm staying here. Is that okay with you?"

"It's always okay with me."

"Thanks."

~ ~ ~ ~ ~

The clock face read 2:27 a.m. Hannibal's eyes popped open out of a dead sleep, and an audible grunt burped from his chest. He stirred, but found he couldn't move. Traci's head was on his chest and her right leg and arm were draped over him. His stirring caused her to shift slightly.

"I want to talk," he whispered.

"I know. You've been tossing like crazy. I figured lying on you might keep you still."

~ ~ ~ ~ ~

Neither of them moved. Traci maintained her position spread out over Hannibal.

"For the first time in my life, Trace, I'm really scared."

"I understand. So am I. Do you realize the position you're in at the moment, though?"

"What are you talking about?"

"Hannibal, you have at your fingertips the answer to the world's complete energy needs forever."

"I don't have anything yet, Traci. I'm having trouble translating the rest of the tablets and scrolls."

"You'll do it. And then your troubles will really begin."

"If I live that long."

"Darling, if the government finds out you have those photos, you most surely will disappear."

"You think I haven't thought about that already? I'll have to remove them from my office computer before they find out I've got them stored there."

"Do it quickly, while you still have it in your power to do so."

"I'll take care of it later today."

"Speaking of power, Hannibal, do you realize you possess the power to transform the entire world in that handful of photos?"

"Or, potentially, to destroy it completely. But I haven't got squat yet. And right now I'm afraid what Grindstone and this messed-up government will do with it once it *is* rediscovered."

"Grindstone's not the problem, hon. But there *is* a problem."

"What's that?"

"The Chinese already suspect something. And if the Chinese are onto this, you can bet the Russians are too. And don't count the Israelis out, or the Iranians. In fact, if I were you, I'd sooner or later expect agents from nearly every country on earth to come looking for me."

"But we're not even close. I have no idea where to start looking for the tuaoi."

"Sure you do. Finish the translation and you'll know where it is."

"Can Grindstone help?"

"Grindstone can do much to get the technology out to the world after you find it, but you alone hold the power to find it."

"What if I can't?"

"You will. I'll help you if I can. We were a great team before, weren't we?"

"We still are. I guess I need to finish the translations. But in order to do that I'd have to find some kind of Rosetta stone. I have only bits and pieces, not the whole set. It's a very sophisticated language. I have no idea where to start looking for any answers except by comparing the three languages that have grown out of the Naacal's."

"Well, you did say the languages were similar, right?"

"It's not that easy, Traci."

"Sure it is."

"I need to be alone and undisturbed. I can't have Kirby looking over my shoulder and asking me questions every two seconds. After I've finished, I'll tell him everything. Until then —"

"I can keep him away. I can try to drag him back down to Mexico, if that'll help."

"Just keep him away from me for a while. Can you do that for me?"

Traci raised her hand and caressed Hannibal's face.

"You're my greatest weakness, Hannibal. I'd do just about anything for you."

CHAPTER 15

Traci returned to her office and daily life, realizing there was nothing she could do to help Hannibal any further except to do as she said and keep Kirby away from him for the time being.

With privacy achieved, Hannibal instantly fell into self-sequestration, secluded in his apartment, absent from the world. He spent nearly every waking hour meticulously combing over the photos of the stone tablets and scrolls, determined to make a breakthrough in their translation.

Even studying the strangely shaped stone tablet he had removed from the Australian vault didn't surrender any useful clues to understanding the complex language.

Frustration was his haunting companion. It seemed that just at the moment he thought a real breakthrough had arrived, it would slip away, leaving him only exhausted and more aggravated.

He found himself most often lying on the floor of his still messy living room, staring up at the ceiling and seconds away from screaming his head off in bitter disappointment.

It was the small, undecipherable pieces of the dead language that prevented a breakthrough, small but critical. Based largely upon symbols looking more like bastardized hieroglyphics than anything else, the language was impossible to connect together into a cohesive story.

Lacking his own Rosetta stone, he found himself most times only guessing at the words' meaning. Like Douglas Rawlinson's translation of the Sumerian Behistun Inscription, completed in 1849, he needed just one tablet or scroll that contained an identical copy of a story in more than one language he could read to put it all together.

Of course he was never going to find such a tablet or scroll, he mused, lying on his back staring up at the ceiling. That would be too easy. For him, life was all about the struggle — the challenge, not the reward. He didn't really believe that, of course, but that was what it seemed like most of the time.

While so many of his college mates had gone on to make incredible finds and become quite famous and wealthy in the process, Hannibal had always seemed to be on the cusp of something great and wondrous, only to find in the end that such accomplishment was just out of reach.

Like Atlantis, for example. From all his profound research, logical thinking, and sound reasoning, he had come to the conclusion that he might have discovered the mythical land's location. His evidence was strong. He was certain he was correct, but just when he was about to announce his findings to the world, a competitor stepped in with his own "supporting" data, trumping him with a horribly conceived theory and corrupt reasoning. He tried to shout out his discovery, but no one would hear him. His voice was only a whisper.

Of course they didn't hear him; he lacked all the showmanship his competitors possessed. As Richard Grendel had pointed out so unceremoniously, archaeology is part research and part entertainment, with entertainment being the key component to obtaining the financing necessary to make a grand discovery. To Hannibal, it was only the research that counted, and that stalwart but misguided thinking was holding him back from making those astonishing discoveries. To the investors, it was mostly the show.

A light flashed and he found himself standing in the middle of the main ring of a circus. He looked down and saw that his clothing had changed to the baggy, red-polka-dotted pants of a clown, complete with over-sized blue shoes. Instinctively, he reached up to his face and found the large sponge nose.

Next to him was Grendel, dressed in a tuxedo, wowing the crowd with a wonderful story. The crowd cheered loudly at his wild, animated gestures illustrating exciting scenes of his story.

Grendel turned toward Hannibal. In his hands he cradled a huge seltzer bottle.

"And for this clown?"

"In the face!" chanted the frenzied and delighted crowd.

With that, Grendel aimed the nozzle of the bottle directly into Hannibal's face and squeezed the trigger, soaking him with the seltzer.

Hannibal jumped up from the floor he had fallen asleep on. He was dry. He was dressed normally. All was well.

"Damn!" he muttered.

He sat down at the table, knowing that he was right about Atlantis. He was right about there being a global civilization in the past, too. Hell, he even reasoned that the people of Atlantis and the Naacal could be the same race of people. He was nearly certain of it. And yet here he was again, on the cusp of a great discovery and falling short once more, the answer to the greatest puzzle in archaeology just out of reach.

Without completely translating the language and finding the location of the firestone, if it still existed, he would remain mired in the obscurity of irrelevancy, just as Grendel had said, all the time knowing that no matter his skill or his discoveries, the game was played differently at the varsity level of archaeology. To gain the respect he deserved, he would have to become the model of what the sponsors and the Smithsonian thought was the quintessential archaeologist.

"Or crack this damn code!" he bellowed loudly.

He thought about his colleague, Dr. Hector Gonzalez. What had he found that was reason enough to get him murdered? Perhaps he had found what Hannibal had been searching for. Perhaps he had stumbled upon the Naacal's Rosetta stone.

"That's it, Hannibal. Just swim around in the sea of conjecture. That should really help solve the problem."

But if not the Rosetta stone, then what was it Dr. Gonzalez had discovered? Obviously, it was something important enough to get him forever silenced.

The more he studied the tablets and scrolls, the more it looked as if someone long, long ago had taken the original language and *purposely* sliced it up into three different sections and then developed them independently into the languages they had become. But if that were true, then another, more important question arose. Why? What would be the purpose in destroying a very wonderful and sophisticated language?

As he pondered that question, only one reason, dragged out into the light from the back of his dark brain, made any sense at all. Someone wanted the language hidden to make it nearly impossible for anyone to decipher the original language. It was beginning to make sense, but not sense enough to solve the riddle plaguing him.

Someone much smarter than he had done this for a good reason. If this was true, then the next obvious question was how could he translate the original? For this answer, Hannibal would have to extract the roots of all three languages. Luckily, for all three there was sufficient data.

As he again recalled, for the Sumerian language there was the initial work done by Douglas Rawlinson starting back in 1835 and the later work of the Irish Assyriologist Edward Hincks.

For the Mayan language he had in his possession the works from the first bishop of Yucatan, Diego de Landa, and the later 1950s work of the Russian ethnologist Yuri Valentinovich, who correctly theorized that the Mayan language was at least partially phonetic.

For Navajo, it was easy enough. He had committed to memory every note ever taken while studying with their great holy man, Black Owl. And Black Owl, through his enlightening demeanor, had provided the impetus necessary for him to learn that intricate language fluently.

With enormous effort, he could lay out all three base languages and match them to the scrolls and tablets. He possessed the skill to do that. But he lacked the key necessary to form the context of the language.

In time, he hoped to discover something that might tie these three distinct languages together. When that happened, he would know for certain where the firestone was and how to use it — or, more importantly, how *not* to use it.

He began to feel the weight of the fate of the world settle down upon his shoulders. Still, the achievement of rediscovering the firestone might finally bring him the recognition and funding he deserved to do so much more for the betterment of humanity.

In that moment he recalled the answer to his reckless response to a question asked by Black Owl.

"Why should I teach you the language of our people?" the Navajo holy man had asked.

"Because my work makes me deserving of understanding this language."

Hannibal, having met Black Owl through a college friend, Douglas Long Lance, bedeviled the already ancient holy man. He was impetuous and pesky about learning the complete language of the Navajo. Generally speaking, Black Owl didn't care for the white man, but he saw something unique in this young, brash, bold graduate student. There was a fire burning brightly in this youth's soul. He couldn't explain it, but he liked Hannibal instantly, from the first moment of Douglas's introduction.

"Hannibal," the holy man finally said in response to Hannibal's flippant answer, "Geronimo was not Navajo, but my grandfather heard him speak one day during a gathering of many tribes. The great man was asked what he thought he deserved from life. 'Sometimes getting what we deserve is what we deserve,' the great man said. And he was right, Hannibal. Sometimes that is exactly true."

Those scintillating words had seemed an ominous warning back then, and they seemed even more fitting now. Instead of recognition and success, he thought, finding the firestone might earn him a bullet to the head for no other purpose than to steal his work. Either way, in the final analysis, his efforts to protect his discovery might not be enough to protect humanity from its final destruction.

Hannibal stood up and wandered around as far as he could in the midst of the chaos that was his living room. He gave up that idea quickly and flopped back down into his kitchen chair and tried to lay his head down on the table, thinking that a short nap might bring him the perspective he needed. A large box prevented him from doing so, however.

He tried pushing the box away, but it was too heavy for a gentle nudge.

"What the hell is this anyway?"

He stared at the box for a few seconds and then recalled picking it up from his landlady, Mrs. Morrison, the night he and Traci arrived home from Australia two weeks ago.

In his exhaustion and his subsequent work trying to decipher the language of the Naacal over the past several weeks, he had completely forgotten about the box. He'd considered it just another box containing more of his artifacts, placed there by one of the workmen returning his belongings to the apartment — just one of a number of items now muddling up his kitchen table that he had to move around from time to time in order to use the table.

He turned it over to read the sender's address. That's when his jawed dropped open.

The sender was Dr. Hector Gonzalez.

He grabbed a knife and cut the string binding the box and then the sealed edges. Opening it carefully and removing all the foam protection, he found a laptop computer and a rubber-banded stack of what looked like field notes. But it was what was under the notes that really caught his attention. Lifting out the notes, he saw a small, foam-wrapped package about fourteen inches square lying on the bottom of the box. He quickly unwrapped it and discovered that it was an encoded stone tablet containing a single story in the Mayan, Sumerian, and original Naacal languages.

He also found a handwritten note from Dr. Gonzalez. He read it aloud.

Hannibal,

I Stumbled upon something of extraordinary importance. I found this tablet, but did not have time to Eksplore the area in more detail. I believe this tablet will be of great help to you doing what you do best.

The cave is located near the small distribution station you found. Seek the guidance of the pauahtun. It is the truest path. It is an Ekceptional path to follow. I buried him there for you, to help you find your way through the Blackness of doubt. He is almost glorious in the 20 meter rays of the rising sun.
I just hope you Understand my honest intent.
I'll be in touch later.
Your friend, Hector

Hannibal lifted the stone tablet and blinked. It was true. It was real. Staring up at him was exactly what he needed. The lines neatly spaced, the language plainly engraved into the stone, the different languages distinctly set apart from one another. There was no doubt about it: the gods had finally heard him calling out and had found him worthy, and sent to him his personal Rosetta stone.

"You gotta be kidding me," he whispered. "It's been sitting here for weeks. Right under your nose, Hannibal."

His cell phone rang. It was Traci.

"Hannibal, how are you doing? It's been a while. I'm getting worried about you."

"Traci, listen to me carefully. I can't talk now. I'm on the verge of something wonderful. I'll call you when I have something more to say about it. Until then pretend that I don't exist."

"Don't be so melodramatic, Hannibal."

"Seriously, I'll call you when I have something to say. Goodbye."

Hannibal pressed the End button on his cell phone, then turned it completely off.

~ ~ ~ ~ ~

Having barricaded himself in his apartment by piling furniture in front of his door and repeatedly refusing to answer any phone call or knock on the door except to shout "Go away! I'm busy,"

Hannibal prepared himself to solve the riddle of the Naacal language.

Mrs. Morrison had checked on him several times over the last month. She was always greeted with the same response. "Go away! I'm busy."

"Okay, dear," she would respond. "Just making sure you're alive. I don't need a dead man in there stinking up the place. Have a nice day, dear."

"Yeah, yeah," was Hannibal's only response.

CHAPTER 16

Traci finally gave up calling and showed up at the door. Beating on it, she called out, "Come on, Hannibal. It's just me. Let me in."

"Not now. I'll call you. Go away!" came Hannibal's terse reply from within.

"Hannibal, open this door immediately, or I *will* have it broken down. I can do it, Hannibal. You know that."

"Fine," came Hannibal's frustrated voice. "Break it down if you must. Just go away."

"Hannibal, I mean it."

"Okay, okay."

She heard the sound of furniture being moved around for several seconds and then the lock turned and the door cracked open. Traci pushed it open and stepped into a room that looked as if a tornado had struck it. But come to think of it, it had looked that way for a while now. Perhaps, she thought, this was the new normal.

"It's only been two months, Hannibal since you sequestered yourself. I see you've finally straightened everything up. Looks great."

Hannibal slammed the door shut and relocked it without responding.

He returned to his kitchen table, hunched over, and went back to work.

She studied him. His hair had not seen a hint of a brush or shampoo. It was matted and in total disarray. His face was bearded with black and gray. His clothing was wrinkled and soiled. She was thinking that it hadn't been changed in several weeks. Perhaps they were the same clothes he'd worn when they returned from Australia, she couldn't remember, but that was eight weeks ago. Overall, he appeared gaunt and thin. And he reeked.

"Do I get a hello from you? Do I get a kiss or a hug?"

Then she sniffed the air.

"On second thought, I'll pass."

"You can sit down and keep very quiet, please."

"God, you are the romantic animal, aren't you?"

She took another sniff.

"Maybe you're just an animal. You certainly smell like one."

"Quiet! I'm on the verge of busting this whole thing open."

Then Traci noticed the laptop and the stack of papers on the table.

"Hannibal? Is that Hector's laptop and field notes I'm looking at?"

"Yeah. He sent them to me before he died."

"Does Kirby know about this?"

"No! And don't tell him! Not yet, at least. Not until I've finished translating everything. Then I'll bring him up to date."

"When did you receive the computer? This is wonderful news."

"I got it the night we got home from Australia."

"You're telling me it's been here all this time?"

"Yes, now please be quiet. I'm on a threshold."

"Honey, you really need to take a shower." She waved a hand across her nose. "This place reeks, Hannibal."

"Stop talking!"

"Hannibal! Listen to me. Stop what you're doing and listen to me. You need to stop for a while and clean up."

"No time. If you don't like it, you can leave. I'm close to solving this. Now shut the hell up or get the hell out."

"How close?"

"On the verge. Very close. Very, very close."

"Sounds exciting."

"Yeah, yeah."

"Have you got a beer?"

He pointed to the refrigerator with his thumb.

Traci opened the refrigerator, pulled out a beer, and twisted the top off. She then noticed the sink filled with dirty dishes. She picked up a plate. It was caked with a discolored remnant of something she could only guess was once food.

"Yep, this is the Hannibal I know and love."

"Why don't you make yourself useful and wash them."

Traci smirked. "That's funny, honey. Really."

Hannibal turned his attention to her. His expression became serious. "Look, Trace, I need to concentrate. It's not just understanding the words that a translator is confronted with. It's understanding the meaning of those words in the context of how they were used at the time they were written down. That's the truly difficult task.

"In very simplistic terms, it's like the phrase 'This is so cool.' In today's vernacular it could be interpreted as this object is very interesting or it holds great interest within it. In a literal sense it would mean that this object's temperature is very low, or it is cool to the touch.

"When someone, let's say in 1880, spoke that phrase, its meaning would have been in the literal context: this object is cool to the touch, or the object is of a low temperature. It is all in the context of the times and the people's expectation of what those words meant to them. Do you understand?"

"Yes, Hannibal, I do."

"Okay. Now let's change the context yet again. 'She is so cool.' Once again, the object of the context helps to determine its meaning. First, it could mean that she is interesting. Or, once again, it could be that her body is low in temperature. But it might also be interpreted as a description of her personality. She is not a warm person; she is rather cool in how she treats other people. Do you understand that?"

"Yes. I see the problem. And I see your problem. You need to step away from it for a moment and give yourself some perspective. Do you understand *me?*"

Hannibal's eyes fell away from her as he considered what she had said. He then glanced up at her.

"You might be right about that. I hate to admit it, but you might be exactly right. I'm too close to it."

"Exactly. At least you haven't lost your power of reasoning."

He sat back in his chair, still considering her words.

"So, how have you fared with the translations so far?"

"Well, I think I did well, considering what information I have. I tried to immerse myself in what I believed was their life. I tried to imagine what was going on at that time.

"Mind you, we have nothing yet that would make the context apparent. We have no structures, no other books or scrolls to tell us what those times were like, or how they dealt with whatever they had to face. We have no history of these people except what I have here and what the legends say about them, and of course what information I found in Australia. That information has been very helpful, because I found that some of the tablets and scrolls told stories about their history and their life, which has helped me understand the context of their times."

"How do you know you've translated the symbols correctly?"

"To be honest, I don't. I think I picked up the essence, but I'll never know for certain until the translation can be verified or tested."

"How do we do that?"

"We follow the directions given in the translation."

"That sounds pretty iffy. Wait! What directions? What are you talking about? Whose directions?"

"Hector's. He might be able to give me what I need."

"Hannibal, he's dead. In case you forgot."

"I know that, but before he died he sent me this box with this stone tablet here. He also sent me an encrypted note basically telling me where he found the tablet — my Rosetta stone. If I've interpreted his meaning correctly, he found something of even greater importance, something that just might confirm what I've translated."

"What note, Hannibal?"

"This note," he answered, handing her the message.

Traci read it carefully. "Hannibal?"

"Do you see it?"

"Not really. It's pretty cryptic."

"It's filled with clues about where we need to look."

"If you say so, but that means we have to head back to Mexico right away."

"Precisely!"

"First, honey, you *really* need to take a shower."

~ ~ ~ ~ ~

As the chopper approached its landing area, Hannibal noticed the many Mexican laborers standing near the edge of the forest, resting on the handles of their shovels.

"Are you sure you're ready for this, Hannibal?" asked Kirby.

"We can't keep it hidden any longer. We have to find whatever it was that got Hector murdered. I've translated everything I can, but we'll have to test the translation. I gotta find more tablets or scrolls. To do that, we have to follow Hector's hints."

"Okay, if you say so. But we're really letting the kitty out of the sack now."

"We were never going to get away with keeping this a secret forever anyway, Kirby. You know that."

"It's your show, partner."

The chopper set down on the cleared hilltop. Traci, Kirby, and Hannibal stepped out and moved directly to the center of the hexagonal distribution station.

The aircraft lifted off and within minutes the drum of the engine faded, leaving the excavation team in the pristine silence of the Yucatan jungle.

A thin Mexican man wearing wire-rimmed glasses approached Hannibal.

"Doctor Storm. I'm Doctor Rafael Menendez, Doctor Gonzalez's replacement. Good to meet you," he said, extending his hand.

"Good to meet you, Doctor Menendez. I'm very sorry about Hector. He was a good man."

"Thank you. So, what do you think you've found?"

"Nothing yet, but that's why we're here."

"Okay. My people are ready to dig wherever you say."

"I appreciate the support."

"If it helps raise awareness of my country, it is my pleasure."

"Okay, let's begin." Hannibal pulled two copies of Dr. Gonzalez's letter from his shirt pocket. He handed one to Dr. Menendez.

"So this is the famous letter sent by Doctor Gonzalez."

"This is it."

Dr. Menendez read the letter silently for a few moments, then looked up at Hannibal.

"There must be some mistake, Doctor. The information in this letter is in error."

"No, it's in code."

"Please explain."

"Better than explaining, let me show you."

Hannibal removed a compass from his pants pocket and stood staring at it, turning his body to the left until the needle lined up with north. He then walked to the edge of the station and marked a spot with his foot, scratching it in the dirt.

"Here. Have one of your men dig here. But tell them to be very careful. Something fragile is buried shallow, I think."

Dr. Menendez yelled something to one of the men with shovels. The man trotted over and began digging carefully.

Hannibal then found the other three directions and marked them in similar fashion, and three other workers began digging.

After several minutes, the man to the north seemed to have struck something hard. He tapped it gently with the point of his shovel. Something hard was down there, all right.

"Carefully," urged Hannibal.

The worker squatted down and with his hands cleared the rest of the dirt away as Hannibal peered over his shoulder.

"Great!" yelled Hannibal. "That's it. Clear it all away."

Minutes later the other workers made the same discovery.

With the dirt removed, they saw what lay in those shallow graves.

"The *Pauahtuns*," said Dr. Menendez.

"Exactly!"

"What does this mean?" asked Kirby.

"It means that Hector did find something incredible."

"Doctor Storm," said Dr. Menendez, "we have another problem."

"I know what you're going to say."

"Please," said the doctor.

"They're in the wrong position."

"*Sí.*"

"Wait, Hannibal. Explain this to me. I'm not an archaeologist," said Traci. "Who or what are the Paw-ah-toons?"

"I've got another short story for you. According to legend, the Pauahtuns are brothers. They are the holders of the heavens who God placed in the four quarters of the earth to hold up the sky after he created the world."

"I don't understand. I need more detail," Traci said.

"I'll make it brief. Typically around Mayan villages, the Mayans planted ritual stone shafts called Acantuns. There were four of them, planted on the cardinal points of the compass. They represented the brothers, the Pauahtun. Jaguars were said to climb on top of the Acantuns during the night and guard the villages from harm. In many royal Mayan tombs there have been found actual stone Acantuns or, in some cases, painted drawings of the brothers. Some scholars think they were provided to give the royal persons, awakening from their sleep and preparing for travel into the afterlife, clear directions for their travel.

"Most importantly here, though, is that they were set in their proper cardinal points on a compass. Chac-pauahtun was typically red in color and was associated with the east. Sac-pauahtun was white and associated with the north. Ek-pauahtun was black and associated with the west. And finally, Kan-pauahtun was yellow and associated with the south."

"Wait!" said Kirby. "The west and the east are the wrong colors, then."

"Damn. I just can't slip nothin' past you, Kirby."

"Please Hannibal," said Traci. "So are they incorrect or not?"

"Yeah, but it's a code."

"I don't understand."

"Hector gave me directions to where he found the tablet. But just in case someone else found the letter, he disguised the clues. You have to understand Mayan tradition to follow the clues."

"Okay. I know I'm going to regret asking," said Kirby, "but what do you make of all this?"

"Glad you asked, Kirby. Proves there's some form of brain matter under that scalp after all."

"Go to hell, Hannibal. Just tell me."

"Hannibal, I'm pretty close to slapping you right now," said Traci.

"Fine. I'll get serious, but only for a moment. The letter said that he found something, but he didn't have time to *ek*-splore the area more. Please note the e-k. Hector had an excellent command of English. He didn't make mistakes. E-k tells me that Ek-pauahtun, the black Acantun associated with the west, is the obvious key. He says that the hidden entrance is located twenty meters in the direction of Ek-pauahtun, but he is on the wrong side. So the entrance is actually opposite Ek-pauahtun. The rays of the morning sun shine away from the east. He also says that he hopes I 'Understand' his honest intent. Note the capital U. He's telling us that the entrance is underground. We're going to have to dig again twenty meters to the west of the distribution station. So let's go kick around and see what we can find."

The area approximately twenty meters to the west was a jumble of stones and undergrowth. It appeared to Hannibal that it was the ancient dumping ground for the material excavated for the distribution station.

After twenty minutes of turning over stones with the tip of her shoe, Traci called out, "Hannibal, this is ridiculous. There's no indication of any kind of a cave entrance here."

"Keep looking, Traci. It has to be here. Look for something large and black. I think that might be a marker."

Seconds later Traci shrieked. "My god, Hannibal! I'm standing on a black stone. It's the only one around here. I think I found it!"

Everyone gathered around her and stared at the solitary black stone beneath her foot.

"Yep. Good find, Traci. I'm betting that's it. Doctor Menendez, can we get your men to start digging here?"

"Of course," came the response.

~ ~ ~ ~ ~

Two hours later, baking in the hot sun of the Yucatan, Hannibal sweated profusely. For the Mayan workers, this was just another ordinary day's labor for them. They remained calm and cool.

Within minutes of starting their dig, they had found the entrance. It was very narrow, but a fit person could squeeze through the opening. Hannibal figured that was where Dr. Gonzalez had gotten in and then recovered the entrance.

Typically, it would be preferable to leave as much of the site as undisturbed as possible. In this case, however, Hannibal believed that the cave could be damaged worse if the entrance was not expanded sufficiently to get both men and equipment inside.

Dr. Menendez agreed.

Thus he had the workers clear a wider area and then expand the entrance before he let anyone inside the cave, including himself.

It was worth the wait.

The makeshift winch made from three sturdy poles stood, with block and tackle, centered over the entrance to the cave. It was ready for the first person to descend into it.

"Doctor Menendez," said Hannibal, "it's your country. Would you do the honors and drop in first?"

"No, Doctor Storm. Without you, there would be no entry at all. We wouldn't even know about this site. Please. It is your honor."

"Thank you, Doctor Menendez. Okay. Hook me up."

Once he was harnessed and set, the workers began to lower Hannibal into the blackness of the cavern. He was into the darkness only a few feet when he ordered the men to halt.

"I'm letting my eyes adjust," he yelled up.

"What do you see, partner?" shouted Kirby.

"I see blackness, Kirby. That's why I want to stop."

And after a few more seconds, "And we're not partners!"

Kirby smirked.

"You two really have to work this out," said Traci.

"You're taking this too seriously, Trace. It's what we do, he and I. It's a guy thing."

"Then I should probably just slap the both of you."

Kirby chuckled.

"That sounds like fun," came Hannibal's retort from the hole, followed by a laugh.

"Hannibal!" replied Traci, finally smiling.

"Okay," yelled Hannibal. "Let me down slowly ... slowly."

The workers inched him down until he shouted again for them to stop.

"Can you see anything?" shouted Kirby. Suddenly recalling the famous question asked by Lord Carnarvon of Howard Carter as he peered into King Tut's tomb for the first time, he grimaced, anticipating Hannibal's expected sarcastic response.

He didn't have long to wait.

"Yes, shit!" Hannibal's shout echoed.

"What?"

"I see shit. Shit everywhere. Bat shit. Bat guano. The cave is full of guano. It's covering everything."

After everyone who understood English stopped laughing and had recovered, Kirby wiped his eyes. "Okay, Hannibal. That one's going into the books as a classic."

"I'm serious, Kirby. There's shit everywhere. It's gonna have to be cleaned out before we can log anything. It stinks like hell down here."

Another round of laughter echoed through the Yucatan jungle.

"Okay," yelled Traci. "Besides the guano, Hannibal, can you see anything else?"

"Yes. Wonderful things," cackled Hannibal.

Everyone snickered at Hannibal's mimicking of Howard Carter's response to Lord Carnarvon's question.

"Ah, come on. Be serious."

"It's amazing, Traci. It's a freakin' treasure trove, archaeologically speaking. But we still gotta get this place cleaned out. You'd be stepping in a foot of guano if you came down here now."

"How do you know that?"

"Because, my dear, I'm standing in a foot of bat shit at the moment."

"Is he always like this, Señora?" asked Dr. Menendez.

"I'm not married, Doctor Menendez, and yes, this is his normal mode."

"Doctor Menendez," Kirby whispered. "Seriously, he's as good as they come. He's simply brilliant. No joke. The man is one of the smartest people I have ever known. Of course, I'll deny it if you ever tell him I said that."

"I heard you, Kirby," yelled Hannibal from the bowels of the cave. "The acoustics are great down here."

"Eat shit, Hannibal."

"That wouldn't be hard to do down here."

Another round of chuckles filled the surrounding air.

~ ~ ~ ~ ~

A full four hours later, the last of the workers came out of the cave on the makeshift pulley system, covered from head to toe with residual bat guano. Dr. Menendez then made the descent, followed by the others.

"*Dios mío!*" exclaimed the good doctor as he turned in a circle. "It is a house of treasure, as you say, Hannibal."

"Sure is."

The cave was brightly lit with an assortment of klieg lights. The guano had been successfully shoveled to an empty side of the cave. The bats had cleared out when the first shovel broke through the cavern entrance nearly eight hours before.

"There's obviously another entrance to the cavern," said Hannibal. "And it's evidently somewhere off in that direction," he added, pointing his flashlight beam toward the far southern end.

"My god," said Traci. "Look at all the stone tablets. They're stacked up like cords of wood."

CHAPTER 17

Had Hannibal not seen the lone stone tablet standing in the corner first, separated from the rest, he might have wasted months translating the other useless tablets. But his luck was changing, and while the others busied themselves with sorting through the many other stone tablets with their mysterious symbols, Hannibal took the opportunity to secretly scribble down what that particular stone tablet had to offer, just in case he wouldn't be able to take it with him later.

He snapped a few pictures and turned to everyone else.

"Remember, folks ... look, but do not touch. Everything has to be catalogued before it's moved." He looked at Dr. Menendez. "Sorry, Doctor. I don't mean to stomp on your authority."

"No, no. You are correct, of course."

"Hey, Hannibal. What're you doing over there?" Kirby asked.

"The same as you. Looking at all these tablets. It's gonna take years to translate all of these."

Hannibal picked up one in particular, a tablet measuring approximately twenty inches square. He studied without comment.

"Can you do it, Hannibal? Can you read it?"

"Not right now, I'm afraid, but in time, perhaps. Wouldn't you agree, Doctor Menendez?"

"*Sí*, Professor. But even I cannot make any sense of the symbols, and I am Mayan. These are not Mayan symbols, but they *are* Mayan symbols. I do not understand."

"Welcome to my world, Doctor." Hannibal smiled and then returned his attention to the tablet he held in his hands.

"Do you see anything special?"

"It's all special, Kirby. We're changing history here."

"I'll have to take your word for it. None of this means anything to me. You're the master of this universe, partner."

"Still not partners, Kirby."

"Will be soon, though. I'm wearing you down."

Hannibal smirked.

"Can you make anything out at all, Hannibal?" asked Traci.

"Only bits and pieces so far, but it looks like some kind of inventory. Of what, I can't be sure. I do see what I believe are symbols for grain and even perhaps gold. But I'm only guessing. I also see what I believe are mathematical calculations. It's gonna take a long time to sort all of this out before we know what these tablets have to tell us. If it can be sorted out at all."

"Holy moley!" shouted Kirby. "What is *this*?"

Everyone perked up and turned toward the CIA agent.

"What is it?" asked Traci.

"You'd better see this for yourselves, guys."

Quickly, they all surrounded Kirby and stared down in awe at what lay underneath the tablet that Kirby held in his hands.

The gold was still bright and clean, protected from any contaminants by being completely covered by the other artifacts.

Traci tapped it with her index finger. "Pure gold."

She tried to lift it, but she couldn't even move it. "Solid gold, too. I can't budge it."

"No!" yelled Hannibal. "What did I say? Look, don't touch! We need to photograph *everything* before we disturb it any further. Everything needs to be catalogued precisely. Don't touch another thing. Kirby, set your tablet back down exactly where it was."

"You got it, partner. Yeah, yeah, I know."

"There's hope for you yet, Kirby."

"You think so?"

"No. Not really."

~ ~ ~ ~ ~

It was very early the next morning when the last chopper lifted off with a sling of crated, catalogued artifacts dangling beneath it. There remained only two artifacts — the stone tablet Hannibal held and the solid gold seal Kirby had found, now crated and lying next to Dr. Menendez.

"If you don't mind, Doctor Menendez, I'd like to take this one with me and get a shot at translating it. It looks to be just another simple inventory, but I'd like to test my code against it."

"Certainly, Doctor Storm. Without you, we would have none of this."

"Thanks. I'll keep it safe and let you know if I can glean something of interest from it. As for the gold seal, though, it's exactly what I've been searching for the past several years. I knew something like this existed."

"It looks to be a great seal that would have been inset on the entrance structure of some major ancient city. But it isn't Mayan."

"I agree, Doctor. Nothing like Mayan at all. It's very perplexing as to why it would be found here in an underground cave with insignificant inventory tablets, doesn't it?"

"It certainly creates another mystery for us to solve."

"Well, you're Chief Archaeologist now, Doctor Menendez. I'm sure you'll discover what you can about it. As for me, finding it can now be checked off my 'bucket list.'"

"You really do not care about fame and fortune, do you, Doctor Storm?" asked Dr. Menendez.

"For me, it's about the discovery; I'll leave the fame and fortune to you. But I'll say this. I'm now fascinated to find what city the seal came from. It surely must have been a major city to have a seal like that over the entrance gate. Why didn't you send it out with the other artifacts?"

"I am not letting this out of my sight. Corruption is everywhere in my country. Do you know how fast this would disappear from our archives if it left my possession?"

"Like a rocket, I presume."

"Exactly. No, this goes on the helicopter with me."

~ ~ ~ ~ ~

"Like your apartment needs one more artifact, Hannibal," said Traci as she stepped through the door.

Hannibal lugged the stone tablet into his apartment and set it down on the kitchen table. He shut the door and blew a deep breath into the air.

"Holy moley, Traci. You're not going to believe this."

"What?"

"This tablet is an inventory, all right, but it's not an inventory of grain or any other commodity."

"You devil, Hannibal. You sneaky little thief. What have you got there?"

Hannibal stared into her eyes and remained silent.

"What?!" Traci asked, her curiosity now completely piqued.

Hannibal remained silent.

"Hannibal! What's on that tablet?"

"Sit down."

"Come on, Hannibal. I'm a big girl. What's on the tablet?"

"It's the inventory of the firestone distribution crystals and their location in this part of the world."

Traci felt her knees go weak. As she buckled, Hannibal caught her and settled her down into the kitchen chair.

"Oh god, Hannibal. Are you serious?"

"I'm serious. I glimpsed all the other tablets as they were carried out of the cave. They're just normal commodity inventories mixed in with a few astronomical calculations relating to planting and harvesting seasons. I can read Naacal, Traci. I can actually read it and understand it. This lone tablet was standing in the corner of the cave all by itself. When I glanced at it, I almost shouted. It was all I could do to keep silent.

"I didn't even want to tell you for fear that you might react the way you did just now."

"Where are the stones, Hannibal?"

~ ~ ~ ~ ~

The specially modified forty-eight-foot DeFever yacht named *Intrepid*, enhanced for special vacations and corporate entertainment functions including its own scuba gear and air filling station pumps, was easy for one person to operate.

Based in Corpus Christi, Texas, the yacht was usually enjoyed close to American shores. Now, however, it floated in the Gulf of Mexico about one mile northeast of Isla Contoy, approximately twenty-four miles northeast of Cancun, Mexico, bobbing gently in the light surf.

Traci and Hannibal sat at a table on the main deck, Hannibal in his now usual position, head down and loupe pressed against his right eye, studying photographs of stone tablets and scrolls.

"I hope you're right about this. Do you know how much this boat and equipment cost per day?"

"Grindstone's paying," said Hannibal, still peering through his loupe. "And it's the perfect boat for us. We don't look out of place here. In fact, we fit right in with the others around us. No one should even notice us, unless they run out of fancy mustard."

Traci chuckled, then asked, "You're sure about this? You're sure there's a cave down there somewhere?"

Hannibal looked up and exhaled strongly. "I'm as sure as I can be, Traci. I've never been here before. But if I've translated the coordinates correctly, there should be an engraved plaque either attached to or engraved directly into the face of a cliff, near the top. I'm still not reading things with one hundred percent accuracy."

"The Naacal surely didn't make it easy."

"Probably for good reason. In their minds, at least."

"But look out there, Hannibal. There's no cliff. Just a nice easy shoreline."

"Sure. Now there is, but twenty-five thousand years ago the shoreline was a cliff."

"Okay, but why put it on top of a cliff?"

"It's not on the top. The tablet says the plaque is ten cubits from the top, on the face."

"Why do that?"

"I'm not clear on that, but my guess is that it would not have been an easy thing for someone to climb down seventeen feet on a sheer cliff face and find it. I suspect it was hidden in some fashion as well. But it was available for those who could manage to do so. They didn't make it impossible, just extremely difficult. You really had to want to get to it. Of course, I'm guessing at their reasoning behind their decision."

"Well, that at least it makes more sense than anything else I can guess at."

"The cliff is offshore now and underwater. We call it the continental shelf wall."

"I gave up diving for a good reason, Hannibal. I feel claustrophobic with that mask over my nose, surrounded by suffocating water."

"Stay topside then, honey. I'll drop down and over the edge of the wall myself. I've got their coordinates already plugged into the GPS. I'll be down and up in no time."

"You shouldn't dive alone."

"I'm only going down fifteen or twenty feet to the top of cliff and then down another seventeen feet or so. I'll be fine."

"Okay. I'll stay here and man the bridge. You be careful."

"Listen, Traci. I don't want you to get too high on hope about this. Twenty-five thousand years of erosion could have destroyed the plaque or broken it free. And even if it is there, erosion most likely destroyed the information on it regarding the cave and its depth. I could end up looking at a piece of smooth stone. You got that?"

"Yeah, I got it. Just come back to me in one piece. That's all I'm asking. I love you, you foolish man."

~ ~ ~ ~ ~

Hannibal long-strided off the fantail and dropped into the water. After making sure his regulator was working properly, he waved to Traci and then let the air out of his buoyancy compensator vest and slid under the waves.

~ ~ ~ ~ ~

Standing on the deck of another yacht some 300 yards southwest of the *Intrepid* stood a burly man sporting a shaved head and a three-day growth of beard, peering through a pair of binoculars and holding a hand radio.

"He's just dropped overboard, sir," he said into the radio.

"Good," came the reply. "I'm on my way. ETA five minutes."

"Very good, sir."

He dropped his binoculars to his chest and smiled.

~ ~ ~ ~ ~

Settling down along the coastal shelf wall, Hannibal dropped until his dive computer read thirty-seven feet. He stopped his descent and grabbed hold of a stony projection on the undersea wall to maintain his relative position according to the GPS. Glancing down, he noted that the bottom was much deeper below him, so deep, in fact, that he caught only a glimpse of the wall descending into the blackness below. He guessed that the bottom was most likely several hundred feet lower, maybe more.

His eyes searched the wall for any sign of an engraved plaque. He saw nothing of the kind. He slowly moved left several yards and, still seeing nothing, he again consulted his GPS. He was in the correct area, but there was no plaque. He slid over to the right and explored the wall, both up and down. No plaque.

Rechecking the coordinates on the GPS, he was certain that if the plaque existed at all, he should be close to it. He moved back to the left and after reaching a point several yards to the left of the GPS coordinate indicated as the location, he dropped ten feet lower and began to move to the right of center an equal distance.

He continued this maneuver for almost an hour, finally descending down to sixty feet. He found neither a plaque nor any sign that a plaque had ever existed.

Frustrated and running low on air, and having spent much of his bottom time at below fifty feet, he reluctantly surfaced to a depth of seventeen feet from the surface and began his safety stop before surfacing completely.

The safety stop was necessary after every dive for the sake of the diver's health. Failing to make the stop could very likely bring on the bends, a diver's term for decompression sickness — a life-threatening condition resulting from dissolved gases coming out of solution into bubbles inside the body on depressurization.

The bends is a very painful condition and often fatal if not dealt with quickly by placing the victim in a hyperbaric chamber. With the aid of the chamber the pressure within the body is brought slowly back to normal, allowing the bubbles of nitrogen in the blood to be absorbed by the lungs and exhaled safely. To his knowledge, there were no hyperbaric chambers within miles of his location, so Hannibal obeyed diving protocols to the letter. If he incurred the bends out here, it would most likely result in his very painful death.

Normally, the requirement for a safety stop was three to five minutes. However, considering the lack of a nearby hyperbaric chamber, to be on the safe side he waited ten minutes, then surfaced near the *Intrepid*'s ladder. Traci was not there to greet him and he heard male voices coming from the deck.

A feeling of doom overwhelmed him and he silently slid back under the water and swam toward the bow, rising slowly to the surface and listening carefully for more voices. He heard them clearly.

He moved to the other side of the bow and immediately saw a very large yacht anchored a short distance from his, complete with a helicopter on the landing pad. He then noticed the dinghy alongside his own yacht.

It all became clear to him. His yacht had been boarded by strangers and they were most likely holding Traci hostage, not seeking fancy mustard. But who could it be, he wondered. Then he remembered the assault by the Chinese agents in Australia.

Maybe more agents had been sent and this time they got the upper hand.

He instinctively ducked back under the water and swam under the boat and toward the island, but at nearly a mile away it seemed pointless to try. Realizing both that he didn't have the strength to make it a mile to shore and that Traci was probably scared out of her mind and hoping he would come to her rescue, he surfaced about a hundred yards from the *Intrepid.*

A tall man standing next to the railing was staring out at him.

"The island is quite a swim away, Professor," he called. "The yacht's much closer, don't you think?"

Hannibal recognized the voice and the man. He exhaled a relieved breath through his regulator and then removed it from his mouth.

"You scared the hell outa me, Bernard."

CHAPTER 18

William Bernard, his former benefactor, stood on the deck of the *Intrepid*. Dressed in a white linen suit, black silk T-shirt, and white Panama hat with a black band, he presented an imposing figure.

"Forgive me, Professor. I didn't mean to cause such terror. I just came for a visit and to make you an offer."

"I don't want to visit with you. Where's Traci?"

"She's on board, awaiting your return."

"I want to see her."

"I asked her to remain below deck so that you and I could have a private conversation. In a manner of speaking, that is."

"If you harm her, I'll —"

"Now, Professor. There's no need for threats. I have simply come to present you with what I think is an extraordinary offer."

"I don't have anything to say to you, Bernard."

"Fine. Then just listen. It's best if you let me talk anyway."

"I didn't know assholes could speak."

"Be civil, Professor. Try to be something other than Hannibal Storm for just a few moments. That's all I ask. Can you do that?"

"Well, I don't know, Bernard. Can you stop being an asshole for a few moments?"

Bernard chuckled. "I thought perhaps it was too much to ask of you. No matter. You sit. I'll talk. Agreed?"

Hannibal remained still.

"Professor, please. Be the man I know you to be and get over here. Miss Jefferson will be comforted knowing you're once again onboard."

Hannibal paddled warily toward the *Intrepid* and then noticed his nemesis, Dr. Richard Grendel, moving over next to Bernard. Grendel's contemptuous grin was justification enough, he thought, for returning to his yacht, if for no other reason than to punch that grin off his face.

"What the hell is *he* doing here?"

"I'm acting as a consultant, Hannibal."

"You, Grendel? A consultant? You really must be in trouble, Bernard."

"You have no idea, Professor. Come now, it must be grueling for you out there in the scorching sun. Come aboard, relax, have a nice drink, and let's chat. Well?"

"Coming."

"Excellent!"

Hannibal had thought the matter through calmly for a change and had come to the realization that he was trapped and that Bernard would surely sit and wait him out if he didn't return to the boat.

When he arrived at the fantail a few minutes later, a hand dropped down in front of his face.

He handed his equipment to the reaching hand. The equipment jetted out of the water and soon after, the hand returned.

A large crewman wearing a starched white nautical uniform grabbed Hannibal's extended hand, pulled him up onto the fantail, and handed him a towel, grinning at him.

"Someday I'll smack that smile right off your face, friend."

"Professor, please. Stop molesting my crew. Come, sit down, relax."

Hannibal climbed aboard, sat down in a chair opposite Bernard, and wiped the towel across his face. "Traci had better be okay."

"She's just fine, I assure you."

"I'd like to see her if you don't mind."

Hannibal stood up and started for the stairs. He was instantly blocked by the giant crewman who had hauled him out of the water.

"Someday, big boy, I'm gonna put you on the ground and you ain't gonna get up again."

The crewman smirked at the thought of Hannibal taking him down. Hannibal gave it a quick thought as well. His challenge didn't make much sense to him either. "I don't know how I'm gonna do that at present, but when I discover how, you'll be the first to know."

Bernard laughed. "Professor, you are entertainingly impulsive. And if I had more time, I'd indulge you. But I don't. So please calm down and quit this irksome Hannibal routine. Just for a while. Is that really too much to ask of you?"

Hannibal turned and walked back to the chair. Dropping down into it, he glared at Bernard.

"So, Grendel," he said, agitated and wanting to start another argument, "how's your expedition coming along? You ever find your dick?"

"You're so witty and colorful, Hannibal. You're insignificant as an archaeologist, but you are witty and colorful. How's your search for your ancient global civilization going? Find it yet?"

"As a matter of fact, I believe I have."

Grendel began to smirk but stopped, considering that Hannibal might be serious. But his penchant for voicing sarcasm won out over his better judgment. "Where's your evidence, Hannibal? I don't see it anywhere around here. Hey, maybe it's at the bottom of the ocean. Is that where it is? Well, it might as well be there because, face it, Storm, Diffusionism has no basis in reality. It's never been proven. Nor will it ever be proven. And would you like to know why? Because it cannot be proven. There hasn't been discovered one single shred of evidence to show that there was ever a widespread dispersion of culture and civilization by ship or trade routes. Not one, ever! And Diffusionists like you are discredited every time you open your mouths to discuss it. All you offer are wild claims and supposition. Your kind has never presented anything tangible or supportable."

"And it's Isolationists like you that choose to walk around blind and deaf, unwilling to even consider the possibility that you might be wrong. If you ever took the time to examine the evidence that surrounds you worldwide, Grendel, you'd know. You only need to open your eyes to see and your mind to reason. But that's obviously asking too much of you, I guess.

You and those Smithsonian opaque-minded illiterates calling themselves doctors of archaeology. I can't wait for the day when you finally realize that oceans are highways, not blockades."

"Gentlemen, please," interrupted Bernard, waving his arms high in mock surrender. "A spirited debate no doubt exists between you two. But I have no more time for it. And quite frankly, your sniping and griping are becoming quite tiresome. Now, Professor Storm, for my proposal."

"What are you offering? If it's to toss Grendel overboard, I'll agree immediately and we can get it done."

Bernard snickered.

"I'll consider that an option. No. I have a sure thing for you."

"I've got a sure thing for *you.*"

"Professor, I thought we agreed that I would be doing the talking and you'd be doing the listening. Don't go Hannibal on me now. He's such a boorish brute at times like this."

"It's hard for you, isn't it, Hannibal, to turn off that obtuse and barbaric Hannibal within," said Grendel, grinning.

"Professor Grendel, I'm thirsty," said Bernard. "Would you pour me a scotch over ice, please? Professor Storm? Would you care for a drink?"

"I'm good."

"Mister Bernard," said Grendel, "I'm not a bartender, sir."

Bernard cut Grendel a look that anyone would have found overwhelmingly intimidating. Grendel realized his mistake instantly. "A scotch on the rocks. Yes, sir. Immediately."

Hannibal smirked.

"Now, Professor Storm, where were we? Ah, yes. A proposal. My proposal is a simple one. Lots of money to you in return for your giving me what I want. Sounds pretty good off the top, I should think."

Hannibal sneered at Bernard in response, then dropped his eyes to the deck.

"Lots of money for virtually doing nothing, Professor."

"Who do you think I am? Your lackey Grendel?"

Bernard chuckled. "Ouch, Professor."

Grendel cut Hannibal a hateful look.

"How about this? A million dollars for doing virtually nothing."

Hannibal looked back up into Bernard's eyes.

"That's right. You heard me correctly. A cool million, Professor. For doing practically nothing. Does that sound good? Just nod your head if you agree."

Hannibal sneered.

"Well, I'll take that as a Hannibal 'yes.' You see, I know what you're searching for. I don't claim to know what you're doing out here in the Gulf, of course, but knowing you as I do, I think you're searching for evidence of something I'm extremely interested in. Dare I say it aloud, Professor?"

Another silent stare from Hannibal is all he received in response.

"I'll take that as a 'yes' also. The firestone, Professor Storm, the tuaoi. I'm very interested in possessing the firestone. I think you know where it is. Tell me where it is and I'll deposit one million dollars into an account for you anywhere you say. It's that simple. No fuss, no muss, no need for blood and body parts all over the deck. A million dollars. What do you say?"

"What the hell are you talking about, Bernard? I don't know anything about a firestone."

"Come now, Professor. Don't be coy with me."

"I have no idea what a tuaoi is either."

"Do not treat me like a fool, man. I'm not one you want to anger."

"You're right. I take you more for the idiot type, because the firestone is a myth, Bernard — a made-up story. No such stone ever existed or ever will. Oh, I agree there is such a thing as zero-point energy. And I admit that I'm not a physicist, but I'm quite certain you're not going to find that kind of energy source in a quartz crystal. It's impossible."

"I know you're looking for it. And I believe that it, or information concerning it, must lie somewhere in this area, most likely below the surface, am I correct?"

"There's no such thing as a firestone, Bernard. I'm diving here because I heard there are possibly some Mayan artifacts. But I just spent a wasted hour looking for them. It was another bust. One of my many, as I'm sure you've come to know well."

"No, Professor. You're searching for the location of the firestone."

"What makes you think that?"

"I've heard about your little expedition into the jungle with your CIA buddy. I have eyes and ears all over. I pay very well to be kept informed. As a result, I have influence in many sectors."

"I see," said Hannibal. "Does that influence extend directly into the CIA as well?"

"In truth, I can't say that, but there are many others who bow to the dollar."

"I'm sure of that, Bernard. But I'm not one of them. I'll say it again. There. Is. No. Firestone."

"There's an awful lot of money being spent to study a marble building in the middle of the Yucatan jungle, Professor. One of my associates heard you call it a power station."

Bernard stared at Hannibal in silence, gauging the archaeologist's reaction to the revelation. Not getting the response he had expected, he pressed once more. "A million dollars, Professor. And from what I've heard about your little eviction incident, you could use the money."

"You have me confused with your lapdog there," said Hannibal, nodding toward Grendel. "I'm not for sale, Bernard. But even if I were, do you really think I'd trust a promise from you?"

"I thought as much. How about cash, then?" Bernard raised his hand. Another guard standing behind him with a large, thick briefcase immediately stepped forward and laid it down on the table, opened it, and turned it toward Hannibal.

Hannibal's eyes opened wide.

"That's right, Professor. Cash on the barrelhead, so to speak. One million dollars. Just tell me the location of the tuaoi and it's yours. Then I leave your boat and you never have to look at me again. What do you think?"

"Stick your money up your ... that's a million dollars? ... No! How many times do I have to say it? There's no such thing as a firestone. It's only a legend."

Bernard leaned forward and closed the lid of the briefcase. "But there is, Professor. And I believe you're searching for it."

"I'm looking for Mayan artifacts. That's it."

"I do believe you, Professor. Does that surprise you?"

"Nothing you do surprises me, Bernard."

Bernard chuckled. "I really do. I just happen to believe that those *Mayan* artifacts will lead you to the tuaoi."

"There's no firestone."

"Well, then, how are you doing finding your Mayan artifacts?"

"You don't listen very well," replied Hannibal. "I told you, it was a bust. I found nothing."

"Who's funding this little expedition, Professor? No one from the usual players I'm aware of, I know that for certain. I know something else. You personally haven't any money. I know Grindstone Energy is stuffed with cash. Sort of narrows it down, doesn't it?"

"That's none of your business, Bernard."

"How about I fund your adventure, Professor, your own Mayan artifact expedition? Beginning right now. Whatever you need. How's that?"

"I don't need your money. I do need you to get off my boat, though. Now!"

"Okay, Professor. Have it your way. I'll leave your boat, but I'm not leaving this area and I'll be keeping a watchful eye on you every second."

"Do what you want, Bernard. You don't intimidate me."

"I'm not trying to intimidate you. I'm just giving you time to come to your senses. I want to be close by when you change your mind."

"Why don't you have your trained dog Grendel find the firestone for you, if you believe it exists? I'm sure he'd be only too delighted to do it, wouldn't you, Rover?"

"There's that charming wit again, Hannibal. Perhaps your wit will save you from being sacked, too," said Grendel. He smiled and arched his eyebrows.

"I'm serious, Bernard. He obviously meets your expectations of what an archaeologist should be"

"Grendel's an idiot, Professor Storm," said Bernard. "We both know that. He couldn't find his head with both hands a second time. Why would you even suggest that?"

Grendel's patronizing smile disappeared. Hannibal noticed its departure and chuckled.

"Then why do you fund him and not me?"

"He makes me money. It's that simple. Is that what you wanted to hear?"

Grendel did not smile. He stood shamed, but he suddenly felt the need to defend himself. "Mister Bernard, sir. May I remind you —"

"Shut up, Grendel," said Bernard without looking at him. "You're in no position to remind me of anything. Now be quiet. Important people are talking."

Hannibal chuckled again.

"Is that better, Professor?"

"Not really, but it doesn't matter. There's no such thing as a firestone."

"Professor Storm, you're an odd egg, you're unmanageable, you're a real pain in neck, but you do know your stuff. And if you stop and think realistically, you're going to be famous for your discoveries someday. Grendel's not worthy to be your apprentice, but you still have a lot to learn about the business of archaeology."

"Quit trying to blow smoke up my ass. It's not working."

"You know it's true. You're the best. So here's another offer for you. Two million. One million now. This cash. And another million upon receipt of the firestone's location. How about that?"

"What bullshit are you trying to lay on me now, Bernard?"

"You're not well liked in the archaeology community, Professor. You have no friends at the Smithsonian either, but you know that already, don't you? That, Professor, makes it very difficult for me to find investors to fund expeditions for you. And without investors, I don't make money. See how simple that is. You're not going to last long in this field without support. But find the tuaoi for me and you can fund your own expeditions for quite a while. Doesn't that make sense?"

"It makes no sense at all, Bernard. If there was such a thing as a firestone and I did find it, we both know it would be worth a whole lot more than two million dollars."

"Four million, then, Professor. And I'll consider that only seed money. I'll make you disgustingly wealthy. Regardless of what you believe, Professor, I do believe in you. And you've just become an investment to me. I take great care of my investments."

Hannibal stared silently into Bernard's eyes.

"Come, Hannibal. A business arrangement. Can we do it? Can we make a deal today?"

Hannibal thought for several seconds. "Half now, half upon completion. That's the deal. If you're truly serious, then that's what it will take."

"Done." Bernard grinned as he pushed the briefcase toward Hannibal and opened it again.

"That's a million dollars?" Hannibal asked.

Bernard chuckled, then reached into the inside pocket of his jacket and withdrew a checkbook. He sat down at the table and wrote out a check for a million dollars, signed it, ripped it from the checkbook, and handed it to Hannibal.

"Here's a check for the balance of the down payment. Consider the briefcase a gift."

Hannibal picked up the check and stared at it disbelievingly. Then he turned his eyes back to the briefcase. "This is really a million dollars?"

"You give me the location of the tuaoi and you can fill up many more of them before we're finished, Professor."

"Holy ..." Hannibal's voice trailed off.

Bernard stood up and started towards his skiff, but stopped and spun around on his heels. "Oh, Professor? You're not thinking of betraying me, are you?"

Hannibal sat in silence staring at the cash, then at the check, then back at the cash. "This is a million dollars?" he murmured.

Bernard's eyes turned toward his giant guard. "Thomas. If you please."

The big man disappeared down the steps of the main deck and soon returned with Traci, gripping her arm. She was gagged.

Their eyes met and Hannibal jumped to his feet.

"What are you doing, Bernard?"

Hannibal started for Thomas, but the giant guard stepped in front of him.

"What are you *doing*, Bernard?!"

"Just securing some insurance, Hannibal. I'd like Miss Jefferson to be my guest while you're searching for the tuaoi. I'll take good care of her. You can trust me."

Hannibal tried to go around the guard, but it was of little use. The guard took hold of him as if he were a rag doll and tossed him backwards to the deck.

"Easy, George. Don't damage him. We need him healthy and fit."

"This is bullshit, Bernard! Our deal is off. Take your money back, you piece of shit."

"Can't do that, Professor. A deal is a deal once it's accepted."

Traci's eyes showed fear, as did Hannibal's.

Hannibal shot to his feet and charged at George, but soon found himself hanging in midair and George's hand holding him up by his chin. A second later, he found himself returned to the deck of the *Intrepid* on his behind. He didn't bother to challenge the guard again as Bernard negotiated his way into the skiff and sat down.

"You're a chickenshit, Bernard!"

Bernard just smiled calmly at Hannibal. "And you're a four-million-dollar investment to me, Professor."

Hannibal started for them again, but stopped short when George withdrew his .45 and pointed it at his chest.

Traci shook her head no, trying to stop Hannibal from doing what his heart and mind urged him to do.

"You're a real piece of work, Bernard. You know that?"

"Miss Jefferson will be well looked after, Professor. Not a hair on her head will be harmed. I give you my word. Just give me the location of the tuaoi and I'll send her back to you safe and sound and with the balance of your money."

"She may be safe, Bernard, but you're not. This isn't over. You're dead. You are ever so dead."

"Don't be droll, Professor."

Hannibal spat at Bernard, but it dropped harmlessly into the Gulf of Mexico.

Grendel stepped on board Bernard's launch and turned toward Hannibal. He smiled, trying to be coy. He didn't pull it off convincingly.

"Why don't you leave your stooge with me, Bernard?"

"I have other uses for Professor Grendel. He makes a wonderful Tom Collins. Call me with some good news soon, Professor."

"As for you, Grendel, this ain't over. I'm gonna enjoy kicking that smirk off your face."

Grendel stopped smiling and Hannibal noticed a slight discomfort in his eyes. He dismissed it, though, not feeling any compassion for the man at the moment.

When they reached Bernard's yacht, George removed Traci's gag. "Hannibal!" she yelled. "Just find it. I'll be fine. Hurry, Hannibal. I love you!"

"I love you, too! I'll be coming for you. You can count on it. And I'll be coming for you too, Bernard. You can count on that also."

After the launch was hoisted aboard, Bernard's yacht pulled up anchor and motored away. Hannibal stood on the fantail of the *Intrepid* until he could no longer see Traci.

"Good job, Hannibal," he said to himself. "Now you're really in it deep."

CHAPTER 19

Hannibal paced the deck of the *Intrepid* nervously, talking into his sat phone. "I'm telling you, Kirby. I only made the offer because I didn't think he'd actually agree to it. I mean who parts with a million dollars in cash like that? He treated it like it was ten bucks. What am I going to do now? ... I know you're not the FBI, but shouldn't I contact them? Technically, he's kidnapped her, yes? ... What do you mean I should keep this quiet? ... What's *wrong* with you? This is Traci we're talking about, and it's already been four hours since Bernard took her. I'd like to find him and — ... Fine. Okay. We'll do it your way, but if he harms her ... Yeah. Yeah. ... Okay. I'll see you."

He hit the disconnect button and tossed the phone onto the deck sofa. His mind raced with thoughts, most of them about the frightened look on Traci's face as Bernard's yacht pulled away.

"You did real good on this one, Hannibal," he said.

~ ~ ~ ~ ~

The rhythmic, droning drum of a distant helicopter engine made Hannibal look up. From over the coastline he could see the dark dot against the reddening sky just above the huge red ball of the descending sun, growing larger each second. It had been four hours since he had called Kirby for help.

Within minutes the chopper settled onto the sandy surface of Isla Contoy and Kirby stepped out. He glanced at Hannibal and then reached back into the chopper for a stuffed duffel bag and a rifle pouch. He placed them on the sand, then pulled another heavy crate off and dropped it onto the sand next to the bags.

With a quick hand signal he ordered the chopper back up into the air and then turned and crouched low until the chopper was up and away and the swirling sand had fallen back into place.

Hannibal approached from the surf.

"I know you ain't glad to see me, Hannibal, but we're partners now, like it or not."

"Thanks for coming, Kirby."

"What? No smart-ass comeback?"

"No. Just thanks for coming."

"I don't know what to say."

"Don't say anything. That would be perfect."

Kirby grinned. "*There* you are. Thought I'd lost you for a second."

~ ~ ~ ~ ~

"So you're sitting on a million in cash?" asked Kirby.

Hannibal moved toward the bar, stepping around the crate and duffel bag lying on the deck, and pulled out the briefcase. He walked back to the table and laid it down, opening it.

"Whoa! You ain't kidding."

"Right now, Kirby, it means absolutely nothing to me."

"I understand, Hannibal, but as long as we've got it, let's use it. It looks like the only way to get Traci back is to find the damned firestone."

"Can't you make a call to the agency and pull some strings? Can't they send out Delta and rescue her? Can't you do anything?"

"Of course I can. I can have a Delta or SEAL team on his ass within hours. But where is he, Hannibal? More importantly, where's Traci being held? Can you tell me that? I mean, where do I send the SEALs?"

"You can find him. I know you can. Find him and waterboard his ass to locate Traci. I don't care. I just want her back."

"So do I, partner. But we gotta know where she is first. That could take a lot of time. And it could get really messy. He'd be missed. I can't just whack 'im, even though I'd love to do just that."

"I know, I know," said Hannibal.

"In the meantime, let's change our bargaining position. Let's find out where the Naacal put the shittin' thing."

"You're right."

Hannibal moved back behind the bar.

"Can I get you something?"

"If you've got some Sky Vodka and orange juice back there, I wouldn't object."

Kirby dropped his hand onto the stone tablet resting on the table in front of him.

"So, has this tablet given up any secrets yet?"

"I haven't been able to look at it much since Bernard took Traci."

"I understand." Kirby bent over and stared at the tablet, along with some photographs of other stone tablets spread out across the table in front of him.

"You really know how to read these symbols?"

"Sure do, partner."

Kirby stopped reading abruptly. "Wow. Partners, huh?"

As he looked up, he faced the business end of a .45.

"What the *hell*, Hannibal! What's this for?"

"It's for you, Kirby. You're a real piece of work. You know that? And now that I have you here, I can get Bernard to bring Traci back and trade her for his little spook."

"What do you mean? What's going on? Have you hit your head on something?"

Hannibal walked over to the table pointing the weapon at Kirby.

"The cat's outa the bag, Kirby. I know about the call you made to Andy Anderson's sat phone. So tell me, how long have you been working for Bernard?"

"Bernard?! You think I'm working for that piece of shit?"

"Stop jerking me around, Kirby. I'm in no mood for your spy dance right now. How long?"

"Hannibal, calm down. I'm not working for Bernard."

"You called Andy. Why?"

"To find out if you made it there okay. You weren't answering your phone."

"Bullshit. I never told you where I was going."

"Hannibal, think about it. Don't you think the Company knows where you are at all times? You're working on a very sensitive project for us. Don't you think they'd track you? Especially when you spirit yourself off to a foreign country? Come on, Hannibal. It took me less than a minute to figure out who you went to see there. I know about your relationship with Anderson. I've got a file two inches thick on him."

"Why is that?"

"Because you know him. If *you* know him, then *we* know him. Get it?"

"Then why didn't you ever ask me about him after I got back?"

"Because I know he never showed up."

"How did you know that? I never said a thing about it."

"How? You're asking me how I knew you never met with Anderson? Are you serious? Get real, Hannibal. You really brought me out here to trade for Traci? Really?"

"Don't bullshit me, Kirby. I asked you a question."

"Traci. That's how I knew. What the hell is wrong with you? Are you losin' your freakin' mind?"

"Traci told you about me not meeting with Andy?"

"Of course. She still works for us, Hannibal. I thought you, of all people, would have known that. Hell, you do too, even though you won't admit it. Once you're in the agency, you're never out. Christ, Hannibal. What the hell is going on?"

"You bugged the phone I was using."

"Of course I did. Is that really a surprise?"

"It was to me."

"Grow up, partner. I was watching out for you. That's my job."

"I don't believe you, Kirby."

"Well, that's a news flash. Look, I know you're still pissed off that I left you out in the desert of Iraq. I get that. But I had no choice in the matter and I know you know that. Quit blaming me for something I had no control over. I'm tired of it. You hear me? Tired of it. Now, if you're gonna shoot me, then just get it over with. I really don't give a shit anymore. And I'm not gonna explain it to you again. But if you want Traci back home safe and sound, then let's get to work. Just remember one thing. You called me, I didn't call you."

Hannibal thought about it for several seconds.

"But you knew we were here."

"Of course we did. Who do you think's paying for this rig? Grindstone? Where do you think Grindstone gets the money? And don't tell me you didn't know that. Of course I didn't exactly count on Bernard showing up when he did, but now that he's played his hand, we're gonna be on him like glaze on doughnuts next time he shows up."

"So you know about Bernard, too?"

"Come on, Hannibal. Of course I know about Bernard. I know things you don't know. Put that gun away and I'll tell you all about what a real piece of work he is."

Hannibal held the pistol on Kirby, running everything through his mind, trying to decide if Kirby was lying.

"Damnit, Hannibal. We've got work to do. Cut the shit."

"Screw you, Kirby."

"Screw you, Hannibal! You wanna know about Bernard or not?"

Hannibal finally walked over to where Kirby sat and dropped the gun on the table.

"So what do you have on him?"

"First of all," said Kirby, "thanks for scaring the crap outa me with that cannon. And secondly, you really brought me out here to trade for Traci? That was a real thought in that Hannibal head?"

"Shut the hell up. I don't know what to believe anymore."

Kirby laughed. "This has got to be the best one yet, Hannibal. You were serious?"

"I said shut up. Tell me about Bernard."

Kirby laughed again. "Well, partner, for starters, his name ain't Bernard."

"What?"

"Bernard is his great-grandmother's maiden name. His real name is William Douglas Billington, and his great-grandfather is the one suspected of killing off the Herzog expedition after he stole all the files and artifacts."

Hannibal's face turned white. He collapsed into the nearest chair and rubbed his face with both hands.

"You have got to be kidding me, Kirby. I thought it was Billings or something like that."

"Well, it's Billington."

"So you know about Herzog as well? You know all of this to be true?"

"As true as it gets. Bernard's been trying to find the firestone for decades. He must have his great-grandfather's notes and files. And we suspect he's also got the missing artifacts that supposedly were destroyed in the fire."

"Then there never was a fire?"

"Oh, there was a fire all right, but only to hide the theft of the files and artifacts."

"How does the CIA know all of this?"

"The firestone is nothing new to the Company. They've known about its existence for a long time, but they've never been this close to finding it until now. That airliner crash was the catalyst to everything. That's why you were brought into it. The Company knows you're the only one who's got even a chance at figuring out its location."

"So it's fair to say you know the rest about Australia as well?"

"I know all about it. I haven't told the Company about it yet. You have Traci to thank for that, but it's not important unless it gets us closer to the firestone."

"If you open that vault, you'll destroy everything, Kirby."

"I promise you, the vault stays untouched and its location stays with the three of us. I want the firestone. The archaeology is yours. You've already changed history, Hannibal. Hell, you've knocked history on its ear. You know that, don't you?"

"Yes."

"You're going to be famous as hell."

"Only if I tell the world about the Naacal, Kirby."

"Why wouldn't you?"

"They destroyed their own civilization, and they were the ones who discovered the firestone. Can you imagine what the idiots running things today would do with that much power? They'd turn the planet into a cinder. I don't think we're ready for this information, Kirby. I plan to keep my mouth shut about it."

"Well, partner, that's entirely up to you. But I'll tell you this. It's better for *us* to have the firestone than for anybody else to have it. That's the way the Company sees it. And if we can't own it, we'll destroy it."

"That's not such a bad idea, Kirby."

"That decision is above my pay grade, Hannibal. I'm tasked with locating it. That's all I'm trying to do. The morals of using it are none of my business."

"That's the problem. It *is* your business. The people who discovered it couldn't stop it from being misused. If I find it, I intend to hide it forever or destroy it myself."

"Find it first, Hannibal. If you do, then the other decision can be made. If other governments find it first, it'll no longer be our decision to make. We can't let that happen. *I* can't let it happen. So tell me, how did you find out about this place?"

"That little odd-shaped stone tablet there on the table."

"What about it?"

"You notice the odd shape?"

"Yeah. It's almost like a puzzle piece." Then Kirby's eyes opened wide. "It *is* a piece of a puzzle, isn't it?"

"That's what I think."

"And you think another piece of it is around here somewhere?"

"You got it. In an underwater cavern near here, I think. The other piece of it is back home safe and sound. I hid it away."

"Where did you get the other piece?"

"Remember the odd-looking tablet I retrieved from that cave near the distribution structure, the tablet I asked to take with me?"

"Now that you mention it, yeah."

"It was the crystal inventory portion of the puzzle."

"You sneaky little shit! Does Menendez know about it?"

"No."

"Well done, Hannibal. So this is where the firestone is?"

"No. This is where the distribution crystals are supposedly hidden."

"What about the firestone?"

"Haven't found it yet. I'm hoping that another piece of the puzzle tablet is hidden below, with the firestone's location on it. You see, I'm thinking the Naacal split up the puzzle and hid the pieces all over the place here in the new world. Finding one piece presents no danger. One would have to find all the pieces before the location of the firestone is revealed."

"Well, partner, I gotta hand it to you. You're the best. So what's on this little stone tablet here?"

"This one only describes the cavern location. It came from the Australian vault. The first time I saw it I figured it was part of a larger puzzle. I just don't know how large the final puzzle is."

"The Naacal really spread the pieces around, huh?"

"Yeah. I'm guessing it was their hope that all the pieces would never be brought together again to give away the firestone's resting place until mankind was ready to rediscover it. I mean, if they really didn't want it discovered and used again, they would have destroyed the firestone and all references to it. So I have to believe that they left it for a future generation to find."

"And here we are."

"I don't believe it was meant for us, but for a generation that has learned to live in peace. A future generation."

"Well, Hannibal, I operate on the theory that if we find it, we are meant to have it."

"I can't argue with your reasoning, Kirby. And I can't answer the question of why the Naacal left all these clues. Maybe they left it for us or for some future generation. Maybe they were just too precise and deliberate for their own good. Or maybe they just couldn't bring themselves to destroy it. I don't know. Maybe they just plain lost track of it."

"How could they do that?"

"I have a simple theory about it. Maybe they left it intact, thinking that a future Naacal nation would bring it out and use it wisely, but those who knew where it was stored died before they could pass on the knowledge of its location. With them gone, the location of it became lost to time. It's happened before with other things of value."

"That's not a bad theory, Hannibal. At least it sounds reasonable to me. So where is this underwater cave? And don't get smart and tell me it's underwater."

Hannibal chuckled. "Damn. You stole my line."

"That's been my problem so far," he continued. "But I'm hoping I've got it solved."

Just then Hannibal's sat phone rang. He answered it, listened to the caller, jotted down different sets of numbers, thanked the caller, and hung up.

"I knew it," he said.

"Give."

"The tablet that gave me the inventory also had a set of coordinates on it. The coordinates were to a supposed plaque on a cliff face directly above an underwater cave. Its intent was to give the vertical location of the cave entrance located on the cliff face about fifty-three feet or so down from the plaque. The entrance is, or at least was, hidden from obvious view."

"There was an entrance to a cave in the middle of a cliff wall?"

"That's what it says."

"How would they get the crystals into the cave to begin with?" asked Kirby.

"Flying machines or levitation, I guess. It doesn't matter anymore, though, because that entrance would now be underwater. Deep underwater."

"I'm following you."

"I figured that the noted depth was wrong because after the global glaciers melted, the ocean level rose by almost two hundred feet."

"Okay. Makes sense."

"I couldn't find the plaque. After thinking more about it, I realized my error. You see, the coordinates from the tablet that I plugged into the GPS were wrong because the coordinates were based on the placement of the stars."

"Got it," said Kirby. "The coordinates were based on the positions of the stars as they were twenty-five thousand years ago, right?"

"Exactly. The phone call I got was from a buddy of mine who's an astronomer. I called him while I was waiting for you. He just gave me the correction calculations. I need to plug them into my calculations from the translation and then key them into the GPS."

"Great. Let's do it."

"That's the good news. The bad news is, even if I find the right location, the cave entrance is now about two hundred fifty to two hundred sixty feet below the surface."

"I see." Kirby thought about Hannibal's words.

"You still want that Sky Screwdriver?"

"I surely do now. In fact, make it a double."

Hannibal picked up the .45 and chuckled. "I'm sorry, Kirby."

"Forget it. I see the problem, though. I'm not a scuba diver, but isn't two hundred fifty feet well beyond what a diver can safely dive?"

"True. On air, that is. But on tri-mix or a mixed-gas rebreather, it's not a problem at all."

"What the hell is a mixed-gas rebreather?"

"It's a specialized kind of scuba gear. The SEALs use it for deep-water dives."

"Then we don't have a problem, Hannibal. If the SEALs use it, I can get it. Tell me what you need."

~ ~ ~ ~ ~

"Are you sure about this?" yelled Kirby as the helicopter departed after winching down the large sealed tube of equipment onto the deck of the *Intrepid.*

"I'm certified for a mixed-gas rebreather, Kirby. How do you think I got those photographs for Bernard in Bimini?"

"I've never dived before, Hannibal, let alone gone down over two hundred fifty feet. What if something happens to the air supply or the equipment malfunctions?"

"Hell, Kirby. At that depth don't worry about it. If something like that happens, we're dead. So get over it."

"Thanks, partner. That makes me feel so much better."

"Look. I'll go over everything with you. We'll go down slow and steady. Then the worse that can happen is you'll blow out your eardrums because you can't clear 'em."

"Jesus Christ, Hannibal! Your bedside manner sucks."

"Look, it's a mixed-gas closed-circuit rebreather. All you gotta do is breathe nice and slow and it'll all work out. We'll be in full face masks, so we can communicate."

"That sounds better. Yeah, okay, that doesn't sound too bad. I can do that."

"Just know this. At two hundred feet or so, it will go pitch-black down there. We'll have lanterns, so we can see what's ahead of us, but if something dangerous comes at us from behind, we won't see it probably until it's too late — if we see it at all."

"Jesus Christ, Hannibal!"

CHAPTER 20

Hannibal popped up out of the water and smiled up at Kirby.

"I found the plaque. It was exactly where the corrected coordinates said it should be."

"Did you get the coordinates for the cave?"

"I did. We'll have to move the boat about five hundred yards north."

"We can do that."

~ ~ ~ ~ ~

Their descent to the cave started off well. Hannibal found a second plaque he didn't know about, but that only proved that the GPS was exactly on target.

As the dive computer read out two hundred feet, Hannibal stopped the descent. It was nearly totally dark.

"Can I turn on my lantern now?" Kirby asked nervously.

"Let's do it. If we find the cave entrance quickly, we should have plenty of battery power to do what we need to do."

Kirby flipped his on and exhaled. "I don't mind telling you I'm scared half to death."

"You're doing great, Kirby. Just keep breathing slow and steady. I told you, you've got air to spare. We can go six to eight hours on these babies. So just keep breathing normally."

"If you say so."

"And keep using the rock wall to slow your descent like you've been doing. The cavern should be coming up in fifty more feet or so."

"Okay. Let's get down there before I chicken out."

Hannibal chuckled.

They continued their slow descent.

After several more seconds had passed and they had descended another thirty feet, Hannibal glanced over at Kirby, who looked ready to panic.

"You doing okay, Kirby?"

"NO! I'm not."

"Good. You sound okay to me. I just wanted to make sure you aren't narced."

"What's *narced?*"

"Suffering from narcosis."

"I don't even want to know what that is."

"That's okay, you're not suffering from it or you wouldn't be able to answer me."

Kirby reached out and tapped Hannibal on the shoulder and shook his head.

"This is damn scary, Hannibal."

Hannibal grinned, then pointed toward the bottom.

"Hang in there, Kirby. We're almost there."

"I wish you would have shot me earlier."

Hannibal chuckled. "Nah, you're doing good."

Several tense minutes later a large opening appeared near their feet.

They glanced at each other.

"We did it, Kirby!"

"I can't believe it."

"Believe it, buddy."

Hannibal reached the entrance first and moved into the cavern slowly. His guess was right. The cavern opening was enormous, larger than he'd expected, about fifteen feet in diameter. He dropped to the bottom and pulled himself along it, occasionally glancing behind him at Kirby.

"How you doing?"

"I'm doing better now that we're not dropping through the darkness. How far in do we go?"

"The entrance tunnel is approximately two hundred twenty-six cubits deep. That puts it at about one hundred eighteen meters, or roughly three hundred eighty feet."

"That's a long way to swim."

"Would you rather stay here and wait for me?"

"Hell no!"

"Then keep moving and don't stir up the silt any more than you have to. If you do, we won't see what's ahead of us."

"Don't be so damned honest right now, Hannibal. Lie to me a little."

"We'll be just fine if we take it slow."

"That's much better."

Hannibal moved slowly along the entrance tunnel floor, trying not to stir up any more silt than was absolutely necessary. Kirby followed nervously behind, trying not to touch the bottom at all.

The lanterns' beams, although very powerful, disappeared into the blackness that stretched out ahead of them. They inched forward for what already seemed like several hundred feet before Hannibal spotted a familiar reflection of light ahead. He recognized it as wave action. That meant he was nearing the surface of an underground pool about twenty feet above them.

"Up there, Kirby. Do you see it?"

"Yeah. What is it?"

"Surface waves of an underground pool, I believe."

"Great! Get me to dry land."

Hannibal motioned to Kirby to start upward, and within minutes, after their required safety stop, they broke through the surface.

"Leave your mask on, Kirby. Let me test the air first."

"No problem. You can be the guinea pig. I don't mind."

Hannibal slowly broke the seal and took a shallow breath. The air was sweet and fresh.

He fully removed his mask and took a deep breath.

"Fresh air, Kirby."

Kirby pulled his mask off and sucked in a lungful of air. "Holy cow, Hannibal. I thought I was gonna die."

"You did great! I told you it would all work out if we just went slow."

"I'm not looking forward to going back up."

"Well, there's definitely fresh air, so there has to be some kind of vent to the surface. There may be small fissures in the rock, too small to crawl in and out of but enough to get air down here. We'll have to check them out to know for sure."

Hannibal directed his lantern around the cavern and spotted the shoreline. He swam to it and crawled out onto fine black sand.

"Just as I thought."

"Just as you thought what?"

"This is a lava tube. Notice the smooth walls. We're below the limestone sediment layers, at least in this part. And there're no bats. The fissures that let air in must be tiny, too small for bats to come and go. It would be a perfect place to store something very valuable. It's dry. It's protected. There's no light pollution. And it's hidden away where no one could just stumble upon it."

"How far down do you think we are, Hannibal?"

"I would guess about two hundred thirty feet or so below the land surface. Let's drop our equipment here and do some exploring."

A few minutes later, following the natural course of the lava tube, Kirby asked, "Hey, Hannibal. How do these tunnels form? Does the lava just melt its way through the rock?"

"These particular tubes formed near eruptive vents. They were once open channels with running lava. With time, the channel edges built upwards and eventually arched over the stream, forming a roof and becoming a lava tube."

The tube suddenly began an upward slope of about fifteen degrees.

"You sure know some interesting stuff, partner."

"I don't know about interesting, but it *has* proven to be helpful over the years."

"You ever find any gemstones or gold in your digs?"

"All the time, but it would take mining engineers to dig 'em up in any useful amounts."

"Very cool."

They continued walking for nearly fifty feet before coming to the mouth of the tube. Hannibal directed the light into the blackness. Both men's jaws dropped wide open.

What stretched out ahead of them was the most incredible thing either man had ever seen. Perfectly formed clear quartz crystals, eight to twelve feet long, lay in numbers too many to count quickly.

Stone tablets were stacked up by the dozens alongside several solid gold seals like the one in the cave near the distribution station.

Realizing what they had found, both men burst out laughing. Hannibal immediately grabbed his GPS recording device and tried to record the coordinates.

"No signal."

"Let's find a way to get up nearer the surface if we can."

"Sounds like a plan. But before we do, let's photograph as much as we can. Look at those footprints, Kirby. I'm guessing they were made tens of thousands of years ago and haven't been touched since."

"Is that possible?"

"There they are. What can I say?"

"If there's air movement, shouldn't they have been eroded or erased over that time?"

"One would think so, but apparently not, and that tells me the air inlets must be micro-fissures. No way out of here except back through the underwater cave."

"That doesn't make me happy."

"Sorry, Kirby."

"What now?"

"We record."

Hannibal shot photo after photo for a good long while. When he thought that they had enough for future reference, they moved about the cavern looking for a place where they could get a GPS signal. They couldn't find one.

They then returned their attention to the field of large crystals.

"So these aren't firestones?"

"No. I don't think so, Kirby, but I could be wrong. Let's check out some of those tablets against the wall over there."

Hannibal studied several tablets, reading and scribbling notes onto his android tablet with a stylus, which he'd pulled from a water-tight case on his back. Finally, after a good two hours, he stood up and looked around the cavern.

"Nope. These are only the distribution crystals. The firestone has to be someplace else."

"Are you sure?"

"I've been reading for two hours. I haven't seen anything that indicates these crystals are anything other than for the distribution of the energy. Without the firestone to power them, these are nothing more than big, pretty quartz crystals."

"Can you take some time and read a few more tablets?"

"It could take weeks or months to go through them all carefully. We don't have enough supplies to do that. I can only scan them at best. But I'm not finding anything critical. And the batteries in these lanterns won't last much longer. You wanna go back through the tunnel in total darkness?"

"No! Can we move them out of here to be read later?"

"Not really. I don't know which ones are important enough to take. Some of those tablets could be engraved with worthless information. At least worthless for our immediate need. No, until I can sit down and go through them, they're better off sitting right here."

"I'm feeling helpless right now, Hannibal. Is there anything you need that I can get?"

What I need is equipment. Lights and generators. Things like that. That way I can take my time and scan all the tablets."

"I can get that. I can have this place lit up like Times Square if you want, but if I make that call, the Company will want to know why I need that kind of equipment."

"I don't think we want anyone knowing about this just yet. Know what I mean? I'll have to move the equipment down here during the night so we don't draw any unnecessary attention to ourselves. And it has to be delivered in waterproof containers. I want to be self-contained down here."

"Agreed. But the kind of equipment you're talking about is expensive. The Company will want an accounting of it."

"We've got a million bucks up top."

"That's right! No problem, then. I can make a call and have the equipment brought out by private contractor. I know just the guys to call, too, and they're my assets. They know how to keep their mouths shut."

"Kirby, I don't think we should tell another living soul about this until after we find the firestone. It could turn ugly real quick if the wrong person gets wind of this place. Doctor Menendez has enough to keep him busy for months, maybe years, with the tablets we found earlier. He can't translate them yet. And he doesn't know that I can. I've got the Rosetta stone. He doesn't know about that either. Without it, he'll just go around in circles trying to piece three languages together. And remember, he doesn't speak Navajo. And he most likely doesn't even know it is Navajo. Unless he figures it out and they bring in an expert in Navajo, he'll never be able to put it together. Even if he does, he'd have to understand the context of the words before it makes any sense. And that's the hardest part and that's our advantage."

"I don't get it. You're an archaeologist, not an ancient language translator, right?"

"I minored in ancient languages."

"I'll give you this, Hannibal, you're one smart mother —"

"Look at this!" Hannibal said as he pointed to a tablet.

"What is it? Is it important?"

"It's *all*-important, Kirby. Don't start asking stupid questions again. You were doing so well."

"Sorry. I'm working on that."

Hannibal chuckled and picked up the eighteen-inch-square tablet with the six-inch-square missing piece in the lower right-hand corner. As soon as he did, he saw it was a puzzle-like piece, exactly as he'd expected.

"Oh my, Hannibal! Is that what I think it is? Another piece of the puzzle?"

"Sure looks like it, but we won't know until we get it back to the *Intrepid*. But if what I'm seeing right now is correct, then it confirms that the firestone is somewhere up north."

"Why's that?"

"Well, Kirby, because it says so. Look. Seriously, we can't say anything about this cavern. If asked, we never found anything. We searched and searched and found nothing."

"Fine. I'll keep my reports vague."

"Kirby, I mean *no one*. No reports at all, or report that we've found nothing. Let's head back to the surface. I've got something you need to see."

"What about this stuff?"

"Well, it's been here for twenty-five thousand years. I think one more night shouldn't be a problem."

"Yeah. I guess. But that means we gotta dive down here again."

"Is that a problem?"

"Yeah."

"You can stay above if you want. You've seen enough to know what I have to do."

"That would be awesome. You can have this diving stuff. I like it on the surface just fine. I'll get the equipment you need, then you can do your thing down here. I'm staying on top."

"You're a real pussy, Kirby. I never knew that about you."

"I am. And I like it that way."

~ ~ ~ ~ ~

Hannibal was sitting at the table on the yacht scribbling notes when Kirby came up from the galley, rubbing a towel over his head with one hand and holding a drink with the other.

"Nice shower. Nice screwdriver. And no decompression sickness. I like to end my day that way."

He plopped down in the seat opposite Hannibal.

"So. Is it a part of the puzzle?"

"Absolutely."

"What next?"

"Can't say for sure until I finish translating what I have."

CHAPTER 21

Kirby sat completely mesmerized. The ice in his drink had long since melted, his drink untouched. The deck of the yacht was a jumble of photos of stone tablets and scrolls.

"So that's the story of the Naacal as it was told by the stone tablets and scrolls?"

"So far, Kirby. You're almost up to date, but you haven't heard the best part yet."

"Holy Christ, Hannibal. You mean there's more?"

"Yep. But listen to this. By luck, I photographed some incredible tablets and scrolls. After you piece everything together, there's one more part of the story: what happened to the Naacal. This will blow your mind."

"Like you haven't already?"

"I've saved the best for last. I'll give you the *Reader's Digest* version. When the hostile feelings finally led to blows and the war started, the Children of the Law of One realized that the Sons of Belial were going to use the unbelievable power of the firestone to destroy them. They set up some kind of deflectors to direct the rays of the firestone back down into the earth.

"When the Sons of Belial fired the weapons, that's where the energy went. Straight down into the island. Without knowing it, the Children of the Law of One created their own destruction."

"How's that?"

"What they discovered some months later, after the cessation of hostilities, was that by reflecting the energy beams of the firestone down into the earth, they, for all intents and purposes, granulated the substrata that supported the island — turned it to sand. The island literally began washing away right under their feet, through a process known as soil liquefaction."

"What the hell is that?"

"Soil liquefaction describes a phenomenon where a heavily saturated soil loses substantial strength and stiffness in response to an applied stress, usually an earthquake or some other sudden change in stress conditions, causing it to behave like a liquid. The dirt turns to mud and mixes in with the water, and that's it for an island."

"Wow! That's what happened to their island?"

"Essentially, yes."

"Incredible! So you're saying there used to be an island in the middle of the Gulf of Mexico?"

"That's what the scrolls and tablets say. A large earthquake struck one evening and the whole island just washed away.

"After the firestone attack, scientists from both sides discovered what had been done to their island and they were able to prepare for the final disaster. Prior to the fateful event, the people were moved to the surrounding mainland or to the other Naacal nations — India, Australia, Egypt, et cetera, and, of course, Atlantis. Thus ended the primary Naacal nation."

"You mean you found Atlantis?"

"No such luck, I'm afraid. Nothing I've found so far locates Atlantis. Leastwise, no island nations were called Atlantis. It might be a name invented by Plato."

"When did the earthquake take place?"

"The destruction of their island appears to have occurred twenty-five thousand years ago. But get this. I have information written in stone that says the Naacal have been around and in this area as far back as two hundred fifty thousand years ago."

"Wow, Hannibal! You've just rewritten the history of mankind."

"Not me, but it seems that all we have ever known about mankind has just been trashed. You ever hear of a guy named Juan Armenta Camacho?"

"No. I don't think so."

"A very quick story, then. In 1959, Camacho discovered stone artifacts and fossilized animal bones near a place called the Valsequillo Reservoir, near a town called Puebla, about seventy miles southeast of Mexico City. What he found was amazing. He found artwork carved into the jawbone of a mastodon, and the engraving was determined to have been made while the bone was fresh, like right after the beast was killed. Do you see the implications there?"

"Yeah. Didn't those animals die out thousands of years ago?"

"Twenty-five thousand years ago, in fact, and that puts the existence of man in these parts back at least that far. Most mainstream archaeologists will tell you that man has been in the New World for only thirteen to sixteen thousand years. But Camacho's find sets man's existence here back much farther, if found to be true. There's still some controversy regarding the accuracy of the dates."

"That must have bent some feathers."

"You got it. And to make matters worse for the mainstream archaeologists, sometime in 1961 Camacho found a spearhead embedded in the jawbone of an elephant. Testing on that artifact, and other work done in that area by another archaeologist, Cynthia Irwin-Williams, all yet to be confirmed, could put mankind in this area as far back as a half-million years."

"I can just hear the screaming from those establishment types."

"The Smithsonian folks are in a panic. But what these tablets and scrolls have confirmed, what I've just confirmed from this new information, is that man has certainly existed in this part of the world for at least two hundred fifty thousand years. This is gonna crush their world."

"It also seems to confirm your theory of a global civilization."

"I guess it does, at that."

"You're gonna be famous, Hannibal."

Hannibal stood up and walked to the rail along the port side of the boat. He stood silent for several minutes. Kirby let him contemplate for a while, but then grew impatient.

"Hannibal, you did it."

"No, Kirby. I didn't."

"Are you crazy? You're gonna knock everyone right on their ears."

"Kirby, no one can ever know what I've discovered. Beyond you and me, here and now, no one can ever know this. It will rock the very foundation of mankind, turn everything we think we know upside down. It could destroy the very fabric of our societies. And if I do succeed in finding the firestone, I could go down in history as the man who destroyed the world."

"You're getting melodramatic, Hannibal. Besides, if the world does get destroyed, who'll be left to know it was you?" Kirby laughed.

Hannibal smirked. "Good point, I guess."

"Partner, the way I see it, your discovery will force a change to some understandings that need changing. You've proven all the previous theories wrong, Hannibal. Stand on your mountain and shout it to the world: Hannibal Storm was right and he's one hell of an archaeologist!"

"Thanks, Kirby. I appreciate it very much, but I learned something important long ago."

"And what is that, Hannibal?"

"Never be someone who needs a friend; be someone your friends need."

"Nice words, partner, but I don't get it."

"I was a guy who needed to make this find, to show the world that I was for real and not the screw-up most people believe I am. The world doesn't need that guy right now, Kirby. The world needs a real friend — a protector. I don't want good people to die because of me."

"The world, ol' buddy, is not that gracious, I'm sorry to say. The world sucks and it's run by people who couldn't care less about anyone other than themselves and their own needs. I admire what you're saying, Hannibal, I truly do. I've always seen that spark of true grace in you. And no doubt you'd be making a hell of a sacrifice by keeping all of this to yourself, but the word is already out worldwide that the firestone may be real. If not you, partner, then someone else with a lot less integrity might find it. For my money, I'd rather it be you."

"If I find it, Kirby, I'm going to destroy it."

"That's your call, partner, and yes, good people have already died over this, like Hector. But other good people are going to die before it's finished and there's nothing we can do about it."

"There it is, Kirby. There it is. Don't you see? As I said before, when good people are allowed to die without justification, we are all guilty of murder."

"I get it, Hannibal. But a lot fewer good people may die if you find it before someone else. Do you get *that?*"

"I do get it. And you're right. If I find it first, I might be able to stop all the insanity before it begins."

"Correct. And I gotta say, you tell a great story, Hannibal."

"Traci might argue that point with you."

"Tell me this if you can. What happened to the Naacal people who stayed in this area?"

"The information I have doesn't say precisely, but there are passages that tell the story of how terrible the Naacal felt about destroying their own nation. It indicates that they dismantled the firestone along with the distribution stations and hid the crystals. They intended to erase their entire history so they wouldn't be blamed by future generations for the horror they'd inflicted upon themselves. They effected the breakup of their language into three distinct tongues, creating the Mayan, Sumerian, and Navajo languages.

"Those original people who moved to what is now the American Southwest changed their race's name from the Naacal to several other names over the years in an attempt to bury their history. I've found no records to prove it, but I think these people became the Anasazi, the Mogollon, the Mimbres, and others before the Spanish came along and called them the Navajo around the sixteenth century, a name that stuck. I think the Hopi were an offshoot. What is clear, though, is that the native people were here far earlier than current archaeological thinking has them here. Much, much earlier.

"Their island was called the First Naacal Nation. Their name for it was *Mu'un Naacal.* Australia was the Second Naacal Nation, or *Na'un Naacal.* The third nation was called *Tri'un*

Naacal and it apparently was located on a great island to the east."

"Atlantis?" asked Kirby.

"They only called it *Tri'un Naacal*. That one stumped me for some time. I thought it was pronounced 'try-un," not 'tree-un.'" It sounds like a small thing, but it makes a big difference. I won't bore you with how that's so, but it does matter."

"So from one nation they created three?"

"Actually, five. The fourth nation was *Qua'un Naacal*, located in 'the valley of great mountains.' I'm guessing that is Nepal today, from the description of the valley. The fifth nation, called *Qui'un Naacal*, was located somewhere on a great land mass to the south, perhaps South America or Antarctica. I'm not sure, but the way it was described, if I had to guess, I would say South America."

"What about Africa?"

"I don't know, Kirby. I told you what was engraved on the tablet. There are no records of the Naacal people after this time anywhere that I've discovered."

"Amazing, Hannibal. So, five nations in all?"

"No. The five I just named were apparently the main nations, or, as the tablets describe them, the "Mother Nations," but the tablets and scrolls also claim there were twenty-one 'lesser' nations, including the newest area to be rediscovered. We know it as Gobekli Tepe. They called it *Saté'nin Naacal*, or the Twenty-sixth Lesser Nation of the Naacal. They saw these other nations as more like provinces. How about that for synchronicity? The archaeologists excavating Gobekli Tepe have no idea what they've uncovered."

"And we're not going to tell them either, right? You're a freakin' genius, Hannibal. Are you giving thoughts to going back to Australia to open up the Second Naacal Nation vault?"

"I think we should just leave it buried for now. They abandoned the city for some reason. I believe we should honor that. Besides, I think I got from it everything really important.

What's left is more about their life and times. It's more cultural than technological."

"Hannibal, the Company won't allow you to just leave it buried if they even *think* information regarding the location of the firestone is there. If going back to Australia and tearing open the vault would answer that question, they won't hesitate. Do you realize what having control of the firestone technology would do for the nation that possesses it?"

"Like I've been saying all along, it'll probably bring about massive destruction."

"Why?"

"Have you been listening to me? It destroyed an entire nation! And every nation on earth would try to get their hands on the technology, by hook or by crook. There's no way any major nation would allow another nation to hold that technology alone."

"You'd be right about that, but I expect it will be us that controls it."

"Yeah? You think China is going to stand by and allow that? Do you think they're missing their agents yet?"

"The Chinese have locator biochips embedded under their skin. I suspect their government knows where they last were."

"Oh, Christ, Kirby! Do you think they'll find the underground city?"

"I don't know, Hannibal. My guess is no. The mountain most likely blocks the signal. But there's no way to be certain, I guess."

"That's just great. I didn't even think to check the bodies for communication equipment. I'm an archaeologist, not a spy."

"Don't worry about it. I think we can take care of the Chinese, but there's something else. Since you're the only one who understands the language right now, that puts you at risk — big risk."

"Only you and Traci know I can translate this stuff. Are you gonna sell me out, Kirby?"

"Shit, Hannibal. I do my job on one mission and you don't trust me the rest of my life. That really blows."

"I know you did the right thing. I just didn't like having to get my ass out of there alone. Like I told you, I'm no secret agent."

"Yeah, you keep reminding me of that fact, but you did just fine and we got the data before anyone else. Mission accomplished. Sometimes you gotta take one for the team, Hannibal."

"I took mine."

"Yeah, you did. And I've always given you full credit for that. I've never said anything else. Doesn't that count for something?"

"It does, Kirby. Let's put it behind us and never speak of it again. Agreed?"

"It's about time. Agreed. ... So what are we gonna do about that undersea cavern down there? We can't keep it secret forever. I'm sure Bernard knows we found something already."

"How's that? He's nowhere around here."

"Trust me, Hannibal. He's most likely got eyes on us right now."

"Seriously?"

"Yep."

"Could he be listening to us right now?"

"I did an electronics sweep already. We're clean. I do know how to do my job."

"Yeah, I know, Kirby. Sorry. ... I've got to head back down to the cavern tomorrow morning and see what more I can find."

"You found something today, didn't you? Something you're not telling me."

"I found something, but I don't really know what I found. That's why I want to go back down. I need to study it before I can say what it is."

"You're gonna tell me, though, right? We are partners again, right?"

"Yeah, Kirby. We're partners again."

CHAPTER 22

It had been remarkable to watch Kirby work his magic and get the equipment he requested brought out to the boat in the dark of night. To avoid prying eyes, they'd had to move the boat to a location nearly twenty-five miles away from the coast, deeper into the Gulf. But they returned to their original position by one o'clock in the morning, allowing Hannibal plenty of time to get it all ready for the dive. He was amazed at what $300,000 cash on the barrelhead could accomplish using the right people. It was a good investment.

By four a.m., Hannibal had already made several trips from the tube entrance to the cave's interior, getting the needed equipment in place. He was glad to have had Kirby up on top dropping the gear over the side of the boat and sending it down to him by way of a rope secured to the bottom of the entrance. It went faster than he had anticipated.

He flicked on the switch to start the generator and within seconds the entire cave was brightly lit — perfect for what he had to do.

The light allowed him to wander about the cavern inspecting the large distribution crystals with more precision. They appeared undamaged, but he didn't know for sure, having never seen them in action, what they should look like.

The crystals could wait. What couldn't wait were the tablets. He had many of them to look over and time was an issue, for the lights wouldn't stay bright forever. He photographed every one of the tablets first, making certain that he had the best angle to see the symbols later. Some of them initially seemed very important, but he wouldn't know for sure until after studying them in more detail.

He then decided to walk through the cavern and explore it more fully. He found a few more scrolls, but they were so fragile that he dared not lift them from where they lay. Other than some interesting artifacts, there was nothing more of value than what he had already discovered. But what he had discovered and photographed was more than enough for a lifetime.

It was nearly nine o'clock in the morning when he decided that he had done all he could do. Just then, the generator ran out of fuel and ground to a halt. Darkness returned and on came his lantern.

He smirked. "Good timing."

He made the choice to leave the lighting equipment there; having served its purpose, it was of no further value. Gathering up what he needed to take with him took another half hour. It was time for him to gear up and head back to the surface.

He regretted that decision.

As he neared the surface, he thought he heard explosions above him. A second later he saw bullets streaking through the water.

After his safety stop, he slowed his ascent and moved very near the yacht as his head broke the surface.

A full-on firefight was in progress, and automatic rifles were being fired at the *Intrepid*.

Kirby was obviously firing back. Hannibal couldn't do a thing to help, because both hands were filled with inflatable lift bags carrying three stone tablets each. The rapid gunfire continued unabated.

He tied off the bags to the fantail platform and tried to climb aboard. A trail of splashing bullets streaked past, narrowly missing him. He ducked back behind the yacht just as more bullets splashed near him.

Seconds later, more gunfire riddled the yacht and surrounding ocean.

"Kirby, what's going on?!"

"Hi ya, partner," came Kirby's voice from somewhere on the deck. "Can't really chat right now. I'm entertaining guests."

"Can I do anything?"

"Yeah. Don't get shot."

Hannibal heard Kirby return automatic fire.

He peeked around the fantail platform and saw the other yacht, with men still firing automatic weapons at the *Intrepid*.

"The guests don't seem too happy there, Kirby."

"Ah, you know me. I have a way with people."

"Sounds like it!"

"We're working it out."

"Did you see Traci?"

"Not with these types. They're more the worker bees."

"Got it. Give me a weapon."

"It's on the fantail, Hannibal. I had a feeling you'd probably want to join the party."

"I'm going under."

"Have a nice swim."

"Do me a favor. Keep your fire to a minimum."

"Will do, partner. If I can, that is. These guys love to party."

Hannibal inched around, and sure enough Kirby had laid a single brick of C-4 and a digital detonator on the fantail for him. He reached up for it just as a wild round zipped over his head.

After collecting the goodies, he refitted his mask and slid under the water.

He drifted down thirty feet and moved toward the distant yacht. Bullets streaked through the water, but they did not penetrate deeply enough to cause him harm. Still, to be certain, he dropped down to fifty feet.

It took him a while to get into position, and since his rebreather didn't produce any bubbles, he felt he could remain invisible until he could make a difference.

He came up under the center of the other yacht, then slid out to the edge. He set the timer and raised himself out of the water far enough to fix the C-4 to the bow's exterior about where he believed the engine and fuel tanks were, and then slid back under the water.

He gave himself five minutes to drop down deep enough and far enough away to escape the shock waves from the explosion. Drifting at nearly fifty feet, he covered his ears and waited.

The explosion lifted the yacht a few feet out of the water and disintegrated it. From his vantage point he saw lifeless bodies splash into the ocean above him. Within seconds, heavy pieces of the yacht also splashed down and drifted past him on their way to the black depths below.

He waited patiently until he felt that no more pieces were sinking towards him and then drifted upward to the floating bodies.

From the condition the bodies were in, he determined that there was nothing he could do for any of them and swam back to the *Intrepid*.

Surfacing at the fantail, he saw Kirby standing over him, a wide grin etched across his face.

"You throw a hell of a welcoming party, Kirby."

"Yep, but they were dying to leave."

"Right."

"Hey, Hannibal. Are we about done here? I'd like to leave before the authorities stop by for a visit. It would be a little hard to explain the wreckage and bodies, even for me."

"We can leave right away. Hey, I've got a surprise for you. I need some help, though."

Hannibal untied the lift bags and handed them to Kirby.

"Be real careful with these. They're more valuable than we are."

Kirby took hold of the bags and lifted them out of the water.

"Damn, Hannibal. Are these what I think they are?"

"I think so, but we won't know until I have time to finish the translations."

Hannibal climbed the stairs, pulling himself out of the water. After dropping his scuba gear on the deck, he squinted at Kirby.

"May I assume that our guests were associated with Bernard?"

"You may. We had a bit of a disagreement over the issue of you having some kind of evidence for them. I told them we didn't and invited them to leave. They didn't take it too well."

"Bernard's going to be a bit upset when they don't show up."

"Oh, I think he already knows he ain't gettin' his boat back."

"How's that?"

"I can feel him, Hannibal. He's out there somewhere watching this whole show."

"Then we gotta get outa here pronto. Back to Corpus Christi?"

"Might as well. It's as good a place as any."

"Think the owner will mind the bullet holes?"

"It's a Company rig, Hannibal. They expect it every time she goes out."

Hannibal chuckled.

"Well, I'd hate to disappoint them."

"We won't."

~ ~ ~ ~ ~

The *Intrepid*'s engines fired up and the boat cut through the waves and debris of the demolished boat, heading north.

From the distant shore of the Yucatan Peninsula Bernard lowered his binoculars. "Well, well, I'm guessing Hannibal found something."

"Sorry about the boat, sir," offered one of his minions.

"Cost of doing business, Mister Evans. It's just the cost of doing business. After I get my hands on the firestone, I'll be able to buy a million of them on just the interest alone. Bring her to me."

Moments later, Traci was standing next to Bernard.

"So there *is* something down there, it seems," he said.

"That's news to me, Bernard."

"Indeed. He just brought something on board. I can't see what it is from this distance, but it looked heavy."

"Heavy could mean anything."

"It could, Miss Jefferson, but I'm guessing it's connected with the firestone."

"Maybe, but knowing Hannibal, it could be a piece of junk."

"And I'm supposed to believe you? Come on. You can do better than that."

"I've seen it before, Bernard. He's like a child. He's fascinated with shiny objects. And he has the attention span of a two-year-old. I wouldn't be surprised if he found something off a cruise ship that looks like an artifact. He's done it before."

"Miss Jefferson, I assure you I'm no fool. And despite what you think of me and my methods, I know how to manage people. Some people require special motivation to realize their full potential. Professor Storm is one of them. Before I met him, I had heard of him and his uncanny brilliance. When I did finally meet him face to face, it was all instantly confirmed. In my opinion, he is the most capable, determined, intelligent man I've ever met. He is crafty, inventive, and, may I say, a most dogged individual when it comes to working his craft.

"I know you don't believe this, but I have the deepest admiration and respect for his intellect and abilities. He's a fighter, a battler. He loves a challenge. Challenge his intellect and motive, and you incite a dynamo toward greatness. He *will* find the firestone, Miss Jefferson. I'm absolutely certain of it. I just need him to focus and be motivated to find his true purpose, and you've given me that. Thank you, Miss Jefferson."

"I was wrong about you," Traci said. "I see that now. You're brilliant in your own way. And you are so right about Hannibal. Set his course for him. Create an insurmountable challenge, set an impossible task before him, and then get out of his way. Obviously, you know him as well as I do."

"And I have the advantage of no emotional ties with him. Regardless, I know how to manage people. That's the key to success in any business, Miss Jefferson. Knowing the people who work for you and what they can and cannot do is essential to success. Knowing precisely what motivates them, how to discipline them, how to incite them toward their own goals. This is how you manage people."

"You may have created a monster for the cause."

"Not a monster, Miss Jefferson. Your lover is a bloodhound, and it's a true privilege to watch this dog hunt."

"He *is* tenacious."

"He is that and so much more. He'll find the firestone for several reasons, not the least of which is to save you, and also because no one believes he can. He has a wonderful chip on his shoulder, and I am using that chip to my greatest advantage."

"You could have accomplished all that without kidnapping me."

"Kidnapping? You're a *guest*, Miss Jefferson. There are no shackles on you. I'm offering you a ringside seat to watch the brilliance and tenacity of a real archaeologist in action. Enjoy it while you can, because this opportunity will not last forever."

"That sounds ominous."

"All I'm saying is that your presence requires certain resources I think could be better used elsewhere, Miss Jefferson."

"Then why not let me leave right now?"

"Your departure would reduce the professor's bountiful motivation. No, I'm afraid I must insist that you stick around a bit longer. But sooner or later, it shall become necessary to part company in some fashion."

"Look, Bernard. You consider Hannibal an investment and possibly a form of entertainment. But I love him. He's definitely a handful at times and he's a zany guy, but he's my kind of zany. I don't want him harmed in any way."

"I've never threatened him, Miss Jefferson. I need him alive. And after he finds the firestone, I'm still going to need him alive. I assure you, I take excellent care of my investments."

"That's just the point, Bernard. He's far more important to me than an investment. And as for the firestone, it may have existed long ago, but the people who discovered its use obviously couldn't control it. I think they realized its terrible potential and destroyed it. I don't think the firestone actually exists any longer. I think you're on a wild goose chase, and so is my darling Hannibal."

"If so, then why were you out there with him?"

"I love him. I would do anything just to be around him. If he wanted to find the man in the moon, I'd go there with him just to be near him."

"That's good, Miss Jefferson. Well played. I didn't think you had it in you, but you're good. That came across as very convincing."

"Go to hell, Bernard. I never knew how much of an ass you were before, but now I believe it's true what I've heard about you."

"And what is that?"

"You'd kill your own mother if she got in your way."

"You're absolutely right, Miss Jefferson. I'll do whatever it takes to succeed. That's the difference between me and everyone else. I don't impose limits on myself. That's why I'm so successful.

"As for my dear mother getting in my way, well, that old bitch knows better."

CHAPTER 23

Kirby sat down at the deck table and sipped his drink. Hannibal looked up from his loupe and peered over one of the stone tablets he had removed from the underwater cave. "Who the hell's steering the boat, Kirby?"

"It's on autopilot."

"I didn't even know it had an autopilot."

"How are you doing? Discover anything new?"

"As a matter of fact, I have."

"What have you found?"

"Well, that second trip to the cavern paid off. I noticed something interesting on this tablet down in the cave. That's why I brought it out with me. Do you see this symbol here?"

"It's so tiny, I can't see it clearly. How did they carve such tiny symbols into stone like this?"

"I wish I knew," Hannibal said as he handed his loupe to Kirby. Kirby put it to his eye and bent over the tablet studying it. Finally he looked up at Hannibal and smiled. "Yeah, what about it? It looks just like the other two right next to it."

"You see, Kirby, that's why you're a spook and I'm an archaeologist. Look closer. There are differences. This one has two hexagonal patterns surrounding the circle and a vertical bar coming out of the center, with arrowhead points. This one is largest of all and has no bars. You see it?"

"Yeah."

"Look at this one. Same pattern as the others, but it has four radiating bars."

Kirby studied the tablet again. "Yeah, there *are* differences. I see that now. Are they significant?"

"I think this one without the lines must be the firestone. The primary crystal. See how it sits all alone in its own column? The other columns are segregated. And it's the largest one. This one with the arrowheads has to represent the distribution crystals. And this one with the four outward lines must represent the boosting crystals. I'm guessing, of course, but it seems logical to me."

"What's all the writing under the symbols?"

"I'm working on that."

"I thought you could read these things already."

"I haven't seen these symbols put together like this before. Would you care to take a stab at it?"

"I'll stick to being a spy, thank you."

"How long before we reach Corpus Christi?"

"We should be there in about twenty hours. Why?"

"Good. If you go steer the boat and leave me completely alone, I just might have time to work this out before we hit port."

"Okay, okay, I get it. I'm gone."

~ ~ ~ ~ ~

The sun was midpoint in its morning arc toward noon and the *Intrepid* was still about ten hours from Corpus Christi. Hannibal had worked through the night making good progress with the translations.

He had been staring at the stone tablet through the loupe for the past couple of hours. To give his eyes a rest, he looked up and out over the stern and noticed a distant high-speed boat. He stared at it for several minutes. It neither gained nor fell back.

He found that odd, because that type of boat had the capacity to race past them at will. He stood up and continued to peer at the boat. It made no change to its speed or direction.

Worried, he returned the loupe to his pocket and walked to the bridge, where he found Kirby sitting in the captain's chair calmly reading a book.

"Uh, Kirby ... you expecting company?"

"No. Why?"

"We've got company. A fast boat is following us. I think they're pacing us. Does that make any sense to you?"

"No, but don't worry."

"Something's wrong. I don't know what it is exactly, but I feel vulnerable out here."

"Relax. One radio call and I can get fighter jets out here from Corpus Christi Naval Air Station to take care of anyone who might threaten us."

"That's what really bothers me, Kirby. The fact that we might *need* jet fighters."

"I've got it covered, partner."

"Okay. If you say so."

Hannibal returned to the fantail and noticed a second boat slipping in and out from behind the first. This one was larger and substantially further behind the first by almost a full mile.

He returned to the bridge.

"How fast can you get those fighters out here?"

"Pretty darn fast. Why?"

"There's a second boat now. I feel a real panic attack about to begin."

"Let's take a look at 'em first before we go scrambling fighters."

Kirby and Hannibal walked back to the fantail. Kirby picked up a pair of binoculars and stared at the boats for several minutes.

Finally he brought them down to his chest and sighed.

"Hannibal, ol' buddy, will you do me a favor and stop being right all the time?"

"Is it Bernard?"

"The first boat is Russian. The other boat might be Bernard. It's too far away to be certain. Either way, I think a buzz by two fighter jets might get them to back off."

"Good. Call them. Call them right now."

"How long have they been following us?"

"I don't know. I was translating the tablet and looked up and there they were."

"Okay, Hannibal. Go to the bridge and turn the wheel to the right. Hold it for about twenty seconds and then turn it back to the left and hold it for about forty seconds. After that, just let go of it and come back here."

"I can do that."

As Hannibal left for the bridge, Kirby put the binoculars back to his eyes and peered at the Russian boat again. Sure enough, it followed the *Intrepid* through her maneuvers. When the autopilot took over again and put the boat back on course for Corpus Christi, Kirby lowered the binoculars and set them down on the table. He moved to a gun bag lying on the deck and withdrew an M-16 from it, slapped a thirty-round magazine into the receiver, and chambered the first round.

He held it up for the Russians to see.

"That's right, boys. We have our play toys, too."

Hannibal returned to the fantail to see Kirby's display.

"No, Kirby. Not this time. Just call the jets, please."

"Hannibal, have you taken photos of all the tablets?"

"Yes, several of each."

"Have you by chance sent copies to your computer at UCLA as a backup?"

"You know about that, too?"

"Did you?"

"Yes. I did that right away. Why?"

"Keep everything you have here handy."

"How about my camera?"

"Keep everything close. We may have to send the whole lot overboard real quick."

"Overboard?!"

"Yes."

"*Everything?*"

"Everything."

"Okay, Kirby."

"Now grab the other M-16 over there and let's show them that we're willing to party. Let's see what they do."

Hannibal did as he was bid and soon both men stood defiantly on the fantail staring back at the lead boat.

"Is this going to work, Kirby?"

"We should know in a minute."

~ ~ ~ ~ ~

A bullet ripped through the fantail couch. A second one tore into the front of the bar and shattered some bottles on the other side.

"Well, partner, that shooter can't aim for shit. Looks like this is gonna work out just fine. Hit the deck and return fire."

Without hesitation, Hannibal lay down on the deck and began shooting.

"This is what you call 'working out just fine'?"

"Hell, yeah! We're establishing communication here."

"Just what are we communicating?"

"That we love a party. What else?"

"Call the jets, Kirby! Call the jets!"

"Ah, we can handle these guys, Hannibal. Just keep it on semi-automatic and take your time."

"The sea is choppy. I won't be able to hit a thing."

"They can't do any better. Keep firing."

Hannibal looked through the telescopic sight and tried to line up his shot, but the sea bobbed him up and down. His first several shots were either high, whizzing over the boat completely, or they splashed into the water several yards in front of the boat.

The Russian returning fire didn't fare much better.

But Kirby was finding his mark. After several misses, his shots were now at least hitting the Russian boat more consistently, but they were doing little damage. Still, the boat's pilot started a zigzagging maneuver to avoid Kirby's bullets.

"These little two twenty-threes ain't doin' shit. Keep 'em busy, partner. I'm going to up the stakes a bit."

Hannibal did his best to find the boat in his sight, but it was rough going. A moment later he caught sight of a huge barrel in his peripheral vision. He turned his head to see Kirby settle down onto the deck with a Barrett .50 caliber sniper rifle.

"Holy Christ, Kirby!"

"If I can hit the boat, this baby will do some damage. Plug your ears, partner. She's a screamer."

Kirby took careful aim and pulled the trigger. The explosion made Hannibal's ears ring even though his index fingers were jammed into them.

"*Damn*, Kirby!"

The shot ripped through the bow of the boat, sending huge chunks of it into the air.

"Yep. This won't take long," Kirby said with a grin.

Hannibal watched as Kirby lined up his second shot and fired. Another chunk of the bow disappeared.

The Russians realized their folly and turned their boat sharply toward port. It was a bad move; their turn brought Kirby's third shot straight in line with one of the fuel cells. He fired and the boat disintegrated.

"Holy Christ!" yelled Hannibal.

Kirby calmly turned his attention and the telescopic sight toward the second boat. It was still far enough away that his shot might not have reached it, but he didn't have to pull the trigger. The boat turned sharply to starboard and picked up speed. Within minutes it was over the horizon and gone.

Kirby grinned. "I think we'll leave the jets at home. What do you think?"

"Yeah, Kirby. Yeah. Leave 'em at home. Wow! I've never seen that rifle in action before."

Kirby patted the heavy rifle and smiled. "When she speaks, people die and things go boom."

"What will the Russians do now? I mean the Russian government?"

"We're in international waters. They won't do anything. It never happened."

"I just wanted to translate the tablet. I didn't plan on any of this."

"I did. That's my job, partner."

~ ~ ~ ~ ~

For several hours afterward Hannibal kept a nervous watch for other boats as he continued his translations. Kirby had settled back on the bridge with his book, cool as a cucumber.

Finally, he slammed the book shut and wandered back to where Hannibal sat.

"Anything new, partner?"

"Look how all the data line up in columns."

"Okay. Now don't go yelling at me, but how is that fact helpful in locating the firestone?"

"In and of themselves, the numbers aren't helpful at all, but used together they help pinpoint the firestone, or maybe the boosting stations. I'm not certain of anything just yet."

Kirby awaited Hannibal's further explanation, but after several seconds he grew impatient. "Yeah, okay. And that means what?"

"Sorry. My mind slipped away for a second. The data are longitudes and latitudes. I'm guessing that if we calculate the reciprocal of all these distribution stones, if that's what they are, we'll find the exact location of the source. That focal point has got to be where the firestone is, or at least where it was twenty-five thousand years ago. At this point I'm not sure which it'll be."

"What does that mean?"

"It means we'll find where it was either before or after it was moved. I don't know which."

"Goddamn brilliant, Hannibal. Great work."

"Not really, Kirby. We have to plot these exactly on a digital map before we can fix the reciprocals. I need access to a very special computer. When we get back to Corpus Christi, we've gotta go to Denver. There's one computer there that can help me plot these points with incredible accuracy. I think I've translated them correctly, but it's gonna take me time to confirm them."

"Fantastic! Well, you've got about six hours before we dock. Better get working on it."

"Gee, Kirby. Is it okay if I take a piss now and then, or maybe get a bite to eat?"

Kirby caught a hint of a smile on Hannibal's lips.

"You've got a nasty mean streak about you, partner."

~ ~ ~ ~ ~

The University of Colorado stretched out stoically in the center of Boulder, an amazing place of learning in one of the most beautiful settings imaginable. The computer lab, a key component of the School of Geology, contained an extremely sophisticated computer system housing a mapping program unlike any other in the country. Its uniquely high-definition pixel capability allowed a user to pinpoint a location within five feet of the actual site anywhere in the world.

"It's helpful having that pretty little badge, Kirby. Thanks. No one else just walks in here and is granted instant access to their computer."

"It does have its advantages now and then. I never leave home without it. Impresses the ladies, too."

"And if you were straight, it might pay off on occasion."

"Funny guy, Hannibal. You're a funny guy."

"I'm still not sure about you, Kirby."

"Go to hell, Hannibal. I'm so straight you could shoot me from a bow. So tell me again. Why did we have to come here?"

"Because of the uniqueness of this program's accuracy. I told you before that the Naacal did not estimate anything. Their exactness extended to the laying out of the crystals in the distribution grids. This computer program will allow me to input these calculations with a degree of accuracy that can't be achieved on any other computer that I'm aware of."

"So you're saying we couldn't just plug them into Google Earth and achieve the same accuracy, huh?"

"Funny, Kirby."

"Do you still have the same problem as before, the coordinates being for the positions of the stars twenty-five thousand years ago?"

"No. These coordinates are based on longitude and latitude. They're fixed. But I have to input each one individually."

"It's gonna take a while, I guess."

"Yeah. Go get a coffee or something. I need to concentrate."

"Just keep typing. I'm gone."

Hannibal began punching in all the coordinates that he had translated. About an hour later, he stopped typing and glanced up at Kirby as he returned.

"I'm done. If I translated everything correctly, I hope we're gonna see exactly where the firestone is, or was. Would you like to do the honors and press the button?"

"No. You do it."

"Okay." Hannibal pressed the "Enter" key. The computer began to plot the ley lines. One by one the lines began to form a perfect intersection.

"Damn!" exclaimed Hannibal.

"What? What's the problem?"

"Look at it."

"I am. I see a perfect intersection building. Congratulations, Hannibal. I'm impressed."

"Kirby, for Christ's sake, look at it. We're screwed."

"How so?"

"Look at the intersection, man. It's in the middle of the Gulf of Mexico. We're back to square one."

"You're telling me the firestone is lying at the bottom of the Gulf?"

"No. I'm saying this was its position twenty-five thousand years ago when it was still on the island — before the island sank into the Gulf. We don't have squat now."

"That's just great, Hannibal. Now what do we do?"

"I truly don't know. If I can't glean something from what we have right now, we might never find the firestone."

"How about Australia?"

"No. I've got everything concerning the crystals out of there. What's left is for cultural archaeologists."

"Okay. Back in any of the other caverns, then?"

"Look, Kirby, I know you're trying to help. I understand that, but you'll just have to believe me when I say there is nothing anywhere that can help us now. I already have everything about the firestone I could have gotten. The answer is here, staring back at me, but I just don't know what to look for to find it."

"What about using another crystal?"

"Are you asking whether it's possible to use another crystal as a substitute for the firestone?"

"Yeah. They found some big crystals in Mexico. Could we use one of them?"

"I think you're referring to the Giant Crystal Caves in the Naica Mountains."

"That's the place."

"No, we can't use them. Those crystals are gypsum, not quartz. We can't grab just any crystal and stuff it into a hole and call it a firestone. The firestone is unique. Got that?"

"Got it. I was just fishing."

"The only answer is to find the firestone, Kirby."

Hannibal sat motionless, staring at the monitor for several minutes without speaking. Finally something caught his eye.

"Kirby! Look at the radial patterns. Most of the closer sites are line of sight. Then they radiate out from secondary line-of-sight stations. Look at the generations of expansion. Twenty-six generations, except for one site which sits all alone. One could say it appears to be the first generation. All by itself. See it here?"

Kirby studied the monitor and then raised his eyebrows. "Yeah. I see it, but could that just be because the terrain is so different?"

"I know that area. It *is* very different. It's in the northernmost area of Arizona. It's Monument Valley."

Hannibal typed some information into the computer. The picture expanded until it clearly showed a large red sandstone butte.

"That's Eagle Mesa, Kirby. The point is right in the center of that mesa."

"You're saying a crystal was sitting on top of a mesa?"

"Not me, pal. That's what the computer calculations are indicating."

"The firestone?"

"Not necessarily. It could just be another distribution point."

"How would we know? Is it described as a distribution point?"

"No. The tablet only describes it as a single point. Perhaps it was the northernmost point in the distribution system. Remember, back twenty-five thousand years ago most of this continent was covered by glaciers."

Hannibal rubbed his face with both hands a moment and then grinned up at Kirby. "Wait a minute!" He opened his backpack and pulled out several photos of the stone tablets. He sifted through them until he found one in particular. He studied it carefully, silently, for several minutes. Then he smiled. "I forgot about this."

"Forgot about what?"

"The marking here has been changed."

"Changed how?"

"It's like it was erased, scratched out, or adapted. The symbol has been modified somehow. And there's an additional set of coordinates that I thought were just duplicates. But the tablet could have been modified after the island sank. The symbol here could be where they moved the firestone to after the tragedy. Maybe I'm wrong about this, but we won't know unless we ..." Hannibal fell silent and remained so for several seconds.

"Unless we what, Hannibal?"

"Unless we make our next stop Monument Valley."

CHAPTER 24

The black Tahoe pulled up in front of the Navajo hogan and stopped. Hannibal and Kirby exited.

"What if you're wrong about this, Hannibal?"

"Then I'm wrong and we can check Monument Valley off the list."

"Tell me again what we're doing here. I just want to hear you say it."

"For the third time, Kirby, we need permission to go into the area."

"No, Hannibal, we don't need anything. I have full authority to go anywhere I want. This may be Navajo land, but the U.S. government has first claim to it. This place is under my jurisdiction."

"You didn't listen to a word I said on the way out here, did you, pal? We're not here for Navajo permission. We're here for permission from Great Spirit. Black Owl is a personal friend of mine, and he's also the Great Holy Man of the Navajo Nation. Only through his blessing can we safely venture out onto Navajo lands."

"Hannibal, please. Is this the reason we had to stop and buy the tobacco?"

"Yes. You never visit a *Hatalii* without a gift, and tobacco is the traditional gift."

"A what?"

"I told you already, *Hatalii* is what the Navajo call their holy men, their medicine men. He's a Singer."

"You mean like Sinatra?

"No. A Singer is a medicine man, a healer. A Singer acts as a facilitator who transfers power directly from the sacred Holy People to the patient to restore balance and harmony. Most Singers only know a few chants, a few ceremonies, because it takes a long time to learn and perfect each chant and there are sixty ceremonies. Black Owl knows them all. He's the most senior Singer in the Navajo Nation."

"I see. I guess."

"I think you should stay outside, or this might not go well."

"I'm going in, Hannibal."

"You don't understand. Black Owl was a Code Talker in World War Two. He was on ultra-secret missions with the Marine Corps. So secret, in fact, that his name doesn't show up on the registry of known Code Talkers. He earned the Congressional Medal of Honor, but you won't see his name anywhere in those records either."

"Partner, you forget who you're talking to. *I* can find his name in those records."

"Listen up, Kirby. Since his return from the Great War he has shunned virtually all contact with both the white man and the white man's government. He collects his monthly check from the government, his lifetime benefit for having earned the Medal of Honor, but other than that he has little regard for anything of the white man. In fact, his monthly check goes to the local school. He has a Christian name, given to him by the Marine Corps, but he never uses it and forbids it to ever be spoken aloud."

"So?"

"You're missing the point, Kirby. He doesn't trust the government."

"Nobody trusts the government anymore, Hannibal."

"And for good reason, too."

"Yeah, yeah. That's above my pay grade. So go on. What's the big deal? Why do we need his blessing?"

"I won't try to explain it to you. We just do. Stay here, please."

"I'm going in, Hannibal. Just knock on the damned door."

"Fine, Kirby. Have it your way."

Hannibal knocked on the wooden door and then stepped inside.

Black Owl sat stoically at a table and his eyes opened wide when he saw Hannibal. A big smile formed on his face as Hannibal presented the *Hatalii* with the package of tobacco. The holy man spoke some words in Navajo to Hannibal. Hannibal smiled and nodded.

"What did he say, Hannibal?"

"He gave the traditional welcome blessing to Man Who Speaks with Stone People."

"To who?"

"That's the English translation of my Navajo name."

"You've got a Navajo name?"

"I do, Kirby." Then Hannibal spoke some words to Black Owl, who smiled.

"Okay, tell me. What did you say now?"

"I introduced you to Black Owl using *your* Navajo name."

"What would that be?"

"Man with Head of Stone."

Hannibal burst out laughing. Black Owl chuckled.

"Funny, Hannibal. Very funny."

"Black Owl," said Hannibal, now serious and for Kirby's sake speaking in English, "this is Kirby Hansen. He's with the CIA, but he's my partner. I ask you to welcome him."

Black Owl spoke some Navajo words and then motioned for them to sit at the table.

"Hannibal?"

"Relax, Kirby. He just welcomed you, that's all. Sit down."

Hannibal then spoke Navajo to Black Owl and received an approving nod.

"I asked him if he would allow me to tell you more about him. He gave me his permission."

"Thank you, sir," said Kirby to Black Owl.

Black Owl nodded to him.

"Okay, Kirby. Black Owl was born on January 1, 1920. He believes that the spirit of Manuelito entered his body at the moment of his birth."

"I'm sorry, who?"

"To the white people he was called Manuelito, but his real name was Ashkii Diyinii, or Holy Boy. He was a great Navajo war chief who died of measles in 1893."

"His spirit was restless and did not wish to stay in the shadowlands," said Black Owl.

"He speaks English?" Kirby asked Hannibal.

"Of course he does, but he usually chooses not to. He must like you, although I can't imagine why."

"I'm honored, Black Owl. Thank you."

"I see your spirit and have been talking with it since you arrived," said Black Owl. "It is a good spirit to talk to."

"I don't know what to say."

"Say nothing, then, Kirby, and I'm serious," said Hannibal. "It's a spirit-to-spirit thing and not really meant for human ears anyway. Be grateful that he speaks to us at all, because he feels he betrayed his people when he worked with the government during the war. He feels that Manuelito speaks through him on occasion, and Manuelito tells him to avoid white people altogether if he can. So I'm very grateful that he speaks to me."

"Hannibal," said Black Owl, "beware of Coyote. His breath is upon your shoulder."

"I hear the words of the *Hatalii*, and that is why I am here."

"What about a coyote?"

"Not *a* coyote, Kirby. Black Owl is referring to Coyote, the Ancient One."

"I don't understand."

"Coyote represents himself as a trickster and has done so since the days of creation, but he was also a friend to ancient humans, for he stole the secret of fire from the gods and gave it to us. Still, he cannot be trusted. He shows himself in many forms. Right now, I think Black Owl is talking about Bernard."

"He knows Bernard?"

"No. He doesn't know who Bernard is, but he's warning me about someone he says is close by. The trickster is near. I'm only guessing it's Bernard. I've had this feeling that he's been tracking us ever since we landed in Corpus Christi — he or someone working for him. Black Owl feels it too, I think."

Black Owl nodded in agreement and said, "He is silent like the eagle, as powerful as the bear, as deceitful as a serpent." He then said something in Navajo.

"Hannibal?" asked Kirby.

"He said She Who Confronts Her Enemies, that's his name for Traci, is nearby and may be in danger."

"Okay, Hannibal. I'm glad we stopped by to speak with Black Owl. It was worth it. But I told you before, for us to help Traci, I need to know where she is. For now, not knowing, we have to move forward on our mission. Now, do we get his blessing to go to Eagle Mesa or not?"

Hannibal thought for a moment and then pulled out some photos of the underground city, the power station, and the scrolls.

"No, Hannibal! Need to know." Kirby put his hand on the stack of paperwork. "Classified, partner."

"He can help us, Kirby. Right now I think he's the only one who can."

"Hannibal, this is way out of line."

"It's the only way, Kirby."

Kirby thought a moment. "You're certain?"

"As I can be."

"Okay, partner. I trust you."

"And I trust him."

Kirby nodded. "So did Uncle Sam once. Okay."

Kirby removed his hand. Hannibal pushed the pile of paperwork in front of Black Owl.

Black Owl opened the folder and stared at the top few documents. A second later he pushed them all away, closed his eyes tightly, and mumbled a chant. Finally he opened his eyes and looked straight at Hannibal, visibly shaken. "I cannot look upon these."

Hannibal pulled the photos away from the holy man and remained silent.

"Do not continue this, Hannibal. This will bring you much unhappiness and many problems."

"I understand, Black Owl, but I must travel this path until the end. It is my destiny."

"It will prove the end of all things if you succeed."

"Only if misused once again."

"And it will be used as it once was."

"Wait! Does he understand what he's looking at?" asked Kirby.

"I know this thing which is sought. It bears the blood of the ancients. It bears the blood of my people."

"Black Owl, do you know where the firestone is?" Kirby asked boldly.

"It is hidden and it must stay hidden, or the world shall end."

"I must seek to find it so I can destroy it," Hannibal said.

"You will never be allowed to do this. If you find it, they will use it, unless blood is given in sacrifice."

"A part of me wants to shout out loud. Announce it to the world and make it available for all. If my shout is loud enough, perhaps they will be forced to use it for the benefit of mankind."

"You are thinking like a child, Hannibal. It is better that you forget what you know. Bury what you have. Bury it someplace where no one will ever discover it again. And do it soon," warned the holy man.

"Perhaps if I destroy the instructions for how to energize it instead, once I find them? Without knowing how to use it, it would remain only an amazing curiosity."

"If they discover it, they will find the way to use it. Destroy what you have and forget that you have ever seen it."

"That can't happen," said Kirby.

"I promise you, Black Owl. I'll either destroy it or I'll make it so no one ever finds it again."

Kirby squinted at Hannibal.

"You son of a bitch! You know where it is, don't you?"

"Not exactly."

"Bullshit! You know exactly where it is. You've known for some time, haven't you?"

"Do not seek this thing any longer, Hannibal," pleaded Black Owl.

"I have to. I have to know I was right."

"Hannibal, I need to know where the firestone is. I'm not kidding, partner. I need to know right now."

"I'm not ready to tell you yet, Kirby. I'm thinking on it all. This is important to me, too. It's my career and reputation at stake as well."

"That is pride speaking, Hannibal," the holy man said. "And it is the madness that lives within you. Following the madness may lead us all to a disastrous end."

"Hannibal! Pride or madness, I'm ordering you to tell me where the firestone is. I'm serious, man."

"No. I'm not telling anyone. I'm not sure I know exactly where it is anyway. But if I find it, I'm gonna move it somewhere else for safekeeping, or I'm going to destroy it where it is, if I'm able."

"That's crazy talk. You can't do it without my help. I'm the one keeping the bad guys at bay. And I won't go along with this little stunt of yours. This is too important to let one man make a decision like this."

"It's too important to let anyone else *but* me make this decision, Kirby."

"Hannibal," said Black Owl, "it has been hidden safely for all these years. You will only expose it if you attempt to go to it."

"I'm plagued with indecision. The firestone could be the answer to the world's energy needs for all time."

"Or it will destroy the very people you wish to help."

"Or it could do that also. I'm very confused, Black Owl, very conflicted in my soul. I feel like I'm on the edge of a cliff and I don't know if I should step into the void or turn around and walk away."

"Hannibal, for the sake of our friendship, tell me right now where it is. I'll get it secured immediately. No one will touch it or try to make it work without your personal participation. You have my word on it."

"It's not you I have a problem with, Kirby. It's the guys over you who I can't trust. If they get their hands on the firestone, they'll destroy everything just trying to get it to work."

"Don't make me play hardball, Hannibal!"

"What are you gonna do, Kirby? Waterboard me?"

"They won't let you move it. You know that."

Hannibal looked at Black Owl. The two men stared at each other for several seconds. Then Black Owl nodded.

"What?" asked Kirby.

"Black Owl agrees with me, Kirby. The government cannot be trusted. And you know it as well, partner. You know full well that if they get their hands on it, they'll experiment with it."

"They won't know how to energize it. You said that yourself. They'd have to have the instructions. So when you find the instructions, destroy them."

"Kirby, wow! That, coming from you."

"Look, Hannibal. I understand your concerns, but finding it is one thing, knowing how to turn it on is another. If we can get hold of the firestone itself, then at least we know where it is and that no one else can use it. Doesn't that make sense?"

"To a CIA agent it does," said Hannibal. "But to me, it makes more sense to destroy both the firestone *and* the instructions. That way, nothing can be done — ever. Failing that, hiding the firestone so that it can never be found again, after destroying the instructions, makes sense too."

"But you'll have proved your theory, Hannibal. You'll have proved there was a global civilization long before anyone could have guessed. You'll be rich and famous. You'll have what you've always envisioned you'd have — enough funding to last a lifetime."

"That's true, Kirby. That's all true."

"Then make it happen, Hannibal. Only you can make it happen. Think about Traci. Think about how she'd feel about you succeeding. Think what it could mean for her."

"Again, all true. But there's one thing you've failed to mention. What if it's used to destroy? I'd be responsible for that as well. How could I live with that? What about you, Kirby? What if it were your decision to make? Could you live with the fact that you had a chance to save the world and didn't do it?"

"I follow orders, Hannibal. I just follow orders."

"Funny thing, Kirby. That was the argument made at Nuremberg, too."

"What do you want me to say, Hannibal?"

"Nothing to say, Kirby. ... Black Owl, could I sit outside for a while and think?"

Black Owl nodded. Hannibal walked outside. Kirby followed.

"Hannibal?"

"Kirby, go take a walk or something. Leave me alone. I need to think."

"Fine. I could use a walk anyway."

~ ~ ~ ~ ~

A half hour later Hannibal sat in a chair outside Black Owl's hogan, staring up at the mountain range to the west silhouetted against the star-filled sky. He was in quiet meditation when Black Owl walked out and sat down in a chair next to him. The holy man sat quietly, allowing Hannibal to begin the conversation if there was to be one.

Several minutes passed and then Hannibal sat forward in his chair and rested his elbows on his knees. He sighed. "Sometimes I'm not sure why I became an archaeologist."

"To learn from the Stone People, of course. You have a great calling — a gift to hear the words of the Stone People. You need to follow their voices."

"Already I've made a great discovery, but I can't tell anyone about it. What I might find next could either destroy the world or wonderfully change it. I don't know what to do."

"I hear your spirit crying out. That is why the ancestors called upon me to come out here and speak with you."

"I can use all the help I can get, Black Owl."

"This thing you seek, Hannibal, the tuaoi, it is not something you should be searching for. Because the hearts of humans have not changed from the old days, the tuaoi will fall into the wrong hands again if you make its location known. Of this I am certain.

Of this the old ones are also certain. And this time it will destroy the entire world, completely and forever."

"I know, but it could also do so much good. I'm so conflicted. I know what I should do, but I still feel compelled to find it. I've been losing most of my life. I'd like to post a W in my column just once."

"The old ones have a more personal question for you. How much do you trust this man Kirby?"

"I'm not sure I can trust anyone anymore."

"You both need to be very certain about this. Because if you continue down this road toward the discovery of the tuaoi, you may find that you need each other more than you can ever know now in this moment."

"So you believe I'll find it?"

"If you listen to the Stone People, I am sure of it."

"I've done the work, Black Owl. I have a right to finish my search. I have a right to find it."

"Because you have a right to find it does not mean it is right to do so. This shall be a test for you. A great test you must not fail."

"Why, Black Owl? What do you see?"

"This government man will be put under great pressure. His superiors will put great pressure on him to tell them what he knows. This is the same government that lied to my people as easily as it suited them to do so. They cannot be trusted on any matter."

"I know, but I seek it not for any other reason than I feel I must find the tuaoi for my own vindication. I am laughed at and scorned. I want my victory, Black Owl, even if it turns out that I'm the only one who will ever know about it. If I do, then I can handle all the mockery, knowing that I succeeded. I don't care about fame or fortune. I just want to know some self-respect. I tired of not getting my dreams fulfilled. Can you understand that?"

"I understand the pride of a man, Hannibal. But it is your pride that will kill us all if you are not prepared properly."

"It isn't a question of pride, Black Owl, it's a question of honor. Surely you are one to appreciate honor."

"What does this world care for your honor, Hannibal? What should matter most to you is keeping the world safe. The ancient ones were a brilliant people. They discovered the power of the tuaoi, and yet not even they could control it — they could not prevent their own destruction.

"Why would anyone think that its destructive powers would be any safer in the hands of the U.S. government? Whether it is oil, diamonds, gold, or the energy of the tuaoi, madmen use them to gain wealth and power. The good nature of these things is only a fortunate side effect for the rest of us.

"The tuaoi was removed from the world, Hannibal, because the ancient ones could not find a way to restrict its use for peaceful means. Those living today do not carry the full blood of the ancients, have less intelligence and even less control over their emotions — less honor. If the power of the tuaoi is ever resurrected, the cataclysm created by its rebirth will surely end all of history.

"Again, I caution you against seeking this thing. Eat your pride and honor, Hannibal. Leave that bitter taste behind for the taste of the sweetness of doing the right thing. "

"You also know where it is, don't you, Black Owl?"

"Like you, I have never looked upon it, but also like you, I, too, can partially read the symbols left behind by the ancient ones on the stone tablets. They have left behind their symbols all over this land and they have been with the People a long time."

"The question is, is it still in the valley?"

"No. The question is, what will you do with the knowledge you have been given?"

"I don't know the answer to that."

"Hannibal, hear my words. Great Spirit has given to you an abundance of both intelligence and skill to make great discoveries. I tell the ancient ones that you also possess the necessary wisdom, but they still question.

"I tell them that I know your heart and I am certain you will do what is right. I tell them that you do not listen to your pride and that your honor is greater than you now think it to be. But they question still. I tell them that I know Man Who Speaks with Stone People very well. They tell me I do not know him well enough to speak about what he will do.

"We are in a great contest together over you. But I am confident, while they remain unsure. I think I will win."

"Thank you, Black Owl. Your faith in me means a lot. More than you know. But I deserve the chance to make this discovery. And if I do my very best, for all the right reasons, will I not be forgiven for wanting to become something special?"

"I do not know the answer to that question. But I do know this much. Be forever grateful that forgiveness exists in this world, for if we all got what we truly deserved, we would all have bullet holes in our heads."

Hannibal nodded. "True enough. That's why I came to your hogan today, Black Owl. Your wise counsel has always guided me in matters of spirit."

"We have spoken enough. Now we will smoke a pipe together. We will listen to the songs of the night as one. We will sing some ourselves. We will watch the moon rise. Then we shall sit in silence to think on all that has been said this night."

Hannibal nodded as Black Owl pulled a long pipe from his belt. He opened the pack of tobacco Hannibal had given him and smelled it.

"It is good tobacco. I think tonight we will have a good smoke."

CHAPTER 25

Hannibal couldn't sleep. He glanced at the clock on the nightstand: 2:14 a.m. He had been tossing and turning since going to bed at eleven. He listened carefully and heard the rhythmic snores of Kirby in the room next to him. He was envious. Kirby could sleep like a baby. Nothing ever disturbed his sleep. When it was time to crash, Kirby did it peacefully and deeply. Hannibal would give anything for that ability right now.

He relented to wakefulness, rolling out of bed and giving up on sleep. He got dressed. Why not? Nothing better to do, he reasoned. He surrendered to one more fact — the coming sunrise would greet him much the way the moonrise had the night before: filled with angst.

He stepped out from his room at the Gouldings Trading Post hotel and walked to the overlook. There, staring across the black desert landscape, with stars filling the clear night sky above the mesas of Monument Valley, he wondered if he could make the correct decision about what to do with all the knowledge he had gained about the Naacal and the firestone.

Staring at Eagle Mesa, directly in front of him, he even questioned if what he had read was true. Could the actual firestone have once stood on top of that great mesa? After 25,000 years of relentless wind and rain erosion, could evidence of its honored place still exist? If he climbed up onto the mesa's summit, would he discover the hexagonal seat of the firestone? Or, more likely, would he make a fool's climb to a fool's discovery?

Despite the cool breeze of the early morning, more questions burned deeply in him, the same questions over and over. Should he be doing this? Should he be following his dreams, or was Black Owl correct when he'd questioned his right to discover the very thing that could potentially destroy the world?

What was really going on with Kirby? Why had he suddenly backed off from trying to get Hannibal to tell him where he believed the firestone was located? Was this some new strategy?

Perhaps he realized that trying to bully Hannibal into talking wasn't going to work and he was going to soft-sell him into it.

Either way, it wasn't going to work. Hannibal believed that he alone had to make the final decision about what to do with both the firestone and the knowledge of the Naacal civilization. To make matters worse, the more he struggled to find the answer, the further away from him it moved.

He walked back to his room and closed the door. He wasn't feeling tired, so he sat down in a chair.

The phone rang.

Hannibal looked again at the nightstand clock. It now read 3:27 a.m. The phone rang again. He picked it up and put the receiver to his ear. "Yeah?"

"Professor Storm, sorry to wake you."

"I wasn't asleep. Who is this?"

"The messenger is unimportant, Professor. The message, however, is. You will drive to a place I designate and you will say nothing to anyone, especially your colleague, Kirby Hansen. Am I clear so far?"

"So far you're not saying shit."

"Then let me be more to the point."

A second later Hannibal heard a female voice on the phone. "Hannibal, run! Don't listen to him."

"Traci?" Hannibal asked, now sitting up alert.

"Am I 'saying shit' now, Professor?"

"You bastard! You'd better not harm her in any way or I'll—"

"You'll what, Professor? Tear my head off? Rip my heart out? Kill me to death?" The voice chuckled. "Well, then, do it. Oh, only one problem, though, right? Where the hell am I? How can you save your precious lover if you don't know where she's being held? Please, Professor, let's not be droll about this. I understand you know the valley area well, am I correct?"

"I swear, you bastard ..."

"Please, Professor. Let's move past the macho phase of this conversation. You're out of your league on this one. Answer my question, please."

"Yeah, okay. I know the area pretty well. So what?" Hannibal spat out.

"You're familiar with Oljeto Road?"

"Yeah."

"Fine. Follow it left from the Gouldings Trading Post and then north for approximately seven point six miles till you come to Piute Farms Road. Got that?"

Hannibal thought for a moment.

"Professor?"

"I know where Piute Farms Road is."

"Excellent, Professor. Turn onto Piute and travel exactly one point three miles to Holiday Mesa Road. Drive about three hundred feet on Holiday until you see a lighted pole. Stop there and wait for further instructions. Once again, Professor, say nothing to anyone or Miss Jefferson will suffer for your indiscretion. You have fifteen minutes and not one second more."

"I don't have the keys to the car. Kirby has them."

"Already anticipated, Professor. Outside your room is a red Ford Edge. Keys are under the driver's floor mat. Fourteen minutes and forty-five seconds, Professor."

The caller hung up abruptly.

Hannibal did exactly as he was told. He ran out and found the Ford, found the keys, and sped away from the hotel without telling Kirby.

~~~~~

Eleven minutes and thirty-eight seconds later, Hannibal stopped the car in front of the lighted pole. Traci was tied to the pole and gagged.

He leapt from the automobile and ran to her, stopping short after seeing the wire fence and the many trip wires surrounding her.

"Traci! Are you okay?"

Being gagged, of course, Traci could not answer him. That didn't prevent her from shouting muffled reactions to Hannibal's arrival.

"Don't worry, Trace. I'll find a way to get to you."

Traci was in a rising state of panic. She blinked her eyes and nodded her head frantically at Hannibal.

"What, Traci? Are you trying to tell me something?"

She nodded more frantically now, blinking her eyes faster, glancing repeatedly to Hannibal's right.

Hannibal finally figured out her message. She wanted him to turn around.

His head made it halfway around before a hand flashed into his peripheral vision, a wisp of mist danced in front of his eyes, and then it was lights-out.

~ ~ ~ ~ ~

Hannibal opened his eyes, but he couldn't see. Everything was blurry and foggy. His head was spinning and he felt that he was only seconds from losing his supper. He tried to sit up.

"Slowly, Professor," a low male voice cautioned. "Go slowly. The drug will wear off quickly now, but until it does, move slowly. I know it seems very confusing at the moment, but in a few seconds everything will be better."

"What ... what happened?"

"You took a short nap is all. Hang in there. All will be normal in just a few more seconds."

The voice was right. His vision began to clear quickly. Everything around him came into sharp focus. His head began clearing up, his thoughts became organized once more. Within a few more seconds, he was himself again.

Sitting in a chair halfway across the room was a large man with smooth facial features, sporting pure white hair combed straight back and dressed all in black: a fine-looking specimen of a bodyguard. Or a killer.

"Who are you?" asked Hannibal as he sat up on the edge of a bed.

"My name, Professor, is ... well, just call me Mister Falcon, or just Falcon, if you prefer. Labels are just labels, aren't they, Professor? They don't really define a person, do they?"

"I recognize your voice. It was you on the phone."

"Most perceptive, Professor."

"And I smell Bernard."

Falcon chuckled. "He did say that you were a man of keen wit, with a wicked tongue to match."

"Where is that piece of refuse?"

"Mister Bernard will join us shortly."

"Good. I've got lots to say to him."

"And he'll have much to say to you as well, Professor. I assure you, you'll want to listen carefully to what he has to say."

"As for you ..." Hannibal rose quickly from the bed and dashed toward Falcon. But for a big man, Falcon was fast. In an instant, he too stood up. To Hannibal's great surprise, Falcon stood over seven feet tall. Somehow, he'd missed noting that attribute before charging.

Hannibal changed his mind about attacking the giant, but not quickly enough. His gangly assault was greeted by a single right hand, nearly the size of a catcher's mitt, catching him by the throat and picking him up off the floor as if he were a feather.

As Hannibal awkwardly hung choking, his feet dangling a foot and a half off the floor, Falcon smiled.

"You're predictable, Professor. Are you enjoying this?"

Hannibal shook his head, trying to breathe, his face turning blue. He was not enjoying himself at all.

Falcon lowered Hannibal to the floor, and his choke hold became an instant fistful of shirt right under Hannibal's chin.

"Are we going to continue this unnecessary, uncomfortable dance, or will you behave?" Falcon asked with a wide grin.

"Behave," Hannibal rasped.

Falcon let go of Hannibal's shirt collar and stood back, still grinning. "Now isn't that better, Professor?"

"I had to try," replied Hannibal, his voice clearer now.

"I understand, but another attempt at such foolishness will get you hung up on that hook." Falcon pointed to a large metal hook attached to a ceiling beam. "Are we clear on that issue?"

Hannibal glanced up at the hook and then back at the giant before him. He gulped. "We are eminently clear on that issue, Mister Falcon."

"Wonderful. I think we'll get along famously."

Hannibal looked around him. The room had only one door and it was metal. There were no windows and the walls were steel as well, painted battleship gray. But aside from its austere construction, the room was furnished with plushy, modern, ergonomically designed furniture and was decorated in light, comfortable earth tones. If he hadn't been a prisoner, Hannibal would have enjoyed this room immensely.

He then noticed familiar artifacts sitting on inset shelving, behind a glass door. He noted three distinctive stone tablets and about a dozen scrolls shining in the spot lighting.

Hannibal glanced at Falcon. "May I?"

"Actually, Professor, if you could just be patient for a bit longer, Mister Bernard will be only too happy to let you study them all you want."

"Herzog Expedition, I presume."

"Can't say, Professor. Don't know anything about a Herzog Expedition. But I'm certain Mister Bernard will answer all your questions. He should be here any moment."

Just then Hannibal heard the metallic sound of locks and latches being moved.

"Here he is now, I believe," said Falcon.

Sure enough, the door opened and in stepped Bernard.

"Speak of a piece a shit, and it drops at your feet."

"Now, now, Professor. Is that any way to greet your most admiring benefactor?"

"No, but it's the way I greet you."

Bernard chuckled. "You are one of the most predictable people I know, Professor."

"Yeah, Falcon said the same thing as he was choking me."

"Ah, yes. Were you being Hannibal, Professor?"

"I was."

"May I assume that is now finished?"

Hannibal glanced up at the hook and then at Falcon, who nodded and smiled.

"You may," replied Hannibal.

Bernard stepped forward and raised a hand toward the hook.

"He's ... ah ..."

"He's aware, sir."

"I'm aware I'm not a side of beef," added Hannibal.

"Wonderful. Now we can begin in earnest."

"Not just yet, Bernard. Where's Traci?"

"She's safe and unharmed, Professor. I do honor the terms of my contracts."

"You'd better."

"May we begin to have some fun?"

Hannibal nodded.

"You have, no doubt, already spotted the artifacts."

"Herzog?"

"Exactly, Professor. Only one problem — for me, that is. I can't read or understand the damn things. And I have hired the best linguists money can buy. They are completely stumped. Until you tumbled into my life, Professor, I thought them completely undecipherable. But you've cracked the code, haven't you? You can read them as well as you can read a letter from your mother. Am I right, Professor?"

"There's more to just reading the words, Bernard."

"I know, I know, Professor. Context. To understand what is being said, one must first understand what is actually being transmitted and why. Am I correct?"

"You got it."

"And you have deciphered the context, haven't you?"

"That's the problem, Bernard. I haven't. I can read the words, but I don't understand the framework for their thoughts. I don't know what the author was thinking when he wrote them or what the words meant to him. This has been just as big a problem for me as I'm sure it has been for your other linguists. This language has been dead for a very long time. There is no one on earth today who speaks it. To get into the mind of the writer may not be possible. It's not only a complete language unto itself, it's all written in code. I think it was intended that way to make it extremely difficult for anyone to decipher."

Bernard smiled knowingly. "I just love your mind, Professor. You toy with people; it's a game you enjoy playing. And the thing is, Professor, you're smarter than almost anyone I've ever met in my life. Except for me, of course."

"Of course."

"I admit that I do not speak Navajo, Professor, but I did hire several men who did. You are correct. There is a code built into the words. It's like the Japanese trying to decipher the Code Talkers' code. But you've done it, Professor. I know you have. That is how you got here. That's why I built this impenetrable room here in Monument Valley. My linguists deciphered that much, at least. Now, where in this vast valley did the Naacal hide the firestone that has eluded everyone but you?"

"If you only had given me this much credit before, Bernard, I would have brought treasures to your door."

"But I'm not interested in treasures. I'm only interested in the firestone."

Look, Bernard — or should I call you Billington?"

"Ahh, you *are* brilliant, Professor."

"Not me. Kirby Hansen knows all about you and your great-grandfather's little secret and your great-grandmother's maiden name. In fact, the Company's building a hell of a file on you."

"Why do people always think they're breaking some astonishing news to me about that? I've known for a long time that the CIA, NSA, and FBI have huge files on me. But they have no evidence that I have ever done anything wrong. And they certainly don't know about my small collection here. But now, Professor, you do. Are you ready to have at them?"

"I really hate you, Bernard."

"Don't hate me too much, Professor. I'm about to make your dreams come true. You're going to be more famous than Howard Carter could only have dreamed of being. And rich! Don't forget the wealth you'll amass. You'll have your own funding for the rest of your life — several lives over. Now, make yourself comfortable at that table and Mister Falcon will bring you the first of the tablets ... or would you prefer a scroll?"

Hannibal capitulated and sat at the table. "That stone tablet there, on the left. I'd like to study that one, if you don't mind."

"Mind, Professor? I've been dying to have you here for the longest time. Please, Mister Falcon. Would you be so kind as to accommodate the professor's wishes?"

Falcon moved to the glass door and pulled a key from his pants pocket. He opened the door and stepped inside.

"Oh, Professor. Just for the sake of full disclosure, Mister Falcon is the only one who has the key to the artifacts room. And the glass is bullet-proof and shatter-proof. You can look, Professor, but you can't touch unless Mister Falcon allows you to do so. I just wanted to be clear about that."

Falcon returned to the table and laid the tablet gently down in front of Hannibal, then locked the door again.

"He'll be here with you every minute, Professor. I'm sure you'll grow to enjoy each other's company. You'll be very comfortable, unless you prefer to spend your time on the hook." Bernard pointed to the hook on the ceiling beam.

Hannibal glanced up at the hook once again and then directed his eyes back to Bernard. He shook his head.

Glorious. Mr. Falcon is here to see to all of your needs and to assist you should you require assistance. I have stocked this building with just about everything you could possibly want. I'm leaving now. I'll return later for your progress report."

"What about Traci? Now that you have me, you don't need her anymore. How about letting her go?"

"Not yet, Professor. I assure you, she's still quite comfortable. And your continued cooperation will guarantee her continued comfort."

"What about Kirby? He'll soon find out I'm gone, if he hasn't found out already."

"Mister Falcon has already seen to him, Professor. No need to worry about Mister Hansen."

"You killed Kirby?"

"Of course not, Professor. My, you *do* have a low opinion of me."

"Are you telling me the truth?"

"Right now, Professor, Mister Hansen and Miss Jefferson are having a delightful breakfast together. They are both well and unharmed. I would hope you'd wish them to remain that way. Am I wrong?"

Hannibal shook his head.

"You see, Professor, what mutual respect and consideration can achieve?"

"I want to speak with Kirby right now. I don't trust you. I speak to Kirby or I sit here and do nothing."

"Mister Falcon, my hat is off to you. You were absolutely correct in your assessment of our professor here. As predictable as they come. If you don't mind?"

Falcon pulled his cell phone from his pocket, pushed a button, and waited for an answer. "The spook," he said and handed the phone to Hannibal.

"Hannibal?" asked Kirby.

"It's me. Traci with you?"

"Yep. We're fine. Having a lovely breakfast. You?"

"I'm good. What do I do, Kirby?"

"It's your call, partner. You'll figure it out. I'm sorry I can't help you. I blew it."

"You didn't blow it. I'll work it out. You know how I love to entertain guests."

Falcon pulled the phone from Hannibal's hand and disconnected the call.

"You *will* work it out. You're no dummy. Good day, Professor."

Bernard opened the door and started to step through, but stopped and turned back toward Hannibal. He smiled. "Have a glass of wine and enjoy life. It's all what you choose to make of it anyway."

He shut the door. Hannibal heard the locks and latches presumably being put back into secured position.

He turned to Falcon. "So, you wanna be an archaeologist, do you?"

Falcon looked at Hannibal as if the eccentric archaeologist had lost his mind.

CHAPTER 26

Traci lifted her coffee cup to Kirby in welcome. "So tell me, Kirby. How did an amateur get the jump on you?"

"You know, Trace, I think you've been hanging around Hannibal too long. That biting sarcasm is so unlike you."

Traci smirked. "I think you're right. He does have that effect on others, doesn't he?"

"Yeah, doesn't he? To be truthful, a knock on the door awoke me. I thought it was Hannibal. I opened the door, something went 'pssst,' and here I am, wherever *here* is."

"It's sunny, that's all I know. Last night I was tied to a pole trying to warn Hannibal that someone in a black mask was moving up behind him, and the next thing I knew I woke up here, like you. I hope he's all right."

"He sounded fine. Knowing Hannibal, though, he'll do something to piss Bernard off. He's good at that. He always seems to know the perfect thing to say to get under your skin and itch," Kirby said with a smile.

Traci chuckled. "God, how well I know that."

"Gotta hand it to Bernard, though. He got his hands on Hannibal. I didn't think he would, but he's a crafty bastard."

"So now you're admiring him?"

"I admire his ability. I hate his guts."

"Do you think Hannibal will give in to Bernard's demand?"

"I think Hannibal will discover what he needs to discover and try like hell to sabotage Bernard's plans. And if he gets half a chance, he'll send Bernard on a wild-goose chase."

"Why would Bernard risk everything and hold us hostage? Does he really think he'll get away with it?"

"If he finds the firestone, Trace, it won't matter. He'll possess the power to hold the whole world hostage. And I'm afraid he has both the money and the brains to pull it off, too. But what I'm most afraid of is that he'll offer a sample of the firestone's power before stating his demands, and there's no saying what will happen if anything goes wrong. I believe Hannibal: that thing could destroy the world in a heartbeat. It could also be the best thing we've ever had. I really do understand why Hannibal is agonizing over what he should do. I don't envy him his decision."

"Kirby, do you believe we could ever use the power of the firestone only for good purposes? Are you really that naïve?"

"Not by a long shot, Trace. I think we're more likely to turn this whole planet into one big charred cinder. My only hope is in Hannibal pulling this off and stopping Bernard from getting his hands on it."

"Hannibal knew that about the firestone right off, Kirby. If he can, he'll do the right thing. I know him."

"It's funny, you know? The fate of the world rests in the hands of a man who wants nothing from it except a little respect. Go think on that and see if your head doesn't explode."

"I'm sure if he thought of the irony, he'd be howling with laughter. But seriously, I don't think he'll let the firestone or the knowledge of how to activate it fall into Bernard's hands. Or anyone else's, for that matter. I have to believe that."

"I hope you're right, Traci."

~ ~ ~ ~ ~

Hannibal sat hunched over one of the stone tablets staring through his loupe. Falcon sat next to him scribbling notes on a tablet of paper.

"You see, Falcon? You see that round symbol with the curved line wavering through it?"

"Yes."

"What do you think it means?"

Falcon hesitated.

"Come on. After all we've done today, you should recognize it by now, or at least make a good guess."

"Well, Professor," Falcon said, thinking and staring at the symbol, "if we surmised correctly before, that those other symbols next to it might indicate the structural framework required for the support of the output force, then I would have to say this symbol might represent the force itself, emanating as the active force, but not the residual force indicated by this symbol here." He pointed to another symbol on the tablet. "Do I have it correct?"

"Perfectly, Falcon. And you didn't believe you had the understanding to be an archaeologist."

"I have to say, Professor, I find this stuff fascinating. And you're brilliant at interpreting it, too. I can't believe your understanding of ancient languages. Maybe after this whole affair is finished, you might consider taking me on as an apprentice?"

"I would, Falcon. You seem to have a natural talent for this. Too bad you wasted so much time studying better ways to kill people, or I suspect you'd be out in the field right now making incredible discoveries."

"To be honest, Professor, ancient history has always held a great fascination for me."

"It shows, Falcon. It truly does. Now let's get back to the tablet. We've got a lot of work to do. This tablet could be the key I've been looking for."

Hannibal stopped and looked up at a distant wall, thinking. Finally he glanced at Falcon. "Do you think Bernard's great-grandfather had any idea that this tablet he stole might be the key to the whole mystery?"

"I don't think anyone truly knew what they had found, Professor. I think the Herzog guy just found some cool shit and decided to keep it. How could anyone know what they had discovered, Professor? The existence of the Naacal were hardly even imagined back in those days, right?"

"Right you are, Falcon. Very perceptive of you to make that observation."

"Thank you, Professor." Falcon felt honored by Hannibal's words.

"You're very welcome, Falcon. Well deserved, certainly. You have a very keen and delving mind. Excellent attributes for an archaeologist to have."

"You might be right, Professor. Perhaps I do have an innate desire to be an archaeologist. I never considered that aspect of myself before."

"Well, on that note, I have to piss."

Falcon chuckled. "You know where the bathroom is, Professor."

Hannibal stood up and patted Falcon on the shoulder. "Well, partner, why don't you see what else you can decipher on that tablet. Think hard, though, because there will be a test," he said, walking away from the table.

Just before he entered the bathroom, he turned back to Falcon and chuckled. "Just kidding."

Hannibal closed the bathroom door. Grabbing a glass, he filled it quietly with water and began pouring it into the toilet a little at a time, pretending to urinate. At the same time, he began going through Falcon's toiletry bag while carrying on a conversation to hide the noise.

"Do you know what I hate most about growing old, Falcon?" he shouted.

Falcon looked up, but didn't get the chance to respond before Hannibal continued. "Pissing. It takes five times the effort to produce a quarter of the results you got when you were twenty, it takes five times longer than it did when you were fifteen, and when you're supposedly finished, which it seems you never are, you feel no satisfaction."

Falcon chuckled. "You're very weird, Professor," he shouted back.

"I hear that a lot."

While talking, Hannibal located what he had hoped to find. In Falcon's toiletry bag was a prescription bottle filled with white capsules. He had seen Falcon taking them before. He read the label carefully: zolpidem. He said under his breath, "So, the Falcon has trouble sleeping. I'll fix that."

Hannibal finished his monologue. "Nope, Falcon. I don't care for this growing-old thing."

He removed four capsules from the bottle and shoved them into his pants pocket before returning the bottle to the toiletry bag. He flushed the unused toilet, washed his hands, and returned to the table.

"So tell me, have you mastered the tablet yet?"

"Not even close, Professor."

"It may take us a few days to go through everything here. You know what I need right now, Falcon?"

"What's that, Professor?"

"A screwdriver."

"We have a small toolbox where the tablets are stored. I'll see if I can find one for you."

Hannibal put his hand on Falcon's arm, stopping him from rising.

"Not that kind of screwdriver, partner. I'm more partial to the vodka–orange juice kind."

Falcon smiled and then nodded.

Hannibal walked to the bar.

"How about you, Falcon?"

"I'm on duty, Professor."

"So am I. You don't see it stopping me."

"Well, I don't know. Mister Bernard is pretty —"

"Pretty much a chickenshit, if you ask me."

Falcon chuckled. "I was going to say strict."

"And I'm going to repeat, he's a chickenshit. Now, would you like your screwdriver tall or short?"

"Well, I guess a short one would be all right."

"One short screwdriver coming up."

~ ~ ~ ~ ~

The door to the room unlocked from the outside, and Bernard stepped into the room from the hallway accompanied by a burly bodyguard.

"It's the madman."

"I'm getting used to being greeted with criticism, Mister Hansen. Professor Storm has laid the foundation nicely for that. I can't say that I like it, but I am getting used to it. I accept the fact that it goes with the territory. ... Miss Jefferson? Are you enjoying Mister Hansen's company?"

"It's better than yours, I must say."

"Ooh, the knives of unkind words do thrust deeply. Good thing I'm immune to that form of steel."

"That's too bad. I was going for the sweet spot."

"Been hanging around Professor Storm a lot lately, I see. Well, despite the lack of appreciation for the comfort I have provided you, I come bearing news regarding our favorite archaeologist."

He walked to the closet and opened the door. Inside, hanging on the bar, was a set of formal clothing.

"But first. For dinner this evening. I insist on proper dress. For all my barbarity, I do have one or two less barbaric qualities. I think you'll find they fit properly. Dinner is at six. Please be prompt."

Bernard shut the door to the closet and moved back to the center of the room.

"Well, speaking for myself," said Kirby, "I couldn't give a rat's red ass about dressing for dinner, but it's good to know that Hannibal's well."

"Safe and having a gay old time, if I'm still afforded the right to use that term within its original context."

"What about Hannibal?"

"It seems, Miss Jefferson, that he and Mister Falcon are getting along famously. And that Hannibal is deciphering one of the stone tablets with amazing speed. It will, no doubt, be a couple more days before he discovers fully what lies hidden in those symbols, but I'm confident he will succeed. He's an amazing man. Quite brilliant, really. It's such a shame. Such a tragic shame."

"I'll bite," Traci said. "Why's that?"

"The immutable laws of the universe, Miss Jefferson. The brightest suns burn out the fastest. But then there always has been a high price to pay for brilliance."

"Hannibal's not a star, except in my heart."

"Well said. I like that. I have nothing to add to that, Miss Jefferson. But that doesn't change what is. Professor Storm dooms himself. He possesses the highest integrity I've ever seen in an archaeologist. At least in any I've ever worked with. So many sell out so very quickly, and are rather cheap about it as well. But not Professor Storm. And that, I'm afraid, is going to be his undoing. It's certainly going to be a great problem for me."

"Why don't you just encourage him, instead of threatening him?"

"As I said before, Miss Jefferson, I know how to manage people. I have him now at his peak performance. It's only a matter of time before he breaks through and makes the greatest discovery in history."

"You've got *me* very curious about something now, Bernard," said Kirby.

"And what might that be?"

"What's for dinner?"

~ ~ ~ ~ ~

Hannibal sat staring hopelessly at one of the tablets. Something about this particular sixteen-inch-square tablet was special. Just how, he wasn't yet sure, but the symbols on it appeared to be unlike any on the other tablets in the room, or any he'd studied before. It had been two days since he had achieved his last breakthrough. Frustration was evident on his face. Even Falcon was becoming irritated.

"What do you say we just forget the whole thing, Professor? I'll call Mister Bernard and explain to him that the code cannot be broken with what we have."

"Patience, Falcon. It's one of the special traits of great archaeologists. The answer is here."

"Look, I'll attest to the fact that you've searched through every scroll and tablet we have."

"But this is the tablet with the answer. I'm staring at it. I just have to think more like the Naacal and less like Hannibal Storm."

"The devil you say."

"The devil indeed, Falcon. I say drag the devil into the light. He's been hiding long enough."

"I say we break the tablet into a million pieces," suggested Falcon, rising from the table and pacing back and forth across the room.

Hannibal's eyes opened wide with surprise.

"Mister Falcon! You, sir, are a genius."

Falcon stopped his pacing. "What do you mean?"

"That's the key to this! It's another puzzle. It's another damn puzzle! The whole of the tablet is a puzzle within itself."

"How is that possible?" asked Falcon, returning to the table.

"I've been studying the tablet as if it contained a single continuing message. That's not what it is, though. I see that now. It's a puzzle built from several messages. And through that realization I now see that there's a whole other message on this tablet."

"I have no idea what you're talking about, Professor. I can't even begin to grasp how you see what you say you see."

"You're not expected to, Falcon. That's my job. Now, may I ask for some private time to see if I can translate the text?"

"Sure thing, Professor."

~ ~ ~ ~ ~

Several hours passed without Hannibal saying a word or leaving his chair. He sat slumped over with the loupe to his eye, jotting down notes and trading time between the tablet and running his fingers over a map of the valley and its many mesas. He finally dropped his loupe onto the table and rubbed his eyes with both hands.

"Professor?" asked Falcon. "Are you okay?"

"Yes," replied Hannibal, still rubbing his eyes. "But I can't break it. I can't put the puzzle together. The language I understand. I know what the words are, but I don't know how to decode the message. I'm missing the context of it. I can try to think like the Naacal, but I'm not one of them. I'm missing the point. It seems to be an ancient story, but without understanding their culture, their views, their beliefs, the story is without coherence.

"In short, Falcon, it's kicked my ass. I need a drink. How about joining me? I could use some companionship and support."

"Sure, Professor. Maybe taking a break is the best thing you can do right now."

Hannibal rose from the table and went to the bar. "Shall we stick with our usual, Falcon?"

"Screwdrivers forever, Professor."

As Hannibal prepared the drinks, Falcon bent over the tablet and studied it. Hannibal went on. "There's no break, Falcon. I'm finished. I don't know what any of it means. The story on the face of it is of no consequence. In fact, it's not even very interesting. The underlying message — the real message, I believe — is incoherent at best. I have no idea what any of it means. It's a story out of their history, and unless you know their history the way they obviously knew it, the story means nothing. I'm finished. I'm defeated."

"Keep at it, Professor. You'll find the answer."

"It was your idea to quit a while ago," Hannibal reminded him.

"That was before you made the breakthrough about the puzzle within the puzzle."

Hannibal chuckled. "You're thinking like a true archaeologist, but one of the definitions of insanity is performing the same task over and over and expecting different results each time. I would be insane if I continued to work on this translation. I lack the essential knowledge of a civilization that ceased to exist over twenty-five thousand years ago. Without knowing who those people truly were, I'll never solve the puzzle. You'll have to tell Bernard that even I, the great Hannibal Storm, lie defeated amid the rubble of the effort."

"He won't like hearing that, Professor."

"I don't like having to admit defeat. But it seems we will both have to learn to deal with our disappointments, or we'll both go plumb mad. I for one do not wish such a fate to befall me."

Hannibal returned with Falcon's drink.

They clinked glasses and drank.

"I must say, Falcon, you have been anything but a thug. I appreciate that, and I have to admit that I've enjoyed your company. It's nice bouncing ideas off someone who isn't asking stupid questions every minute."

"I have an admission as well, Professor. You're much more than the bubbleheads I've had to babysit while working for Mister Bernard. And you're right about Professor Grendel. He's a complete moron."

"It seems you have good taste as well, Falcon. Here's to good taste and morons." They clinked glasses again and finished their drinks in one great swallow.

"Damn, that hit the spot. How about another?" asked Hannibal.

"Why not?"

Hannibal returned to the bar and mixed another round of drinks as Falcon returned to staring at the tablet. "What do you say, Professor? Would you mind taking one more look at it as a favor to me? Just to be fully certain?"

"As a favor to you, Falcon. Why not?"

Hannibal finished making the second round and poured the drinks into fresh glasses. He moved toward Falcon and handed him his drink. Then he sat down at the table and pointed to the tablet. "You see, Falcon, I can spot, I think, thirty different passages. But ordering them in a way that they tell a coherent story eludes me."

"I understand, Professor." Falcon chugged his drink completely and then settled down next to Hannibal.

"Can't you make rubbings of each individual passage and then just move them around on the table until you get the right set of them together, Professor? Until the story makes sense? You know, just by accident?"

"Mentally, I've tried to do just that. Do you understand mathematics, Falcon?"

"I'm afraid I'm not very good at math."

"Do you know what permutations are?"

"No."

"In brief, permutations measure the possible combinations within a group of numbers. In this case, with thirty passages put together in thirty possible configurations, the probability of putting them into the right order is approximately one in two point six to the thirty-second power. That's two point six with thirty-two zeroes after it. Do you understand how difficult it would be to do what you're suggesting by *accident*?"

"Approaching impossible, if I understand you correctly."

"You're right."

Hannibal took a sip from his glass and noticed that Falcon's glass was empty. "Another drink?"

"No, Professor. I'm feeling sleepy."

"That must be the result of the four sleeping pills I put in your drink. I didn't realize they'd take effect so fast."

"Sleeping pills?"

"Yes. I found them in your toiletry bag a few days ago. Zolpidem, I believe, is pretty effective and I've been waiting for the right time to use them."

Falcon's eyes began drooping heavily.

"Tell Bernard that I couldn't break the code, so I saw little reason to stick around."

Falcon tried to reach out to Hannibal, but it was too exhausting for the big man. His hand slumped to his side and his head landed on the table next to the tablet. His eyes closed. He was out.

"Rest well, Mister Falcon."

Hannibal went through the big man's pockets and found the keys to the door. He took Falcon's cell phone and stuffed it into his pocket and then put the stone tablet under his arm.

"Maybe I can't find any answers right now, but I'm sure as hell not leaving this here for Grendel to work with," he muttered.

He went to the door and unlocked it. The key cabinet on the wall next to the door held only one set of car keys — those for the Ford. He grabbed them and went out the door.

In the distance he saw tall mesas silhouetted against the clear night sky. He was still in the Monument Valley area, just as Bernard had said. He took a moment to get his bearings and figured he was somewhere north of the main valley. He glanced at the cell phone face. The time was 1:06 a.m. There was little reason or ability to search for Kirby and Traci. He wondered where he should go now. Going to the police was out of the question, he knew that much. But where? He was on the run with no place to go. Then his eyes brightened. His destination set itself into his mind.

CHAPTER 27

Falcon lifted his head off the table and picked up the landline phone. Wearing a big smile, he dialed and waited. A voice answered.

"He bought it hook, line, and sinker, sir. And I believe he cracked it. He said to tell you he didn't, but I think he did. He took the tablet with him, muttering something about not wanting Grendel to work with it. You were correct, sir. He thought the sugar capsules were the real thing; thought they knocked me out. ... Yes, sir, he took the Ford."

Falcon picked up a tracker unit and clicked it on. He smiled.

"Yes sir, I'm tracking him now. I have a clear, strong signal. ... I'll let you know, sir."

Falcon hung the phone up, smiled, and shook his head. "You're as predictable as they come, Professor, but I'm really going to miss you."

~ ~ ~ ~ ~

Hannibal stopped the car in front of a modern-looking home. He looked at Falcon's cell phone. It read 2:18 a.m.

He crawled out of the car and walked up the walkway to the house. Without hesitation, he rang the doorbell several times. He waited impatiently and then rang the bell again, persisting until he saw a light come on inside.

A large silhouette approached the door. A second later the door opened.

A tall Native American man stood in the doorway in pajama bottoms. He stared at Hannibal sleepily at first, but then his eyes opened wide in recognition.

"Hannibal? Hannibal! What the hell, dude!"

Hannibal rushed past him. "Close the door, Doug. I'm in trouble. You're in trouble. Hell, man, the whole world's in trouble."

Douglas Long Lance, Hannibal's roommate at UCLA, shut the door and watched as Hannibal paced nervously around his foyer.

"That's a great conversation starter, pal, but what the hell are you talking about?"

"Dougie, I need your help. I'm into something bad and I'm about to go out of my mind."

"I'm an attorney, Hannibal. Dealing with something bad is what I do for a living. What can I do for you?"

"Make a big frickin' pot of coffee and sit down. You are about to have your socks blown off."

Douglas glanced down at his bare feet.

Hannibal noticed. "See, I told ya. They're already blown off."

Douglas chuckled. "You're still very weird, Hannibal."

"Yeah, I'm hearing that a lot these days."

~ ~ ~ ~ ~

An hour later Douglas sat staring wide-eyed at Hannibal.

"That's about all I can tell you, Dougie, without dragging you deeper into this."

"That's enough, Hannibal!"

"Yeah, I know. I'm deep in it right now."

"Man, I don't know what to say. I never knew something like that was located anywhere around here. Hell, I never knew anything like that even existed."

"Well, all the wrong people do, I can assure you of that. Can you help me?"

"Sure ... I guess ... I don't know. I'm an attorney. I can represent you."

"That's not what I need, Doug."

"What do you need?"

Hannibal pulled Falcon's cell phone from his pocket and brought up the picture of the tablet. "Do you see this?"

"Of course."

"I have it right here. The location of the firestone. It's right here. I haven't told anyone about it except you. Now I need to find it. I need to go and locate it for real."

"Where is it?"

"I only have directions, I don't have a map. But the directions say there's an entrance to a vast underground cavern under the valley. The entrance, I believe, is on top of Eagle Mesa."

"Well, I guess we can hire a chopper that'll put us up on the mesa."

"No, Doug! A chopper will only attract attention."

"Well, the only other way up there is to climb. Are you prepared to do that?"

"I haven't rock climbed since we were in college."

"I still climb, Hannibal. Once a month I pick a mesa and climb it. I've got all the equipment."

"When can we start?"

"I'll get dressed and we can go now. You'll need some climbing gear and clothes. I've got some that should fit you."

"Thanks, buddy. I was hoping I could count on you."

"Forever, Hannibal. You should already know that."

"We have to stop and talk to Black Owl first."

"It's 3:30 in the morning, Hannibal."

"It can't be helped. I must speak with him."

"Okay," Douglas said with a shrug. "If you say so."

~ ~ ~ ~ ~

Douglas's Escalade stopped in front of the holy man's small hogan. A light inside immediately clicked on.

"He's awake, Doug."

"Looks that way."

Hannibal and Douglas climbed out of the car and walked toward the hogan's entrance. The door opened.

"Black Owl, I need your help."

"You are in great danger, Hannibal."

"I don't doubt that."

"It is good to see you, Black Owl," said Douglas.

" *Yá'át'ééh abíní, shik'is.*" ["Good morning, my friend."]

They stepped inside the hogan.

"I have made a special tea for you, Hannibal. It will help you to complete your quest."

"Then you already know I've begun my search for the firestone?"

"I know this also. The ancient ones have told me this. But tell me of your true search."

~ ~ ~ ~ ~

An hour later Hannibal finished retelling the story, as much of it as he could.

"So now, Black Owl, I have no choice. Traci and Kirby are depending on me, the Navajo are depending on me, the whole world is depending on me to do what's right."

"It is a hard task for you. But you are capable of accomplishing this."

"I wish I could say that, Black Owl. I wish I could walk in the certainty of being the kind of man you think me to be."

"Hannibal, hear my words and understand. That which you seek, seeks you also."

"What does that mean? I mean truly, what does that mean?"

"If you seek goodness, then the force of goodness will seek to do its work through you. If you seek evil, then it is the force of evil which will seek to do its work through you. You alone must decide which force will be allowed to work through you to its end."

"Fine words, my friend, honestly spoken, but they seem hollow at the moment and only add to my burden."

"To fly upon the wings of destiny, you must make hard choices. To fall upon the spires of fate, you need do nothing at all."

"Then I suppose I must choose to make a friend of such a decision, or else suffer the painful ills of fate."

"It has been my experience that most friends are but for a season only. Very well do I remember the friends of my spring who became the ghosts of my autumn."

"I'm afraid I can say that also, but if not as a friend, then how shall I greet my decision? Shall I gather together all that I know and let such knowledge decide?"

"Be careful what you choose to accumulate."

"What do you mean?"

"Knowledge gained is wisdom won. But wisdom alone cannot decide what you are to do. Your actions taken or refused based upon that wisdom will determine whether it is your destiny or your fate that you encounter."

"Well, you know I would rather be prepared and enjoy destiny than be unprepared and suffer fate. But if I don't find the firestone, someone else might. If I find it, I can make it so it will never be used again."

"If you do this thing and you succeed, then that is how the memory of you shall be written in the book of life by the Great Hand."

"A man once wrote that stories are merely the recording of life. But what I want to know, Black Owl, is who will ever know that what I did saved the world if I do what is right? For that matter, will there even be a page created for me in the book of life?"

"Together we *are* the book of life, with each of us a single page. Absent any page, we dare not call ourselves complete."

"Again, Black Owl, well-spoken words, but what if my page is not missing but written falsely? How will the book of life record the goodness I sought if my deeds are not known? I have always wanted my page to be written boldly. I wanted the ink to be bright. I wanted the words to say that I was a good man, that I strived to do good with the blessings given to me. I've always tried to walk in the brightness of certainty and not in the shadow of doubt. But if I choose to do what is right, I will surely be ridiculed and forgotten, or worse, ridiculed and remembered. There will be no recording of my sacrifice; there will be no songs sung of my good deed."

Hannibal chuckled and then added, "I know there has to be wisdom hidden in there somewhere, but it escapes me at present."

Black Owl smiled. "Wisdom in obscurity is wisdom lost."

Then he grew quiet and sat in silence for several moments before lifting his eyes and looking deeply into Hannibal's. "A great question often arises in the hearts of men, as it has arisen in mine also at times. Will I choose my destiny or fall to fate? Will I live in the brightness of great deeds or perish in the blackness of irrelevancy? So tell me, my friend. What shall it be for you?"

"I wish I could say. I don't know what to do." He looked at Douglas. "What do *you* think?"

"Hannibal, you're gonna do what you're gonna do. You don't need my two cents in the mix, mucking it up."

"What if I do?"

"Then you're worse off for it. What the hell do I know about your destiny or your fate? For that matter, buddy, what do I know about anything? You were always the one who knew exactly where you were going, knew precisely what you would do with your life. I just followed along because it was always interesting being around you. I'm not the thinker you are."

"I keep hearing the words of Grendel in my head. He's right. I'm not a showman. I'm not ever going to be the successful man he is. I'll be reading my written page in the book of life and it'll be nothing more than a sidebar to all the archaeologists who followed their hearts and made the discoveries."

Black Owl picked up a handful of dirt from his floor and tossed it at Hannibal, striking him in the chest.

"You need to come back down upon the earth, Hannibal Storm. Hear me. Do not listen to the whispered lies of men. Walk in your own truth. Write your own page into the book. All things done are written into the book of life by the Great Hand.

All things done cheaply and all things done at great expense are written down equally."

"I'm not afraid to be unknown. I'm afraid to be insignificant," said Hannibal.

"Young one, there is no shame in being insignificant. There is, however, great shame in knowing that you could have made a difference and chose not to get involved."

"You're right, of course, Black Owl. Your counsel has always been wise. That's why I came to see you before beginning my quest. I need your blessing."

"Look, Hannibal," said Douglas, "I've got the climbing equipment. Let's go find your damn firestone so you can destroy it, because we both know that's what you're gonna choose to do."

Hannibal glanced at Black Owl, silently seeking his approval. Black Owl nodded. "Go and destroy this thing before it destroys you."

Hannibal nodded in agreement.

CHAPTER 28

Standing at the base of the northern side of Eagle Mesa, Hannibal arched his back and stared up at the red sandstone walls towering some five hundred feet above him, now black and smooth against the star-filled pre-dawn sky.

Hannibal clicked on his helmet lamp. "Tell me again, Dougie. What the hell am I doing this for?"

"Following that *destiny* thing you talked about." Douglas made final adjustments to his climbing equipment and turned on his own helmet lamp. "Keep your mind on climbing, though, or you're gonna end up doing that *fall to your fate* thing. Got it?"

"Got it. It's gonna be a long climb, Doug."

"I expect it would be a short fall, though."

"Did you really have to say that? Was that really necessary?"

"Just keepin' it truthful."

"Do me a favor, Doug. Lie to me now and then, okay?"

"We can turn back right now, pal."

"No, we gotta get up there. The entrance is up there. I feel it. So, like it or not, that's where I've gotta be."

"Okay, but if you haven't done this kind of climbing since college, what makes you think you can make it? Climbing this thing in *daylight* is dangerous enough; climbing it in the dark is just plain stupid. It'll be a miracle if I can negotiate this wall without killing myself. Tell me again why *I'm* doing this."

"You're my friend?"

"Damn. ... So, how do you wanna start this?"

"Carefully, I should think. Very carefully."

"I mean, who first? Me or you?"

"You! You're leading. Absolutely, you."

"Well, I guess we should get started, then."

"Hey, Dougie? Are we being dumb asses about this?"

"Of course we are, Hannibal. Only dumb asses would be attempting this climb in the dark."

"Okay. I just wanted to be sure I wasn't deluding myself with lofty thoughts of being courageous. Let's go."

"Give it no more thought. We're *definitely* acting like idiots. Are the packs tied off?"

"Yep."

"Then up we go."

Douglas lifted himself onto the first foothold on the cliff face and reached up until he found the first handhold.

Hannibal chuckled as he watched Douglas climb. "We could wait until sunrise, Doug, but then we might as well just go ahead and announce our intentions to the world."

"Is that really such a bad thing?" Douglas found another handhold to pull himself up on. "I mean, won't people see us up on top anyway during the day?"

"Now that you mention it, I guess they will." Hannibal took hold of a stone projection and lifted himself off the ground.

"Well, people are always climbing rocks out here. It shouldn't be a shock, I think."

"You can bet if Bernard finds out where we are, he'll have snipers peeping at us." Hannibal found another projection and pulled himself upward farther onto the cliff face.

"Was *that* really necessary to say? Damn, Hannibal."

"Relax. We're over five miles from the nearest set of rocks a sniper could set up on. All they'll be able to do is watch us."

"I don't know how I feel about that; somebody spying on me through crosshairs. Has anyone ever told you that you have a nasty way about you sometimes?" Douglas continued to hoist himself up.

"As a matter of fact, yes. You used to tell me that quite often," answered Hannibal, staying close to Douglas.

"You're right. I did. What the hell is wrong with *me*?"

"You're my friend."

"Oh, yeah. That defect again."

Douglas was up a good fifty feet now, with Hannibal maintaining an interval of ten to twelve feet. Hannibal had the benefit of climbing on the rope that was secured by the camming devices Douglas had fixed in the small crevices on the wall. Douglas was doing the real climbing and he was an excellent climber. Hannibal felt safe and secure, which gave him the impetus to keep things light.

"Would you mind picking up the pace some, Doug?"

"Why's that?"

"I had about four beers at your house."

"Good thing I'm above you, then."

Hannibal snickered.

~ ~ ~ ~ ~

Bernard approached Falcon, who was lying on his belly staring through a night vision scope. They had set up an observation post on the top of a high rock formation near Gouldings RV Park to appear unassuming to anyone who might spot them, highly unlikely given that they were so high above the park. But people had been known to climb along the ridge to get into a nice position for sunrise. So to anyone who might be curious, they wanted to look like tourists just getting a better view of the majesty of the valley in the coming dawn.

"Good morning, Mister Falcon."

"Good morning, sir. You're up early. It's only five thirty."

"Wanted to get a good start on my day. You've certainly picked the perfect spot, Mister Falcon. You can see forever up here. The campers below won't be any the wiser even if we are spotted. And speaking of spotted, can you still see them?"

"No, sir. While I was on the phone with you, they went around to the north side of the mesa and out of view."

"How long ago was that?"

"Well over thirty minutes."

"And you haven't seen them since?"

"That's correct, sir."

"Are you certain they're still at the mesa?"

"Nothing in the scope. I'm using this to track them now."

Falcon picked up his tracker and flipped it on. An audible warble and a blinking light assured him of Hannibal's continued presence on the north side of Eagle Mesa.

"He's there. At least that's what my cell phone tells me."

"I've got to hand it to you, Mister Falcon. A true stroke of brilliance, bugging your own phone."

"Thank you, sir, but *you* knew he would take it."

"Thanks to his predictable nature."

"Yes, sir."

"You really think the professor cracked the code, Mister Falcon?"

"Yes, I do. Why else would he be out in the valley at this time of morning, sir, except to hunt down the clues he discovered? Nothing else makes any sense."

"What does Eagle Mesa have to do with the firestone, I wonder."

"I obviously can't say, sir, but he seemed to be studying all the mesas pretty intently, Eagle Mesa more than any other. It must mean something. And I did observe them carrying climbing equipment to the car from Douglas Long Lance's house."

"I've had dealings with that lawyer before. Can't say that I liked it much. He's too honest. So you think they'll attempt to climb that mesa?"

"In truth, sir, I think they've already started."

~ ~ ~ ~ ~

"Damn!" said Hannibal, staring between his legs down the cliff face. "I can't see the ground anymore. We've gotta be up a couple hundred feet by now, maybe more."

"Stop looking for the ground. It's down there, trust me. You're making me nervous. Besides, it should start getting light soon. It's gotta be nearly six o'clock by now."

"We're doing great, Doug. Sure glad you brought all those camming devices."

"I just hope we don't run out of them before we get to the top."

"Not a problem. I've got plenty, but I'm hoping we run out of cliff face first," Hannibal said with a chuckle.

"Is everything a joke to you?"

"Pretty much, I guess. I mean, come on, Dougie, think on this, buddy. We're in our mid-forties, we're hanging on the face of a five-hundred-foot cliff trying to get to the top of the mesa to look for the entrance to an underground cavern where a giant crystal that destroyed an entire civilization twenty-five thousand years ago may be hidden. Not to mention the fact that we could plunge to our deaths at any moment. Now tell me, how is this not hilarious?"

"You have a real strange sense of humor, Hannibal."

"At least I still have a sense of humor."

"Are you sure the entrance is up there?"

"I'm not sure of anything, but that's what the puzzle indicated."

"I still say a chopper would have been easier."

"We've already had that discussion."

"I know, I know. I still think it would've been better, though."

"Come on, Doug. We needed a new adventure anyway."

"The one I had in mind includes swimming pools and drinks with little umbrellas."

"That comes later."

~ ~ ~ ~ ~

Bernard opened his eyes from his nap and stared up at the new morning sky. He yawned. "Well, have you seen anything of our daring duo, Mister Falcon?"

"Nothing yet, sir. Did you have a nice nap?"

"I did, thank you. Would you by chance have any coffee?"

"In the pack, sir."

As Bernard went through Falcon's backpack he noticed Falcon's tracking device lying silently next to it. "When was the last time you looked for their signal?"

"Just minutes ago."

"And?"

"Signal still strong and steady, sir. They're definitely on the mesa wall."

"Unless he dropped your cell phone."

"No, sir. The elevation is changing. They are most definitely climbing the mesa. And considering the time they probably started, they must be getting near the top by now. We should see them soon, I think."

"Let's hope you're correct, Mister Falcon," said Bernard, sipping his coffee.

~ ~ ~ ~ ~

Three hours had passed from when they began to climb. The top was now in sight.

Mother Nature had performed her work well over the millennia; the fractures in the rock were perfect for the type of camming devices Hannibal and Douglas carried. Hannibal continued climbing behind Douglas, aided by pulleys and ascenders, and every so often he would stop climbing and haul up both heavy packs next to him and tie them off.

"I'm trusting you, Doug. I just wanted to remind you of that fact. I'm counting on you placing those camming devices just right."

"You're telling me that *now*?"

"I'm just sayin'."

"You're getting scared? Is that what you're saying? What the hell took you so long?"

"I'm not scared. I'm just sayin' keep doing things right. Now that it's light, I can see the ground crystal clear. Christ, this a sheer face! If we fell now, we wouldn't hit anything till the bottom."

"Will you quit bitchin'? Just keep doing what you're doing, Hannibal. We're doing fine."

"We're hanging nearly five hundred feet up on a sheer rock face! I've got a right to bitch."

"What happened to the hilarious part of this, Hannibal?"

"I'm laughing, I'm laughing. It's an inside kinda laugh right now, but I'm laughing."

~ ~ ~ ~ ~

Twenty minutes later, Douglas was sitting comfortably on top of Eagle Mesa watching the sunrise as Hannibal walked the mesa top staring down at the rock surface.

He stopped and stared out over the valley as sunlight crawled across the landscape. He chuckled. "You know, Dougie, from here I think I can see the freckles on God's face."

~ ~ ~ ~ ~

"Well, I'll be!"

"I can't believe it myself, sir," replied Falcon, drawing his eye back from the high-powered scope. "They made it. That had to be some climb."

"Admire them later, Mister Falcon. I want to know what they're doing up there."

"Right now, sir, they're just standing there staring out over the valley. Sir, what if they just climbed the mesa to climb the mesa? Hannibal *did* say he couldn't translate the text. Could he have been telling the truth?"

"Don't be gullible, Mister Falcon. It makes me look silly for having hired you, and I don't like looking silly. They're up there for a good reason. You keep watching them. If anything unusual happens, you let me know. I can have a chopper up there within minutes."

"That will surely attract a crowd, sir."

"Yes, it surely will. But I don't care."

"The firestone can't be up there. Not on top of the mesa, sir."

"I hired you to track the professor, Mister Falcon, not give me your opinions about the firestone. Keep me informed. I've got some arrangements to make just in case our two explorers do find something." He stood up and walked away.

"Roger that, sir."

~ ~ ~ ~ ~

"Let's get looking around, Doug. If the entrance is up here, it won't jump up and introduce itself."

"Hannibal, we could be standing on top of it right now and I wouldn't know it. What are we looking for?"

"Look for a capstone, Doug. Big or small, it should look a bit out of place, I would think."

"You mean like us standing up here right now?"

"Funny."

"How do you think they got the firestone all the way up here?"

"Levitation, I suspect, or possibly they used their airships to get it up here."

"It's hard to believe, but okay. If you say so."

They continued walking slowly over the top of the mesa, looking for the slightest stone out of place. The windswept rock, however, was smooth, the years of erosion having erased any defect in the stone that might have once existed.

Two more hours passed and neither man could see anything that could be even remotely construed as an entrance to the interior of the mesa. As far as Douglas was concerned, there was no entrance and Hannibal had been wrong about the whole thing. He finally sat down and raised his arms in mock surrender.

"Look at this mesa, Hannibal. There's no sign of an entrance. We've been from one end to the other. I'm ready to call it a day. How about it?"

"Get on your feet and keep looking. It has to be here."

"Let's look at it differently, Hannibal. If you were the Naacal, where would *you* put a hatch?"

"I don't really know, but remember how many centuries the wind has swept over this mesa top. It could have easily worn down any projections."

"How big do you think it would be?"

"I have no idea. I would expect it to be at least two feet wide, but hell, it could be tens of feet wide for all I know. The text doesn't say."

"What if we find the hatch and it's too thick to break through?"

"You're just a continuous ray of sunshine, Doug."

"Hey, I came up here with you. Don't rain on my rainy parade."

Hannibal chuckled.

"If you came up here thinking this was going to be easy … well, it's not. Look, I have no idea what the entrance will look like. Hell, knowing the Naacal, they might just as easily have lifted off the entire top of the mesa and reset it."

Douglas chuckled and shook his head.

"What? You think shearing off a mesa top was beyond their capabilities?"

Douglas shrugged his shoulders. "I don't have any idea, Hannibal."

"I sure don't think so. For all I know, they could have hollowed out the entire mesa. We gotta keep walking and looking, Doug. That's all we can do. If the entrance is here, we might find it. If we quit, we're guaranteed *not* to find it. And the others who might eventually be following us might not quit as easily. I don't want to take that chance."

"I'm not saying that we stop, but I've been banging on rock with this rock hammer for over two hours trying to find a hatch. There ain't no stinkin' entrance. There ain't no stinkin' hatch. *There ain't no stinkin' capstone, Hannibal.*"

"It's here, Doug. The text says it's here. And I feel it in my bones. I know it's here somewhere."

"Why didn't they record the entrance on the stone tablet?"

"What better way to hide something so dangerous than not record its exact whereabouts? The tablet indicated that a capstone was built by their craftsmen. It supposedly covers the spot where the firestone was installed after it was moved from the Naacal's island nation."

"I still wonder why they simply hid the records of the firestone's existence instead of destroying them."

"Damn good question, Doug. I've been wrestling with that one myself. I wish I had an answer for it."

Douglas picked up his rock hammer and tapped lightly against the stone mesa as he continued his reasoning. "Doesn't make sense to me. Why here in Monument Valley? We don't have any caves or underground grottos that I'm aware of. Everything around us at the base layers is bedrock — solid rock. Where the hell could they put it but inside a mesa? And if so, why Eagle Mesa? Why not some obscure mesa? Hell, Hannibal, there are hundreds of other mesas around here far out of the public eye. Why here?"

"I can't answer that either, Doug. Their reasoning remains a mystery."

"*It just doesn't make any sense!*" Douglas shouted, slamming his hammer down onto the mesa.

The hard strike resonated. Both heard it distinctly.

"Doug! Did you hear that?"

"I did!"

He slammed his hammer down several more times and each strike brought another reverberating return.

"Christ, Hannibal. I think I'm sitting on the hatch."

"I agree. Look for any congruous lines in the stone."

Both got down on their hands and knees and searched meticulously for any indication of hatch lines they might have overlooked before. Hannibal scratched at the surface with the pick blade of the rock hammer, beginning where Douglas had sat and moving in a straight line away from that point.

"Do what I'm doing, Doug. Pick a point, any point, and scratch a straight line outward with the pick point. If there is a hatch line, the pick point will find it."

Douglas did as instructed and slowly scraped the pick point into the soft red sandstone, but it was Hannibal who made the first find.

"Here, Doug! I found something. It looks like a cemented crack, but it has length and I believe it has symmetry to it as well."

Douglas joined Hannibal and both scratched into the joint and then moved away from each other.

Douglas came to a turn in the line first.

"It looks like it could be a turn in a hexagon, Hannibal! A damn big hexagon."

"Sure looks that way."

"Hannibal! Do you think this would fit the firestone?"

"If it does, that makes the firestone frickin' huge."

"It's getting pretty light. Someone's bound to see us up here."

"We're tourists enjoying a climb. Keep going."

CHAPTER 29

Traci Jefferson sat very still in a chair, her mind calmly calculating, scheming, planning. Kirby Hansen was doing the same as he paced back and forth across the room.

Traci finally looked up at Kirby, smiling. "Is this the new Kirby? I've never seen you pace before."

"I've never felt so helpless or useless before. Hannibal is out there by himself. I have to do something. I've been thinking."

"So have I. I've got a plan."

"So have I."

They both smiled. "You first," said Kirby.

~ ~ ~ ~ ~

Bernard crawled up alongside Falcon.

"Welcome back, sir."

"What have they been up to?"

"They had been scratching and hammering at the summit for over two hours before they moved beyond the crest to the northern side of the mesa. I've lost sight of them."

"How long has it been since you saw them last?"

"Thirty to forty minutes now. I'm sure they're still there, though. I can see their climbing gear."

"Excellent, but I've got to get eyes on them. I've got to know what they're doing up there."

"I know it's your party, sir, but it'll be getting mighty hot up there soon, if it isn't already. They'll have to leave the summit soon, and they'll have to use the climbing gear to get down. I suggest we just wait them out. If they spot anyone observing them, they might just cut and run, sir. The firestone is our objective. Leave them thinking that they're safe and unobserved, and maybe they'll be less likely to get scared and run. I'm confident they'll lead us to the firestone if we don't rabbit them."

"Very well, Mister Falcon. I most certainly don't want Hannibal hightailing it with what he must know. We'll do it your way for now. Besides, you're right. Where can they possibly go?"

~ ~ ~ ~ ~

Within twenty minutes Hannibal and Douglas together had exposed the joint sufficiently to see that they had indeed discovered the capstone. It was an immense hexagon, measuring fully twenty feet across.

Both men stopped scratching and stood in awe at what they had uncovered.

"Jesus, Hannibal, will you look at that."

"We did it, Doug. This is it."

"How the hell do we get it open?"

"Yeah, that. I'm working on it."

"Even after all these years of weathering it still could be feet thick, Hannibal. We're probably gonna need drills and dynamite."

Hannibal chuckled. "*That* would put on quite a show. A bit more than just a typical day here, wouldn't you say?"

"Sure would. And of course we'd be arrested immediately. And everyone in the world would soon know that there's something unique going on up here." Douglas smirked. "I just took the joy right out of it, didn't I?"

"You sure did, pal."

"If we can't blow it open, Hannibal, how the hell are we going to get it open?"

"Time to go to the Naacal for the answer."

Hannibal moved up over the crest and toward his climbing gear. He opened his backpack and withdrew the stone tablet he'd taken from Bernard, and then dropped back over the crest.

~ ~ ~ ~ ~

"Got something, sir."

"What is it, Mr. Falcon?"

"Hannibal appeared again, pulled the tablet from his backpack, and disappeared back over the crest."

"Now we're getting somewhere." Bernard brought his binoculars up to his eyes. "Come on, Professor. Give up your little secret. What are you doing up there?"

"Just guessing here, sir, but I think he must have found some markings and is trying to interpret them. Maybe the markings describe where the firestone is."

"Guessing isn't cutting it, Mister Falcon."

"No, sir."

"There is definitely something up there that brought him all the way up a sheer cliff, and it is not insignificant."

"Agreed, but what?"

"If I had that answer, Mister Falcon, I'd have a chopper up there right now."

~ ~ ~ ~ ~

Hannibal sat reading the tablet.

"Why did you cart that thing up here, Hannibal? Wouldn't a photo of it be just as good? That thing must weigh a ton."

"You're right, but a photo might not have been as clean to look at. To the Naacal, details mattered. If I can just interpret this puzzle a bit more, it might give us the answer to getting inside."

~ ~ ~ ~ ~

Kirby held the pole of the standing light firmly by one end as he placed the other between the bars on the window. He pulled and the bars bent.

"Kirby, when you said your plan was better, I didn't think it would include scaling down the side of this building."

"Traci, our Hannibal would say, you are of little faith." Kirby smiled and then winced as he applied more pressure to the bars. The bars opened wide enough for him to slip through. He laid the pole down gently.

"There, that should be enough."

"So, how do we get to the ground? Without falling, that is."

"You just have to know every little detail, don't you?" Kirby grinned.

"It would be nice."

"Okay, Trace, here's what we do."

~~~~~

Douglas lay on the mesa playing with a chunk of broken rock as Hannibal sat next to him, his eyes glued to the tablet. Douglas finally raised his eyes to Hannibal.

"I'm not criticizing you, Hannibal, but it might have been helpful if you had worked all this *opening the rock cover* thing out before we climbed all the way up here. You know what I mean? It's hot as hell and we're running short of water. You've been staring at that rock for over an hour now."

"You're starting to sound like Traci."

"I'll take that as a compliment."

"The answer is here, Doug. I'm looking at it."

Hannibal continued to stare for several more minutes before he finally looked up in frustration. "Just open the hell up! *Shee-it!*"

There was slight shift in the cover. It wasn't much, but both men felt it.

"What was *that*, Hannibal?! What just happened?"

Hannibal stared at the capstone and then at the tablet and then back at the capstone. "Look! The joint has cracked open!"

Douglas sat up and ran his hand over the nearest section of joint. "It sure has. Something happened."

"It's sound, Doug. Sound, audible frequencies, musical notes, tones. Something like that opens the capstone. Certain sounds or tones, in some kind of sequence, I bet ... Wait! I've got it! Now I remember. In the vault in Australia I found some scrolls with unusual symbols on them that I came to understand were musical notes. I see those same symbols here. I couldn't understand before. I thought they were the notes of some ceremonial song, but they're a code. It's laid out right in front of me — the notes I need to open the capstone. Be real quiet, Doug. Let me read for a moment."

Hannibal read the tablet for several more minutes and then looked up at Douglas. "Ready?"

Douglas nodded.

"*Shee no gul nik si go shee it tu guy no.*"

Nothing happened.

Hannibal looked at the tablet again. "Ah, damn. Wrong line."

Douglas chuckled.

"*Shee gul nik go nak go soon may gee shee it.*"

The instant rumble made both men jump back.

"Something's happening, Hannibal!"

"I know that, Doug! It's opening!"

"I can see that."

The capstone began descending straight down. After dropping some six feet, it moved to their right, eventually disappearing under the thick rim of red rock to reveal a decidedly deep hole.

"Hannibal, you did it! You're a frickin' genius! You the MAN!"

They high-fived one another and then stepped forward and peered down into the blackness.

"Does the tablet say how far down the shaft goes?"

Hannibal read. "Not exactly."

"Well, does it say how we get down there?"

"I don't know."

With the capstone gone, they saw that the mesa was a hollow shaft, as if someone had used a giant drill bit to make the hole.

"That's a big hole, Hannibal! What are we gonna do? I can't fly and I ain't jumping into *that.*"

"I told you, I don't know."

Hannibal read some more. "Ah, I missed it. More notes."

"Well, start singing, maestro."

"*Go chee mak soon get my get soo long.*"

An instant later a short set of stone stairs slid smoothly out from the rock wall. Douglas peered down at them.

"Ah, hey, buddy, there's only about twelve steps there. I think we're a little short. Do you see that big gap in the stairway?"

"Yeah, yeah. Just a minute." Hannibal began reading again.

"Damn!" said Douglas. "Maybe you'll have to sing all the way down."

"No, I got it. Let's get our packs. We're going to need them."

"It looks like it's gonna be a long walk down."

"You could always jump, Dougie. I'm sure it'd be quicker. Of course it would include some flying, screaming, and crashing, too."

"You're a funny guy, Hannibal. A little mean-spirited at times, but funny."

"Just get your pack and follow me."

"I will so long as it doesn't include any jumping, flying, screaming, or crashing."

~ ~ ~ ~ ~

"Sir, we have movement."

Bernard rolled over and put his binoculars to his eyes. He watched as Hannibal and Douglas picked up their backpacks and strapped them securely to their backs.

"Are they getting ready to climb back down?"

"It certainly looks that way, sir."

They watched intently as both climbers disappeared back over the crest.

"Damnit," said Bernard. "I can't do this anymore."

He pulled his cell phone from his pocket and dialed. A voice answered.

"Get the chopper ready. We're on our way."

He clicked off the call. "Let's get going, Mister Falcon. We're done here. It's time to take this little game to the next level."

~ ~ ~ ~ ~

A knock on the door got Traci's attention. She turned away from the window just as the door opened and a guard entered the room, carrying a large tray with food and drinks on it. Two other guards followed him. They carried short automatic rifles.

"Oh, my!" Traci said, startled.

The first guard immediately noticed the window bars pried apart. He dropped the tray to the floor, shattering glasses and launching food rockets through the air. The other two dashed to the window to look for Kirby.

The closet door opened and a blow to the side of the first guard's head with the light pole sent him tumbling to the floor unconscious. Kirby stepped out and swung the pole toward the head of the next-nearest guard. Another clean shot and another body hit the floor.

Before the third guard could react, Traci sent a crushing kick to his right knee. His face contorted and he writhed in pain. He didn't feel it long, though, for a second later Traci's other foot snapped up and into his chin, sending his eyes rolling up into his forehead and his unconscious body dropping to the floor with a thud. It was over just like that.

"Not a bad plan, Kirby. I gotta give you that one." Traci bent over and picked up one of the rifles.

"Thanks, Trace."

Kirby picked up the other rifle and checked the chamber, making sure a round was ready to fire.

She chambered a round with a swift slap of the charging bolt. "You're sure there were only three guards?"

"I haven't seen any others. You?"

"Not that I can recall. So, what do we do now, Kirby?"

"Hannibal was keen on Eagle Mesa. He mentioned it several times before we got separated. I guess we start there after I call in the troops."

"No troops, Kirby. No one else, please."

"It's protocol, Traci. You know that."

"Damn protocol. Hannibal wouldn't want it."

Kirby thought for a moment. "Ah, Traci, we shouldn't do it that way. Bad stuff can happen quickly in this game. You know that."

"I understand, but it's what Hannibal would do."

"I hate it when you're right."

~ ~ ~ ~ ~

"So, you gonna start singing, or what?" asked Douglas. "We don't have all day."

"You're sounding more and more like Traci every minute."

"I wish she was here. She would insist that you have a better plan than just winging it."

"You just have no faith in me at all, do you?"

"I've got faith, Hannibal. It's just that we're gonna need more than twelve steps to get down to the rest of the stairway. So how about you get your voice on and fill in the gap?"

"I need to finish reading this tablet first."

Hannibal read for several minutes, shaking his head from time to time and occasionally nodding.

"Gonna tell me what's going on?"

"No. Be quiet."

Hannibal read some more and then glanced up at Douglas.

"Down we go," he announced and started down the stairs.

"Where? Go where? We aren't jumping, are we? I mean there's none of this 'leap of faith' crap involved here, is there? Because I don't know if I've got that kind of faith, pal."

Hannibal didn't answer.

"A water slide! Hell, I'd love a water slide, Hannibal."

"No water, Doug."

"Details, details."

Hannibal reached the last step. From there it was a drop into blackness. He pulled out his flashlight and flicked it on.

"Get out your flashlight, Douglas. It's about to get really dark."

"Hannibal? Tell me what's going on, please. And don't you even *think* about jumping."

"Hang on to something, just in case."

"Just in case what? Come on, Hannibal. Don't do this to me!"

Hannibal sang out another group of notes. A second later the capstone moved out and back up into place. At the same time another set of stairs opened out of the wall, completing an in-line section of the steep staircase.

Once the capstone closed, the only light they had to navigate by was from their flashlights and helmet lamps.

"Oh, Hannibal! Oh, this isn't good." Douglas reached out his left hand to touch the wall and his hand went into a small trough with something thick and gooey in it.

"What is this sticky stuff?"

"Keep your hand away from it."

"Why? What is it? What is it, Hannibal? What did I just touch? Is it poisonous?"

"Will you just wait a second? It's not poisonous. Geez."

"Well, then, what the hell is it?"

"Hold your horses, Tonto!"

"That ain't funny. And you're *not* the Lone Ranger."

Hannibal reached into a side pocket of his pack and withdrew a small lighter. He flicked the flame into existence and touched it to the trough. The material lit immediately and scooted down the trough that spiraled toward the bottom of the carved-out mesa walls.

Within seconds the flames grew brighter, revealing a staircase descending as far as they could see.

Douglas smiled. "Now that's what I'm talkin' about."

"Happy now?"

"I am. Yes, I am. Very pleased. I like that tablet. Keep reading, but holy cow, it's a long way down."

"Conserve your batteries, Doug. Turn off your lights, but be careful. One small trip and we'll arrive at the bottom doing that flying, screaming, crashing thing."

~ ~ ~ ~ ~

Bernard stepped into the chopper. The groundsman shut the door and the aircraft immediately lifted off, rising quickly. Bernard placed the headset over his ears and moved the microphone into place.

"Go out north first, keeping away from Eagle Mesa."

"Yes, sir," replied the pilot.

"I just lost their signal, sir," announced Falcon.

"Just like that?"

"Just like that, sir. It was there and then it was gone."

"Could he have fallen?"

"I suppose it's possible and the phone shattered."

"Oh, I hope not, Mister Falcon. I hope not."

"Yes, sir. Let's hope not."

The chopper worked its way directly north from the airfield near the Gouldings Resort Hotel. It passed Eagle Mesa and then made a slow turn back toward it.

Falcon raised his binoculars to his face. Bernard did the same.

Neither of them spotted the climbers on the wall. There was nothing. Not even their ropes. Bernard then searched the top of the mesa, but saw no sign of them there either.

"I don't get it, Mister Falcon. Where the hell are they?"

"I don't see them either, sir."

"Pilot, fly over the top of the mesa, please."

The pilot nodded.

By the time the aircraft reached the mesa, they were staring down at the top without needing binoculars. There was no sign of either man.

Down below was Douglas's Escalade, parked near the base of the mesa.

"Okay, Mister Falcon, I'm stumped. Any thoughts?"

"None, sir. I don't know what to say."

"Well, they can't just disappear."

"True enough, sir."

Bernard's phone rang. He answered and listened in silence for a moment and then replied, "Thank you, Mister Thompson." He clicked the phone off.

"This day is not getting any better for me. Mister Hansen and Miss Jefferson have made their escape."

"Are we shut down, sir?"

"Of course not. Why would you ask that? Do I give the appearance of a man who quits anything?"

"No, sir. I'm sorry. I didn't mean —"

"Enough. Let me think for a moment."

After a minute or two Bernard pressed his microphone button and continued. "It's possible that Mister Hansen has already called in his associates by now. If so, it won't be long before we have CIA choppers surrounding us. But I'm going to gamble that he didn't. This is more personal for him now, and my gut tells me he's keeping mum for the time being. We'll keep searching." Then to his pilot, "Make a sweep completely around the mesa, please."

"Will do, sir."

"Where are you, Professor?" Bernard asked under his breath.

~~~~~

Hannibal and Douglas continued their descent with ease. Although steep, the stairs were comfortably wide and easy to negotiate.

"Look at the walls, Hannibal. Look how smooth they are. How did they do this?"

"With a technology we don't have today, that's for sure."

Douglas ran his hand across the surface. "Touch it, Hannibal. It's like glass."

Hannibal laid his hand against it. "Sure is. It looks like the pores were sealed at the time the mesa was carved out. It's almost like it was carved by something that melted the stone and sealed the pores in the process."

"These stairs aren't too bad."

"Not too bad at all, Dougie."

Hannibal stepped on a stair and there was a slight rumble. They stopped and moved against the wall for support. They were down about a hundred feet and the sound they heard was the upper portion of the stairway moving back into the mesa wall.

"A built-in security system, it seems," said Hannibal.

"Damn smart people."

"I'll say."

"Hannibal? Do you think the firestone is here?"

"It's seeming more and more like the perfect place for it."

"Yeah. Who'd ever think it would be hidden inside a freakin' carved-out mesa?"

"The tablet says they built the caverns below for the sake of a room they called 'the vault.'"

"The vault? I wonder if that means what I think it means."

"We'll find out, I guess — if it still exists."

~ ~ ~ ~ ~

Almost fifteen minutes later, they came across some carvings in the wall.

"Wow! Hey, Hannibal, will you look at these."

"Amazing."

"Can you read them?"

"Yes. They're depth callouts. This one says we're five hundred feet from the bottom. Of course the measurements are in cubits, but that's the conversion."

Douglas ran his fingers over the engraving. "I can't guess how old it is."

"Have you ever heard of the Winnemucca Lake petroglyphs?"

"No."

"They were discovered a long time ago, but in 2013 a team went out there and dated them. To their great surprise, the carvings were between ten thousand five hundred and fourteen thousand eight hundred years old. They're currently and officially the oldest known petroglyphs in North America. You just touched a petroglyph that predates those by over ten thousand years."

"Wow!"

"I'm really starting to understand this code now. It's a great puzzle. Absolutely ingenious. It says that the Naacal hollowed out the mesa before their island sank under the Gulf. Just before the sinking, they moved the firestone to this location and operated it for a time before shutting the whole thing down because they feared they would destroy everything again if they didn't. It doesn't say how long the firestone operated here, but this is the last place it worked. We're making history with each step we take, Doug."

They continued their descent, noticing other glyphs as they went.

"Thanks, Hannibal."

"For what?"

"For bringing me along. This is the most wondrous thing I've ever seen. And to be one of the first to see this after all this time blows me away."

"Doug, I don't want to rain on your parade, but I haven't read anything confirming that they hid the firestone here. Just that it operated here last. I've got a feeling, though, that we're going to see something much more awesome than this hole after we get to the bottom."

CHAPTER 30

The helicopter completed its sweep around the mesa with no sign of the climbers.

"I don't mind telling you, Mister Falcon, I'm perplexed."

"Me too, sir. I just don't understand."

"Pilot, put us down on top of the mesa, please. I want to get out and walk around."

The pilot nodded and within moments the chopper settled down onto the mesa's top. Bernard and Falcon stepped out and walked the immediate area.

"If you don't mind, sir," Falcon yelled above the growl of the helicopter's engine, "I'd like to explore the area where I saw them last."

Bernard nodded, his mind racing with the enigma of how two men could have disappeared off the summit of a mesa without a trace.

Falcon wasn't gone long before he trotted back looking very excited.

"On me, sir. I found something."

Bernard signaled to the pilot to cut the engines, then followed Falcon to where the capstone sat as if it had never moved, its open joints forming a huge hexagon.

Bernard stared at it silently for several minutes, shaking his head occasionally. Finally he sighed. "It's a hatch and he opened it, Mister Falcon. The professor opened it and he's inside."

"It sure looks that way, sir."

"But how?"

"I certainly have no clue."

"It was a rhetorical question, Mister Falcon. But it does seem that I may have to put hope, however unjustified it may be, in our Professor Grendel once more."

"That's very disappointing, sir. With all due respect, Grendel's an idiot."

"I agree, Mister Falcon, but it seems an idiot is all I have available at present. Go back and retrieve our pet. I'm afraid we're going to need him out here."

Falcon nodded and headed back toward the helicopter, leaving Bernard standing in the middle of the capstone shaking his head.

"You're brilliant, Professor. And I'm going to tell you so. Right before I kill you."

~ ~ ~ ~ ~

Kirby steered the SUV, borrowed from Bernard's stable of vehicles, through the valley brush as he directed it toward Eagle Mesa.

Suddenly he hit the brakes. The SUV skidded to a stop. He pointed to the mesa top as a helicopter lifted off and began moving toward them.

"That's gotta be Bernard's chopper."

"What makes you think that?"

"I don't know. I'm guessing."

Moments later, bullets riddled the ground near them.

"I hate it when you're right, Kirby. Get us out of here."

More bullets hit the ground surrounding them as Kirby punched the gas and spun the vehicle around. Traci leaned out the window and returned fire with her automatic rifle, causing the helicopter to veer away sharply.

"Yeah," she yelled, "we can play too!" She fired several more rounds at the fleeing helicopter.

"We gotta find a place to hide, Trace. We can't fight them like this. They have the advantage. There ... over there."

Kirby jammed on the brakes. They jumped out and fired a few rounds at the helicopter as it made another run directly at them.

"That large outcrop over there, Trace. We can hide behind it and give 'em hell from there."

They dashed toward the outcrop and made it just as bullets walked across a large boulder next to them. The chopper roared over their heads and settled into a hover a great distance away. From the protection of the boulder, they watched an unknown gunman point the muzzle of a large-caliber machine gun at their parked SUV and pepper it with bullets until the tires exploded, the windows shattered, and steam rose from the hood.

"Damnit," said Traci, aiming carefully. "It's almost out of range. It would be pure luck if I hit anything worthwhile. Still, it would be nice to return the favor."

She adjusted her aim and fired several rounds at the distant helicopter. Kirby joined her, knowing that with any kind of luck at all the helicopter would leave the area. As for the busted-up vehicle, he knew they would be walking out of the desert valley. It was fortunate they weren't more than three or four miles from Gouldings Resort.

Traci's final shot caused the chopper to pitch violently as her round hit the canopy directly in front of the pilot. It immediately veered away.

"Looks like you gave them a message, Trace. Nice shot."

"I don't think I hit anything critical, but a message is a message, right, Kirby?"

"You got that right."

Traci lowered her rifle and looked at the smoldering SUV.

"Looks like we're walking back."

Kirby chuckled.

"Yeah, but after we get back, I'm going to make a call and even up these odds a bit."

"Kirby. No."

"Not them. I've got other friends who don't mind making some noise now and then."

~ ~ ~ ~ ~

Bernard held his phone to his ear.

"I'm through pussyfooting around, Mister Falcon. Get the C-4. We're opening this hatch tonight."

"What about them?" Falcon asked, referring to Kirby and Traci.

"Forget them. In another hour we'll be inside this mesa and they'll still be walking out of the valley. I can't worry about them. I've got to concentrate on the matter at hand. This nonsense has gone on far too long already."

"You still don't think they'll call in the Feds?"

"Not a chance. This has become even *more* personal for them. They're right where I want them to be. At least we know where they are for the moment."

"That's true. Okay, sir. I've got Grendel with me in the chopper now. I'll grab the C-4 and we'll be leaving the compound soon. I expect to be back to you within fifteen minutes."

"Mister Falcon, if you see our friends wandering about in the valley and have a few minutes to kill, do so."

~ ~ ~ ~ ~

Forty-two minutes after Hannibal and Douglas started down the stairs they stepped off the last of them and onto the sandy floor of the cavern.

Hannibal read the depth engraving on the wall next to the final step. "For the record, Doug, we're down around twelve hundred feet from the top."

"For the record, pal," Douglas said, panting, "I ain't going back up them steps. So you'll just have to find another way out of here."

"That may be harder than you think."

"Then you'd better wish me back up on top or be prepared to carry me, 'cause I know I won't make it back up there in this lifetime."

Hannibal heard Douglas's comment, but his eyes had fallen to the sandy floor and the thousands of ancient footprints in it. His hand flew out and against Douglas's chest, preventing his friend from stepping on the footprints.

"Stop, Doug! Look down."

Douglas looked and his eyes opened wide in astonishment.

"Someone else is down here?"

Hannibal smiled.

"*Was* down here. About twenty-five thousand years ago."

"Whoa!"

"What's important is that the prints are still here, Doug. Nothing has gotten in to disturb them."

Douglas shook his head and looked back at the staircase.

"If nothing's disturbed them, that means there can't be another way in. And if there isn't another way in, then there isn't another way out. That means we have to go back up those stairs."

"Don't get your panties in a knot. It could just mean that there's some blockage in the passageway that needs removing. Let's not create a peck of monsters just yet."

"A peck? Did you just say a peck? Who the hell talks like that anymore, Hannibal?"

"Fine! Don't create a pack of them either."

"You're weird, dude."

"So everyone keeps reminding me. Let's follow the footprints and see where they leads us."

Just then the flames from the trough died away and complete blackness returned. They switched on their flashlights and Hannibal's eyes opened wide as his light struck a stone tablet about sixteen inches square, sitting inside a carved inset in the red sandstone wall. He immediately moved toward it.

"What do we have here?" he said, reaching out for the tablet.

Douglas's hand struck his forearm. "Wait!" he said. "I've seen this kind of thing before. It could be booby-trapped."

Hannibal chuckled.

"You've been watching too many Indiana Jones movies."

Hannibal pulled the tablet from the inset. Nothing happened. He grinned at Douglas.

"Okay, okay. Just read the damn thing and stop gloating."

Hannibal sat down on a step, rested the tablet on his knees, and began to read silently as Douglas explored the cavern.

Finally Hannibal stirred. "Wow," he said, "this is amazing. It's directions to the vault."

"Great news. How far in is it?"

"If I'm right about the meaning of these symbols, it's a few miles into the caverns. These caverns wander about under the whole valley. At least that's what I think it says. These symbols give us only a general direction to follow, with some landmarks to guide us."

"You *did* say miles, right?"

"Miles, Dougie. It's a few miles in, according to this information."

Hannibal laid the tablet down against the step, slipped his backpack off, and removed the other tablet that he had taken from Bernard's room. He calmly grabbed it with both hands and then smacked it against one of the steps, breaking off a chunk.

"And you did that because ..."

"Except for this part with the notes on it to get out later if we have to go back up the stairs, we don't need it anymore, it's too heavy to lug around, I don't want it falling into the wrong hands. Which reason do you like best?"

"All of the above. I just wondered."

Hannibal shattered the rest of the tablet and tossed the largest pieces in several directions.

He stuffed the small section of tablet into his backpack and swung the straps over his shoulder.

"There's only one way to go from here, it seems," said Douglas.

"Then our choice is an easy one." Hannibal pointed in the direction of all the footprints.

Douglas stared at the prints for a second or two and then grinned. "We're off to see the wizard," he said as he walked away. Hannibal smiled and shook his head.

"And you call *me* weird."

~ ~ ~ ~ ~

Even though their flashlights were powerful, the cavern was much too large for the lights to illuminate anything but a fraction of it in any given direction.

The footprints in the sandy surface led them a thousand feet or so until Hannibal stopped and held his hand up.

"What?"

"Do you hear that?"

"Hear what?

"It sounds like water; like a river. Like a river somewhere in the distance."

"Oh, yeah. Hey, a river is good. We're almost out of water."

"No, it's not ahead of us. Listen. It's off to our right, I think."

Hannibal walked toward the sound of rushing water until he came to the edge of a cliff.

"Holy crap!" said Douglas. "That's quite a cliff."

"Yeah. Do you hear it?"

"Clear as a bell now."

"There's a river flowing down there."

"How far down do you think it is?"

"Let's find out," said Hannibal, looking around for a heavy stone in the sand. Finding one, he lifted it up and held it out over the cliff. He let it fall and counted.

They heard the large splash after several seconds.

"At thirty-two feet per second per second, that means the river is about three hundred feet down."

"I've never heard of an underground river in these parts."

"Well, Doug, you've heard of it now."

"I don't see a way down, and like I said, we're running short on water. It's gonna get serious if we don't find some soon."

"I bet we find a spring somewhere along the way. You keep following the footprints. I'll keep reading the tablet."

~ ~ ~ ~ ~

Two helicopters lifted off from the airport runway near Gouldings Resort. Falcon and Grendel, in the lead helicopter, led the way directly to Eagle Mesa.

Falcon's eyes scoured the landscape whizzing past under them, warily looking out for any evidence of Traci and Kirby, but there was no sign of them. Better yet, no bullets impacted the chopper. He breathed noticeably easier as the copter scooted over the burned-out hulk of the bullet-riddled SUV he had ordered destroyed earlier.

Within minutes, the helicopters settled down on the mesa's summit. Falcon jumped down and moved toward Bernard.

"No sign of our two shooter friends out there, sir."

"Too bad. But I guess I'll have to live with my disappointment. Let us now turn our attention to the more important task ahead."

"We'll have that hatch blown within thirty minutes, sir."

"That would be delightful, Mister Falcon."

Falcon moved away toward the hatch just as Grendel walked up to Bernard.

"Thank you for inviting me out here, sir. I'll —"

"Yes, yes, Professor. Just try to be useful. Can you do that?"

"Yes, sir. Of course, sir. I'll give it my best effort."

"Fine. Study the photo of the tablet, Professor. See if you can discover how Professor Storm got through the hatch."

"There's a hatch?"

"Over there, Professor." Bernard pointed to the gather of armed men who had stepped out of the second helicopter, the civilian model of the Black Hawk, the Sikorsky S-70A.

Grendel walked away toward the group surrounding the hatch.

He weaved among the seven armed men in black assault clothing, including face masks, and came to stand next to the capstone. As he stared down at it, his eyes grew wider.

"Well done, Hannibal," he mumbled to himself.

One of the armed men bumped into him.

"You need to move out of the way, Professor. We gotta get these charges set."

"Of course, of course," he replied, stepping away.

The group of men worked quickly and silently, setting up their equipment next to the capstone.

Within minutes drills began whirring as wide-gauge diamond-tipped drill bits cut into the capstone. The work was accomplished methodically and with delicate precision until several holes were filled with high-tech explosives and the detonating wires were attached and connected to the electronic detonator.

The whole operation took just over thirty minutes.

While the work was being done, Grendel stared haplessly at the photograph of the tablet. Despite his best effort, he had no understanding of what he was seeing. Knowing that Hannibal must have successfully translated the symbols and opened the capstone only added to his frustration. And though he hated Hannibal for doing what he himself could not do, secretly he was filled with admiration for the man, or at least for his amazing accomplishment.

Bernard, who had been staring out over the darkening landscape during the explosives' preparation, now turned back toward the capstone when he heard one of the men in black announce that the charges were set and ready to blast the stone into pieces.

"Professor?"

Grendel looked at Bernard, lifted both of his arms in surrender and shook his head. "I'm sorry, sir. I have no idea what any of the symbols mean."

"As I expected." Bernard motioned toward Falcon with the fingers of his right hand, imitating an explosion.

Falcon nodded.

"Please move back, Professor. We wouldn't want pieces of you all over the place."

They all moved a safe distance away, ducked their heads, and covered their ears.

The man holding the detonator looked at Falcon for permission to flip the switch.

Falcon looked at Bernard.

Bernard thought for a few seconds and then nodded his head.

Falcon turned his eyes to the man holding the detonator and nodded. "Fire in the hole!" the man yelled and then pressed the button. The capstone disintegrated upward into thousands of tiny pieces.

After the rain of rock subsided, they all moved toward the now gaping hole in the mesa's summit.

Staring down into the blackness, each man gulped and sighed. Finally, one of the dark-clothed men whistled. "I ain't believing this."

"Well, believe it," said Bernard. "There it is in front of you, and Professor Storm already has one hell of a head start on us."

He turned away nonchalantly, as if the wondrous sight was no surprise to him. "Mister Falcon, would you kindly find a safe way to the bottom, please?"

Falcon, still feeling the shock and awe of the mammoth hole staring up at him, finally nodded his head. "Right away, sir." Then he smiled. "Well done, Storm."

~ ~ ~ ~ ~

Traci sat with a sweater draped around her shoulders as Kirby exited his hotel room and walked over to where she was staring out from the viewpoint at Gouldings Resort directly at Eagle Mesa.

"Did you get through to your friends, Kirby?"

"I did. The cavalry will be here in a few hours. And they're coming ready to do bat —"

Just then a bright light flashed upward from the top of the mesa.

"What was *that*?!"

Seconds later, the muffled blast wave vibrated past them and then all was quiet, still, and dark again.

"Something blew, Kirby. Do you think Hannibal is in a fight with Bernard up there?"

"No. It looked more like a single explosion. They're more likely up there blasting rock."

"Damn! Can you get your guys here any sooner?"

"I'm afraid not. It'll be about ten o'clock before we can get a chopper up there ourselves."

"Do you think anyone else saw the explosion?"

Kirby looked around. No one else seemed to have noticed. At least no one in their vicinity.

"I can't believe it, but it doesn't look like it. I guess it could have been mistaken for thunder and lightning. At least I hope so."

"I hope Hannibal's okay."

"Me, too, but we'll find that out after we get out there on top of that mesa."

~ ~ ~ ~ ~

The explosion reverberated throughout the cavern, stopping Hannibal and Douglas in their tracks.

"Looks like we're about to have some company, Dougie."

"Yeah, and they don't sound like the patient, singing type."

"Good point."

"Wish we had some weapons."

Hannibal slipped his backpack off his shoulders, opened it, and reached into it, pulling out a .45 pistol.

"Sweet. Anything for me?"

"This is it, I'm afraid."

"Hannibal, they've got explosives."

"I heard," he replied nonchalantly, stuffing the pistol into the back of his jeans, under his belt.

"And I'm sure they've got rifles, too."

"No doubt."

"Well?"

"No time to dillydally now. They're coming fast and hard. In an hour or so they'll be on us. We're going to have to pick up the pace."

Hannibal walked away quickly.

"That's it, Hannibal? That's all you've got to say?"

"We're going to have to pick up the pace *substantially*."

"Pick up the pace?" Douglas jogged after Hannibal. "Can you outrun a bullet? I know I can't. We're going to have to have a better plan than *picking up the pace*, Hannibal!"

"Have you got one?"

"A plan? No, I haven't got a plan."

"Then picking up the pace is the best we've got."

Hannibal burst into a sprint. Douglas kept pace.

They dashed through sand corridors with twenty-foot ceilings for what seemed a full mile before finally coming to an opening in a red stone wall.

"Look for something that might close the door on your side, Doug," said Hannibal, panting hard.

"What door? I don't see a door."

"Maybe it's hidden away in the wall?"

Hannibal looked for any indication of a mechanism on his side, hoping he could close off the corridor once they were through the opening. There was no such mechanism. Douglas searched his side of the opening.

"Nothing here, pal."

"Damn. I was hoping for some way to slow them down."

"No door. I think our luck is running on low, buddy, along with our water."

"Looks that way. I guess we need to put as much distance between them and us as possible. The tablet says the corridors branch off in different directions and there are doors that close throughout. I guess this isn't one of them, but there's only one way to the vault. So let's head for it."

"How far is this vault from us now, you think?"

"I'm only guessing, but I'd say another mile, more if I end up taking a wrong turn. There're so many different corridors we could end up in by mistake. It's really confusing down here. Especially running through them like we are."

"Let me make this simple. Don't take the wrong turn, Hannibal."

"If we do, it won't be because I'm trying to."

"No. Just don't do it at all. Okay? I don't want to face bad men with rifles with just my boyishly charming grin, if you catch my drift."

"Got it."

The caverns started looking all the same after several more minutes of running. Hannibal used the large number of footprints as a guide, hoping that whoever had made that many footprints knew where they were going. It didn't always work and he was forced to stop several times and consult the tablet for the correct general direction.

"Okay, Doug. I see it now. I'm reading it better. We should be okay if we stay on this heading. The opening in the wall was one of the landmarks. I missed that. My bad. The next one, though, is a sealed door with a small waterfall in a great wall nearby."

"Great. We need the water. I'm almost dry."

"I know, I know."

Hannibal took off again, jogging through another large opening in the wall and then suddenly skidding to a halt just before tumbling over the edge of a cliff.

"Whoa!" he bellowed as he came to a stop only inches from the cliff's edge. Douglas had to dig his feet hard into the sand to avoid running into Hannibal.

"Oh, god! Oh, god, that was close, Hannibal! That was way too close."

"No kidding. I think I got the directions wrong."

"You think?"

"Would you like to give it a try? Maybe you can do better."

"No. Just don't be wrong."

"I'm doing my best."

Hannibal studied the tablet again and then shook his head.

"No, I just have general information and landmarks to spot on the way to the vault. There are so many different corridors to pick from down here, I'm just not sure which one is correct. I was following the largest number of footprints in the sand until —"

"I guess that wasn't such a bad idea *until.*" Doug inched forward and looked over the cliff. "I wonder if they stopped in time."

"You're a bundle of chuckles, Dougie. Let's backtrack a bit."

They headed back toward what looked like a main corridor and then worked their way through another maze of twisting and connecting passageways and openings until Hannibal noticed a highly disturbed path marked by many footprints. He followed them, trusting that they were the correct path leading deeper into the cavern and eventually to the vault.

~ ~ ~ ~ ~

"How many steps do you think there are?" asked an armed man nicknamed Headshot as he followed Bernard and Falcon down the stairs.

"As many as it takes to get us down to the bottom, I reckon," answered their explosives man, Blaster.

"We've been climbing down for over a half hour," said the man furthest back, Zippo.

"And you'll climb another half hour if that's what it takes," boomed Bernard's voice from the lead. "Now shut up!"

Falcon followed Bernard step after step. "The lad's right, though. I've been wondering just how deep into the mesa we are. These helmet lamps and flashlights don't penetrate very far."

"I've seen symbols on the wall as we've been descending. If we could read them, we'd probably have the answer."

"Agreed, but from the readings I'm getting on the tracker, Hannibal's over three hundred seventy-five feet lower than us, and if I'm right, I believe we've descended well below the base of the mesa by now."

"At least you're getting the signals again."

"Yes, sir, but they're also indicating that he's at least three miles ahead of us. I just hope he doesn't figure out the phone is bugged."

~ ~ ~ ~ ~

Nearly fifteen minutes later, Bernard stepped down onto the red sandy floor of the cavern.

"Finally," he said as he pointed the beam of his flashlight in every direction. The area was littered with the rubble of the exploded capstone. "The cavern is enormous, Mister Falcon. And from the looks of the walls, it appears that it wasn't formed naturally."

"Agreed, sir."

"I can only imagine what kind of power they used to carve out the guts of an entire mesa. I'm in awe, Mister Falcon, and now I'm even more determined to get control of that energy. I don't care what it takes. You find the professor and the firestone and I'll make you so wealthy you'll only be able to wonder how much money you have."

"I like the sound of that, sir. And don't worry, we'll find him and the firestone, both intact."

"Make me believe it, Mister Falcon."

Just then Bernard's wandering flashlight discovered the empty wall inset and shards of the broken tablet.

"Well, it seems our wayward professor is intending to make this more difficult. Radio up and ask Professor Grendel to join us, please."

"Sir, with all due respect, he's been of no help so far. He's better off up top and out of the way. I mean, he's an imbecile, sir."

"As you continue to remind me, Mister Falcon, but even an imbecile has value now and then — for certain tasks. Possibly even Professor Grendel."

CHAPTER 31

"Boss?" asked a young man dressed in heavy assault gear, his vest webbing filled with the assorted paraphernalia of someone who worked extensively with high explosives.

"Yeah, Boomer," replied Kirby, fastening the last buckles on his Kevlar vest.

"The chopper's winding up. We're ready to go when you are, sir."

"Thanks, Boomer. Tell the men we'll be with them shortly."

"You got it, sir." The young man turned to leave when Kirby halted him.

"Boomer?"

"Sir?"

"Do we have the ordnance on board?"

"All set, sir."

"Good. Tell Crankshaft to expect the LZ to be hot and smoking. I don't expect they'll want any visitors dropping in on them unannounced."

"Will do, boss."

Kirby turned to Traci, who was cinching up her vest. "There's no reason you need to do this, Trace. We can handle the rough stuff without you."

"I'm going with you, Kirby. For Hannibal."

"We don't know where Hannibal is. We're just going up on the mesa to get Bernard and his guys. Why don't you sit this one out until we hear from Hannibal?"

"Kirby, I was in the field for fifteen years. I can handle a little gunfight. I think I've established that already."

"You have, no doubt about that, but Hannibal brings out something else in you, and I don't want you to get distracted. It could get pretty hairy up there."

"I'm a big girl. I'm going."

"Okay, fine. Let's get out there and get our hands on Bernard. He's bound to know where Hannibal disappeared to."

"If nothing else, I'll get to punch him in the nose."

~ ~ ~ ~ ~

Grendel sat on the mesa studying the photographs of the tablet now in Hannibal's possession. Frustrated by his inability to make sense of the symbols, he made small growling noises from time to time.

Finally one of the security team members had had enough. "What's the matter, Professor? You's soundin' like you's a tiger havin' a bad day. Or you's in heat." He chuckled. The other three team members laughed.

Grendel glanced up at the man. "It must be hard for you, Mackie, being around so many people so eminently more gifted with superior intellect and ambition. Tell me, do you ever consider putting the muzzle of that rifle into your mouth and squeezing the trigger?"

Mackie chuckled. "That was a good one, Professor."

A radio call interrupted the beginnings of a verbal sparring match.

"Get the professor's ass down here. The chief wants him."

"Roger that."

Grendel smiled. "He wants *me*, Mackie. He doesn't need *you*, apparently. You, I guess, don't matter as much as you thought you did. Does that hurt just a bit?"

"You's a trip, Professor." Mackie's smile disappeared. "Now attach that rope to yer harness and git down there before I toss yer ass into that hole without it."

"Delighted," Grendel retorted.

"NOW!"

Mackie's loud command ended the pleasantries. Grendel realized that the guard might be serious about tossing him down the hole and then claiming he'd forgotten to cinch him to the rope. With playtime clearly over, Grendel immediately placed the photos back into his leather valise and slipped the long strap over his neck and under one arm. He moved toward the hole.

"Might as well get down there," he said, feigning nonchalance. "The fun has obviously ended here."

"Ain't been no fun here, Professor. You's a damned idiot and I's glad we's done with babysittin' yer ass. You been goin' on and on about how good you is, but if you was half as good as you thinks you is, you'd have been with the team making the initial penetration. But ya ain't as good as all that. Now get secured to the rope or I *will* toss yer ass into the hole without it, just for shits and grins."

"Nicely stated, Mister Mackie," said Grendel, wearing a condescending smile. "Took advantage of that college education, I see."

"Yeah. College of hard knocks, Professor." Mackie brought a clenched fist up to Grendel's face and gritted his teeth. "You want a lesson or two?"

Grendel's eyes fell to the ground at his feet as he humbly ceased his witty remarks and secured himself to the rope. He strapped his helmet on and then grabbed the rope in a death grip as he stepped toward the black hole. Mackie moved up behind him. A sudden wave of nausea swept over him, making him dizzy and terribly uncomfortable. He could almost sense Mackie's desire to push him over the edge and delight evermore in doing so.

"They called for me, Mackie. Don't do anything rash."

Mackie smiled. "They didn't say they needed ya alive down there, Professor."

Mackie checked Grendel's harness and made sure all was ready to go.

"But they do. Mister Bernard does need me alive. Maybe someone else could check my harness. I don't exactly trust you."

"Too bad, cause I's all you got. And get this. Ain't nobody here likes you, Professor. That's no lie. But you's on my team, like it or not. And I take care of my team. Now don't you let us down, Professor." Mackie chuckled devilishly. "If only they didn't need ya alive ..."

Mackie pushed Grendel hard in the back, sending the already terrified man tumbling into the abyss.

It was certain by all who witnessed it that Grendel's screams were shrill, highly effeminate, and heard by everyone in the cavern and perhaps even by the spirits of the dead Naacal themselves. They echoed for what seemed like hours but was, in reality, only seconds. To Mackie, it was the sweetest of sounds.

Mackie grinned and, being a bit inclined toward sadism, took what pleasure he could from Grendel's terror, but he was also a disciplined professional, and his measured grip on the rope allowed Grendel to fall only ten or twelve feet before coming to sudden, jolting stop. Grendel was able to swing over and catch the makeshift handle the first group had drilled into the rock below the retracted staircase after only a few oscillations as a human pendulum.

Grendel recovered his wits enough to get his feet planted solidly on the rock steps, but finding his voice proved impossible. He crumpled to his rump upon a step and sat for a minute shuddering from fear and staring at his trembling hands, having never before experienced such terror.

He finally gathered himself together enough to glance up at Mackie, who stood staring down at him, grinning like the ghastly ghoul Grendel was now certain he was. "After all these days together, I can't tell you how good that felt, Professor," hollered Mackie. "If only they didn't need ya alive." He cackled and then disappeared.

Grendel was still visibly shaken, but he heard Mackie's voice above, obviously on the radio, reporting to those down in the cavern. "Professor's inserted and on the steps. He'll be down shortly, I reckon; faster if he takes a tumble. Mackie, out."

It took a few more moments before Grendel recovered sufficiently to unharness himself and begin a wonky descent down the steps.

Grendel was finally alone and felt reprieved to be away from that torturous and maleficent beast above, but he peered uneasily into the void below.

"What the hell were you thinking, Richard?" he mumbled to himself. "You know better than to toy with an imbecile like that."

He reached up and clicked on his helmet lamp and took another hesitant, careful step.

~ ~ ~ ~ ~

Mackie walked over to where the other mercenaries had gathered. "I's glad we's done with that sumbitch."

"How long do you think we'll have to hang out here?" asked Cutthroat, a tall man with a bulging chest and rippling muscles, covered in bright tattoos of dark avenging angels and frightful scenes out of some horrific and apocalyptic nightmare.

"Did ya always ask such stupid questions when you was out in the middle of Afghanistan lookin' for the Taliban, Cutthroat?"

Cutthroat smirked.

"We'll be out here as long as it takes, y'all. With the big bucks comes big responsibility. Now y'all shut the hell up!" Mackie scowled at the men.

"Shit, responsibility," argued a man called Nasty, for the obvious reason. "We're sitting on the top of a stinkin'-ass mesa. What kind of responsibility is this for fighting men of our caliber? This sucks. I want some action."

"You keep talkin' like that and you're gonna call the shit down on our heads. We're getting paid, Nasty," said a fourth mercenary nicknamed Barber, for all the close shaves he had been in and had the scars to prove it. "Who cares if all we have to do is sit and wait? I think it's about time we got a cushy gig for a change. At least there ain't nobody named Mohammed taking potshots at us or some kinda shit. This is easy money, man. Don't fart on our gig here."

"It sure is hot out here on this rock," said one of the pilots, called Hitchcock for the simple reason that he remained mysterious about his past. "Ain't no shade or nothin' up here, I'll tell you that."

"That figures, coming from a pilot," quipped Nasty. "Why don't you crawl back into your chopper and kick on the AC, you pussy wussy."

"Bite me, Nasty."

Nasty and the others chuckled. All this banter was standard operating procedure for men of this ilk. God forbid anyone would ever say something kind to one another. If so, then all manner of ill speak would rain torrents down on that wretched soul.

The other pilot, named Scooter for reasons unknown, turned his head upward and around. He spun in circles and then stared out over the valley before finally bellowing, "Hey! Hey! You guys hear that?"

"Hear what, Scooter?"

"I'm not sure, but it sounds like another chopper. I can't see nothin', though."

The others listened intently for a few seconds and sure enough, the distinctive whump-whump of distant helicopter blades became more audible.

"Look alive, animals!" yelled Mackie. "We's got company inbound."

"Damn!" yelled Barber. "I don't see shit yet."

"You think it's the law?"

"I can't say, Nasty," replied Mackie. "But they ain't gonna be the friendly types. I'll say that much."

Six sets of eyes stared out from the mesa in different directions, and it was Nasty who made the discovery of not one but two helicopters tracking in from the west on a level with the top of the mesa. "There! Coming from the west. Straight out!"

All eyes turned in that direction and confirmed the two choppers coming straight at them.

"I think it's about to get very nasty, boys!" Nasty bellowed.

"Looks like," said Cutthroat.

"Time to get the choppers up and out of here," Hitchcock yelled.

"And just where's y'all plannin' to go?" Mackie asked. "If it's the law, they gonna follow yer asses to where you land and cuff y'all nice and tight right there."

"I'll still take my chances in the air," said the pilot. "I'm not trained to do my fighting on the ground."

"I'm with Hitchcock," yelled Scooter. "We'll leave the ground fight to you boys. Let's wind 'em up, Hitchcock."

"You don't gotta tell me twice, Scooter."

"We'll be back for y'all if y'all's still in one piece after this."

"Go on — run, ya cowards!" yelled Mackie.

The pilots climbed into their choppers and started their engines. The blades slowly started to rotate when the first rounds from one of the inbound choppers began peppering the summit of the mesa accompanied by a familiar whirring.

"Ah, shit!" yelled Cutthroat. "I know that sound."

"That's a goddamn mini-gun!" bellowed Mackie.

"Oh, yeah. This shit's gonna get *nasty*," said Nasty.

All four mercenaries fell to their bellies, aimed their rifles at the offending helicopter, and began returning semi-automatic fire in a calm and controlled manner.

And just like that, the firefight began in earnest.

~ ~ ~ ~ ~

From his perspective, Kirby Hansen felt they had the upper hand the instant the first bullets struck the mesa. He had the confusing element of surprise on his side and it was his intent to take full advantage of their position.

The mini-gun being fired by one of his group with years of experience firing such a weapon, nicknamed Rascal, had caught the lounging mercenaries completely unawares and was causing debilitating chaos among them. Still, he knew that men like these recovered quickly and would return devastating fire if allowed to regroup.

It was Kirby's intent to either unseat them from their occupation of the mesa summit or to kill them straight-out, knowing that capturing them alive was not a an option. Not for these men, who no doubt would consider surrender unacceptable. It would be do or die for them.

He knew the type of men securing the mesa summit. He had employed men like them on countless occasions, for duties very similar to the one they were performing at that very moment. They were fighters, and knowing that they would fight to the death, given no other option, was the reason he'd asked the mini-gun operator to aim *near* their position, not *on* it. Kirby was hoping to force them to evacuate the summit rather than choose to fight. It would be at least a temporary option for them.

He watched through his binoculars as both sets of helicopter blades began to spin the very instant the first red dust of pulverized rock from the mesa's summit rose into the air.

"Come on, boys," he said. "I'm giving you the open door. Take it. Take the option before I have none left to give you."

He saw one of the choppers lift off without the mercenaries. "Come on! Take the option, damn it all."

Just then two bullets struck the chopper's exterior.

"It's getting serious now, boss!" yelled Tripod, the helo's pilot.

"Yeah. Okay, Tripod. I got it." Kirby tapped the mini-gun operator on his shoulder. "Okay, Rascal. Take 'em out. No more mister nice guy."

Rascal nodded and began to decimate the summit at the rate of 6,000 rounds per minute. His first target was the helicopter still on the summit. A steady five-second burst exploded the chopper Scooter piloted. He never knew what hit him.

The mercenaries concentrated their fire on Kirby's copter, leaving Kirby's second helicopter to drop down below the rim and out of the line of fire.

"Crankshaft," Kirby said to the pilot of the second chopper, "work your way below the rim and around to the north until you're behind them. We'll slide around to the south and keep them busy from for as long as we can. Be quick about it, though. I don't want to deal with a lucky round sneaking in on us."

"Roger that, boss. Making my move this time."

"Tripod," Kirby said to his pilot, "give me a little shimmy and shake and get us out of the line of fire, if possible. And don't move in closer, whatever you do."

"I can do that, boss. These Black Hawks are made for this, unlike those fake Black Hawks on the summit."

The mercenaries moved quickly and often, making it nearly impossible for Rascal to zero in on them from his distance. And they knew it. This wasn't their first contact with a mini-gun and an experienced operator. It turned into a four-against-one battle.

From Rascal's perspective, as he returned fire against one mercenary, he left himself vulnerable and exposed to the steady aim of the other mercenaries. And knowing that these men were expert shots, and that at nearly a mile away, it would take a miracle shot to hit him, he gave them kudos for striking the chopper as often as they did. This was not going to be an easy fight. He knew that and so did the mercenaries. Something would have to give soon.

Still, from his position above the mesa's summit, Rascal knew he had the best advantage. All he had to do was lob the rounds high over the summit; gravity would drop them onto the sprawled mercenaries. It wasn't the most accurate way to fight, but it was the best he could do across the great expanse that separated the combatants. And who knows, he could get lucky. The mercenaries, on the contrary, had to use rifles tuned and sighted for closer targets, ones which weren't moving erratically over a mile away and high above them.

For a while it looked like a Mexican standoff, with neither side gaining an appreciable advantage. That is, until another voice came to life in Kirby's headset.

"Ready, boss."

"Roger that," replied Kirby. Then to his gunner, "Cease fire, Rascal. Dragon Slayer gets the glory on this one."

Rascal nodded. "I don't mind, boss." He removed his finger from the trigger. The whir of the mini-gun wound down to a stop, leaving only the drone of the helicopter engine and the whir of the swirling blades.

Rising slowly up from behind the mercenaries, the second chopper came into view.

"Dear god! Is this really necessary, Kirby?"

"The time for compromise is over, Traci. They made that call when they decided to fight instead of evacuate."

Kirby's finger touched the button on the microphone attached to his headset. "Do it, Dragon Slayer!"

"Roger," came the reply from the second mini-gun operator.

All anyone aboard Kirby's chopper could do now was watch in horror as the slaughter unfolded before their eyes.

In the heat of the battle with Kirby's helicopter, the mercenaries had forgotten about the second one. It was a fatally tragic error on their part.

The moment the chopper made its presence known to the four mercenaries was the exact moment when the finger of the second gunner squeezed his trigger, sending a spray of bullets in a sweeping motion across the mesa and into the prone bodies of the mercenaries. In only a matter of three or four seconds a billowing cloud of red mist drifted up and off the summit in the wind.

What Kirby and Traci saw from their position was the clinical nature of a precision surgical strike on a group of snipers. The muzzle fire spitting from the mini-gun was all that was initially seen by those on Kirby's helicopter. They heard no report of the gunfire, for the drum of the engine and whoosh of the whirling blades drowned it out.

The exploding bodies were a scene of pure horror for those observing the ambush.

"Oh god, Kirby. This is terrible," said Traci as body pieces launched into the air and over the side of the mesa, followed by the growth of a bright red stain being spread wide by the wash of the spinning blades.

The bursting flames from the gun ceased.

And just like that, the firefight ended.

"I gave them an open door, Traci," said a somber Kirby, eyes still glued to the tragedy on the mesa's summit.

"I know. I know."

Dragon Slayer didn't need orders to cease firing. It was evident that he had successfully erased the threat.

"Gun secured, boss," came the dry voice in Kirby's headset.

"Okay, Crankshaft, settle down onto the mesa. We're on our way in."

"You got it, boss."

Kirby punched a number on his cell phone and lifted it to his ear. "This is Kirby Hansen. Let me speak to your sheriff. ... Sheriff, this is Kirby Hansen. We are presently secure on the mesa. If I were you, I wouldn't send anyone out here right now. It's a mess, a real mess. I had to use option B." He listened intently for a moment. "Sheriff, it's not a place you'd want to see right now. Let nature take its course for a few weeks and then you get a crew up here to clean the debris off the summit. Trust me, sir. It's not someplace I'd care to be presently and I wouldn't land here if I didn't have to. There's nothing to be done up here." He listened again. "That's great. Good to hear it. Thanks for allowing me to do this my way. I'll remember your assistance and cooperation. Good day, Sheriff."

Kirby clicked his phone off and turned to Traci. "They've got the other pilot in custody already. He gave himself up immediately upon landing at the airport."

"Well, one life saved is better than no lives saved."

"I guess I should look at it that way too, but now we need to find Bernard, and I'm guessing that big hole in the top of the mesa will have something to do with finding him."

"I'm worried about Hannibal, Kirby."

"I don't know who those fighters were on the mesa, but to tell you the truth, if Hannibal is down there in that hole, I'd be more worried for them. Hannibal doesn't take kindly to people messing with his archaeology."

"How well I know that," said Traci.

"My money, though, is on Bernard being behind this — in spades. Still, if he messes with Hannibal, well ... we need to get into that hole fast."

~ ~ ~ ~ ~

Hannibal and Douglas continued following the footprints in the sand until they came to a large sealed door blocking the corridor. He noticed several symbols engraved on the face of it and identical symbols on the wall to its left. He read them silently and then nodded.

"Well, Hannibal?"

"This is it — the landmark and just what we need."

"Ah, we don't need a closed door, buddy. Closed is not a good thing, especially when we have bad men following us. What do the symbols mean?"

"They just identify the doorway and the corridor. It's like Hallway six, Doorway seven. You know, just an identifier. What I need to do is find the tones to open it."

"You're assuming it takes tones to open it, like the capstone?"

"I can't see why they would change mechanisms at this point. Can you?"

"I guess not. ... Well, sing the song already."

Hannibal read the tablet for several minutes and then smiled.

"La, la, la, la," he sang in varying pitches.

The doorway remained sealed.

"That didn't work, Hannibal."

"I was just finding my tones."

Douglas chuckled.

Hannibal straightened up and sang a line of sounds. An instant later the stone slab began to inch slowly upward. It took almost a full minute to completely disappear into the ceiling.

"Nice job, Sinatra!" Douglas flashed a grin.

Hannibal snickered.

As they walked through the doorway, Hannibal motioned for Douglas to move right while Hannibal moved left. "Look on the wall and see if there isn't a physical switch or perhaps some kind of button or the like."

"You mean you can't sing it down?"

"The tablet makes reference to a switch or ... I've got it! It's a lever. Look for a lever of some kind, but it might be buried in the wall

Douglas found it immediately.

"Got it! It's over here."

"Pull it."

Douglas reached for the upper end of the lever and tugged at it. It moved easily, as if oiled. The stone slab began dropping as slowly as it had risen, until it settled gently back into place.

"Now we've got some breathing room, Doug."

"Until they blow it to pieces."

"Yeah, until then."

They heard the sound of trickling water to their right.

"That's a lovely sound, Hannibal."

"It is indeed."

They walked only a few yards and discovered the small waterfall glimmering in the light of their flashlights, trickling down over flattened rocks and into a small pond which overflowed, fell into another channel, and then disappeared into the floor of the cavern.

Hannibal read the tablet again. "Yep. This is one of the landmarks. We must be on the right track to the vault."

"The vault can wait. My canteen is on vapors."

"Mine, too."

They filled the containers to the brim, drank several swallows, and refilled them.

"Tastes great. Now, Doug, let's see if we can find the vault."

"Lead the way, buddy."

Hannibal consulted the tablet once again. "Okay. Straight down the main corridor, I should think."

"We're off to —"

"Shut the hell up," Hannibal said, grinning.

"I sort of feel like I'm in Oz."

"Well, just so long as there isn't a wicked witch."

"Oh, yeah. I forgot about her."

~ ~ ~ ~ ~

They continued down the expansive main corridor for what Hannibal could only guess was another half mile until, on the right, was another sealed door, smaller than the previous one by almost half, engraved with similar symbols.

Hannibal stared silently at the markings.

"Hannibal? The corridor goes on past this doorway."

"Yes it does, Doug, but oh my, I think this is it."

"The vault?"

"The vault, Doug. I think this is it."

"Okay, wow. Well, then, sing like Al Pacino and get us in there."

"Al Pacino's an actor, not a singer."

"Sing like Eydie Frickin' Gormé, then, I don't care. Just get us in there."

Hannibal smirked, then began reading the tablet.

After several anxious minutes, Douglas began to pace nervously. Several minutes later he could take no more. "Well?"

"I don't think the code is on here, Doug. I've read through it several times and I don't see it."

"That's just great. So, what do we do?"

"I don't have the faintest idea."

Hannibal stared at the door, scanning it for any hidden signs or messages. It was then that he spied a small raised area. When he stepped forward and wiped a hand across it, he discovered a symbol that had been filled in with a sand-like substance to make it look like the rest of the red sandstone door.

"Okay," he said, wiping his hand across the face of the stone door and discovering another recognizable symbol. Seconds later, applying the same method, he cleared away nine more symbols. He grinned and pointed to the eleven symbols.

"Yeah," said Douglas, "Now you're talking ... ah, singing, I mean."

"Yep. About to."

Hannibal backed away from the door. "How about this?"

He sang the notes he believed were engraved on the door. It lifted immediately in the same slow fashion as the previous one.

"Well done, Hannipal!"

"'Hannipal'?"

"You like it?"

"No."

They both chuckled until the door lifted high enough that their flashlights illuminated the area just beyond.

The view that greeted them stunned them to absolute silence.

CHAPTER 32

Kirby's wobbly leg reached outward from the last of the stone steps and his foot dropped onto the security of the cavern floor.

"I hope there's another way out of here. I'll never make it back up. I can't even feel my legs except for the burning."

"I'm thankful for my morning jogging routine," Traci said. "That wasn't too bad."

"Shut up," said Kirby. "You're killing me."

Traci giggled and slapped him on the back. "We'll talk about your stamina training later."

"Ha, ha," he shot back. "Everyone's a comedian these days."

After Kirby and Traci landed, three armed men trotted down the steps and around them, immediately forming a defensive perimeter. They, of course, were neither tired nor winded.

"That was an awesome down, boss," said one of the men, nicknamed Hound Dog because he always took the lead position in a column, commonly known as the Point Man position, and also had a knack for "smelling out" the enemy. In a firefight he was the go-to guy, which was why he was the leader of this team. "I'll race you back to the top, Boomer. How about it?"

"Not just yet, Hound Dog. But after we've finished this gig, you're on."

"I bet I can beat both of you," said Wrecking Ball, a giant of a man who had earned his nickname by crashing through a thick wooden door, surprising some bad guys on the other side who'd thought they were safe.

"Shut up, all of you," said Kirby. "And show a little respect for the old guys here, like me."

Everyone snickered. Then Boomer said, "But you're the only old guy here, boss."

"But I *am* the boss, Boomer, and I decide who gets the good assignments around here. Are you on my frequency?"

"Full roger on that, boss man," Boomer said with a smile.

Kirby noticed the empty inset in the wall and the shards of tablet lying in the sand. "Well, Hannibal's down here somewhere," he said.

"What makes you say that?" asked Traci.

He hobbled over to the empty wall inset and pointed to the shards. "Oh, I've just got a feeling."

"I hope you're right, but I'm worried about anyone else that's down here. I'd hate to walk into an ambush."

"Don't worry, ma'am," said Hound Dog. "That's what I'm here for. I'll sniff 'em out and put 'em down."

"Ooh, ooh," the other two men sang out in response to their leader's smugness.

"What do you say, boss?" asked Hound Dog. "Follow the footprints?"

"Yeah. Just give me a minute to get the knots out of my legs. They're having fits."

"We can head out on point, sir. You can follow when you're able," suggested Hound Dog.

"Can't wait to get some, huh?" asked Kirby.

"Hooyah, sir," Hound Dog answered with a grin. "This hound is ready for the hunt."

"Go on ahead, then. If you run across anyone not Hannibal, secure them. If they resist, eliminate them. We're not going to play around with anyone down here. You got that?"

"Roger that, boss. Okay, check communications. If all is well, sing out."

The other two men confirmed that their communications hardware was operating correctly.

"Okay, let's go. Wrecking Ball, you stay behind the boss and keep our six clean."

"I'm on it," said Wrecking Ball as the other two men walked away into the darkness.

"Sorry to keep you behind, Wrecking Ball," said Traci. "I'm sure you'd rather be with your teammates."

"No problem, ma'am. This is my job now, to keep our six clean and safe. It's all good."

"Okay," said Kirby, still hobbling a little. "Let's get moving before my legs completely rebel against me. But slowly, please."

Traci smirked.

~ ~ ~ ~ ~

Though an experienced archaeologist, Hannibal stood completely stunned by the expanse of the blackness that lay in front of his eyes. Douglas stared at what he could not comprehend.

Finally Douglas gathered himself enough to speak, but still not enough to move. "So this is why they called it the vault."

"You can say that again."

Hannibal was the first to regain control of his body and take a step into the enormous room, but it was so large that the beam of his flashlight faded away to nothing after only a few feet.

"How is this possible?" he asked.

"We need bigger lights," said Douglas.

Moving slowly into the room, they soon discovered a set of large stone bins bordering their approach. The flashlights were not powerful enough to expose what Hannibal believed to be several more ahead of them in the murkiness.

Hannibal turned and searched the area around the doorway and found what he expected. A large, empty trough on each side of the door ran back into the vault.

"I knew it. Another lamp trough."

"Just like the stairway, right?"

"Exactly."

"I thought they had electricity."

"They did, but we don't. And maybe this was meant for temporary lighting. I don't know. I'm guessing."

Douglas rubbed his hand inside the dry trough. "Ain't no oil or pitch, pal."

"I'm working with what I think we have. Hang on." Hannibal searched the end of the trough and found what looked like a large stone plug. "Hold my flashlight, please." Douglas grabbed Hannibal's flashlight as Hannibal wrested the plug with both hands. Initially it wouldn't budge, but he gripped it more tightly and gritted his teeth as he twisted harder. Seconds later the stone gave way and as Hannibal pulled it free, a gush of what appeared to be black oil raced down the trough.

Douglas dipped his finger into it and brought it up to his nose. "It ain't oil," he said.

"I figured that, but I can't tell you what it is. Whatever it is, it has the ability to remain fresh for a very long time."

Hannibal went to the other side of the doorway and performed the same technique on the plug above the other trough. It twisted more easily than the first and soon the oil-like liquid gushed down the second trough.

Hannibal removed his backpack and pulled out a long starter wand, clicked it to ignite a flame, and touched it to the oily substance. Instantly it ignited and took off down the trough, creating both flame and light, but no smoke whatsoever.

The full expanse of the room immediately became visible. It was nearly the size of a football field and very level, with a stone ceiling about twenty feet above them. Hannibal lit the other trough and they watched in delight as the contents of the room slowly became visible.

Hannibal's eyes spotted something in a recessed area of the nearby wall. He stared at it for several seconds and then blinked hard, as if he expected it to disappear. It didn't.

"Oh, Doug, look here."

"Hannibal, you need to see this," said Douglas, staring at something in front of him.

"Doug. Look now."

Douglas could not manage to turn his eyes away from what he was seeing.

"No, Hannibal! You really need to turn around."

Hannibal surrendered and turned around. His jaw dropped open.

The glint of gold struck his eyes. The flaming trough lit the room brightly and he saw the stacks of gold bars stretching back into the vault room, covering an area approximately fifteen feet high, fifteen feet wide, and a hundred fifty feet long.

He blinked again; the gold bars remained glistening in the light of the flames.

"Oh my, Hannibal. There's more gold here than I've ever imagined there could be."

"Now I understand what the words on the tablet mean."

"What's that?"

"I thought the words meant that the vault contained the *true wealth* of the Naacal. I expected to find a vault filled with scrolls and tablets. You know, their true wealth, their knowledge, their wisdom. Now it makes sense. It wasn't the *true* wealth, it was the *total* wealth of the Naacal. This is where they brought all their wealth, their treasure, their valuables."

"Why? Why not just move it to wherever they set up their new nations?"

"I think this was their Fort Knox."

"Perhaps, but our Fort Knox is empty.

"Good point."

"On that note, why is it still full? Wouldn't someone in the past have known about it and have emptied it?"

"Over time, those who were responsible for keeping track of it may have died unexpectedly, taking the knowledge of its location with them."

"I guess that makes sense." Douglas walked around to the first bin and then jumped back. "Oh, Hannibal! Come here."

Hannibal walked to the bin and jumped back as well. It was full of diamonds in varying sizes, the visible ones perfectly cut and polished and of flawless quality. The bin was the size of the bed of a ten-yard dump truck and it was bordered by others. The bin next to the diamonds was filled with polished emeralds of varying sizes and shapes. The next was filled with polished rubies, equally varied. The others contained finished topaz, turquoise, sapphires, yellow tourmalines, aquamarines, and other precious and semi-precious stones, all apparently perfectly cut and polished and flawless. They counted the bins. Fifty of them, all filled to capacity.

"This is totally unprofessional of me," said Hannibal, "but I'd be nuts if I didn't."

He removed his backpack, emptied its contents onto a nearby polished stone table, and began shoveling handfuls of stones from the nearest bins into it. Douglas immediately did the same. "To hell with being professional, Hannibal. If you didn't do it, I was getting ready to do it myself."

They added additional handfuls of diamonds until their packs could hold no more. They set the packs next to the doorway.

"We're millionaires," Douglas said with a grin.

"At least," replied Hannibal. "Now look at this," he continued, pointing to the wall inset next to the door.

Douglas's eyes opened wide as he saw what Hannibal was pointing at.

The emerald serpent head stood at least twelve inches high and six inches wide. The highly polished stone twinkled at both men, enticing them to touch it. Douglas yielded first, but Hannibal stopped him.

"No! Don't touch. Look, on the wall above it. It's some kind of warning."

"Okay. No touching. It's amazing, but not as amazing as what's in those bins."

"Are you kidding me? Look at the size and purity of the emerald. It alone is worth millions."

"What's the warning?"

"It says not to disturb the statue or the Great Serpent will seek its revenge."

"Okay. Whatever. That's good enough for me. What do you say we take a stroll back into the vault?"

"Let's do it."

They walked around the vault, weaving among other bins filled with gold statues and figurines, each encrusted with assorted precious and semi-precious stones, until they finally came to stone shelves carved into the walls, full of neatly stacked stone tablets and scrolls. Hannibal pulled out some scrolls, still fresh and pliable, and unrolled them. He read a few passages from each.

"The sum total of the knowledge of the Naacal, I'm guessing. This is greater than the library at Alexandria, I'll bet."

"Can you read it?"

"Yeah, Doug. I understand almost everything."

Douglas then discovered a stone box sitting on another shelf further back.

"Hey, Hannibal. Take a look at this, will you?"

Hannibal walked over and stared at the box for a moment. He wiped his hand over the top of it, revealing another set of symbols hidden by the same sandy material as that on the doorway to the vault. He studied the symbols for a quick moment and then cleared his throat and sang seven notes. The cover immediately opened. Inside the box was a dazzling, life-sized clear crystal skull. Hannibal reached in and pulled the skull out and stared into its eye sockets with awe. Those polished sockets were almost hypnotic, and they held Hannibal's gaze with ease.

Douglas, meanwhile, found a carved tablet about fourteen inches square in the back of the box. He picked it up and saw that it was covered with the same kind of symbols as all the others they'd seen, but carved so small as to be almost impossible to read without a magnifying glass.

"What does this say?"

Hannibal fought to turn his eyes away from the skull to look at the tablet and then handed the skull to Douglas in exchange for the tablet. He reached into his pocket and pulled out his loupe. He read for several minutes and then nearly dropped the tablet. "Do you realize what you're holding in your hand, Dougie?!"

"A crystal skull, of course."

"Not just a crystal skull, but the *thirteenth* skull. And based on the titles and headings here on this tablet, the skull has been encoded with the Naacal's entire history. What's more, it contains the instructions on how to energize the firestone."

"Oh, boy!"

"And now it all begins to make sense to me."

"How's that?"

"Have you ever heard of the legend of the crystal skulls?"

"Yeah. In that ancient history class we took at UCLA, the professor talked about the skulls. But I don't remember what he said about them."

"Well, the legend says there are thirteen crystal skulls. Some claim that twelve of the original have already been located. But the thirteenth has yet to be found."

"So, you're certain this is the thirteenth?"

"Yes, but give me a minute."

Hannibal read for a while longer and then nodded.

"Yep. This is it. In order to energize the firestone, one must raise the stone into its proper place and then bring all thirteen crystal skulls together in a special formation around it. The symbols for the tones used to call the energy into the skulls are encoded in the crystal structure of this skull. Once the skulls are activated, they, in turn, ignite ... wait, that can't be right. Oh, okay. Got it. They *energize* the firestone. Some of the words still elude me from time to time."

Hannibal looked up from the tablet and nodded. "Doug, if this special tablet and the energizing skull are here, I have to think the firestone is here as well."

Hannibal read more symbols and then looked at Douglas. He was all eyes, and they glistened brilliantly.

"Okay, that look is interesting."

"Doug! The tablet says that the Naacal encoded the inventory of all their *craft* into this skull as well."

"Craft? You mean like cars and boats?"

"And aircraft and spacecraft."

"Wow! But tell me, how could they encode their information into the skull in the first place?"

"It's widely known that quartz crystals can hold large amounts of data, but it doesn't say here how the Naacal managed to do it. Maybe I have to keep reading, but that's for later. I'd better keep the skull and tablet with me, just in case."

Hannibal carried them to the entrance, placed them gently into extra pouch sacks attached to the outside of his pack, and then trotted back.

"So where do you think the firestone is, Hannibal?"

Both men glanced around the vault, but the firestone was not immediately obvious.

"Jesus, Hannibal, this place is so big. How are we going to find it, if it's here?"

"We could be standing right next to it and not see it with all this stuff around."

"We haven't even begun to explore this vault. No telling what we're going to find in here."

"Doug, let's spread out and keep looking around. Yell if you find anything special."

"You got it, but it's *all* special to me."

"You know what I mean."

The men separated and walked back into the vault.

After a while Hannibal called out, "Anything, Doug?"

"More jewels and golden artifacts. More stone tablets and a whole other bank of scrolls. Hell, there must be thousands of them, in boxes carved into the walls. How about you?"

"Just about the same on this side."

Minutes later, both men yelled out as one: "You gotta see this!"

What both of them had found were land vehicles, or what looked like land vehicles, lined up in neat rows, about thirty of them.

They came together in the center of the vault at the same time.

"Vehicles, Doug!"

"I see it. I don't believe it, but I see it. Christ, Hannibal. Everything you said about the Naacal was true. They had freakin' *cars.*"

Hannibal laid his hand on the nearest one and rubbed it. "I wonder if we can drive them out of here." He chuckled.

"Maybe." Douglas moved around the vehicle and disappeared down the row as Hannibal continued his silent caress of the Naacal car.

He finally smirked. "I wonder what's under the hood."

Douglas did not reply. Hannibal continued his thought as he worked his way down the row toward the back of the vault.

"I've dreamed of this day, Doug. And I wondered what I was going to say when I found it. But now that I'm staring at the wonder of it all, I have no words to offer. This is more than I ever dreamed it could be. The world — our world — has no clue this ever existed."

Hannibal listened for Douglas's response, but he heard nothing.

"You still with me, Doug? You know, I'm wondering if the corridors could have been roadways into here. Hell, they probably go for miles and miles under the valley, leading in every direction like a subterranean superhighway. Hey, if we get them going, we could have races down here, Naacal style." He laughed. "How about that? We could call it the Naacal Five Hundred."

Still no response from his friend.

He turned and looked all around him, but Douglas was nowhere near.

"Doug! You okay?"

Still no response.

Hannibal became alarmed and walked back to where they had stood before, in front of the Naacal cars. Douglas was not in sight.

He then walked toward the other side of the vault. About halfway over, Doug shouted. "Hannibal! Run! I found it!"

Hannibal instantly broke into a jog and headed toward Douglas's voice. A minute later he skidded to a stop at the crest of a rise and looked down in astonishment at the huge quartz crystal lying on its side.

Douglas was twenty to thirty feet down the slope and standing next to the firestone, with his right hand resting against the enormous crystal. He turned toward Hannibal and grinned.

"I found it, Hannibal!"

"You did that, all right."

"Ain't she a beaut?"

The firestone lay perfectly level on its side, propped up on several evenly spaced supports. It was over seventy feet long and naturally formed into a perfect hexagon. With a diameter of over fifteen feet, it towered over the two men. The quartz crystal was clear and flawless.

"Oh, my, my, Doug, it was all true. Everything I found out about it was exactly true. This has to be the greatest archaeological discovery of all time."

"You did it, Hannibal! When everyone called you crazy, you did it, buddy. No one can ever take this away from you."

Hannibal buckled to his knees as he stared at the firestone. "I did it! I really did it. I'm finally somebody. I'm really somebody. A global civilization existed that gave rise to everything we are and I have now proved it."

He rose up off his knees and walked down the slope, reaching out toward the firestone. Drawing next to it, he put both hands gently against the crystal and lowered his head in reverence.

"Does this mean that Atlantis really existed?"

"No, Dougie. Not the way history has painted it, but I have no doubt that a similar place did indeed exist."

"Could Atlantis have been the island of the Naacal that sank into the Gulf?"

"It's more likely now that the Naacal's island could have been the impetus for the legend. 'My mission divine, my purpose complete, my destiny secured.'"

"It sure is, pal. You did good, Hannibal."

"Not me, Doug. That was a passage written on one of the scrolls I found. It was recorded by one of their high priests who was largely responsible for getting the firestone dismantled. 'To save the world, I gave my all to the cause. My mission divine, my purpose complete, my destiny secured.' It was a plea to all the Naacal, a requested sacrifice, to leave all they had known behind and go forth and start over. He knew that such a sacrifice had to be made if humans were to ever survive. It seems our world owes great gratitude to Ho' Cha' Malia Di, High Priest of the Mu'un Naacal — 'a sacred land that once was but now is lost forever.'"

"Wrong, ol' buddy. It ain't lost. It lives again through your discovery. You can now bring their sacrifice into the light."

Hannibal hesitated and then turned to Doug. "No, Doug. *I'm* the one he warned his people about. I'm the 'Great Hypocrite,' the 'Great Deceiver,' the 'Man of Lies.' You see, I want to shout this to the world, Doug. I want to scream out from the highest peak: '*I was right about EVERYTHING!*'"

"And you were."

"But I can never say anything about this place. I wasn't sure how I'd react if I found it. Now that I have, I'm scared half to death to reveal the discovery. Not now, at least. Not for a very long time, most likely. The world is simply not ready for what lies in here. From the riches to the wisdom to the firestone itself. We're just not ready. These were great people. They chose to fall into obscurity rather than cause their descendants to suffer the ills of their own arrogance. We're not as great."

"Hannibal, what the hell are you saying? This vindicates you! You're completely exonerated! It's your choice where you want to go and what you want to do with the rest of your life. No one can ever speak against you again. You're going to be a god in archaeology. You're going to make the world forget there ever was a guy named Howard Carter."

"That vindication must stay unrealized, Doug. I see that now. I finally understand that I *must* either destroy the firestone or destroy any record of where it is. No one can know about this place. No one must ever see this except us if that's at all possible."

"Don't do this to yourself, pal. You deserve to be recognized for your accomplishment. Like no other, I might add."

"No, Doug. Black Owl was right when he talked about what we all might truly deserve, and the world doesn't deserve this. Not the effects of this. Not for my sake. And I've blown it. I should never have tried to find this place. I should have destroyed every bit of evidence I found. If the firestone gets energized and it ends up destroying the world, I'll be the one to blame."

"That's nonsense. And yeah, maybe the world isn't ready for it today, but someday it might be. Don't be so hard on the world, Hannibal. Don't kill a chance to use this power to help make lives better. There must have been a reason the Naacal didn't destroy it."

"It's not that, Doug. What I mean is that the whole world doesn't deserve to get itself blown to pieces by the greed and ignorance of those few who wish to control it. Those in charge won't use it for good. They're not enlightened enough to use this wisely. The rest of the world should not have to suffer for the improprieties of a few evil-minded elitists — or a selfish archaeologist who wanted the glory of the discovery. No, Doug. We as a species, as a race, are not ready for this. So we, you and I, have to decide whether we destroy the firestone or see to it that no one ever finds the vault again. At least not for a *very* long time."

"What about the gold and jewels, Hannibal? A lot of good can be done with them."

"Not if they fall into the wrong hands. No, the vault as it is must disappear — again. I will not go down in history as the man who destroyed the world."

"I don't want to sound argumentative, buddy, but we've got heavily armed guys about to find us. How are you planning to keep them outa here?"

"Destroy the firestone. Then it won't matter."

"What about the gold and jewels?"

"We can destroy the entire vault."

"How's that?"

"The emerald serpent head next to the door. The one I told you not to touch. I'll have to read it again, closer this time, but I believe it gave a pretty clear warning. Perhaps it's a warning that the vault will be destroyed if it's touched."

"So you're gonna touch it?"

"If that's what it takes to keep everything out of Bernard's hands, yeah, I'll destroy it all."

"Okay. I'm with you, but let's make sure we can get out of here before you go destroying anything. I'm not ready to play martyr just yet."

"I'm heading back to the serpent head."

"Wait! Maybe there's another way hidden in the scrolls or etched on one of the tablets. Like a ... what do you call it? Like Captain Kirk on the *Enterprise* when they don't want the ship to fall into the wrong hands. You know?"

"Are you talking about a self-destruct switch?"

"Yeah. That's it. Maybe there's a self-destruct song or something."

"That's not a bad idea, Doug. They seem to have had everything else figured out. Let's go check it out."

~~~~~

An hour after his frightfully unconventional entrance into the cavern, Dr. Richard Grendel exhaustedly descended the last of the cavern stairs to find Falcon seated on the last step, waiting patiently for him. Grendel took a seat next to him.

"I'm glad it was down and not up."

"Indeed, Professor. That'll come later."

"I hope not for a while."

"Mister Bernard and the others have gone ahead. He couldn't wait. We'll start out after him in a minute. First, however, he wanted you to look at these fragments and tell him if these were once part of the tablet you have photographs of — the one taken by Professor Storm."

"Okay, but I need to rest a bit first. I'm not in the condition I thought I was in. That was a lot of stairs."

Falcon callously rose to his feet. "You can rest later, Professor. Mister Bernard was very clear about you doing the job he's paying you for and hasn't received any benefits from."

"But I —"

"*Now*, Professor!"

Grendel peered up into the eyes of the giant man staring down at him with contempt. "You don't like me, do you, Mister Falcon?"

"I have neither compassion nor affection for those who regard themselves as more than they are, Professor. And even less for men of low honor in high places."

"You're employed by such a man, you know."

"And I have come to have little regard for him. But I've chosen to work for him, so I've damned myself. Now start doing your job."

Grendel rose painfully to his feet and took a few torturous steps toward the tablet shards, but his legs seized up. "Ow!" he bellowed and collapsed back onto the step. "I'll have you know, sir, that I'm a well-respected archaeologist at the university. I'm not accustomed to such treatment."

"You're an idiot, Grendel. And next to Professor Storm, you're a *sorry-ass* idiot. You're no better than the rest of us who have surrendered our souls to the devil. If it were left to me, I'd put a bullet in your idiot head right now and leave your worthless carcass here to rot. Now enough chitchat, Professor. Do your damn job!"

~~~~~

Grendel and Falcon rushed through the corridors aided by their lamps until a wavering light far in the distance alerted Falcon. He stopped quickly and grabbed Grendel's arm. Grendel finally noticed the bouncing light in the distance.

"Is that Mister Bernard?"

"I don't know who it is, Professor. Get down and stay quiet until we know for certain."

The light continued toward them and then a voice called out. "Mister Falcon? Is that you, sir?"

"Yeah?"

"It's me, sir. Zippo."

"Okay." Falcon stood up. Grendel arose as well and stood silently as Zippo approached them.

The young man came to a stop in front of the two. "Mister Bernard sent me back to find you. It's getting pretty hairy up ahead; lots of twists and turns, several intersecting corridors. It would be real easy to get lost down here. I've marked the way back to the others, but you'd have to know what to look for. To be safe it would be best if both of you stayed close behind me."

"Okay. Proceed." Falcon motioned for Grendel to go ahead.

Grendel obeyed and walked past him.

Falcon followed for a few yards and then stopped, turned, and pointed his light beam back toward the entrance. He listened intently, eyes closed, thinking he'd heard a noise. There was only silence. He opened his eyes, stared back into the darkness, then turned toward the others and jogged to catch up.

CHAPTER 33

Hannibal was studying all the scrolls and tablets he could, trying to discover any way he might seal the door permanently without bringing it all down onto their heads. He wasn't having much luck.

In truth, he realized that Black Owl was right; he never should have come here in the first place. Now it would clearly be his fault if anyone else discovered the vault.

He read a passage from one of the scrolls and smirked.

"What's that?" asked Douglas. He was seated next to Hannibal, being respectfully quiet and still.

"This passage here. Makes me feel like a piece of garbage right about now. It says: 'Trust not in the good intentions of evil hearts.'"

"Why does that make you feel like garbage?"

"It's from a larger passage that discusses the merits of keeping the firestone active despite having destroyed their nation with it. The author is addressing whether or not enough goodness still lies in their collective hearts sufficient to make the right decision about the firestone. You could say it is a treatise on ethics. Man, have I failed that test. And here I am, trying to justify my own good intentions in light of the evil of my deeds. I wanted to make this discovery, Doug. I willingly sacrificed all my ethics so I might stand proudly before the Board of Deans and the world and announce that I had finally discovered something of great worth; that I wasn't a fool or a 'waste of resources,' as both the university and Bernard called me in so many words. Pretty pathetic, huh? I've certainly accomplished something, all right — exposing all of this to other evil hearts so that everything we have now can be destroyed in the name of progress. Yeah, buddy, I'm so very proud of myself right now."

"Don't be so damned hard on yourself, Hannibal. You're an archaeologist. It's your job to make discoveries. You're not responsible for the ethics of others. And I believe in you. You'll do what's right. You'll find a way to protect all of this from those *really* evil hearts. Have a little faith in yourself, Hannibal."

~ ~ ~ ~ ~

When Falcon and the others heard the faint sound of drills and saw light beams flashing all over like air raid lights, he picked up the pace and dashed to where he saw Bernard and the other men preparing to blow open the heavy stone door blocking the corridor.

Grendel managed to make it past the group and stand before the great door. He stared at it in awe.

Bernard walked up to him. "So, Professor. Did Hannibal smash the tablet?"

"Yes, sir. Most definitely. It was the same tablet he stole from you."

"He didn't steal it. No one steals from me. I let him take it."

"Of course, sir. Sorry."

"Do the markings on the doorway make any sense to you?"

"He did it!"

"What's that?"

"He did it, sir. Hannibal Storm discovered the lost global civilization he always said existed. He was right. He was right about everything, it seems."

"So now you're a fan?"

"I hate him, but he was right. I have to give him that."

"So it would seem, Professor. You can't read those symbols, though, I presume?"

"I have no earthly idea what they mean, sir. I'm sorry. I have no knowledge of these people at all. In fact, they can't have existed. There are no archaeological records that support their existence."

"And yet here we stand in front of an artificially constructed doorway that must have been built by an extraordinarily advanced civilization tens of thousands of years ago. How is the archaeological establishment going to explain this?"

Grendel just shook his head and stared at the stone door before him. "Frankly, sir, I have no idea. They'll probably deny its existence."

"I'll tell you this much, Professor. Professor Storm will certainly know how to break the news. And he'll be perfectly eloquent about how these people existed, and when, and what marvels of technology they had command of. He won't do it using all the showman techniques used by people like you, Professor. He'll just walk out onto the world stage, state his case perfectly, and blow the socks off of everyone."

"I'm sure he will."

"Oh, by the way, Professor Grendel, I'm canceling your expedition, and I expect any money not already spent to be returned promptly."

"Of course, sir. I understand."

"You've proved most disappointing to me, Professor."

"I've disappointed myself, sir."

Zippo walked up next to Grendel as Bernard walked away.

"Ain't it something, Professor?"

"Yes, Zippo, it is. ... By the way, may I ask why they call you Zippo?"

"Sure. It's because when I'm asked how many enemy I've left alive in the field after a firefight, my answer is —"

"Zippo, yes, I understand."

"You got it, Professor."

"How very quaint."

"I'd get back a ways, Professor. They're gonna try some C-4 and attempt to blow the hell outa that door. But I don't know why they think that'll work. They can't get a drill bit into it. They even used diamond-tipped drills. They all shattered. But they're gonna tape the C-4 bricks to it anyway. It should be interesting. Anyway, cover your ears, it's about to get loud."

Grendel retreated further away and squatted onto his haunches, lowered his head, and covered his ears.

A minute later, he barely heard the shout, "Fire in the hole!" The area lit up brightly and the blast reverberated throughout the cavern, nearly vibrating Grendel's teeth out of his head.

After the blast, everyone gathered around to see what effect the explosion had on the door. It had no effect at all.

Grendel approached to within twenty feet of the group as the men discussed their next move. He couldn't make out the conversation, but after several minutes Zippo returned.

"What gives, Zippo?"

"Apparently, it ain't any kind of rock anyone's ever seen before. So they're gonna try thermite. That shit will damn near cut through anything. It's gonna get hot as hell, though, if you're standing too close. Get far away and stay low, Professor. Oh! And don't look at it. You'll go blind."

"Mister Bernard?" Grendel shouted. "Can you wait just a moment, please, before trying the thermite?"

Bernard held his hand up and stopped the ignition from occurring. "What is it, Professor?"

"May I have a look at the door?"

"Make it quick."

"Thank you." Grendel walked to the door and rubbed a hand across it. Zippo was partially right. It wasn't constructed of stone at all. The more he rubbed his hand across it, the more he felt that the door could be opened electronically, if not through other vibrational methods. What was certain in his mind was that the material would not yield to any kind of conventional explosive or thermal force. He pulled a loupe from his front pants pocket and studied the material up close, looking at it in various places.

"Well, Professor?"

"Sir, I don't think your thermite will have any effect on this material. Rather, I think you'd have better luck opening it by applying aggressive vibratory energies or high-energy electronic pulses. Sound, being vibrations, of course, is the most logical. But we might explore electronic pulses as well.

"It's rather obvious that Storm got through somehow. And he managed to open the door without employing these tactics. I therefore suggest that we explore methods other than explosives or trying to melt a hole through it."

"Is that it?"

"With the proper equipment and some time, I might be able to duplicate the vibrational sequencing necessary to open the door … if that is what opens it, of course."

"Stand away, Professor. We have neither the equipment nor the time to debate this any further."

Grendel moved away quickly.

"Mister Blaster. Melt that door, please."

Blaster nodded and flipped the igniting switch, which sparked to life a gas-fueled jet of flame which, in turn, ignited the thermite. The flame grew quickly to 4,500 degrees Fahrenheit and everyone felt the instant blast of heat.

The light rapidly grew so bright that everyone except Blaster, who was wearing welding glasses, had to turn their eyes away.

The burn continued furnace hot for several minutes until the thermite burned itself out, leaving a puddle of molten chemical at the base of the door.

The door, however, was undamaged and unmarked except for a black residue, which fell away immediately upon being touched.

"Okay, Professor Grendel. That round went to you. But we still don't have any equipment to perform your other suggestions. So I appeal to you, sir: find the correct sounds from whatever source you can, but get that door open."

"I'll do my best, sir."

"Let's hope that this time your best will be enough."

Grendel pulled out the photographs of the tablet once again and began reading, or more to the truth, began staring at the symbols.

After some time he winced. "Goddamn you, Storm," he muttered. "How did you do it?"

~ ~ ~ ~ ~

Traci had walked next to Kirby silently for the last thirty minutes. Her mind was a mess of incomprehensible thoughts. The singular filament connecting all those wild thoughts was Hannibal Storm's well-being.

She opened her mouth to speak just as a deafening explosion blasted a force wave through the cavern and the associated flash lit up nearly the entire cavern. Kirby's clenched fist shot up into the air and the five-person column came to an instant stop just as the blast wave hit them, giving them quite a jolt.

"What the hell was that?" asked Traci in a whisper.

"That was C-4 or Semtex, ma'am. Somebody's trying to blow something up," Boomer whispered back.

"Okay, boss, we've located the opposition," whispered Hound Dog. "Now what?"

"You do a quiet look-see up ahead and report back here. We'll wait."

Hound Dog nodded and slipped away, disappearing quickly outside the range of the flashlights that were turned toward the wall so that no light beams headed towards Bernard's group.

They crouched down and quietly awaited his return.

About fifteen minutes later, Kirby heard the shuffling of sand up ahead and Hound Dog soon appeared in front of him.

"Boss, we got three guys in black, one professor type, one extra-bad type, and one hotshot. One of the guys in black has got a night scope. He's a pro and he's looking to blow skulls."

"What were they blasting?" asked Traci.

"There's a door, ma'am, a big-ass door blocking the corridor. They were trying to clear it. It's still standing. I suggest we find a good hide for a while. It looks like they're gonna try thermite next. It's gonna get bright in a big way real quick."

"Will it work?" asked Kirby.

"Don't know. The professor-looking guy was trying to talk them into finding another way to open the door about the time I left."

"Okay," said Kirby. "Find someplace low and dark and stay put in case Grendel failed to convince them."

Everyone spread out and found a safe place and waited.

They didn't have to wait long before the light produced by the thermite illuminated the cavern a second time. No one moved a muscle until the brilliant light had subsided back into blackness.

They gathered back together.

"Can we take them into custody without getting bloody?" asked Kirby.

"I don't see how, boss. The guy on the night scope is dug in tight. I don't think we can make a clean approach in a group."

"Damnit. No other way to do this without putting their lights out?"

"The night scope's hot and well placed, boss."

"Can you take him down, Hound Dog?"

"Can do, boss. If I go alone."

Kirby sat thinking.

"You want me to do this, boss?" asked Hound Dog.

"You're sure you can take him?"

"Roger that, sir. Found a nice hide and can do my thing from there. It's not a problem. I can take the other two blacks as well, but I'd like some quick company right after the third shot. I won't get a chance at a fourth if they come at me."

"Okay, you're go. Boomer, Wrecking Ball, you both slide up into support positions with Hound Dog and take out anyone you need to. Got it?"

"Got it, sir. We're on it."

As the three team members moved out of range of the light, Traci laid her hand on Kirby's arm and whispered into his ear. "I feel we're getting really close to Hannibal. He's on the other side of that door. I just know it."

"I feel him, too. But we're going to have to get past that door as well, and it sounds like it's gonna be tough to do that."

"Hannibal will just have to find us, then."

"Hang here a moment, Trace. I'll be right back."

Kirby moved forward, disappearing into the darkness.

Traci waited calmly alone in the dim red glow of her flashlight buried against her chest. Several minutes later she heard the soft shuffle of sand and heavy breathing coming from somewhere in front of her. Seconds later Kirby reappeared.

He leaned in close and whispered in her ear, "Move up next to the wall here, Traci. The boys are about to light up the place." His hand shot up to his earpiece. He listened intently for several seconds. "Okay," he whispered. "Take the blacks out. Do not harm the civilians. Proceed when ready. You're clear."

Traci tapped her earpiece. "I don't hear anyone."

"Sorry. We went to channel four. It's encrypted."

Traci thumbed her radio knob and clicked to channel four.

Over the course of several tense minutes, she heard only whispered back-and-forth transmissions from the men slowly getting into position.

She finally heard one of them announce that they were going green, they were turning on their night vision equipment.

Everything then went deadly silent. She reached out and dropped her hand on Kirby's arm. He turned his head toward her. "Pretty quick, Trace."

Pretty quick it was. A second later massive gunfire erupted, making flashes of light on the cavern walls nearly three hundred yards ahead of them. The gunfire was loud and steady for about ten seconds and then it was over, with only loud voices — frightened voices — reverberating throughout the cavern shouting their surrender over and over.

"Let's move, Trace."

Just as she stood up she heard a voice on the radio. "All secure, boss. Come on up."

Minutes later, Traci and Kirby saw the bright lights of many flashlights all pointed in one direction, illuminating three men with their backs against the undamaged corridor door, their hands raised above their heads. One man was almost sobbing as he continually voiced his surrender and begged not to be shot.

Traci smiled, recognizing the blubbering man. "Grendel. The lion of archaeologists."

As they approached the men, the horror of the brief firefight stretched out in front of them in the form of blood-soaked sand

and the bullet-riddled bodies of Bernard's assault team. Traci and Kirby came to a stop before the three prisoners.

"Mister Bernard, how lovely to see you again."

"Miss Jefferson. Mister Hansen. Nice getaway, by the way. I'm impressed."

"It didn't take much, I'm afraid."

"True, Miss Jefferson. I must admit it. A failing of mine, hiring incompetents as I have. I'll be more studious in the future with my hiring practices. I do learn from my mistakes."

"Hey, Falcon. Got any more of that magic knockout gas on you?"

"Fresh out, I'm afraid, Mister Hansen."

"Too bad. Now I know the other two wouldn't think of moving a muscle, so this is directed at you, Falcon. Twitch without permission and you'll be dead an instant later. Are we understanding each other?"

"No twitching. Got it."

"Splendid. Hound Dog, would you secure these gentlemen, please?"

"Sure, boss, but we only have three ties. We weren't exactly counting on taking prisoners."

Bernard smirked. "How delightfully witty."

Moments later Boomer stepped up alongside Kirby, who was studying the large stone door in front of him.

"You want me to blow it now, sir?"

"Give me a minute, Boomer."

"Roger that."

Boomer stepped away just as Traci came up next to Kirby.

"Stunning, isn't it?" she asked. "What's it made of?"

"It's nothing I've ever seen before."

"It can't be drilled either," offered Grendel, reaching his tied hands up to scratch the end of his nose.

Traci motioned, and Wrecking Ball brought Grendel to Kirby.

"Tell me about this, Professor," said Kirby.

"It can't be drilled. The drills they used broke without making a scratch on it, even the diamond-tipped drills. My question is why didn't they make the summit capstone out of the same material?"

"Good question. Maybe it wouldn't have eroded the same as the sandstone around it and would eventually stick out like a sore thumb, calling attention to itself."

"That actually sounds like a very plausible and reasonable answer," said Grendel.

"Do you know what this material is?"

"No, Mister Hansen. I'm an archaeologist, not a metallurgist. It's something I've never seen before either. It's made to look like sandstone, of course, but it isn't. It isn't at all. My best guess is that it's some kind of super-alloy never seen before in the modern era. The explosion didn't touch it, and the thermite only temporarily discolored it."

Grendel moved to the door and wiped his cuffed hand across the black residue left by the thermite. It wiped right off, leaving no trace. "Look carefully," he continued. "The thermite had no effect on it whatsoever. As far as I can tell, it didn't even heat up during the thermite burn."

Kirby stepped forward and touched the door. He could see that it remained flawless.

"Wow! I wish Hannibal was here to explain this."

~~~~~

Hannibal felt the vibration rumble through the sand against the soles of his feet. He stopped reading and twisted his head around, trying to locate the source.

"Hannibal! Did you feel that?" asked Douglas, stepping up to him from the bins.

"Yeah."

"Any idea?"

"Lots of them, but I suspect reverberations of an explosion."

"I didn't hear any explosion."

"Neither did I. You think it was our new friends trying to get through the door?"

"That would be my guess."

"Doesn't sound like they succeeded. I wonder why."

Feel like taking a walk and finding out?"

"Sure. I need to refill my canteen again anyway."

They walked to the entrance of the vault and listened carefully for any other sound. It remained still and quiet. Hannibal started walking away from the vault, but stopped.

"What?" asked Douglas.

"We can't leave the vault like this."

"Got it! Gonna close it?"

"I think it's wise to do so, Dougie. No telling who has come to visit, but I'm guessing they ain't the friendly type."

"I spotted the lever earlier. It's over on the right, just inside. I'll get it." Douglas started to reach for the lever, then stopped. "Oh, wait!"

"What?"

Douglas moved into the vault and returned carrying the backpacks, the two pouches containing the crystal skull and the tablet hanging from Hannibal's. He moved to the other side of the corridor, fell to his knees, and began digging into the sand. Hannibal pulled the lever to lower the door and then kneeled down next to him and began to dig also. "Great thinking, Doug."

"Just thought I should, in case you can't sing it open again."

"Or wouldn't want to."

"Same. Same."

The stone door slowly dropped as they dug a hole deep enough to drop the packs into and then covered it back up and made it look undisturbed.

Hannibal wiped a sleeve across his brow. "Now let's go back to the door and see if our visitors are having any luck opening it."

~ ~ ~ ~ ~

"Okay," yelled Boomer. "Everyone stand back and cover your eyes. It's gonna get real bright." He pulled the cord and ignited the fuse and then ran back to the others.

Everyone watched the fuse burn toward the coil of thermite and saw it fire off into a brilliant light. The heat generated by the thermite hit them like a giant sun. The flames crawled along the strips of thermite and ignited them, creating more light and heat.

After several minutes the chemical burned itself out and darkness re-enveloped the area. Flashlights flicked on again as Boomer moved toward the door. "Wow!" he bellowed. "Not a scratch or a scorch mark. Nothing. The professor was right. It did nothing to it."

Kirby and Traci joined him at the door. They looked disbelievingly at it. "Amazing! You sure you set the line right, Boomer?"

"I set it right, boss. This shit just don't burn."

"What are we going to do, Boomer? Any other tricks in your bag?"

"No, boss. I got nothing that'll touch this door."

"The Naacal seem to have beaten us all, Mister Hansen."

"Not all of us, Bernard. Hannibal made it through. He's on the other side of this door. I know it."

"Perhaps, Miss Jefferson. But perhaps it was his crossing of the threshold that triggered the door to shut in the first place. Perhaps he's trapped on the other side, as helpless now to get out as we are to get in. Perhaps there are other booby traps that he didn't know about. Perhaps he's dead already."

"And *perhaps* you should shut your mouth before I put the butt of this rifle into your nose."

Bernard bowed his head and remained silent but retained the hint of a contemptuous smile.

It seemed that her threat came too late. Bernard's words had gotten to her, and she was faced with the possibility that he might be right and Hannibal was either hopelessly trapped on the other side of the door or had already met his end by some nefarious Naacal booby trap. In a sudden burst of emotion, Traci slammed the butt of her rifle into the door. "Damn!" she shouted. The metallic echo reverberated throughout the cavern.

She suddenly had an idea.

She hammered a series of taps on the door and then waited.

"'Hannibal' in Morse code. Good move, Trace. I take it he knows Morse code."

"He taught *me*, Kirby."

There was no immediate response, so Traci tapped out her own name.

Seconds later she heard a response in the form of a hollow tapping sound. Kirby heard it too.

"Did you hear that?" he asked.

"Yes! It's Hannibal. It said 'proof.'"

Securing the butt of her rifle, she tapped out another Morse-coded word.

"'Poseidon'?" asked Kirby.

"Shh, listen."

Seconds later she heard the response. "'Deliberate'!" she announced.

She then tapped on the door again, this time speaking the letters aloud as she did. "J-U-P-I-T-E-R."

Moments later the door shifted slightly and began to rise slowly. Jubilation exploded in the air at the same time as the gunfire. In seconds, Kirby's assault team lay dead and Falcon held a smoking rifle in his hands, slamming a new magazine into the receiver and homing the charging bolt.

Kirby and Traci immediately dropped their rifles and put their hands up, feeling especially fortunate not to have been killed already.

Grendel rose to his feet with his tied hands still protecting his face. And Bernard stood smiling sardonically.

"You do move quietly for a big man, Mister Falcon. Would you mind cutting me loose now?"

Falcon moved to Bernard and cut the plastic tie.

"Pocketknives. Such deviously delightful gadgets and so easy to hide." Falcon raised his left leg, placed the knife back into the cuff of his pants, and returned his foot to the sand. He grinned. "No one ever checks the cuffs. Go figure."

Bernard then stooped to pick up a dropped .45. He stuffed it into the back of his pants.

The stone door continued its rise until the shocked expressions of Hannibal and Douglas greeted them.

Traci flew to Hannibal and wrapped her arms around his neck and kissed him hard. He returned the kiss with equal fervor.

"I'm so glad to see you, you goofball."

"Professor Storm," said Bernard, moving toward the startled men. "So kind of you to assist us. Miss Jefferson seems to be glad as well. Uh, one thing. Are you armed by chance?"

Hannibal pulled his .45 and dropped it to the sand at his feet.

"Thank you, Professor. Mister Long Lance?"

"I got nothing."

Falcon pointed the muzzle of his rifle toward Kirby. "Mister Hansen. You mentioned something earlier about twitching, I believe."

"Got it." Kirby put his hands on top of his head and locked his fingers.

Traci, Douglas, and Hannibal did the same.

"What have you been up to, Professor Storm?"

"Oh, you know, Bernard, a little drinking, a little gambling; the usual stuff. I guess the party's over, though, huh?"

"I have so missed that wit of yours. Did you find it?"

"Find what?"

"Professor, Professor, you were doing so well. Tell me, please, before I run out of patience. It's been a rather trying day thus far."

"Oh. You're asking about the firestone? Nah, sorry. Haven't found it yet."

"It would make it so much easier if I believed you, but alas, I do not. You accomplished quite a climb earlier, by the way. Quite impressive."

"I told you I felt eyes watching me."

"You did say that, Dougie."

"Gentlemen, please, let us end this chitchat and get down to the truth of the matter. How did you open this door?"

"A little birdie told me."

Bernard considered the options as Falcon directed the others to move against the wall.

Finally Bernard glanced up at Hannibal. "Touch, Professor?"

"I'm sorry?"

"Touching the correct symbols on the door in a specific order, perhaps?"

Hannibal turned his eyes upward to the slot into which the door had disappeared. "Well, you could try."

"Indeed," said Bernard, his eyes following Hannibal's. "Not very practical, is it? Possible for raising it, but not for lowering it. No. Touching is not the key."

Bernard studied the symbols next to the door, running his fingers over them. He glanced at Hannibal and then shook his head. "Not these either, I suspect. I'm guessing sounds, then. Sounds, notes, tones, certain auditory vibrations? As Professor Grendel suspects. Sounds in a specific order lift the door, correct?"

"Gee, I hadn't thought of that. Sounds good."

Bernard chuckled. "That wit again. You're an absolute delight."

"Uh, this adulation of yours for me isn't gonna lead to us kissing or hugging, I hope."

Bernard laughed hard while shaking his head no.

"I'm glad I can entertain you so easily."

"And you do, Professor, you do." Bernard wiped the laugh tears from his eyes and exhaled. "Mister Falcon, would you be so kind as to put a bullet into Miss Jefferson's knee for me?"

"Right or left, sir?" asked Falcon, smiling.

"Indulge yourself."

"Sounds!" shouted Hannibal. "Sounds in a specific order lift the door. A lever on this side lowers it."

"Excellent, Professor. We do get along so much better when you cooperate, do we not?" He turned to Falcon. "Bring the others along. We may need them to bargain again with the good professor here."

"Hands," said Falcon. "Bury your hands into your front pockets; we apparently have no more ties. If I see any part of a wrist, a part of a head is going to explode. Are we clear on this?"

Hands were instantly buried into front pockets — deeply.

Falcon aimed the muzzle of the rifle at Kirby and Traci and motioned them toward the open doorway.

"Mister Long Lance. Navajo Nation attorney and Professor Storm's friend. I have not forgotten about you. Please join the others, and if you please, lead the way back to where you both were last. I don't think Professor Storm would volunteer that information on his own. And I do tire of threatening beautiful women."

"Sure. I'm easy to get along with. Especially when I have the muzzle of a rifle in my face."

"Indeed. It does tend to persuade one toward good behavior. Let's see what you two have discovered."

"Ah, excuse me, Mister Bernard," said Grendel. "Would it be too much to ask that I be cut loose, too?"

CHAPTER 34

In a tight single file the group arrived at the vault door.

"Wonderful, Mister Long Lance. Thank you. Now, Professor. If you please, the notes."

"That's just the problem, Bernard. I can't find the notes. I've been trying for hours to sing my way in, so to speak. No luck so far. The notes are not on the tablet here. I'm open to suggestions."

"That tablet is the one you removed from the wall at the bottom of the stairs, I presume?"

"The very same."

Bernard nodded and moved to the door. He ran his hand over the joint between the door and the wall. He moved to the other side and did the same thing. Then he moved to the center of the door and stood silent for several minutes, rubbing his hand over the symbols on it.

He glanced back at Hannibal and smiled. "Correct, Professor. They're not on the tablet. They're right here. And you can read them."

"I can read the words, Bernard. They're in code. Just like the tablet. I can't break the code."

"Ah, I see. Context again, right?"

"You got it."

Hannibal glanced at Douglas and then at Kirby and Traci. Their faces remained impassive, but the message was clear: he had been inside.

Bernard studied the doorway again and then turned toward Hannibal. "Professor, would you please explain these footprints in front of the door?"

"Footprints? There's nothing to explain. They're mine and Doug's. We were trying to find a way in."

"Despite what you may think of me, Professor, I am a student of observation. Such a talent often puts me at an advantage during negotiations. So, in that vein, tell me, please, why would there be footprints leading away from the door?"

"I don't understand."

"Look here, Professor. The prints run straight out of the doorway, right over several other prints. And notice the gait. A normal gait, I should think; as if someone made their exit from inside the room while walking out in a normal stride."

Bernard turned his eyes toward Falcon.

"Mister Falcon, it seems the good professor requires repetitive stimulus to learn. Therefore, please, a bullet to the thigh of Miss Jefferson. Your choice once again."

"Goddamn you, Bernard. Fine. Have it your way, you bastard."

"I always do, Professor and 'you bastard' should probably become my middle name, I hear it so often." Bernard held up a hand to Falcon, once again stopping him from carrying out his order. He then rubbed the symbols on the door. "Sing, Professor. You do know how to sing, don't you?"

Hannibal walked to the center of the door and sang the notes. The door began slowly rising.

When it rose high enough for all to see inside, everyone gasped audibly, including Bernard.

The trough of fire was still ablaze and the entire vault was illuminated. Bernard staggered a bit, then caught himself.

"Dear god, Professor. You truly are a genius, an absolute marvel. Will you look at this."

Bernard walked through the door and went straightaway to the first bin. He stabbed his hand into it and brought up a handful of diamonds and let them slip through his fingers.

Next he wandered over to the bins filled with the rubies, emeralds, and sapphires and did the same thing. Then he stopped and stared up at the stacks of gold and shook his head. Finally, he walked back toward the others, still standing outside the vault. He motioned everyone inside.

"Riches beyond imagination, Professor. I salute you. Of course, they are but trinkets next to the real prize, aren't they?"

Then Bernard noticed the emerald serpent head on the shelf next to the door. "Oh, my, my," he said, moving toward it.

"Stop, Bernard! Don't touch that!"

Bernard stopped in his tracks. "Thank you, Professor. What was I about to do? Bring the roof down upon us?"

"I don't know exactly. The markings above it are some kind of warning, though. I haven't had time to translate them completely. Just don't touch it, *please!*"

"I won't. ... And so, back to the subject of this endeavor. Where is it, Professor?"

"It's here, Bernard. At the back of the vault."

"The vault? Is that what they called it?"

"Yes."

"Aptly named, I'm sure. In the back, you say?"

"At the far end, about three hundred feet or so. You won't miss it, I promise."

"You won't mind if I —"

"No. I don't mind. It's quite a sight. It's something you'll want to experience alone."

"Very gracious of you, Professor. I feel obliged to do just that." Bernard nodded to Falcon and then pushed both hands into his own pants pockets and strode toward the back of the vault, whistling an unidentifiable tune. He then stopped and turned back toward Hannibal.

"Professor. You wouldn't be trying to get me to walk into some kind of trap, would you?"

"I would love to do just that, but it wouldn't do me any good right now. It's back there."

Bernard nodded, turned back toward the rear of the vault and began walking again, whistling once more.

~ ~ ~ ~ ~

It was a full twenty minutes before Hannibal caught sight of Bernard returning slowly, his head bowed. He came to a stop in front of Hannibal and the others, who were now seated on the floor of the vault up against the wall. He stood very quietly for a long time, his hands still shoved deeply into his pockets. Then he raised his head and stared at Hannibal.

"I know you despise me, Professor, and I understand why you would."

"I don't despise you, Bernard. Loathe you, detest you, hate you. Yeah. That would better describe it. I hate you."

Bernard chuckled. "I understand. But I give you my word on this matter. You, sir, are going to be filthy rich. Filthy rich and world famous. I promise to give you the full credit for its discovery. I'm impressed beyond anything I could ever have imagined from you."

"I wish I could be as impressed with you, too. But ..."

"I accept your interim judgment of me and my actions. But I set yet another task before you. A mighty task, to be sure, considering your personality, but one even more suited to you than finding the firestone. Help me announce it to the world."

"Again, Bernard, I'll pass on the accolades. Just leave this place and pretend you've never seen it. If you do that, I'll be a good boy and live behind the veil. I won't squawk about Grendel being the face of any expedition. And I'll make discoveries for you that will rock your world. I give you my word on that. But leave the firestone here. Leave and forget it. We're not ready for it."

"If you don't mind, Bernard. I would very much like to see it for myself. It's been quite a journey for me as well."

"Not at all, Miss Jefferson. In fact, why don't we all take a walk and have a look at it. It's the least I can do."

"I'll pass, if you don't mind," said Hannibal. "Been there, done that."

"As you wish, Professor. Go ahead, the rest of you. Please. Go see what marvel rests at the end of this amazing vault. Mister Falcon and I will keep company with the Professor. Oh, and don't get any cute ideas, please. Try to remember that Mister Falcon holds the only weapon on your favorite professor."

"Ah, Mister Bernard? May I —"

"Yes, yes, of course, Professor Grendel. Be off with you."

"Thank you, sir."

They proceeded between the bins, each stopping, as expected, to run their fingers through the gems as they headed toward the firestone.

"Actually, Professor, I'm glad you wanted to stay. It gives us a moment to talk."

"I don't really have anything to say to you, Bernard."

"Nonsense. Your every thought is consumed with how to talk me out of bringing the firestone into the light, so to speak."

"Since you put it that way."

"It's indescribable, Professor. One of the most indescribable things my eyes have ever seen — quite beautiful."

"It's been my experience that beautiful things don't last long in this world, but then neither do the ugly."

"True enough, I expect, but then, no matter how striking the beauty of a thing, without light upon it, does not the beauty remain hidden?"

"I suppose so. 'What you choose to see is that which will be seen by you.'"

"Well stated. And I see your point. We often choose for ourselves what we wish to see."

"That didn't come from me. I read that on one of the many scrolls discussing what to do about the firestone."

"Tantalizing. And who is it that spoke such eloquent words, Professor?"

"The high priest was telling the people that things will be for them as they choose them to be. If they choose to see the wisdom in burying the firestone, then they will see their future as brighter and safer."

"Ah. Great wisdom in those words, to be sure."

"And so it can also be said for knowledge and vision."

"I agree, in part, though to appreciate the full power of something wonderful does not always require one to see it. Is that not also true?"

"Sure. Electricity, the wind, a well-planted suggestion, for example. But is it any safer because we can't see it?"

"Not always, I concede. In the case of radiation, for example. The fact that we cannot see it actually makes it more deadly. But what is your point?"

"The point, Bernard, is this. We learned how to detect the presence of radiation with the creation of Geiger counters. With their help, we've learned how to avoid its deadly effects. Although we didn't witness the destruction of the Naacal nation, through these records we've — I've — learned how we can avoid the deadly effects of the firestone. And that is by not energizing it."

"A good point. But then with all new discoveries there's always a learning curve. What we've learned from the Naacal is to be careful where we direct the energy flow. You see, Professor, I know something of the Naacal and their destruction. Not as much as you, obviously, but more than most."

"Then I have nothing more to say."

"Please, Professor. I was enjoying our intellectual sparring. It's not often I meet someone with whom I can spar. Indulge me, please."

"You get your jollies from someone else, Bernard. The Naacal were honorable people. Fools sometimes, but when it counted most, they proved themselves wiser. Can't say the same for you, I'm afraid."

"The Naacal were fools for giving up. And let me remind you that they used the firestone quite effectively for a very, very long time — thousands and thousands of years — until they used it improperly, of course. I won't make that mistake. And isn't that what truly defines science, Professor? Learning from the mistakes made by others? In that spirit, then, do not the ends justify the means?"

"Not always, Bernard. Sometimes the ends are just ends that should be respected for what they are and left alone. 'I've always tried to walk in the brightness of certainty and not in the shadow of doubt, never afraid to fail but always afraid that I might fail to try.' Words again from the high priest explaining his decision to ask that the firestone be hidden away."

"Gallant words, but of empty value. 'Knowledge gained is wisdom won.' Isn't that what your friend Black Owl said?"

"How do you know what he said?"

"Please, Professor. We've covered that already. I pay well to stay informed."

"Then act informed, Bernard. Use the wisdom won. Leave the firestone where it is."

"With the power of the firestone we could literally go to the stars. Now isn't that, alone, a worthy and noble endeavor, something to take pride in?"

"Pride? Isn't that something that comes before a fall?"

"Clever. I do so enjoy our little repartee. But you're missing the point, as usual. We could do so much more good with the firestone than we could ever do without it."

"The good of it. The bad of it. The right and wrong of it. You're missing the greater point of it all, Bernard."

Bernard turned toward Falcon and smiled. "Listen, please, Mister Falcon. This is going to be good, I assure you." He turned back to Hannibal. "Please explain, Professor."

"The only reason we're a civilization above the primal level of survival is because of our laws and words of guidance. More so, it is because of our faith in and respect for those laws and philosophy that we find ourselves here in this very room today trying to resolve what we should do.

"Those magnificent ancient minds had the foresight to see where mankind was heading if they didn't set down good laws and wise words to live by. But it's the understanding of what those fine words mean in the context of preserving life that gives us our direction and shows us how we must live in order not only to survive, but also to flourish and grow as a civilization."

"Professor, Professor. It's in the spirit of those laws and ancient words that we are operating now. I'm only exercising the wisdom they left for me to use."

"None of this has your name on it, Bernard. No one assigned you to exercise anything. You're living under your own self-induced illusion. You are only one man — a part of the whole. You're not the whole unto itself no matter how much you may wish it to be so."

"My dear man, sometimes there is but only one person to seize the moment. Take Caesar, for example, or Napoleon. They saw the moment. They recognized the instant that destiny called out for someone to act, and they answered."

"Not good examples, Bernard. One was murdered and the other lived out his life in exile because they tried to seize what was not theirs to seize."

"Wrongful action, Professor. That is what brought them down. Wrongfulness and selfishness were their undoing."

"But you're different, right? You see yourself as a hero, do you? The savior of mankind?"

"Destiny has called me to action, and I have answered. I have been preparing myself my whole life for just this moment. Why should I be denied my moment of destiny?"

"You're not the answer to destiny, Bernard. You're a coward at best. 'To know what is right and not to do it is the worst cowardice.' So said Confucius."

Bernard chuckled. "You sling words about as if they were razors, Professor."

"I'm just speaking the truth. If the truth cuts, so be it. You don't yet possess wisdom enough to understand the moment of destiny's call. But if I haven't yet convinced you to walk away from the firestone and leave it hidden, then I guess I've failed destiny as well."

"Quite to the contrary. You've given me every reason *not* to leave it buried and hidden away. Exposing it and all the harm it can do will give mankind the perfect reason to keep our civilization thriving. The potentially destructive nature of the firestone and the history of the Naacal will serve as a compelling reminder of how we must live as a civilized society or perish as a despicable race of undeserving animals."

"I've wasted my words, Bernard. I see that clearly now. And we still find ourselves at odds over what to do with this great discovery."

"Anyone ever tell you that you have a tendency toward pessimism, Professor?"

"Only people like you, Bernard. People who choose to remain blind and deaf to the truth because they choose to remain ignorant to the true nature of evil men. 'Trust not in the good intentions of evil hearts.'"

"Wonderfully clever, Professor."

"I read it in another scroll."

"It was directed at me, no doubt. But we're only at odds, Professor, because you refuse to see all the wonderful possibilities the firestone would bring to the world. Therefore, it is left to me to bring the joys of limitless energy to the world — to reignite the destiny of mankind."

"Tell me, Bernard. Do you ever get lonely in your private fantasy?"

"Words as razors, Professor."

"I tried reason. It wasn't working."

Bernard laughed. "There's that wonderful wit bubbling to the surface again. But wasn't it your friend Black Owl who said that one should be ashamed knowing that one could have made a difference and chose not to get involved?"

"Damn, you must pay a fortune for your informants, but once again, you're missing the point of those words. They were intended to stay a man from making an error, not to encourage him toward manifesting it."

"You've got it all wrong, Professor. The error would be in not seizing the opportunity to do something wonderful with all the wisdom gained from any disaster."

"I wonder if someone said that very thing twenty-five thousand years ago, just before the island sank."

"Your wit is chilling. But I'm a fan of humankind. I want to free man from the shackles of his own disbelief in himself."

"Didn't the devil say something like that at one time?"

"Very clever, but we do agree on one important point. The nature of evil men must be arrested and bound — bound so that man's greatness can be unleashed — unleashed to realize the full potential of the strength of his character in action."

"The Naacal couldn't make that happen, Bernard. They saw the folly in that effort. But they loved mankind so much that they sacrificed the benefits of their own civilization, broke it up and took it back almost to the technology of the Stone Age in order to preserve it. Now *that* is love, Bernard. *That* is wisdom. *That* is strength of character in action."

"More gems, Professor, but let me ask you this. If they so loved mankind, why didn't they simply destroy the firestone in the first place? Why didn't they shatter it into a million pieces or let it fall to the bottom of the sea along with the remains of their island? Why did they preserve all their knowledge and supposed wisdom in scrolls and on tablets? If you *can* answer those questions, to my satisfaction, I'll gladly walk out of this vault and never speak of it again. Can you make me believe they didn't preserve all of this because they held out some hope that one day, far in the future, mankind would grow into a civilization that could use the firestone without all the destruction? Can you make me believe that?"

"I can't make you believe anything, Bernard. You'll either choose to believe it or not. But I can say this. I've read their words. I've been inside their heads. I've heard them crying in despair, I've felt their despondency for what they considered despicable behavior on their part. I've read their self-curses, shared their feelings of self-condemnation. And I've also read their other words, the words filled with love, hope, and admiration for what their leaders chose to do for the sake of preserving mankind on 'this precious little blue pebble stone held up on high by a loving creator in the midst of the black sea of eternity,' as one scroll's author called our planet. Do you have any idea what strength of character it must have taken for them to dismantle all the technology they had available to make their lives easier? Do you realize the hardships the leaders returned to their people so that we might exist here today? Are you capable of understanding *any* of their motives or appreciate the magnitude of their sacrifice? I don't pretend to know why they chose to hide it and not destroy it. But let me ask you this. If it is truly meant to benefit all mankind, as you say, then why not make it free? Free for all to use. Without constraint or limitation, except in regard to safety."

"You're playing naïve, Professor. Would you prefer that someone else — someone not interested in the good it can do but rather how much money they can make — control it?"

"It's all about the money for you, and even more importantly, the power."

"Power naturally follows success, Professor. Would it be so bad if I controlled the use? I could protect mankind by restricting how it is used."

"So we've come back to the savior thing again. You'd be the great protector of mankind, would you?"

"Everyone has their place in this world. Some just don't realize it till late in their lives. I've always known my place as a great man."

"Keep telling yourself that, Bernard. Someday you just might believe it yourself. What was it Hitler said? 'Tell the biggest lie often enough and everyone will eventually come to believe it'? You've been listening to yourself too much. And I'm not going to give you the chance to destroy everything. Not you. Not *you*, by god."

"So melodramatic, Professor. So passionate. So full of vim and vigor to protect mankind. So full of shit, too. If anyone is guilty of anything here, it's you, Professor. Why didn't you destroy the tablets, the scrolls? Why did you tenaciously pursue that which you supposedly didn't want found? I'm here because of your own greed and lust for the glory of making the discovery. What is it the wise man said? 'Fool, if you are brave enough, point the finger at yourself; the rightful reason of your own wretchedness.'"

"You got me, Bernard. You're absolutely correct. I am at fault here, but I would be at greater fault if I stood by and allowed you to compound my foolishness into a tragedy while knowing that I could have done something to prevent it."

"Take heart, Professor. Your efforts merely granted the knowledge back to the world. Your job is done. Mine is just beginning."

"That wasn't my intent."

"Intent or not, here we are. And I cannot sit by and watch this opportunity slip through my hands. I'm not cut from that cloth. I seize opportunities. I didn't have anything to do with what my great-grandfather did all those years ago, but I'm going to maximize the occasion given to me by his actions."

"'Many speak loudly. Few act bravely.' More wisdom from the Naacal, in case you're wondering."

"Another jewel of wisdom. But now it's time for our conversation to end, because I can see that we will remain forever irreconcilable on this issue. I expected it, but I hoped it would not come to this. Now, if you'll excuse me, I'm going to collect your comrades."

Bernard departed, leaving Falcon and Hannibal alone.

Making sure that Bernard could not overhear him, Falcon said, "I understood all you said, Professor. And I even agree with you. But I have to know. Is it truly spectacular, the firestone?

"Go down there and see it for yourself. You helped find it; you should see it."

"How did I help find it?"

"You were a great sounding board while I was trying to figure out what the symbols meant. That helped a lot. I would say thanks, but it's hard to thank someone when they've got a rifle pointed at you. Oh, by the way. Sorry about the sleeping pills. No hard feelings, I hope."

Falcon chuckled. "Sugar pills, Professor Storm."

"Ah. Guess who the fool is, then."

"No hard feelings on your end, I hope."

"Nah. We're good. An actor or an archaeologist; I think you could pull either one off well enough."

Falcon laughed. "That was a good one."

"Shall we go see the firestone?"

"Would you mind leading the way?"

Hannibal nodded and then strode toward the back of the vault room, passing the bins of gems.

"Oh my," said Falcon, obligingly dipping his hand into the bin of diamonds. "If I could only fill a single pocket."

"Go ahead."

"If I could."

"Why can't you? You think anyone will know a handful of diamonds is missing from that bin?"

"I guess not." Falcon grabbed a handful of diamonds and stuffed them into the front pocket of his Dockers. He glanced at Hannibal, as if he was suddenly concerned that Hannibal might mention it to Bernard.

Hannibal outguessed him. "Grab another handful. Who's gonna know but you and me?"

"Mister —"

"To hell with Bernard. Go for it."

"Why not?"

Falcon lifted another handful from the bin and dumped the gems into the same pocket. He smiled at Hannibal. "Between us?"

"Absolutely. Diamonds are a guy's best friend, too. And gold, and emeralds, and ... well, you get the point."

Falcon chuckled. "Let's go see the firestone now, Professor."

"Like you said, Falcon, why not? That's what rich people do, right? Go see things."

Falcon laughed. "I really like you, Professor. I hate Grendel. He's an idiot."

"There may be some hope for you after all, Mister Falcon."

CHAPTER 35

Tears streamed down Traci's face as she stared up at the firestone resting silently on its supports. Kirby walked back up the rise and stopped next to her.

"Hannibal was right," said Kirby. "He was right about everything."

"While you've been down there examining it, I've been standing here trying to find a description for it. It's beautiful, Kirby. It's stunning, awesome, frightening, spectacular, but those words aren't enough."

They heard sand shuffling behind them and turned to see Bernard's awestruck expression as he stood staring up at the firestone himself.

"I heard you, Miss Jefferson and I agree. It's beyond description."

Grendel approached them, still awestruck himself. "It's amazing. It's the greatest archaeological discovery of all time. I too have been trying to describe it. I can't find the words."

"Of that I have no doubt, Professor. But even without a proper description, here it sits, and you had nothing at all to do with it."

"So kind of you to keep reminding me of my failures, sir."

"Indeed. A point I will keep making from time to time. Shall we head back now, please?"

Just then Hannibal and Falcon arrived.

"Ah, delighted with your presence, Professor. What made you change your mind?"

"I'm afraid I did, sir. I wanted to see it for myself."

"So then, what is your assessment, Mister Falcon?"

"It looks like trillions of dollars to me, Mister Bernard."

"Excellent observation, Mister Falcon. Indeed it does, and that just might be the description that has eluded every one of us thus far. Trillions of dollars. It does seem the perfect description. How about you, Professor? Does that description befit the firestone?"

"You're asking me, sir?"

"Hardly, Grendel. You're not worthy of offering a description. The question was put to Professor Storm."

"A bringer of death. That's how I see it."

"There's that pesky pessimism again. I so much prefer your charming, albeit biting, wit."

"Please, Bernard, I'm begging you. Leave it where it lies."

"We've finished that discussion. And I'm sorry you won't be able to share in its announcement to the world. Now, if you please, let us head back to the entrance. Would you lead the way, Professor Storm?"

~ ~ ~ ~ ~

Upon reaching the vault door, Bernard whispered into Falcon's ear. "Escort them all somewhere away from here and see to their end properly. I need them gone forever."

"With pleasure, sir."

Bernard stepped in front of his four captives. "Professor Storm, thank you so very much for your discovery and wonderful debate. You lost, but I shall think about you from time to time, though probably not as often as you would like.

"Miss Jefferson, it's been a pleasure knowing you, in a matter of speaking.

"Mister Hansen, it has not been at all enjoyable knowing you. You cost me a wonderful yacht.

"And Mister Long Lance. I have not had the pleasure of knowing you long, and I do apologize for your suffering such a similar fate simply by association, but I could never trust that you wouldn't hold some Native American grudge against me for invading your sacred land and terminating your friendship with Professor Storm. Goodbye to you all."

Hannibal glared at him. "There are still good people in this world, Bernard. Like Hector Gonzalez and others. You'll lose eventually. The word will get out. I promise you that."

"Yes, Doctor Gonzalez. Sorry about him, Professor. He wasn't supposed to be injured. My man Mackie got a bit inventive and overzealous."

"You'll get yours soon enough."

Bernard looked at Falcon and nodded. Falcon walked over to the four doomed captives and pointed the muzzle of his rifle at each of them. "Normally I would now remind you to push your hands deep into your front pockets and warn you that if I saw a wrist, I'd put a bullet through your head without further notice. However ..."

Falcon turned the muzzle of his rifle toward Bernard. "This is not a normal situation."

"What the devil are you doing, Falcon?!"

"I happen to like Professor Storm, sir. And I also happen to agree with him. This world isn't anywhere near ready for the firestone. And even if it were, this world is not ready for *you* to control it. To be honest, sir, I don't really like you very much."

"You're a traitor! A clueless, dishonorable traitor."

"And you, sir, are a despicable bastard."

Falcon turned to Hannibal. "I can't tell you how long I've wanted to say those words, Professor."

Hannibal chuckled.

"Falcon, you've been paid for your services to date. Handsomely, I might add. But I see your position. I'll make it a hundred times as much."

There was no reaction from Falcon.

"A thousand times. No! A million times more."

Still no reaction.

"Fine. Name your price, then."

Falcon grinned. "Professor Storm, may I assume that you know how to close the door?"

"I do, Mister Falcon."

"Then may I suggest that you activate it now?"

At that moment a single diamond dropped down Falcon's pant leg from a small hole in his pocket and bounced off his shoe into the sand.

"Well, it seems you've collected your bonus already," said Bernard.

Falcon bent to retrieve the gem.

In one smooth motion, Bernard retrieved the .45 from the back of his pants and shot Falcon in the right temple, killing him instantly. "Your services are no longer required, Mister Falcon."

Hannibal made a move toward Falcon's body.

"Now, now, Professor. That rifle will do you no good with a bullet in *your* head."

"I'm not after the rifle, you imbecile. I'm after the diamonds. They need to be put back into the bin."

Hannibal kneeled over Falcon's body and thrust his hand into the front pants pocket. He pulled out a handful of diamonds and showed them to Bernard. At the same time he grabbed a handful of sand with his other hand, hidden from view.

He stood up and thrust the diamonds before Bernard's face. "You see these, Bernard? If these get out of here, the whole thing will be compromised."

Bernard's eyes fell onto the diamonds. He smirked. "What are you talking about? How would they ever get out of —"

An instant later Hannibal threw the sand into Bernard's eyes. Bernard instinctively reached one hand up to his eyes while his other hand raised the pistol. He squeezed the trigger several times, blindly firing in several directions, the bullets striking nothing but stone walls and ricocheting harmlessly in different directions. A second later Kirby was on him, grabbing the pistol with his left hand while sending a crushing right cross to Bernard's jaw, knocking him to the sand.

Bernard struggled to regain his senses and clear his eyes of the sand.

Hannibal tossed the diamonds into Bernard's face. "Here," he said. "You might as well keep these. You're going to be with them for a very long time."

Kirby aimed the pistol at Bernard, but Hannibal put his hand on Kirby's wrist.

"No! We're not murderers, Kirby." Hannibal bent over and retrieved the rifle from the floor. He checked the chamber. A round was in it.

"What am I supposed to do, Hannibal? Take him into custody? He'll sing like a bird to the authorities about this place just to save his sorry-ass skin."

"We don't take him into custody. We leave him here. He wanted possession of the firestone so badly, let him have it."

"You can't leave me here, Professor. It's doesn't equate with your code of ethics."

"Hannibal, what if he gets the door open?"

"Traci, honey, he'd have to read the symbols and sing the notes. Maybe you can sing, but you can't read the symbols, can you, Bernard?"

"But what if he learns?"

"How can he do that Kirby? The symbols are engraved only on the other side of the door. Even if he's memorized them, he can't translate them. The Naacal provided only a way in. They built in an exit security, probably for cases just like this. He's not going anywhere."

"That's true, Kirby," said Traci. "Besides, a bullet's too good for him."

"Okay, Hannibal. It's your discovery. It's your call."

"What do you think, Dougie? Would the ancestors want him running around free or in here?"

"I have no idea what the ancestors would want. But I want his ass to rot in here."

"Don't listen to him, Mister Hansen! He's a lawyer. I have experience with lawyers. Never trust a lawyer."

"He's got me there," Douglas agreed.

"And forget what Hannibal says, too. It's his fault we're here at all. He could have prevented anyone from discovering this place, but he selfishly wanted to be famous."

"Shut up, Bernard," said Kirby, "or I'll shoot you in the face for my own reasons."

"Hannibal, he'll die here," said Traci. "That's not you. That's not right."

"Jeremy Bentham, honey. 'It is the greatest happiness of the greatest number that is the measure of right and wrong.'"

Hannibal walked to the side of the doorway where the lever sat nestled into the wall and pulled it. The door began its slow descent.

"Be one with the firestone, Bernard."

"You can't leave me here! I'll die!"

"Better you than the whole world."

The four stepped through the doorway to the corridor.

"Wait! Please! I don't want to die with him, Hannibal."

"You've been a real pain in my ass, Grendel. But get yours over here."

"Thank you, Hannibal. Bless you. Thank you."

Grendel charged through the doorway, leaving Bernard to stand alone within.

Bernard refused to cower. "Well played, Professor. I get it. You're not going to leave me here. I know people. I know you. You'll open this door and let me out. I may have to wait a while, but you'll let me out eventually."

"Consider this payback for Professor Herzog and Hector. Enjoy the firestone and all the jewels. Oh, one more thing. That emerald serpent head over there on the wall? According to the inscription above it, if you disturb it, it will supposedly release the Great Serpent, the protector of the vault."

"All right, Professor, you've made your point. I'll leave the firestone untouched. I give you my word."

"Your word means nothing to me, Bernard. Falcon was right. You would have done anything to get it. Now you've got it all to yourself. Here's another quote I found in the scrolls. I think it was written just for you. 'Be careful of what you choose to own, for it shall claim you also.' Pretty fitting, don't you think?"

"Stop this right now, Storm. I mean it! I've learned my lesson."

Hannibal pulled out the check that Bernard had written to him earlier. He unfolded it and held it up for Bernard to see and then tore it up into little pieces. "I've kept this with me as a reminder to myself of how easily I could have sold out. Deal's off." He let the pieces trickle between his fingers and fall onto the sand.

The door continued moving downward.

"Oh, that reminds me. I was wrong about that warning on the wall. It just came to me. It's not the *Great Serpent*. It's *many serpents*."

Bernard started for the door. Hannibal fired several rounds from the rifle at his feet, stopping him.

The door was only two feet from closing.

"Hannibal! Stop this nonsense already."

"Gotta run now. Sing, Bernard! Sing! You do know how to sing, don't you?"

The door finally settled down, closing tightly to the ground and severing Bernard's last word: "HANNI —"

~ ~ ~ ~ ~

Douglas pointed his flashlight at the sand and fell to his knees and began digging. Soon he pulled a backpack from the hole and handed it to Hannibal. "This is yours, buddy." He then pulled his own pack from the sand and slung it around his shoulders.

Hannibal opened one of the pouches attached to his pack and withdrew the skull, holding it up for all to gawk at. Grendel's eyes opened wide. "NO! Is that the thirteenth?"

"It is, Grendel."

"Oh my."

"Oh my, indeed. Would you care to hold it?"

"May I?"

Hannibal handed it to Grendel, who stared at it in awe.

Hannibal opened the other pouch and withdrew the tablet. "I will need to study this very carefully. I think it contains something special."

He then slipped the backpack over his shoulders. "Oh, honey. I forgot." He grinned at Traci.

"Yes, dear."

"Would you mind getting my loupe out of my backpack?"

"Sure. Turn around."

"Hey, partner, would you mind catching Traci for me?"

"Sure ... what?"

Traci unzipped the main pack compartment. Kirby caught her as her knees buckled.

~ ~ ~ ~ ~

They headed for the only way out of the cavern — back toward the long, steep staircase. Kirby dutifully led the way, forever the agent in charge. They were in no hurry, though, and it was Kirby who pulled the lever to lower the corridor door. Traci occupied herself with an intensive study of a huge ruby in her hand. Grendel was still mesmerized by the crystal skull. Douglas held an emerald and grinned, while Hannibal read the tablet intently through his loupe. Suddenly his head popped up.

"Holy crap!" he shouted, stopping dead in his tracks.

Everyone stopped what they were doing, came to a halt, and stared at him.

Hannibal fell back into silence and dropped his head down to his loupe. He read for several seconds in silence.

"What, honey? What is holy crap?"

He looked back up. "Did I say that in my outside voice?"

"Yes, you did. Now, what is it?"

"Well, among other things, this tablet contains an inventory of their airships, parked in an underwater cavern near Bimini, along with a list of their other bases and ..."

Hannibal fell silent again as he went back to reading.

"Continue, partner."

"WOW!" chirped Hannibal, head still affixed to his loupe.

"Okay, I'll bite. What is it?" asked Douglas.

Hannibal remained silent and kept reading.

"Come on, Hannibal. Tell us!" ordered Kirby.

Hannibal remained silent, intensely reading.

Finally Traci leaned into him closely. "Give it up, Hannibal!"

Hannibal continued to read.

"Hannibal! Dear! I'm about to slap you."

Hannibal stopped reading and looked up, his eyes on fire with excitement. "Hey! You guys wanna know what's on the back side of the moon?"

EPILOGUE

Bernard sat on a box filled with busts of the ancient Naacal leaders, elbows resting on knees, his mind searching. He had been sitting there for quite some time, waiting for Hannibal to reopen the door. He had waited patiently, but now impatience began to surface.

He sought some acceptable purpose to his punishment, but he could find no justification for being incarcerated for so long. What did Hannibal Storm wish from him, an apology, an admission of guilt for wrongdoing? Or was he trying to scare him into submission, giving him time to think things through and come to admit that leaving the firestone undisturbed was best? Okay, he'd consider that. Or maybe it was to teach him that his methods might have been a bit harsh. Okay. He was big enough to admit that, too.

But years of being in charge, listened to, respected, and feared had created a man not to be toyed with in this fashion. With this realization his impatience grew into agitation. Finally, he raised his head and kicked at the sand.

"Enough is enough, Professor! I'll admit it, I've learned my lesson. Now open the door."

The door remained closed.

"Come now, Professor. Your lesson has been most appreciated and painfully absorbed. Open the door, please."

The door remained in place.

"Hannibal! For Christ's sake already. You win! Okay? YOU WIN!"

No response.

Bernard kicked at the sand again and listened to the ominous silence of the room until he could take it no more.

"You want to hear me sing, Professor? Oh, I'll sing, Storm! I'll learn to sing this door open. You can count on it, you bastard!"

He stood up, turned his back to the door, and reached for his canteen. Unscrewing the top, he drew in a deep breath. "Run, you coward! Run away. One day I'll find you. The world will bow to me. I assure you of that. I will learn to energize the firestone and command all its power by myself."

A sudden fit of laughter overtook him. "I've done it! It's *mine*, Great-granddad! I have sole possession of the firestone."

Then his rage returned. "I gotta get outa here! HANNIBAL!!"

He tipped the canteen up. It was dry.

"This is not over, Hannibal!" he screamed at the top of his lungs. He clutched the canteen tightly with both hands as if strangling it, imagining, no doubt, the neck of Hannibal Storm in his grasp.

His rage continued to fester until it exploded. He turned back toward the door and tossed the canteen at it. It missed the door but knocked the emerald serpent head off its pedestal and onto the sand floor.

"*Oh, no!* No! No! I'm sorry. I'm sorry. I'll put it back. Hannibal! Please open the door. I've done something."

He rushed to the serpent head and picked it up. It sparkled with such beauty that he had to stare at it. But then Hannibal's warning again filled his head.

He was about to set it back onto its pedestal when from the hole left by its absence the head of a very large rattlesnake, tongue flicking wildly as it sensed the heat of its prey, arose.

Bernard dropped the emerald head to the ground and backed up, startled. "No! Go away! No! No! Stop! Go back! No. No, no, no. NO! NO! ... Hannibal, please! I regret everything! Open the door!"

He continued backing away as the six-foot snake crawled out of the hole and dropped onto the sand, coiled and loudly rattling its warning.

"No! Stop! Hannibal! Open this goddamned door NOW!"

Trap doors perfectly hidden within the walls of the vault began opening one by one, a snake's head popping out of each, tongues flicking.

His eyes danced in his head as he tried to count all the snakes that had dropped onto the floor. It quickly became impossible to count them all. Then thousands of small platelets opened, dumping a snake from each onto the sand, adding to the gathering numbers.

"NO! NO! NO! NO!"

He was now crazy with fear.

The roar of the rattling echoed throughout the vault, growing louder with each passing second and with each added snake.

Within a short time, he found himself surrounded by a slithering mass moving toward him. "NO! Stay away! Stay away from me, damn you! NO! ... HANNIBAL!!"

Then the light began to fade as the flames in the troughs slowly died out, surrendering the vault once more to the mastery of the darkness.

"NOOOOOOOOO!" screamed the man who could now truly claim sole possession of **THE FIRESTONE**.

The End

About the Author

Val Edward Simone was born in Seattle, Washington, and has been writing since 1980.

Val has published adult-themed action/adventure novels; historical fiction; western novels; short stories; a collection of thoughts, musings, and observations; a collection of children's short stories; and several children's picture books. He continues to work on many other novels and short stories.

He is also a strong advocate of early childhood reading and continues to work with schools, local libraries, and directly with children through parent-assisted workshops, helping children to discover their own creativity through reading, writing, and drawing.

Val currently lives and works in Colorado.

His websites:
www.ekidslandpublishing.com
www.morningsidepublishing.com
www.morningsidepublishing.com/TwinHorse.html

Connect with Val Online:
Twitter: @valsimone
facebook: val.simone1@facebook.com
Linkedin: Val Edward Simone

Other Books by Val Edward Simone

Morningside Publishing, LLC
Novels
Blood Trackers: One Crazy Love Story
Blood Trackers 2: Revenge of an Angel
About Things I Lost Long Ago ... scribblings from a foolish heart
The Wondrous Life of a Long-Ago Man
Comes the Devil to Crooked Creek
Captain Delightable's Magical Tales of a Minchon Warrior
A Minute of Forever
The Firestone . . . Is Mankind Ready?

Short Stories
Manifest Destiny
The Secret Life of Goner Andling
Love Bytes
Dragons Within
The Problem with Dragons
The Unfortunate Dragon

Ekidsland Publishing, LLC
Children's Picture Books:
Felix
The Gingerbread Pony
The Littlest Bell
Mean Muley McGrudge
Otto and Kevin
Proton Gator
Sammy Sparrow Spy
The Fairy Collection

Short Stories
Through the Waterfall
Fairy Forgotten
Emily's Wish
Kaylee's Secret
The Wizard of Sebastianville

Children's Coloring Book:
Proton Gator & Friends Coloring Book